VOLUME 5

Written by Brandon Varnell

Art by Kirsten Moody

ISBN: 978-1-53545-57-3 (paperback edition 1)
978-1-951904-35-7 (OELN Edition)
978-1-951904-36-4 (eBook)

DEDICATION

This page is made in dedication to my amazing patrons. Without them, my characters would never get lewded by so many wonderful artists:

Aaron Harris; Abraham Madsen; Adam; Alarinnise; Alex Burt; Armando Pastrana; Aaron Cortrighr; Austin; Brendan Smiley; Bruce Johnson; Bryce McClay; ByzFan; Casey G. May; Catcrazy9; Chase Corso; Charles Dorfeuille; Chett Nialo; Christopher Gross; Cody Woodard; CosmicOrange; Daniel Glasson; David Bell; Edward Grindle; Edward Lamar Stephenson; Edward P Warmouth; Eric Bailey; Feitochan; Forrest Hansen; Forrest Hansen; G___Sweet; Grant; Green and Magenta Beast; IronKing; Jacob Flores; Jared B; Jason Wilcox; Jeremy Schultz; Jessy Torres; John Patton; Jordan McDonald; Joseph Snyder; Joshua Hasbell; Manny G; Mark Frabotta; Mason; Matthew Wallace; Max A Kramer; Michael Erwin; Michael Moneymaker; Mike Dennehy; Minocho; MrRedSkill; Nathan S; Norodim; Nyxterrynne; Phoenixblue; Philip Hedgepeth; Rafael; Randgofire23; Raymond T; Red Phoenix; Reent Dopychai; Repooc Ilahsram; Richard Garret; Rob Hammel; Robert Shofner; Rooser45; Roy Cales; Samuel Donaldson; Sean Gray; Seismic Wolf; Smudi Corp; Tanner Lovelace; Thomas Jackson; Thomas Lindsay; Thomas Oconnell; ToraLinkley; Travis Cox; Vincent Frosceno; William Crew; Wizard4Hire; XY172; Zach Miller; Zach Strickland; Zak Whiteaker; Zenn Barger

CONTENT

<u>WORDS YOU SHOULD KNOW:</u>

Onigiri: Also known as o-musubi, nigirimeshi, or rice ball, it is a Japanese food made from white rice formed into triangular or cylinder shapes and often wrapped in nori.

Kyūbi: A nine-tailed fox yōkai found in Asian mythology. The most popular telling about the kyūbi is the legend of the Bijuu.

Ecchi: Often used slang term in the Japanese language for playfully sexual actions.

Sanzu River: A Japanese Buddhist tradition and religious belief similar to the River Styx. It is believed that on the way to the afterlife, the dead must cross the river, which is why a Japanese funeral includes placing six coins (rokumonsen) in the deceased's casket.

Nakama: The Japanese word for a very good friend. Calling someone your nakama is like telling someone you love them in a non-romantic way.

Iaijutsu: A combative quick-draw sword technique.

Shuten Dōji: A mythical oni leader who lived in Mt. Ooe of Tamba Province or Mt. Ooe on the boundary between Kyoto and Tamba in Japan.

Iaidō: A modern Japanese martial art and sport that emphasizes being aware and capable of quickly drawing the sword and responding to a sudden attack.

Shotacon: Japanese slang describing an attraction to young boys and is shota in manga.

Bishōnen: A Japanese term literally meaning "beautiful youth (boy)" and describes an aesthetic that can be found in disparate areas in East Asia: a young man whose beauty (and sexual appeal) transcends the boundary of gender or sexual orientation.

Bishie: A shortened derivative of Bishōnen.

Yamato nadeshiko: The term "Yamato nadeshiko" is often used to refer to a girl or shy young woman and, in a contemporary context, nostalgically of women with "good" traits which are perceived as being increasingly rare.

Seiza: The Japanese term for one of the traditional formal ways of sitting in Japan.

CHAPTER 1

Spring Break

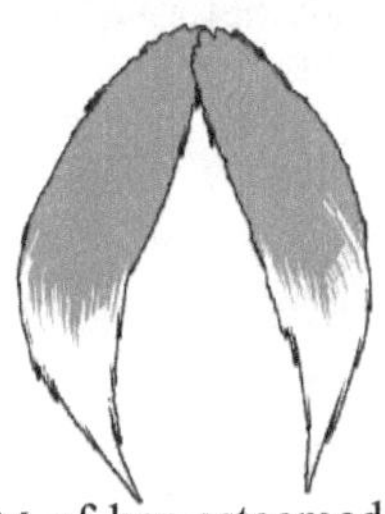

SHE ENTERED THE ROOM of her esteemed mistress. It looked a lot like an office. She wandered across the beige carpet, until she stood in front of a desk made from oak wood. Behind the desk sat her mistress, reading over and filing away documents, a no-nonsense expression on her face. Before this female, who'd built this village with her own two hands, she prostrated herself.

"You summoned me, nya?"

Her mistress didn't even look up from her work. "I did. I have a job for you, one that I feel you are uniquely suited for."

She perked up. She was being given a job? This was an awfully rare occurrence. She was almost never selected for such tasks these days.

"You are to locate and dispose of Lilian Pnéyma, who is living in Phoenix, Arizona."

Phoenix?!

Cassy's breath caught in her throat. Phoenix was where her last job had been! That particular mission, like most she'd taken, hadn't ended very well, and thus, she'd been forced to return home, more disgraced than ever.

If my mission is in Phoenix, then...

"I have been very lenient with you, Cassy Belladonna. However, know this, should you become distracted by consorting with human children while on a mission again, your punishment will be much harsher than it was last time. Do you understand?"

Cassy nodded emphatically. "Understood, nya."

"Then you are dismissed. You leave tomorrow morning, so pack your things and be ready before daybreak."

"Yes, Mistress, nya."

As Cassy left in surprisingly high spirits, she contemplated her next mission's destination.

Phoenix... I wonder if I'll get to see Master again...

***

Kevin Swift, Iris noticed, was a most unusual human. Maybe her perceptions of him were skewed, but there was something about him that seemed off to her.

It was not his personality, nor was it his personal life. He did all of the things that she imagined a normal human boy would do. He went to school, hung out with friends, watched anime and read manga, worked at a part-time job, trained to become capable of fighting yōkai, and spent time with his supernatural girlfriend-slash-mate. While those last two things definitely weren't something ordinary human boys did, the facts remained the same. In all regards, Kevin Swift was an average human teenager.

Except for one tiny difference. His unbending will.

Iris didn't know if this part of Kevin was something intrinsically connected to him, or if he was just odd. She only knew what she saw. Kevin's determination, his will, his drive to succeed—these traits of his exceeded those of anyone else that she knew. All she had to do was remember the time when she'd tried to cast an enchantment on him. No regular human could have thrown off an enchantment like hers—standard enchantments maybe, but not hers.

The **Aura of Allure** was a powerful technique. It was the strongest enchantment in her arsenal. Even three-tailed kitsune could not break it. She knew this. She'd tested it. For Kevin to break free of her enchantment with nothing but sheer willpower was nothing short of astounding.

You could say it put him up a notch in her book. Just one, though.

"Wait, wait, wait, wait, wait! Hold on! Timeout!" Alex made an x-sign with his arms as he stared at Kevin, his bulging eyes and slack-jawed mouth giving him an appearance that made Iris snort. "You're telling me that you and Lilian still haven't done the deed? Seriously? After all this time, nearly five months of dating, and you two haven't fucked like rabbits in heat?"

"The heck is that supposed mean?" Kevin mumbled as he ate. "And it's foxes in heat."

"What?"

"Never mind."

I still don't know what she sees in him.

Iris would admit, if only to herself, that Kevin was decently handsome. He wasn't the best-looking guy at school, but he was cute in his own way. Tousled blond hair swayed as he ate, and eyes of the brightest blue stared at the world with an unusual sharpness, which hadn't been there when they'd first met. Light tan skin, visible beneath his T-shirt and shorts, appeared to have been kissed by the sun.

He'd put on a good deal of muscle, too. As she watched, Iris could see the way his arm flexed as he raised the chopsticks to his mouth.

It was lunchtime. She, Kevin, Lilian, Lindsay, Christine, Justin, Alex, and Andrew were sitting around the stone table. Iris sat beside her sister, silently observing Kevin, whom she'd become fascinated by. She really wanted to see what made him tick.

"Whatever, my point is that Lilian has offered herself to you, and you're not doing anything about it. What kind of man are you? I can tell you right now that if I were in your position, I would have already shoved my hot, throbbing—"

"All right, that's enough out of you," a red-faced Kevin said.

The innocence that Kevin still displayed amused Iris. Sure, they hadn't had sex yet, but he and Lily-pad had shared some passionate moments together. She should know, having spied on them often enough when they thought no one else was looking.

Kevin continued. "Why are we even talking about this? My sex life really can't be that interesting, can it?"

Alex and Andrew shared a look. They were twins, but they looked nothing alike. Alex had brown hair while Andrew was a redhead. Andrew had a lot of freckles, but Alex had none. The only similarity was their height. Like her and Lilian, they were fraternal twins.

"Considering you're the only one among us who even has a sex life, I'd have to say yes. Yes, it is. None of the girls we've dated are willing to put out. You've got a girl who actually wants to do the horizontal mambo, but you're not actually doing anything with her. Do you know how much that pisses me off?"

"What he said," Andrew added.

"Did you ever think that maybe the whole reason no girl is willing to do anything with you is that they know you're only looking for sex?" Kevin suggested. "And Lilian and I do plenty of things together that are, um, not meant for anyone else to know about."

"Oh, yeah? Like what?"

Iris grinned when Kevin froze. "You walked into that one, Stud."

"Shut up," he snapped at her before addressing his friends. "Lilian and I, well, we do lots of things together… things that are… um, you know…"

"No, we don't know. That's why we're asking."

"Ugh. R-right. W-well. Well!" Kevin tried to put on a confident front, but Iris could practically see the gears turning in the boy's head. He was panicking. "That's… it's… how do you say…"

Having heard the conversation from where she was speaking with Lindsay and Christine, Lilian helpfully interjected. "Kevin brought me to multiple orgasms last Saturday when we were taking a shower together."

"Right." Kevin nodded. "I brought her to—LILIAN! You're not supposed to tell anyone that!!"

"Um… whoopsies. I forgot. Tee-hee."

Lilian bopped herself on the head and poked her tongue out. Her red hair swayed from the action, and eyes like emeralds peeked out from underneath her bangs. A green off-the-shoulder shirt showcased her slender shoulders, magnificent bosoms, and flat stomach. Jean shorts covered her small, shapely bottom and revealed her lean legs, which ended in a pair of delicate feet that were encased in gladiator sandals.

What I wouldn't give to kiss that stomach, or those legs. I'd even suck on her toes.

"Don't say that in such a cutesy tone!" Kevin barked. "And don't make that pose! You're not an anime character!"

"Hawa."

"And don't use your mom's catchphrase!"

He makes a surprisingly good tsukkomi.

"Would this be a bad time to tell everyone that you were gnawing on my panties the other day?" Iris asked, her tone nonchalant.

"Oh, shut up," Kevin snapped. "I was not. You shoved those panties in my mouth while I was sleeping—and those weren't your panties anyway. They were your mom's panties. You don't even wear panties!"

Everyone stared at Kevin, who only realized what he'd said several seconds after he said it.

"Uhuhuhu." Iris's grin became the epitome of devilish desire. She looked over at the fraternal twins and winked. "He knows me too well. Ev-ery-nook-and-cran-ny!"

Andrew and Alex were both blown back by nosebleeds. They fell from their seats, blood gushing from their noses like water hoses out of control.

"I-I-I-I do not! SHUT UP!"

"Uhuhuhu… how cute," Iris muttered. This boy was just too easy.

"But seriously, you've changed a lot, man," Andrew said, wiping the blood from his nose as he sat back down. "You used to be a total pansy."

"Guh!"

"Biggest pansy I've ever seen," Andrew agreed.

"Urk!"

"You were so completely pansified that you couldn't even talk to girls without passing out."

"Gurk!"

Iris watched in mild amusement as several arrows appeared seemingly out of nowhere and pierced the blond teen's back. Lilian, being the good girlfriend that she was, carefully pulled each metaphorical shaft out and tossed them to the ground.

"Do you guys really have to put it like that?" Kevin whined piteously.

"Are you denying it?" Alex asked.

"…"

"Thought not. Face it, Kevin, you were a complete loser. Worse than those main protagonists who are all buff and badass, and then get turned into complete wimps because some chick with more estrogen than she knows what to do with got this idea in her head that yaoi fan fiction is art."

Kevin's cheeks puffed up. "You guys are awful!"

"And you shouldn't make fun of yaoi fanfiction," Lilian added.

"Right," Kevin said. "Wait. What?"

"Don't worry, Stud." Iris grinned as she pressed her breasts into Kevin's back. "I don't doubt that you're a paragon of masculinity." She blew on his ear, enjoying the way he shuddered. "In fact, I would love to help you show these peons just how much of a man you are. Right. This. Instant."

Iris could practically feel Kevin's struggle. It was admirable, really. Any other male would have succumbed ages ago. Yet even now he fought against her, denied her. Perhaps that was Lilian's influence, but the fact that her sister and Kevin had yet to have hot, passionate, and raunchy sex suggested otherwise.

"Come on," Iris whispered, her voice suffused with her intent, her lust, her desire. "Why don't you show me just what you're made of, big boy—gya!"

Something hard and strong smacked Iris in the head, sending her sprawling to the ground.

"Iris, stop picking on my mate," Lilian said, her bushy red tail disappearing before anyone but Iris and Kevin could notice it.

"Aw!" Iris pouted at her sister from where she sat, sprawled across the ground. She grinned when Alex, Andrew, and even Justin tried to stare down her shirt. "I was just having a little bit of fun."

Lilian pouted at her, which Iris thought was adorable.

When Lilian realized that Iris wasn't going to apologize, she turned her attention to Kevin, eyes softening in concern. "Are you okay, Kevin?"

"Yeah, I'm fine." Kevin sniffled. He looked at Lilian with big, watery eyes. "Thank you, Lilian. I love you."

Lilian's eyes also went wide, but then, inexplicably, they became warm pools of love and compassion. A smile touched her lips. "I love you too, Kevin…"

"Lilian…"

"Kevin."

"Lilian."

"Kevin!"

"Lilian!"

"Oh, for all the gods' sakes! If you two are gonna get all lovey-dovey like that, then get a fucking room!" Christine shouted.

As per the usual, the yuki-onna was decked out in classic Lolita clothing. Iris didn't understand how someone could wear something so stifling in Arizona, but she had to admit that it gave the girl a certain charm. She looked like a doll. Iris was even tempted to take her home and play dress-up.

Uhuhuhu, maybe I could even get Lilian and the stud to join in. That would be fun.

Sitting on her butt, Iris switched her gaze from Christine to the still hugging Lilian and Kevin. For some reason, whenever she saw them hug like this, she imagined waves crashing against a beach with a sunset backdrop. She didn't know why.

"Is something wrong?" Lindsay asked Christine, tucking a strand of blonde hair behind her left ear. Doe-like brown eyes gazed at her Lolita-clad friend. Lindsay was a cutie, in a tomboyish sort of way. She was the most normal girl Iris had ever met, but cute nonetheless.

The yuki-onna blinked, and then looked at the lithe blonde. "No. It's nothing. I just realized we're missing someone."

Lindsay looked around and realized that Christine was right. "Now that you mention it, we *are* missing someone."

"… Eric…" Justin added unnecessarily. Iris didn't know how he'd heard them. His ears were covered by a pair of headphones, which were as black as his hair. Pale skin made a startling contrast with his dark hair and clothes, lending him a gothic appearance.

At the mention of their perverted friend, everyone began searching. Even Iris peered at her surroundings from her place on the cement. Eric was a lecherous fool with lanky limbs and spiky brown hair. He reminded her of a monkey. Lilian had nicknamed him "Saru" in reference to some anime character with the same personality. Iris didn't get it, but she wasn't an anime nerd like her sister.

Kevin's brows furrowed. "Come to think of it, Eric hasn't had lunch with us for the past couple of days. I wonder what he's up to?"

"Waaaa…"

As if summoned by their thoughts, a loud scream echoed to them as if from a vast distance. In a most unusual form of synchronization, the entire group turned towards the source of the yells.

"… aaaaAAAAHHHH!!"

Naturally, the source of all that shouting was Eric… and the horde of freshmen girls chasing after him, angrily waving around various implements that could be found within a gym—except for one girl, who had a claymore. It was too bad for Eric that the claymore girl was at the front of the pack. Her demonic red eyes glowered at the young man, and she shouted expletives that would have made a sailor cream his pants and proclaim his undying love for her.

"HELP MEEE, MASTER!!"

"Mwahahahahaha! Run, Apprentice! Run! This is all part of your training!"

"How is this training?! They're trying to kill meeeeeee!"

"We're training your endurance, my boy! You must be able to outrun women if you ever want to excel in the art of peeping! Now run faster! Mwahahaha!"

"UUUUUUUUWAAAAAA!"

Heather followed behind the group, laughing like a loon as she goaded Eric to run and spurred on the girls chasing after him. Pretty soon, Eric ran past them, screaming like a prepubescent little girl. The Horde, for that's all they could have been, followed, a large cloud of dust flying off of the ground behind them.

Everyone sat there as Eric disappeared into the distance, listening as screams of terror became squeals of agony. It sounded like the girls had caught up to him.

"So…" Lindsay started again, "… are we still on for spring break?"

Jumping off her seat, Lilian stood on the table, left foot on the bench, right on the table itself. She raised a hand to her face, clenching it into a fist, eyes blazing with an inner fire.

"Of course we are!" she declared, wearing a large, excited smile. "There's no way we're going to alter our plans now! This is my first spring break, and by Inari, we are going to travel out of this state and have fun!"

A grinning Kevin followed his girlfriend-slash-mate's example. He, too, jumped onto the table, imitating Lilian's pose. An excited gleam had entered his eyes.

"That's right! This is something we must do! It's going to be the adventure of a lifetime! There's no way we can pass up on this opportunity!"

Everyone stared at the two with the kind of "WTF?" expression that had become commonplace among them. Iris snickered. Seeing them act like this made her realize that maybe, just maybe, this strange human really was meant for her sister.

Lindsay pressed a palm against her face and sighed. "I swear, it's like Kevin gets more insane every time I see him." Despite her words, the smile she wore blunted any harshness they might have held.

Several months had passed since the incident that had rendered Lindsay's mother in the hospital. She'd had plenty of time to think about what had happened. At first, Lindsay thought that avoiding her two friends was the best idea. This had caused a lot of drama and angst to go on between the group.

Fortunately for everyone involved, Lindsay had come to her senses, thanks to a surprisingly passionate speech from Christine. In the end, the problem was solved with a heart-to-heart conversation that involved talking, hugging, and lots of "hawas."

"I'm beginning to see what you mean," Christine muttered. "And to think, he used to be such a shy, innocent boy." She shook her head sadly. "Lilian's corrupted him."

"That reminds me!" Lilian turned to Kevin, her eyes sparkling. "We need to think of which costumes we should bring with us!"

Kevin's eyes widened. "You're right!" The two raised their hands, pressed their palms together, and laced their fingers. "This is a very important decision. We need to think carefully about which costumes we should bring. We need at least… two? No, three. No, it's two. I'm pretty sure it's two."

"It's two, Kevin. We're only going to Comic-Con for two of the seven days we'll be there."

"Right." Kevin's eyes sparkled. "I can't believe we're going to Comic-Con together!"

Lilian's beaming smile was a reflection of her joy. "Me neither!"

"Oh, Lilian, I love you so much."

"I love you, too, Kevin."

"Lilian."

"Kevin."

"Lilian!"

"Kevin!"

"Stop hugging already!!"

***

"Gravity is a most unusual force. It's different from magnetic forces, electrical forces, and it is connected in some way with the geometric properties of space and time. And that connection is known as the General Theory of Relativity…"

Kevin Swift often wondered why he'd decided to take AP Physics. Every single lecture was filled with overly complicated explanations that explained very little. His head hurt just from thinking about some of the garbage his teacher filled it with. Really, what had he been thinking?

…

That's right. I wanted to get into a good college.

He felt like slamming his face against the desk. Curse his need to excel!

"Before we get into the General Theory of Relativity, we're going to study an older form of gravity, Newtonian gravity, and build upon these lessons first, then expand on the theories behind…"

The man speaking up front, his teacher Leroy Dupout, was an old man. Kevin would even go so far as to say ancient. His skin, wrinkled and ashen, contained multiple sunspots that people tended to get when they aged. That same skin hung off his elbows, gangly, wrinkly folds that quivered as he moved his arms. It disturbed Kevin a great deal.

I wonder what would happen if this guy and Cthulhu faced off.

"So let's begin with the first of Newton's equations: F=MA, force is equal to mass times acceleration…"

He looked over at Lilian, his girlfriend and mate of four months. It was hard to believe they'd been together that long. Harder still to believe that even now, after several months had passed, Kevin felt a thrill go through him at the thought.

"Let us assume that we have a frame of reference…"

She noticed him looking at her and sent a smile his way. Kevin responded with one of his own, even as he felt his cheeks grow warm. There was just something about knowing that her smile was reserved for him that set his soul ablaze, and yet it also eased his heart.

It's such an odd feeling. Is this what people call the springtime of youth? No, wait. I think I heard that in an anime.

"Someone gag me…"

Lilian and Kevin turned at the same time to glare at Iris, who sat behind them. As always, the girl looked like the absolute epitome of sin. The way she sat in her chair like it was a throne, her chest extended, swaying enticingly with every inhale and exhale of breath, all of it was done with the purpose of flaunting her assets. More than half the class was focused on her boobs instead of the teacher—even the girls.

There are going to be a lot of Fs in this class.

Class eventually ended and he, Lilian, and Iris left with the rest of the students.

"Don't forget about your homework just because it's spring break," the teacher called to the leaving teens. "Your papers on the theory behind Newtonian physics will be due first thing next week."

Nobody actually listened to him. Kevin felt sorry for the old man. Teachers really didn't get much respect these days.

"Man!" Iris stretched her arms high above her head, which had the completely intentional side effect of making her chest pop out. "I am so glad to be out of that class. It's so boring. Really..." She brought her hands back down and stared at her sister and him. "Why did you two choose such a boring class?"

"I'm beginning to wonder that myself," Kevin admitted with a shrug. "I think I had a reason when I chose that class, but it seems to have slipped my mind."

"Who cares about class?" Lilian declared. She walked on Kevin's right, her left hand entwined with his right. "Class is over, school is over, and we can go home and prepare for spring break." Her eyes sparkled at the thought. "Spring break. I'm told this is supposed to be some of the best times of a high school student's life." She squealed. "I'm so excited!"

"Maybe a little too excited." Despite the harsh-sounding words, Kevin could clearly see that Iris was every bit as excited as her sister. She just didn't want to show it.

The trio strolled to the front gates, where Kevin's new mode of transportation awaited.

Due to his dislike of buses, he and Kotohime had gone out and bought a bike, one that was large enough to carry him, Lilian, and Iris. It was a three-seater bike with orange trim. Lilian had picked out the color.

"Kevin!"

Before the group could leave, Lindsay ran up to them. Trailing behind her was Christine. While Lilian appeared happy to see her friends, Iris didn't.

"Oh, great. The closet les—oof!" Iris sent her sister an incredulous look. "You just elbowed me!"

Lilian puffed her cheeks out. She would have looked angry if she weren't so cute. "You were going to say something rude about my friends."

"U-ugh."

Kevin thought he saw a javelin randomly spear Iris through the chest, however, when he blinked, the javelin was gone.

I must have imagined it. He resisted the urge to rub his eyes. *I think I've been watching too much anime lately...*

"Hey, you two! What's up?" Lilian greeted the pair cheerfully.

Kevin shook his head. *No, no, no! How can I say that? You can never watch too much anime!*

"We just wanted to tell you there's been a slight change of plans," Lindsay said. "Christine's going to stay at my house tonight, so you won't have to drive to her place tomorrow."

"So, the lesbians are finally coming out of the closet, are they?" Iris's teasing grin was in full form.

Kevin palmed his face as Mount Christine erupted and Kevin palmed his face.

Tsundere Protocols: Activated.

"Le-les-l-le—you! Shut up! Shut up, shut up, shut up! You don't know what you're talking about! I'm not—I-I mean, it's not— WE'RE NOT LIKE THAT!" Christine's face looked like an atomic bomb had gone off on it. "Don't get any strange ideas. I'm only staying at Lindsay's house because we thought this would be easier. I was trying to be considerate, Tit Monster!"

A small black cloud hovered over Lindsay's head. The lithe blonde knelt down, one arm curled around her legs, which were drawn up to her chest. She used her other hand to draw circles on the pavement.

"She didn't have to say it like that," Lindsay muttered lowly. "She makes it sound like we're not even friends."

"There, there." Lilian rubbed her friend's back in a consoling manner. "I'm sure she didn't mean it. You and Christine hang out together a lot. You're obviously important to her."

Lindsay looked at her red-haired friend with hopeful eyes. "You think so?"

"Of course. Christine's just being a tsundere."

"I'm not a tsundere!"

Lilian gave the snow maiden a pitying look, which caused Christine's tsundere protocols to reach power levels that exceeded 9,000.

"I'm not! Y-y-y-you don't, ah, you don't know what you're talking about!"

By this point, even Kevin and Iris were looking at Christine with matching deadpanned expressions.

"You're really not helping your case with that tsundere act, you know," Kevin said.

"Denial is a painful thing to watch sometimes," Iris added.

"SH-SH-SH-SH-SHUT UP! I'LL KILL YOU ALL DEAD!"

Christine's face would not be losing its neon complexion anytime soon.

***

Kevin, Lilian, and Iris arrived home fifteen minutes later. After locking up their bike, they entered the apartment, taking off their shoes and walking further inside. There, they were greeted by their maid—one of them.

Kirihime was a three-tailed kitsune. Her shoulder-length black hair possessed a lustrous shine, and two antenna-like strands poked out from the top of her head. Large, round eyes that were the same color as her hair smiled at them with a comely warmth. Unlike her sister, who preferred kimonos, Kirihime wore a black and white French Maid outfit.

"Lady Iris, Lady Lilian, Lord Kevin," Kirihime greeted the group with a gentle smile and a curtsy. "How was school? Enjoyable, I hope."

"Meh, it was nothing special."

"I thought it was fun."

Iris rolled her eyes at her sister. "You think everything is fun."

While Lilian pouted at her sister's teasing, Kevin conversed with Kirihime. "Did you, Camellia, and Kotohime already pack everything for the trip?"

"Mostly. Yours and Lady Lilian's clothing have not been packed yet. I thought about doing that myself, but then I thought that you might want to choose your own clothes." Her eyes slowly widened in a clear sign of worry. "D-did you want me to pack your clothes? I-I'm so sorry! If you want me to, I'll go and do that right now—"

"No, no," Kevin assured Kirihime with a gentle smile to put the maid at ease. "Lilian and I will pack our own clothes, so there's no need for you to do that. We have to choose which cosplay to bring anyway."

"O-okay." Kirihime slumped in relief.

"You worry way too much, Kirihime," Lilian said. "You should learn to be a little calmer, like Kotohime."

"Oh, no. I could never—my venerable sister is such an amazing woman. I could never be like her."

"Mou, I think you're selling yourself short."

"That's very kind of you to say."

Stepping further into the room, Kevin found what he'd expected to find upon arriving home: Kotohime flittering about the kitchen, preparing dinner. Her four tails were out, extending and retracting, moving in what almost appeared to be at random, but was actually a choreographed dance done with a purpose. One tail reached up and opened a cabinet, pulling out a bottle of spices. Another opened the fridge and pulled out a large slab of meat in a plastic bag. The woman was a bundle of furry activity.

Kevin felt insanely jealous.

I could cook twice as fast if I had that many appendages at my disposal.

Long black hair danced in an unseen breeze as she moved about the kitchen. Her dark eyes were slightly narrowed, adding a sensual allure that didn't fool Kevin one bit. A purple kimono tied together with an obi several shades lighter covered her voluptuous body. The voluminous sleeves had been tied with a tasuki—a long white sash.

"Dinner will be ready in an hour or two," Kotohime told them, even as one tail grabbed a knife. "I know it is not my place to say it, but why don't you three make sure that everything you want for our trip is packed? You will not have much time tomorrow, especially you, Kevin-sama."

"Yeah." Kevin scratched the base of his neck. "I know."

"M-My Lady! Please be—"

"Hawa!"

As one, everybody turned and winced as Camellia crashed to the floor. Her raven hair was in disarray, strands sticking out in several places. Bright green eyes looked at everything with a joy that reminded Kevin of a child, presenting a powerful dichotomy with her adult body, which was beautiful enough to give Kotohime a run for her money.

To think this is Lilian and Iris's mother.

"I'm not gonna say a thing," Iris declared.

"You just did."

"Whatever, Lily-pad."

"Don't call me that!"

"Aw! You're so adorable when you get angry!"

"Iris—wa-wait—kya!"

Iris leapt on top of her sister, dragging the redhead to the floor. There, she proceeded to rub her face against Lilian's left cheek. She also reached underneath Lilian, who was lying on her stomach, and cupped her sister's breasts.

"Hey! Stop! —eek!"

Kevin watched as Iris continued to grope his mate. He wondered if he should stop them.

Lilian noticed him staring and reached out with a hand, no doubt hoping he would take it.

"B-Beloved! Help!"

"But you're doing so well," Kevin said, feeling a strange sense of vindication, almost as if he'd been in the exact same position as Lilian before. Oh, wait. He had.

"But she's trying to rape me!"

"You're exaggerating."

While Iris rubbed her nose into her sister's lovely red hair, Lilian again tried calling out for her beloved. However, Kevin found the whole situation amusing and decided to let things play out. Meanwhile, Kirihime helped Camellia to her feet.

"A-are you alright, My Lady?"

"Hawa, don't worry." Camellia took her fall, like all of her previous falls, with a childish grin. "Camellia's breasts softened her fall."

"Ha…" A trickle of sweat trailed down the right side of Kirihime's face. "Th-that's good… I think…"

"Hawa," Camellia said, seemingly in agreement.

***

"I was thinking; we should definitely bring our matching bushy-brow costumes."

"Mm."

"Oh! And we should definitely bring our Nalu and Jerza costumes."

"Mm."

"But I don't know what other costumes we should bring. What do you think?"

"Mm."

"…You're completely ignoring me, aren't you?"

"I'm still mad at you."

Lilian stood over by the window, arms crossed under her chest, staring at the world beyond their bedroom. Kevin wished she would face him, and not just because he knew that her crossed arms were putting her breasts on an enticing display. While he didn't obsess over it like Iris did, he still thought Lilian had the most adorable pout ever.

Chuckling, Kevin walked up behind Lilian. He slid his arms around her waist and pulled her back into his chest. Leaning forward, he placed a soft kiss on her cheek.

"There. You're not mad at me anymore, right?"

"Mou… you're no fair, Beloved."

Despite her words, Lilian leaned into him. Her hands came up, and she placed them over his hands, which rested on her flat stomach. Kevin was tempted to take things a little further than simple hugging, but he resisted the urge to rub her entrancingly taut belly.

"I sense deep thoughts going on in here." Kevin kissed Lilian on the temple. He was taller than her, so he had to lean down to do so.

Lilian hummed softly, a way of masking her anxiety. "Kitsune are among the largest yōkai population in the world. I don't know exactly how many of us there are—it's not like we actually keep track of our numbers—but there are more kitsune than almost any other yōkai race on the planet."

"I know. Kotohime's been teaching me about kitsune."

"Then you probably know about what goes on behind the scenes? How our politics work?"

"She's… getting there. It's a slow process."

"You know how our social science teacher has been lecturing us on human politics."

"American politics, actually, but I get what you're saying. What about it?"

Lilian hummed when Kevin, unable to resist, slowly rubbed her stomach, reveling in the softness of her perfectly flat belly.

"American politicians… no, human politicians in general, speak with two tongues. They promise one thing and almost never fail to deliver something else, something you didn't want or ask for."

"Kitsune politics are similar in that respect. A good kitsune diplomat speaks with a gilded tongue. They whisper soft words and reassurances in your ear, and then they stab you in the back when you least expect them to, metaphorically and sometimes even physically."

Kevin listened as Lilian spoke. She'd been taught politics from a young age, and though he knew she loathed them with a passion, he also knew that she, like her maid, was a font of knowledge in this regard.

"Politics in the kitsune world are also a lot more… violent. While kitsune rarely fight in combat, that does not mean we're not above killing and murder. It's not unusual for a diplomat or the political leader of a clan to be… dealt with through assassination or other means. There are even some cases of entire clans being annihilated and their position usurped."

"You're talking about how the Vande Clan destroyed the Ślina Clan and took over as the Great River Clan, right?"

Lilian paused when one of Kevin's hands slipped into her shorts. Her breathing hitched.

"Th-there are many other examples. That's just the most recent one. My point is the kitsune world, the yōkai world, is violent. You are a human. You and all of your friends. Our world has never been very kind to humans. For every human/kitsune relationship that ends in joy and happiness, there are ten more that end in tragedy. Our way… it is cruel to humans."

Kevin did not speak for the longest time.

"Are you having second thoughts about us? About our relationship?"

"No!" Lilian twisted around in his arms until she was facing him. Her eyes were wide, and the earnestly pained expression on her face caused a knife to twist painfully in Kevin's chest. "Of course not! Never. I love you so very much, Kevin. You're my mate, and I will never, ever regret this decision." She sighed. "I'm just worried."

"Because of what happened with Jiāoào?"

Five months ago, a kitsune named Jiāoào had kidnapped Lilian. Kevin had gone to her rescue and was nearly killed in the process. Kiara, his combat instructor, had also lost an arm fighting against a Void Kitsune.

Lilian leaned forward, pressing her face against the crook of his neck. She breathed in deeply. Kevin shuddered as her breath tickled his neck. Her scent, a wonderful fragrance that soothed his mind, pervaded his nose. He would never tell her this because it was embarrassing, but Kevin loved her scent. "Yes, when Jiāoào kidnapped me, it reminded me of something important, something that I had been running away from for a while now."

Kevin didn't say anything. He knew his role in this scene. He held her close, and listened as she spoke.

"I am a member of the **Pnéyma** Clan, one of the Thirteen Great Kitsune Clans. The Pnéyma Clan is considered one of the strongest clans in the world. We have field agents in various positions all over Europe, and branch family members who oversee operations outside of our clan compound. While the main family, the family that I come from, is small, we have over one thousand kitsune who live under and abide by our rule."

While 1,000 wasn't a large number by human standards, it was a lot in terms of yōkai. Kevin didn't know how many kitsune existed, but he'd been given a rough estimate by Kotohime, who claimed there were probably around 50,000 kitsune worldwide. That wasn't a very large number, certainly not when compared to the 3.5 billion humans that existed.

"Jiāoào's attempt to kidnap me reminded me that I'll never be free, that I'll always be a member of the **Pnéyma** Clan. No matter how far I run, no matter how hard I try to escape, I'll always be dragged back into that world." Her arms around Kevin tightened. "I'm afraid that you'll end up being dragged into that world with me. I don't want to see you get hurt."

Her words suffused Kevin's heart with warmth. In that moment, she could have told him that there were two thousand other suitors who would be coming for his life, and he wouldn't have cared. For her, he would take on even a Great Clan by himself.

"You worry too much."

"Yes, I worry too—huh?"

"You're worrying too much, you're thinking about this too hard, and you're forgetting something important."

"I-I am? What?"

Kevin paused for a moment, but only to wonder about something. Why was every single expression Lilian made so damn cute? Seriously. Maybe he was being biased, but it seemed like, no matter what facial expression Lilian wore, she always looked adorable… and hot, but mostly adorable.

"You're forgetting that I chose this path. I decided to become your mate. I might not have known about all this stuff, like the politics or the crazy fox-boy stalker, but that doesn't change the fact that this is the path that I've decided to walk."

Lilian looked up at him. Her eyes, wide emeralds that made her look like those impossibly attractive females Kevin saw so often in anime, possessed a sincere hope that made her all the more enchanting.

"Do you really mean that?"

"I wouldn't have said it if I didn't mean it."

It was almost interesting to watch the way Lilian's face shifted into a variety of expressions. First came surprise: the widening of her eyes, the parting of her lips. This was followed by another emotion. Embarrassment? No. Joy mixed with shyness perhaps. Her lovely cheeks gained a beautiful rosy hue. Next came desire. The color of her cheeks darkened. Her breathing grew heavy. Eyes that were once wide became lidded. A hand settled on the back of his head, fingers threading through strands of blond hair.

"Kevin…"

A whispered word from honeyed lips. Kevin stared at those lips, beautifully shaped, slightly parted, pink, and softer than the finest silk. They glistened in the moonlight. Lilian's small tongue darted out and licked those lips, and Kevin found himself envying them.

"Yes, Lilian?" he lowered his voice to a whisper. By this point, Lilian's lips were close enough that he could practically taste them. Her warm breath carried with it the scent of strawberries and cinnamon.

"Kiss me."

Had Lilian said those words when they first met, he would have denied her. Actually, he would have passed out, but it amounted to the same thing. Had Lilian told him to do this as little as several months ago, that first contact would have been tentative, a soft flutter like the petals of a flower caressing bare skin. Had she said those words several months ago, Kevin would not have done what he did that night.

***

"All women have the ability to detect lecherous intent in their vicinity. I call it the Perv-O-Dar. In order to beat this Perv-O-Dar, you must learn to mask your presence, my young apprentice."

Eric Corrompere was only half paying attention to his master. The other half was dedicated to trying to get a peek at the nubile, feminine flesh that lay on the other side of the bamboo fence.

"Yes, Master."

Just then, Eric felt something come over him, an overwhelming and undeniably potent feeling. Eric could do nothing to act against this feeling, for it consumed his very being, enthralling him in its libidinous embrace.

Eric clenched a shaking fist.

And raised it to the sky.

He also shouted very loudly.

"My Lord! Your greatness truly knows no bounds! I AM HUMBLED BEFORE YOUR AWESOME PROWESS!"

"Did you hear that?"

"It sounded like a man!"

"A man?!" La gasp. "Peeping tom! It's a peeping tom!"

"Let's murder him, girls!"

"Well, it looks like this is my cue to leave," Heather said. "You're on your own, Apprentice. Good luck."

"Eh? W-wait! Master, what are you—"

But Heather was already gone. She'd vanished, disappearing like a ghost. Or ninja. Or a ninja ghost.

Eric hated it when she did that.

Just then, several shadows covered his vision. Eric turned to find dozens of towel-clad figures glaring at him with glowing red eyes and hellfire blazing behind their backs. They were holding sharp, pointy implements that he was sure did not belong in a hot spring.

A cold sweat broke out on his face.

Eric whimpered.

"Mercy?"

***

They had become animals of passion, of lust, of desire. Driven only by the unquenchable thirst for each other, they could do nothing more than embrace this need and the fires it had lit beneath them.

Saliva became their sustenance. They shared in the sweet nectar. What little managed to escape their mouths was eventually scooped back up by an errant lick.

Tongues danced to the rhythm of a hundred pulsating drums that obeyed no form of musical theory, driven as it was by the staccato bursts and nasally gasps of their dramatic breathing.

Licking, hooking, twirling, tasting, pushing, and pulling… nothing existed beyond these concepts of action—nothing but the desire, the need, the thirst, the hunger that consumed them, that pushed their eager bodies and battling tongues to greater heights of passion.

Lilian's back pressed against the wall, smashed between the hard surface and her mate's muscular body. Her shorts had long since disappeared, as had her shirt, and Kevin's eager hand had yet to leave its place on her left breast. His other hand had yet to leave its place on her right butt cheek, and Lilian would be damned if she let it move from that spot… unless it was to switch to her other cheek.

Her legs were hooked around his waist. Her body, slick with their combined sweat, rubbed against his bare stomach and chest, generating ceaseless friction that caused her to moan with the desire for more. Their pelvises, the only part of their body still covered by clothing, ground together; the intensity of their rubbing privates caused her body to shudder.

Lilian was lost. Lost in her desire for this human teenager, who evoked feelings she could only experience with him. Her need for him—to feel his body against hers, his warmth pervading her, hands touching her skin—was as inarguable a fact as one plus one equals two. Did he know what he did to her? Could he even comprehend the feelings that the mere thought of him invoked? Probably not fully, but he was certainly beginning to.

"Ahn!"

His mouth left her lips. She would have complained, but that implied that she had the ability to speak. She did not. Anything other than her monosyllabic moans had fled long before his lips ever latched onto her neck.

He licked her. Kevin's tongue glided along the side of her neck, reveling in the salty taste of her sweaty skin. It left a trail, wet and glistening, from the base of her neck all the way up to her ear, which a set of teeth proceeded to nibble on soon after.

"Hnn!"

Hardness. She could feel her mate's arousal. She could feel him pressing against her, caressing a place on her body that only he was allowed to touch—well, that only he was allowed to touch now. She and Iris had experimented before Kevin had come into the picture, but Kevin didn't seem interested in going the harem route. Her lace panties clung to her skin, rubbing against her folds and sending her mind into delirium.

Her small feet touched carpet as Kevin set her down. Wanting to experience another kiss, Lilian claimed his mouth again. Her tongue darted past his lips, where it plundered the inside of his mouth, even as she pushed him onto the bed and used the hardness trapped between her thighs to pleasure herself.

She wanted him. Inari-blessed, she wanted him right now. She wanted to feel him inside of her, to feel him filling her up, sending her over the chasm, as her mind touched upon the maddening ecstasy that could only come after her body had been thoroughly plundered by her mate.

She wanted to have sex with him so badly, but she wouldn't do it. Not now. Not yet. She had promised her mate. Kevin was willing to indulge her need, to satiate her desire; however, there was one line that he didn't want to cross yet.

She didn't understand his unwillingness to have sex—Inari knows they'd done just about everything short of it. But then, Lilian wasn't human. She was a kitsune, and their society did not have the downright stupid taboos about sex that humans did.

She still thought it was dumb to let something like a silly little taboo get in the way of their love, but Kevin had been firm on this. Lilian loved Kevin, so she had promised that they would not take that last step until he was ready—and a kitsune never broke her promise.

Kevin groaned underneath Lilian as she dry-humped him. His body bucked, hips moving to the rhythm she set. He placed one hand against the bed, pushing his body up so he was sitting. The other fell upon her derriere like a baker's hand on wet flour, and her rear muscles clenched at the most welcome sensations.

"Yes!"

She hissed against his mouth, an action only partially repeated by him. Kevin's mind was even more lost than her own. She knew that, should she desire it, she could probably get away with ripping his pants off and having her way with him. Oddly enough, the thought never lasted longer than a fleeting second. Her promise and his love meant far more to her than the transitory pleasure she could derive from such an act.

What began as a slow buildup within her lower stomach reached a crescendo. She could feel it, the tightening of coils in her loins, the impossible peak being reached right before that final release. Her panties were sopping wet by this point, the flowing juices had even stained hers and Kevin's legs. With one final wail, she tipped over the edge—her body shuddering, vision going white. Nothing remained except that incredible feeling of rapture that could only come from an intense orgasm.

Strength ebbing, her mind going strangely blank, Lilian collapsed on top of a just as spent Kevin. She breathed in deeply, basking in his scent and the oh-so-wonderful glow of what they'd done. His hands resting on her back sent tingles down her spine.

"… Lilian?"

"Mm?"

"Thank you."

Lilian looked up, an incredible feat considering her exhaustion, and met the beautiful blue eyes of her beloved mate. Using the last of her strength, she pulled herself up to place another kiss upon his now bruised lips.

"I should be the one saying that," she muttered against his mouth. One kiss turned into two and two into three. Lilian was about to go for a fourth when a voice interrupted her.

"By Inari's sagging scrotum, that was hot."

The warm feelings that had been clouding the couple's minds dispersed like a summer breeze in Antarctica. They turned their heads, slowly, mechanically, towards the door. Iris stood there, leaning against the doorframe. Her hands were covering her crotch. It wasn't hard to realize what she was doing.

"*How long has she been there?*" They would have wondered—except they were still trying to comprehend the fact that Iris had entered their room sometime while they'd been passionately embraced.

"Hey, don't stop on my account. I don't mind being given another show." Iris paused to grin lecherously. "Unless you'd like me to join you."

As the words "join you" passed through her ear, Lilian's mind went straight down the gutter. She envisioned her and her sister ganging up on Kevin, having their way with him. Then she imagined Kevin and Iris ganging up on her!

Several seconds later, Lilian was launched into the air as blood shot from her nose like the thruster exhaust from a Gundam. She slammed into the ceiling, her body going *splat!* She stayed like that for several seconds before, ever so slowly, her body peeled off the ceiling and landed on top of Kevin.

"Oof!"

Kevin released all the air he had in a loud *whoosh!* as Lilian's soft body slammed into his stomach. He gasped, trying to suck in the oxygen that he'd lost to no avail.

Still lying on top of him, her eyes swirling around in her head, Lilian, clearly insensate, muttered:

"Ufufufu, Beloved, Iris, this is my first time… please be gentle, ufufufu…"

After he finally regained his breath, a blushing Kevin glared at Iris who, if the smile she wore said anything, told him that she didn't care if he was bothered, angry, embarrassed, or all three.

Her mission complete, Iris left, her laughter echoing to him as she sauntered down the hall.

Kevin glanced at Lilian, who was still giggling and muttering nonsensically in her unconscious state.

"Ufufufu, Beloved, I promise we won't suck you dry…"

He sighed and stared up at the ceiling.

"That girl is going to be impossible come tomorrow morning. I can already tell."

For some reason, the thought didn't bother him as much as it once did.

***

Within the darkness, Detavio ran through the streets of Los Angeles. The moon hovered above him, and the stars were all but invisible, blocked out by the lights of Los Angeles. He paid attention to none of this, however, and continued running through the docks.

Damn it! Shit, fuck, gods be damned cock suckers!

He had just barely managed to escape from a situation in which everything had gone right but still somehow ended up going horribly wrong. He couldn't believe those damn foxes! They had been waiting for them, setting up an ambush for their little group, and like a bunch of fools, they'd fallen right into it. He could only thank all eight million gods that their leader, and the majority of their members, had not shown up to take care of this deal personally. That would have been a disaster!

However, this did leave him with a problem. He was the only member of his group still alive, and his enemies were now chasing after him.

His short legs carried him as quickly as they could. The bluish-green tone of his scaly skin reflected the moonlight, with several lamps and neon signs adding color to his bald, shining head. Both factors made it easier to find him. Gods, he really hated this state.

If California wasn't next to the ocean...

"I think he went this way!"

"Quick! Don't let him escape!"

Gritting his teeth, breath coming out of his nose in nasal rasps, he pushed his legs harder than he ever had before. He couldn't let these assholes catch him!

He turned a corner, then another, before ducking through the nearest door. Leaning against the doorframe, he let himself rest, silently gasping for breath. He'd never been so exhausted in his life. Damn those kitsune for blocking off the ocean. Didn't they have enough land, wealth, and power? Now they were stepping onto his leader's turf!

Outside in the alley, he could hear them shouting.

"Where did he go? Did you see him?"

"I think he went that way!"

"Let's go!"

He breathed a sigh of relief before noticing where he was. He decided to have a look around while he waited for his pursuers to leave the area.

He appeared to be in a warehouse, which made sense. This block of the city contained nothing but warehouses. All of the deliveries that arrived from out of the country via ship were stored here, in one of the many large buildings, which were shaped similarly to giant seashells. This one appeared to be mostly empty, save for a few large boxes.

He walked forward slowly, cautiously, on the lookout for anything suspicious. He didn't think those kitsune would be able to find him, but it never hurt to be careful.

Reacting to the large jet stream of water that screamed at him from above, he sucked in a deep breath, then launched his own jet of water at it. The two attacks negated each other, blowing apart and spraying water everywhere.

He glared up at the roof, where a shadowy figure with two swaying tails stood. A noise to his left alerted him to another presence. It was another kitsune, this one also possessing two tails—brown ones.

More and more kitsune entered the room, surrounding him on all sides. How had they found him so quickly? And why were there so many? He counted at least half a dozen!

One of them smirked, a two-tails with blond hair and cobalt eyes. Those eyes, they were a trait of the clan these kitsune belonged to. He hated those condescending eyes, which looked down on him, as if he was trash beneath the kitsune's feet.

"Heh. It looks like you fell right into our little trap. Man, I had always been told that you kappa sucked at illusions, but I never realized you were so shitty at them that you couldn't even tell when you're being led into a trap by one."

D-damn these kitsune and their illusions!

He eyed the kitsune surrounding him, even as he backed up. If he could just find some kind of break in their formation, a weak point that he could exploit. Most unfortunately, there did not seem to be one. These kitsune of the Mul Clan, their tactics were as impeccable as he'd heard.

"Well, whatever, this is the end of the line for you, Scaly. You and the rest of your gang should have just packed up and left when you had the chance."

Had the chance? Ha! As if these foxes had ever given them a chance to escape. Just where would they go anyway? They couldn't move inland. They needed the ocean to survive.

He opened his mouth to talk, although he had no clue what he would say. In the end, it didn't matter.

Pain erupted in his back and chest. He cried out in anguish. His vision went white. When his eyesight returned, spots kept him from seeing the whole picture. He felt numb.

Something was sticking out of his chest. It was a claw, made from water, frozen into crystals, and hardened to the density of diamonds. Dark ichor drenched the claw, shining brightly in the sparse amounts of illumination from the overhead lights. The smell, a coppery scent tinged with sea salt, filled his nostrils.

The last thing he saw before everything went dark was another kitsune walking between the group, her three white tails swaying behind her like the abominable tentacles of a kraken.

CHAPTER 2

The Cat Goes Nya

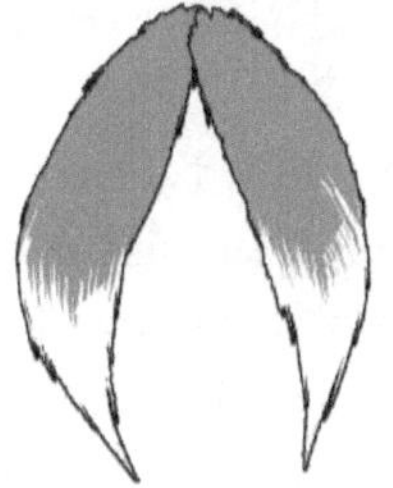

EVER SINCE KEVIN MADE plans with his friends to travel to California, he'd taken to delivering the Saturday and Sunday morning newspaper. With everything he had going on, like his continued training with Kiara, increased studies, spending time with his friends, and making time for his girlfriend-slash-mate, doing extra work wasn't something he cared for. But, he really wanted the extra spending cash for this trip.

That morning, the sun could scarcely be seen as he rode his bike down the street. While the sun had started rising earlier now that spring had come, it still refused to come out at 2:35 in the morning.

A cold chill swept through the air. Kevin's jacket flapped as he tossed newspapers onto the driveways of various houses. He was disappointed to see that his aim still sucked.

By the time he arrived back at the newspaper distribution center, his cheeks had gained a rosy hue, and his face felt like it had been stuck in a fridge. He actually missed the summer heat.

"I hear you and your friends are going somewhere this spring break." Davin Monstrang didn't take his eyes off the money he was counting as he spoke.

"Uh, yeah," Kevin said. "We're heading off to California, Los Angeles, to be exact." His eyes sparkled as he thought about traveling to the beach state. Odd as it might have seemed, he'd never been to California before. "There's a Comic-Con that's happening this coming Friday, so Lilian and I have decided to go. Then we thought, 'Hey, we should invite our friends to come along as well!' One thing led to another and here we are. We'll be leaving about an hour or so after I get home."

Davin grunted as he finished counting the money, then tapped the bills against the table, straightening them.

"California's a dangerous place to be right now." He finally looked at Kevin, who felt a shudder course through him when all six of his boss's chins undulated in ways that defied the laws of physics. "If you and your family really plan on going to California, then you should take as many precautions as possible."

"Um, all right," Kevin said unsurely. Davin slapped the wad of cash into his hands. Kevin blinked when he noticed how many bills there were. "Uh, boss, I don't want to be rude, but I think you counted wrong."

"No. That's the correct amount."

"But it's too—"

"Just take the damn money and be grateful!" Davin grunted, his eyes glowing. For some reason, the air became colder. Puffs of frosty mist were released from his mouth as Kevin breathed.

"Y-yes, sir!"

Rushing out of the building, Kevin heaved a deep sigh. "Dang, I knew Monstrang could be freaky, but I didn't realize he could be that scary." He shuddered. "Better not get on his bad side. Still..." He held the cash up to his face. "Who knew he had a soft side as well?"

Kevin chuckled and walked over to his bike. He put up the kickstand and grabbed the handles. It was time to head home.

"Nya."

Blink.

"Nya?"

"Nya."

Blink. Blink.

Kevin looked at the wall near the distribution building—and nearly squealed upon spotting the small, cute, adorably furry animal sitting on its haunches. A black cat with big yellow eyes stared at him. Its tail swayed behind it, moving left, then right. It opened its mouth, releasing another one of those utterly endearing, if unusual, "nya" sounds.

This cat reminds me of the one that I took home with me when I was in elementary school. It even nyas. How cool is that?

"Kitty!"

Like a child who'd just seen a new toy on Christmas Day, Kevin dropped his bike and went over to the cat, whose large incandescent orbs had yet to leave his face. He reached the feline in record time, and his hand was quick to descend upon its head. The cat didn't seem to mind. Indeed, it reveled in the attention, purring as he gently scratched behind its left ear, which twitched with minute movements.

"Aw! You're just about the most adorable thing I've ever seen."

Lilian's fox form was cuter, but he wasn't going to say that. Cats had pride too!

As Kevin pampered the cat, he realized that he needed to return home. Slowly, and with great reluctance, Kevin stopped petting the cat, which "nya'd" in complaint, and tried to get his attention again.

"Nya?"

"I'm sorry." Kevin struggled not to be blinded by the cuteness as he looked into the cat's eyes. "But I really need to go."

"Nya?"

"D-don't look at me like that. I have… I need to leave. We're planning a trip, so…"

"Nya?"

"Those eyes won't… they won't work on me. I've already been subject to them once. I won't succumb again."

The cat tilted its head.

Kevin squealed like a little girl who'd just been touched by her favorite pop idol.

"Kya! So adorable!"

He scooped the cat into his arms. The cat didn't seem to mind.

"I'm sure it'll be fine if I take you home with me."

"Nya," the cat mewled, seemingly in agreement.

***

Despite having spent a good portion of last night getting into the hot and heavy with Kevin, Lilian stirred in the early morning light. She knew that Kevin had already left. That she was holding a pillow and not her mate testified this. It was disappointing, but not unexpected. While she wished he would stay in bed with her, she didn't begrudge him for starting his day before her. Her mate's mornings were always busy.

As sunlight filtered into the room, she opened her eyes… and found herself staring at another pair of eyes, which were less than an inch from her own.

"Have I ever told you that you look adorable in your sleep?" Iris asked.

"GYA!"

"What the—kya!"

Lilian was so surprised that her body jerked upright. Unfortunately, Iris was leaning over her, so she ended up smacking her head against her sister's.

A loud *crack!* reverberated throughout the room. Newtonian physics came into application and Lilian's head swung backwards for a second hit on the bed. Fortunately for her, the bed was a Tempur-Pedic and therefore sinfully soft. Not that she cared about such things in the wake of her heavy hit.

"Damn." Iris groaned as she rubbed her now sore head. There was a large bruise on it. "Was that really necessary?"

"I'm the one who should be asking that!" Lilian hissed. "What the heck are you doing on my bed?"

"Watching you sleep." Iris rolled her eyes. "I thought that would be obvious."

"Don't watch me sleep. That's creepy."

"Oh, please. Like you don't watch your precious mate while he sleeps."

"That's completely different. Kevin's my mate. I'm allowed to watch him sleep."

That doesn't make it any less creepy.

"See that? Even the author agrees with me."

"Shut up! And you, don't agree with my sister!"

Sorry.

"Now get off me. I have to take a shower."

"Mmm." Iris hummed. "I could do that." A grin that oozed raw sexual energy curved her lips. "But I really don't want to."

Lilian would have snapped at her sister, but she lost the ability for vocal communication at her sister's next action.

With the grace of a feline, Iris arched her back and thrust out her chest. She wore no clothes, so Lilian was graced with the perfect image of Iris's large and perky breasts, her nipples barely hidden by a shimmering curtain of black silk.

Oh, wow. That's, uh, no, wait! Bad Lilian. You can't think about your sister like this! A human like Kevin won't accept this kind of relationship!

Lilian's breath hitched when, after twisting her body in enticing and erotic ways, Iris lowered herself until her nose grazed against Lilian's.

"Hmm?" A delightful hum. "See something you like, Lily-pad?"

"Don't call me that," Lilian whispered. Her voice held a tremor that it had not possessed before. Iris's dark eyes penetrated her soul with their depth. They were like fathomless black holes, dark and alluring eyes that held a most beautiful and dangerous secret.

"Come on, admit it, you like it when I call you that."

Hot breath washed against Lilian's ear, causing a shudder to run down her spine and her toes to tingle.

"No…" she choked. "I don't… I don't like it. Please stop."

"Mmm."

Lilian gasped when Iris's bare crotch rubbed against her left thigh, leaving a wet, glistening trail.

"No, I don't think I will." Dark irises containing a sensual elegance pinned Lilian in place. "I want to spend some time with my lovely sister." Soft, delicate hands, so different from the ones that she was used to, cupped her bare breasts. It was electric. "You're always spending time with that mate of yours. I don't mind, really." Iris tweaked her sister's left nipple. Lilian moaned. "Kevin's at least proven himself a capable person, so I'll accept him as your mate. But still…" Another tweak. Another moan. "I need some time with you for myself. Your poor sister is beginning to feel neglected."

Lilian's mind failed her. A part of her knew that she needed to do something, that she needed to get out of this situation. That part seemed to be growing smaller by the second, however. She had already been ensnared by her sister's intense gaze, which caused her body to heat up with desire.

*D-dang it. And to think she isn't even using her **Aura of Allure**.*

Iris would never use an enchantment on her. That meant these feelings, these desires that were assaulting her from all sides, they were purely Lilian's own body responding to what she deemed as desirable.

"Now… why don't you show your wonderful sister some love, hm?"

Just before Iris could claim Lilian's lips, the door opened and Kotohime walked in. She paused upon seeing them, then raised her arm, hiding her smiling lips behind the voluminous sleeve of her kimono.

"Ufufufu, breakfast is ready, Lilian-sama, Iris-sama. Please be sure to come to the table after you are finished here. You might also want to check your bags to ensure that you have not forgotten anything. Kiara-san has already arrived, and we are only waiting on you two and Kevin-sama."

At Kotohime's words, Lilian snapped out of her fugue. She then flung Iris off the bed. Her fraternal twin squawked as she became a heap of tangled limbs on the floor, but Lilian ignored the Void Kitsune and leapt to her feet.

"Right, I should do that. Thanks, Kotohime."

"Ufufufu, I live to serve, Lilian-sama."

As Lilian rushed into the bathroom, Iris glared daggers at Kotohime, whose placid smile had not left since she'd entered.

"Damn it, Kotohime! You just had to ruin it, didn't you? I was this close…" Iris held up her left hand and pinched two fingers together to indicate just how "close" she had been. "This close to stealing a kiss from Lily-pad's lips."

Kotohime's response to Iris's angry eyes and gesture was a wondrous and beautiful smile. "Ara, ara. This humble servant does nothing but her best to serve Lilian-sama each and every day."

These words did not please Iris. Not in the least.

"All of my hate, Kotohime. All of my hate."

"Ufufufu…"

***

Kevin walked up the stairs to his apartment. Held within his arms was the cat he'd met by the distribution center, who purred as he scratched behind her ears.

He had already noticed that Kiara had arrived while he'd been delivering newspapers. It didn't take a genius to figure that out. All he had to do was look at the large bus. Of course, the term large was just a euphemism. It didn't really describe how big the bus truly was. Obscenely gigantic might have been more appropriate. How she got the dang thing there was another matter entirely.

"Hawawa!"

"M-My Lady Camellia, p-please come back! You shouldn't run around like that, and you still need to take a bath!"

Kevin sighed. Really, that woman was just so…

"Nya?"

He looked down at the cat and smiled. "Don't worry. That's just my family. They're all great, um, people. I'm sure they'll love you."

The cat rubbed her head against his chest, purring. Kevin's inner fanboy released a very unmanly squeal.

More laughter erupted from inside the apartment, along with the worried voice of Kirihime.

"P-Please come back to the restroom, My Lady!"

Kevin opened the door—

"Kevin-kyun!"

—and received a face full of two big, round things as he was bodily tackled by an overly enthusiastic woman-child.

All the air was expelled from Kevin's lungs as his back slammed against hard concrete. He gasped in agonic asphyxia, his mind hazing out after his head cracked against the pavement outside of his apartment.

"Gu…ugh…hu…"

"Hawa! Kevin-kyun!"

"Ugh."

Several seconds were required before he regained the ability to speak. He'd pretty much swallowed his tongue.

"Camellia—ugh!"

"Hiiii!" Camellia greeted him, her five tails wagging like an affectionate dog, and her ears happily twitching on her head.

"Why the heck are you naked?!"

Indeed, Camellia was not wearing any clothes. Bare as the day she'd gained her second tail, the lovely five-tails sat on top of him, palms pressed against his chest, squeezing her breasts together.

Kevin didn't know what was worse: The fact that a naked woman was sitting on him, that this naked woman was his mate's mother, or that his body was beginning to respond like every other hormonal male would to a naked woman sitting on him. Really, this whole situation was screwed up.

"Camellia doesn't knooooow~"

"Lord Kevin!" A distraught Kirihime bowed to him. "I-I am terribly sorry! I was going to give My Lady Camellia a bath when she ran off. P-please forgive me."

"Ugh... j-just get this woman off me, please."

"Mou..." Camellia pouted at being called "this woman." "Kevin-kyun is being a meanie."

"I'm not being mean at all," Kevin snapped, his face flush. "You're just acting weird... er. And what's up with the 'kyun'?"

"Camellia... Camellia heard that boys like being called that."

"You've been reading my manga, haven't you?"

"Um!"

Figures.

He would have facepalmed, but his hands were pinned to his sides by the woman's lovely thighs.

Kevin was eventually let up when Kirihime finally convinced Camellia that she needed a bath. The woman left with a pout.

"But I wanted to play with Kevin-kyun some more."

"M-my apologies, My Lady, but... you really need to take a bath now. We're leaving soon."

"Hawa. Okay."

After Camellia was led away, presumably toward the bathroom, Kevin stepped into the apartment and sat on the couch with a heavy sigh.

"You really do have an interesting life, don'tcha?"

"Kiara."

She sat on the couch with him, her single remaining arm resting on the backrest as she leaned back, and her left leg crossed over her right.

Not much had changed about the woman. She still loved her business suits, still preferred pants to skirts, and her hair remained as wild and unruly as ever. The only difference between now and when they'd first met was her missing left arm, which she displayed like a badge of honor.

"You think missing an arm makes me some kind of invalid? Get real, boya. A warrior shows these scars with pride. I lost this arm in combat against a superior foe and won. This is my badge, the proof that I prevailed against all odds and came out on top."

"Hey, boya," she greeted him with a fanged smirk. "Did you enjoy Camellia's welcome home greeting?"

"Ugh." Kevin buried his face in his hands. "Please, never mention this moment again."

"I make no promises."

That was probably the most he could hope for.

Kevin sighed. Life was so unfair sometimes.

***

The cat Kevin brought home was missing.

"Where'd the kitty go?"

"Kitty?"

Seeing the raised eyebrow directed at him, Kevin explained. "I found a cat and brought her home with me."

A very thorough explanation, indeed.

"Uh-huh," Kiara muttered, apparently no longer interested in his worries. She quickly went back to reading the newspaper on her lap, flipping the pages with her only remaining hand.

Kevin eventually found the cat sitting on the windowsill in the living room. She must have leapt out of his arms sometime after he'd opened the door, but before his face had been smothered by that agonizing bliss that stood somewhere between heaven and hell.

"There you are."

"Nya."

The cat mewled as he lifted her up and carried her to the dining room, where he set her down on the floor. He fetched a bowl and set it on the tile, then poured some milk into it.

"I hope you like milk."

"Nya!"

Kevin wasn't sure, but he could've sworn he saw stars appear in the thing's big yellow eyes. He shook his head.

Must be my imagination.

"Perhaps it would be wise if the cat drank her milk elsewhere, Kevin-sama," Kotohime said, eyeing the critter lapping up the milk. "I do not wish to accidentally step on her tail."

"You're too graceful for that," Kevin dismissed her concern.

"Ufufufu, flattery will get you nowhere."

Kotohime ruffled Kevin's hair, much to his consternation.

It was one of the many changes that had happened within the Swift household. Before the incident where Lilian was kidnapped by the creepy two-tailed brat, Kotohime had treated him with grudging respect. After he'd beaten the crap out of Jiāoào Shénshèng, Kotohime's disposition towards him had changed. She showed more genuine respect, and even a bit of sisterly affection.

She was still a hard ass when it came to lectures, though.

As Kevin pouted at the beautiful woman in the kimono, another figure walked into the kitchen.

"Hey there, Stud." Iris slinked in, hips swaying enticingly. She walked—no, stalked forward, soaking in the knowledge that Kevin couldn't take his eyes off the alluring sashay of her hips. "How was that job of yours?"

Kevin forcefully pulled his eyes away. He'd never been more pleased to see someone sit down.

"Fine," he mumbled. "Is Lilian in the shower?"

"I believe so."

"Gotcha."

Kevin made to walk out of the room.

He was stopped by two arms encircling his chest, and a pair of breasts on his back.

"Gonna go join your mate?" Kevin shuddered. The shuddering intensified when a pair of oh-so-soft lips covered his ear, and a set of teeth gently nibbled on it. "Mind if I join you two?"

Kevin gritted his teeth and pulled out of Iris's grip, wincing as her teeth painfully scraped along his ear. "Yes, I do mind. And stop doing that. I have a mate."

Iris just laughed; it was a lyrical, beautiful, deadly sound. "So?"

Kevin calmed the storm raging within his mind. He wouldn't let this girl get to him.

"I'll be back in a bit."

As Kevin walked out of the kitchen, Kotohime turned to the girl lounging at the kitchen table. "Don't you think you're taking this game a little too far, Iris-sama?"

Iris chuckled. "Oh, no. This game is far too fun for me to stop, and it's only just begun. I'm going to play with him until I've finally accomplished my goals."

"Which is?"

"Uhuhuhu, I can't tell you that. It would spoil all the fun."

Kotohime didn't seem bothered by the lack of an answer. She went back to her self-assigned task of cleaning. Meanwhile, Iris leaned back in her chair. She never saw the person coming up behind her until it was too late.

"What's this I hear about you messing with my student?" Kiara asked, an evil grin on her face.

Iris was given no time to respond before Kiara struck.

"Kya! My tail! Let go of my poor tail!"

***

Steam rose within the shower, swirling motes like zephyrs drifting lazily on the wind. Heat gathered around her, causing sweat to break out on her skin.

Lilian ignored the water spraying her back, ignored the heat and the steam coalescing on the walls and ceiling. Her mind, locked in an internal struggle, fought a losing battle. Her attempt at drowning out the call proved futile, for it obeyed no rationale, this raw, undiluted need. She felt hungry, and this hunger demanded to be satiated.

The door opened.

Kevin walked in.

He wore nothing but a towel.

"Morning, Lilian. Mind if I join you?"

Lilian's eyes dilated as they tracked his movement. Her breathing grew heavy when she looked at his washboard abs and well-defined pectorals—the result of seven months of brutal training. Her mind hazed when he smiled at her, blue eyes admiring her body just as she admired his.

Kevin's smile inflamed her soul. Those muscles made her body yearn for his touch. Her eyes began to gleam.

She wanted him.

She needed him.

She moved to claim him.

Kevin's eyes widened.

"Lilian, what are you—"

Her tongue didn't allow him to say anymore.

***

Kevin and Lilian appeared in the living room, dressed for the day. Lilian, a pair of denim shorts covering her bottom and showcasing her lovely legs, strolled further into the room, bare feet padding against beige carpet. She wore a satisfied smile. Her green off-the-shoulder sleeveless shirt folded as she moved. Kevin walked in with her, a sleeveless shirt and blue jeans adorning his frame. He looked dazed.

"Kya! Get away from me, you stupid mutt!"

Lilian gaped and the lost look on Kevin's face disappeared. Together, they watched as a frightened Iris ran from a laughing Kiara.

"Come on now, girly. Surely you don't think I'm finished with your punishment, do you?"

"Punishment?! Just being in your presence is punishment enough—KYA!"

"Mwahahaha!"

Kiara grinned as she pinned Iris to the ground, on her stomach. She stood over the girl, kneeling on her back, grabbing the young vixen's tails.

"L-let go! —Ah! —Why are—s-stop it! —AAH!"

"No can do." Kiara's eyes gleamed with the wicked light of a sadist. "You see, I've got a problem with people who mess with my disciple. There is only one person allowed to fuck with his mind." A pause. Kiara went back over her statement. "Three people: Lilian, Kotohime, and myself. You are not one of those three people and, for your transgressions against my student, you must be punished."

"No! Stop it! Gya! My tails! Stop grabbing them!" In desperation, Iris looked around and saw Lilian and Kevin standing several feet away. "What are you two—ahn! What are you doing?! Don't just—ah! —don't just stand there! Get this woman off me!"

"But you look like you're having so much fun," Lilian said, her emerald eyes gleaming. Who needed to get revenge when they could have someone else do it for them? "I don't want to interrupt your bonding moment."

Kevin clapped his hands together and smiled with a completely insincere smile. "I'm so glad to see you two are making nice."

Iris's eyes widened as she realized no help would be coming. "Oh, fuck you two! Fuck you-hyyyyaaaa!"

"Language."

"No! Stop! Let go! Iyahn!"

Kevin and Lilian left the squirming, kicking, and struggling Iris to her well-earned torture. Making their way into the kitchen, they were greeted by Kirihime and Camellia.

"Hello, Lady Lilian, Lord Kevin."

"Hey!"

"Sup."

"Lilian, Kevin-kyun, hiiii~!"

"Again with the 'kyun.' Seriously, what's up with that? And why are you extending the last word of your sentences?"

"Camellia doesn't knoooooow!"

"Good morning, Mom," Lilian greeted her mother with a gentle smile and a kiss on the cheek. Camellia gave her daughter that absolutely radiant smile, which never ceased to remind Kevin of a child. Really, it almost seemed as if Camellia was the daughter and Lilian the mother.

Sitting down at the table with Camellia, he and Lilian were greeted by a large, all-American breakfast: scrambled eggs, French toast, waffles, and pancakes lathered in a rich syrup.

Two blinks.

"Whoa, what's with the American breakfast, Kotohime?"

"Ufufufu, can't this humble Kotohime make something different every once in a while?"

She received two blank stares.

"Kiara-san isn't a fan of Japanese breakfasts," Kotohime confessed.

"That's because Japanese breakfasts can't beat a good stack of pancakes," Kiara said as she marched into the room and sat down at the table. Lilian scooted herself closer to Kevin. The woman smirked, and then directed her attention to the food. "You really went all out today, Kotohime. I can't wait to sink my paws into this."

"That was a terrible pun."

Kiara raised an eyebrow at Kevin. "What's that? Did I hear someone say they wanted to spar with me?"

"Guh!"

Several minutes after everyone else started eating, Iris walked into the room. The girl looked absolutely frazzled. Her hair was a mess, her eyes were bloodshot, her ears were twitching, and it looked like someone had stuck her tails in a dry tumbler.

Her steps were ponderous and slow. Every so often she would wince, and her tails would bristle as if they'd been zapped by a Pikachu. It took her nearly a full minute just to reach the table. Only after she had slumped in her seat did the gorgeous vixen notice the stares she was receiving.

"What are you all looking at?"

Everyone looked away and resumed eating.

Breakfast that morning was good. Kevin would have said it was the best Kotohime had ever made, but he knew that she wouldn't appreciate that. She loved Japanese food as much as Lilian loved waffles. When they finished breakfast, the group grabbed their luggage and met at the entrance.

"Hawa! This is so exciting!" The beautiful but clumsy Camellia laughed as she carried her luggage out the door. "Road trip. Road trip. We're going on a road trip."

"My Lady Camellia." A worried Kirihime tried to catch up to the older woman. "Please be mindful of where you walk. You're coming up on the—"

"HAWA!!"

"—MY LADY!!"

Kirihime's eyes widened in horror as Camellia lost her footing and tumbled down the stairs. She probably would've gotten seriously injured were it not for Kiara having preceded the group to prep the bus. She caught Camellia before the woman could fall on her face—or her breasts.

"H-hawa. Thank you."

Kiara sighed. "You really should be more careful."

"H-hawa…"

When Camellia's ears drooped and her tails fell limp, Kiara sighed.

"There, there." She petted the woman's head as if Camellia were a dog. The irony was not lost on her. "No harm was done this time. Just be more careful in the future."

"Hawan…" the blissed-out Camellia muttered, her ears flapping and her tails wagging happily.

Iris palmed her face. "I swear, that woman is a complete embarrassment."

"I-Iris." Lilian looked scandalized. "You shouldn't say that about our mother!"

"Why not?" Iris shrugged. "It's true, isn't it?"

Iris tried to ignore the disapproving glare Lilian sent her in favor of descending the stairs. While she seemed to do a relatively decent job of pretending that the way her sister glared at her back didn't bother her, she could not help but respond to the—by now—familiar fingers almost lovingly caressing her tail.

"Giiiiii!"

"Sorry, sorry." Kiara chuckled. "My hand has a mind of its own sometimes. It really loves how soft your fur is. What kind of shampoo do you use?"

"None of your damn business!" Iris hissed, her face burning with humiliation. She stomped down the stairs, which shook beneath her feet. She didn't want everyone else to see how ashamed she was.

This was why she hated dogs!

The bus was a large vehicle that stood at the same height as a double-decker bus used for city-wide tours. It was also several times longer than those buses, giving it a good deal more space. Silver metal gleamed within the morning light. On each side of the bus was the Mad Dawg Fitness logo—a ripped bipedal pit bull with a fanged grin giving a thumbs-up.

Kotohime turned to look at everyone there, while Kiara climbed inside the bus.

"All of you should make sure you have everything you need. Once we head out, we won't be coming back."

Kevin and Lilian had everything they needed inside of the two black suitcases that Kevin wheeled behind him. They'd been slowly packing for the past two weeks, deciding on the clothes they wanted to bring—and the cosplay in particular. Last night they'd finished packing before getting lost in each other's bodies.

"We're good," Lilian answered for them both.

Kotohime nodded and then turned to Kirihime, who'd been in charge of packing for Camellia, who no one trusted to pack for herself.

"Do not worry, Kotohime." Kirihime's demure smile set everyone around her at ease. "I made sure to pack everything last night—except for the toiletries, which I packed away this morning. We're ready to go."

"What about you, Iris-sama?" Kotohime eyed the small satchel slung over the vixen's shoulder. "Will that be enough?"

"Oh yeah, don't worry." Iris's wicked grin caused Kotohime to do just that. "I've got everything I need right here. And what I don't have in here is in my Extra Dimensional Storage Space."

Kevin groaned. "Not this again…"

"There, there, Kevin." Lilian rubbed his back.

"Don't patronize me."

"All right, everyone!" The automatic doors slid open. Kiara sat in the driver's seat, her face marred by a fanged grin. "Get on board. We're heading out."

"Yes!" Lilian cheered, pumping her right fist into the air. She wore a face-splitting smile, and her eyes sparkled like gems refracting sunlight. "Time for our spring break adventure to begin!"

Wearing a placid smile that made her seem even more beautiful than usual, Kotohime watched as her charge and Kevin boarded the bus. Seeing how happy the young vixen was caused warm feelings to spread through her chest.

"She really has come so far…"

Her eyes then wandered to Kevin, Lilian's mate, whose sunny grin perfectly matched the one worn by the emerald-eyed girl.

"And to think Kevin-sama has come this far as well…"

She did not know what Kevin had been like when he first met Lilian, but she'd heard the stories. Regardless, his transformation, spanning over the six months that she'd known him, had been nothing short of astounding. He'd gone from a boy, unsure of himself and what he wanted, to an upstanding young man. He'd certainly started growing up, that much was certain.

Iris rolled her eyes at the couple. "You two are way too excited. It's just a stupid trip."

"How can you say that?" an appalled Lilian asked. "This is more than just a trip. This is spring break. Our first spring break. We're going to California!"

"The only reason you're so excited is because you get to wear those dumb costumes that you and Kevin spent so much money on."

"They're not dumb! These costumes are amazing! I won't have you say anything bad about them." Lilian's cheeks became large, inflating with her intake of oxygen. They swelled up and became red, like a balloon with too much helium.

"Aw!" Iris squealed. "Look at you! Now I just want to pinch those adorable cheeks of yours."

"Eek!" Lilian covered her rear. They all knew which cheeks Iris was talking about. "No, wait! S-stay back! No! Stay away! These cheeks can only be touched by my beloved!"

Kotohime sighed as Iris chased Lilian onto the bus, her fingers making the creepiest grasping motions known to both man and yōkai, as if already imagining Lilian's buttocks underneath their grasp.

Really, that girl is just so...

Over near the bus, Camellia tried to put away her luggage.

"My Lady Camellia, why don't you let me take care of that for you?"

"Ah, don't worry, don't worry." Camellia smiled at her maid. "Camellia's got it—hawa!"

"M-My Lady!" Kirihime cried out as Camellia's luggage fell on top of the five-tails.

Was it wrong, Kotohime pondered, to be amused by the sight of Camellia-sama being crushed by her own luggage? Maybe. Probably. And yet, wrongness aside, she could not help but feel amused. The suitcase didn't weigh much, maybe a little over twenty pounds, yet Camellia-sama acted as if it weighed over five hundred.

"Beloved, help!"

"Uh, I would love to, but, um, a-actually, I think I heard Kiara saying she had something she needed help with something inside the bus, so I've gotta go. See ya! Bye!"

"Beloved!"

"Gotcha!"

"Iyan!"

From within her place at the driver's seat, Kiara watched the group of kitsune with an amused smile. She had absolutely no clue what the future had in store for her, or them, but knowing this unusual bunch like she did, she knew that there would never be a dull moment.

She was looking forward to an exciting trip.

CHAPTER 3

Road Trip

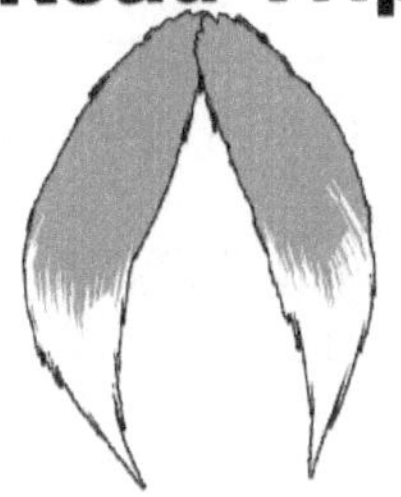

LINDSAY WAS A SIMPLE GIRL. She enjoyed the small pleasures in life: spending time with her friends, playing soccer, and going out. Among the simple pleasures that she enjoyed, one of them stood above the others.

It wasn't taking amusement in watching the antics of Kevin and Lilian, though she had to admit they were fun. Showers. She absolutely loved showers.

Standing under the spray of hot water, she allowed herself this guilty pleasure. A groan of satisfaction escaping her lips as millions of tiny droplets hit her back, relaxing tense muscles, relieving the tension in her body. It was wonderful.

Nothing could possibly beat this.

Someone knocked on the restroom door.

"Hey, Lindsay! Are you done in there? I still need to take a shower, too, you know!"

Oops. I forgot I can't enjoy a long shower this morning.

Turning off the water, Lindsay stepped out of the shower, grabbed a towel, wrapped it around her waist, and opened the door. Christine stood on the other end. Her arms were crossed, her foot tapped an impatient rhythm against the carpet, and her face was set in a scowl. Lindsay thought Christine looked too cute for her own good, but she knew better than to say that out loud.

"Sorry," she said sheepishly, grinning at her friend. "I completely forgot you haven't taken a shower yet."

"You always forget," Christine grumbled. "Every single time I spend the night here, you forget that I also need to take a shower."

Lindsay squirmed under her friend's gaze, trying not to flush. Did Christine even know how intense her gaze was? How it made her feel? Probably not. If she did, Lindsay had no doubt that the girl would be doing that tsun-thingy Lilian kept teasing her about.

"Please tell me you at least didn't use all the hot water this time."

"I… I don't think I did…"

"That's not very reassuring."

Lindsay was pleased to note that she had not, in fact, used all the hot water, though Christine's shower had gotten cool near the end. After they both donned their outfits—Lilian in her pixie pants, sleeveless shirt, and tennis shoes, and Christine in her Gothic Lolita outfit—the two sat at the dining room table and ate breakfast with Lindsay's family.

"Are you sure you two want to go traveling with that Pnévma girl?" her mom asked. Lindsay would have rolled her eyes, but that would have been redundant by this point.

"Mom, we've been over this a hundred times already. Lilian's my friend, and I don't want to hear anything about how she stole Kevin from me. She didn't. I just… wasn't smart in how I approached him."

Understatement of the century. Lindsay knew that she'd screwed up any chance she might have had at being in a relationship with Kevin. At the same time, she actually felt kind of relieved. She really did like him, but a part of her realized that they wouldn't have been a very good match. The only thing they had in common was their love for sports, and they loved different sports anyway. Lilian was much better for him.

She's an anime nerd like him. They're two cute anime nerds who do all those strange Japanese things.

"That is why I told you to sink your claws into him before he could get away," her mom lectured. "Honestly, you were too lenient with him. You should have simply told him that you and he were dating, and that you wouldn't put up with any of his complaints."

Lindsay saw Christine stiffen in her seat at the mention of Kevin and grew a bit concerned. She knew that the yuki-onna still harbored some feelings for him. She didn't necessarily blame the girl. Kevin treated her with kindness and respect and accepted all of her personality flaws, but that was how he treated everyone. She was sure Christine had realized this, but getting rid of those feelings locked in her heart could be tough. Lindsay knew that all too well.

"And in either case, I was not speaking of the redhead. I was talking about that other one. That… that vixen with the atrocious attitude."

Ah, so she's talking about the twin.

"You mean Iris, don't you?"

"Yes." Her mom's scowl made her think of a bomb about to go off. The woman looked like she might explode. "That accursed girl who dresses so scandalously. Ever since I first laid eyes on her, I could tell that she was trouble."

"Well, there's something you and I can definitely agree on," Christine said, scowling. Lindsay almost sighed. While Christine and Lilian had settled their differences, her snow-hating friend and Iris had been butting heads ever since the other girl had arrived.

Not that Lindsay couldn't understand why. Iris might have been the hottest girl she'd ever seen, but that attitude of hers was a serious turn-off. The raven-haired femme was disgustingly arrogant.

"You see? Christine agrees with me. That girl is bad news. If you stick around her for too long, she'll end up corrupting you. Just knowing that girl is living with my dear Kevin is enough to make my blood boil!"

The woman slammed her hands on the table, startling the two youngsters. Gritting her teeth, Lindsay's mom held a clenched fist up to her face. Fire burned within her eyes, a blazing inferno that could scarcely be contained.

A droplet of sweat trailed down Lindsay's face. Her mom got way too excited whenever Kevin was involved. And was it just her, or did her mom look sort of like a demon with that apoplectic expression?

"Who knows what that girl is doing to him right this very second! She's probably corrupting that poor, innocent boy!"

"Uh, I don't think Kevin's all that innocent anymore," Lindsay murmured, too soft for her mom to hear. It would be better not to tell her progenitor what she knew about Kevin's sex life.

"For all we know, she could be having her devious, detestable way with him right this very moment! Yes! I can picture it now! That sickening, shameless girl! She's probably seducing him with her body, tempting him with her wily seductress act right this very moment! It wouldn't surprise me one bit if she's broken into the shower with him, pushing him against the wall and rubbing herself all over his bare, naked flesh… caressing those budding muscles… and… and… oh… Kevin…"

Her mom trailed off, eyes glazing over, cheeks flushing red. Drool started leaking from the plump woman's mouth, which she didn't seem to notice.

Lindsay suddenly felt a very strong urge to slam her face against the table.

Christine leaned over to whisper in the tomboy's ear. "No offense, but your mom really scares me."

"None taken," Lindsay mumbled. "To be honest, she scares me sometimes, too."

Breakfast was an awkward affair after that.

***

Like most of the middle class, Lindsay's family lived in a cul-de-sac. All of the houses looked alike: one or two-story houses, stucco and brick walls, and tiled roofs. There wasn't much differentiation between residences.

The one they arrived at didn't appear any different from any other house. It was one story tall, made of red bricks and red tiles. There were several cacti in the yard, small, squat, round ones. A tree also stood alone, surrounded only by many small shrubs and bushes.

Kevin and the others disembarked from the large bus and walked up to the front door. Lilian, the brightest smile anyone would ever see plastered on her face, pressed the doorbell. There was a second's pause. Then rushing footsteps came from inside. Several shouts could be heard behind the door, which soon opened to reveal a grinning face.

"Lilian!"

Lilian laughed as she and Lindsay hugged, squealing like a couple of, well, like two teenage girls. Behind Lindsay trailed Christine, who was followed by Ms. Dianne. The eldest of the trio caught one look at Iris and scowled.

At least she knows better than to say anything.

"Hey, Christine!" Kevin greeted his friend with a sunny smile.

It was interesting, the way Christine's face turned blue, then went back to pale, almost as if the yuki-onna was undergoing hyperpigmentation.

"K-Kevin," she greeted, "how, um, I hope you slept well."

"I did. Thanks for asking. So, are you two ready for the trip? Got your stuff? Need any help? I wouldn't mind carrying your luggage to the bus."

Christine went back to blushing.

"H-h-h-he… w-w-w-who said I wanted you to help me?! Huh?! Stupid jerk! I can carry my own luggage! Hmph!"

Kevin's shoulders slumped. "What did I do now?"

"Uhuhuhu," Iris chuckled. "Look at you, always jumping the gun and getting angry for no reason. And you wonder why Kevin doesn't like you."

"A-as if I care about something like that!" Christine's eyes could have melted ice, or created ice. Her glare was certainly bone-chilling. "And you're the last person I want to hear talking about my personality!"

"Ho? It seems the snow-prude's claws are out today."

"Bitch!"

"Do you two really have to fight?" Kevin asked.

"YES!" they shouted at the same time.

"Eep!" Squeaking like a little girl, Kevin hid behind Lilian, whose expression was more amused than concerned.

The argument continued unabated.

"You had better take good care of Kev—I mean, my daughter," Ms. Dianne said to Kotohime and the other adults.

"Hawa! Do not worry. Camellia will look after her!"

At the sight of an enthused Camellia, whose eyes sparkled with childish determination, Ms. Dianne faltered. "U-um, erm, yes, that's good to hear… I think."

"Do not worry, Dianne-san," Kotohime assured the woman with a placid smile. "I shall ensure that no harm comes to anyone during this trip."

"I'm pleased to hear that."

"Ufufufu, of course."

"And now I'm not so pleased."

"Why does everyone say that to me?" Kotohime wondered. Meanwhile, the argument between Christine and Iris continued.

"Cow."

"Icicle."

"Skank."

"Dead fish."

"Whore!"

"Doesn't that mean the same thing as skank?"

As Christine and Iris degraded to childish name-calling, Kevin looked at Lilian. "Think you can stop these two?"

"I'm not suicidal enough to get between their arguments," Lilian declared.

He and Lilian then looked at Lindsay, who noticed their stares and raised her hands. "Whoa! Don't get me involved in this. I'm just a regular human."

"Used catcher's mitt!"

"Oh, that's a good one, for a frosty little prude."

We're going to be here a while, aren't we? Kevin groaned.

***

Alex and Andrew were alone in their house. Neither of their parents was home. Their mom was at a club meeting of some kind, and their dad had been called into work due to an emergency. That meant they were on their own, until Kevin and the others picked them up.

"Hey, Andrew?"

"Yeah?"

"You ever get the feeling that our friends are hiding something from us?"

"What do you mean?"

Lazing around in the living room of their humble abode, Alex and Andrew stared at the ceiling. The auburn-haired Alex lay on his back on the couch. His eyes went from the ceiling fan to his fraternal twin brother. The redhead sat on one of the living room's two chairs, his feet propped up on their coffee table. He looked contemplative.

"What I mean is that I can't help but feel like all of our friends know something that we don't. It feels like they're all in on some big secret and aren't telling us for some reason."

"I noticed that you didn't mention Justin," Andrew said.

Alex rolled his eyes. "I doubt Justin even knows what's going on half the time—or cares."

"Hmm." Andrew rolled onto his stomach. "I suppose you've got a point. There's definitely been something happening that no one's telling us about. Kevin's changed, and in a big way. A few months ago, he was just like us, kind of a scrawny kid who could run well and had no luck with women. Now look at him. He's got a hot girlfriend, that goth chick likes him, and he also gets to hang around with his girlfriend's super-hot sister."

"Don't forget about whatever new workout he's been doing."

"Please don't remind me." Andrew sounded depressed. "Just thinking about that makes me feel inadequate. It shouldn't be possible for someone's muscles to grow that fast. Ugh…" Rolling onto his back again, he covered his eyes with a forearm. "I just don't get it. What's going on? And why does everyone but us know about it?"

"Who knows?" Alex shrugged.

The ringing of a doorbell interrupted the rest of their conversation. They answered the door and were greeted by a large amount of pretty… plus Kevin. Really, seeing Kevin with all those gorgeous ladies—more than half of whom he lived with—was just unfair.

"You guys ready to go?" Kevin asked.

Alex and Andrew looked at each other, and then hurried to grab their luggage.

Neither of them knew what was going on. They didn't know why, or even how, their friend had gone through so many drastic changes in such a relatively short time period, but on that day, in that moment, they made a promise. One way or another, they were going to find out what big secret everybody was hiding from them.

Believe it.

***

"Yes, we'll be traveling to California today for spring break. No, I'm not sure when we're going to get there. It takes at least six hours of straight driving to reach Los Angeles. I imagine that means we'll arrive sometime late in the afternoon."

"…"

"We're really going through with this, then? I thought you had adopted a wait-and-see approach? Isn't that the entire reason you had all of those people who tried kidnapping your son's girlfriend disposed of and sent those machines after Ms. Grant?"

"…"

"Well, I suppose it doesn't matter. I'll do whatever you order me to. Justin, out."

Justin hung up the phone after he had finished his conversation. It looked like things were about to get interesting again.

A knock came at the door.

"Justin! Your friends have arrived!"

"… Coming…"

Grabbing his luggage, Justin made his way out of the bedroom. He wouldn't be sleeping there again for a long time.

***

Earlier that morning, Heather Grant had driven over to Eric's place to make sure her apprentice had everything he needed. While his mom had not been pleased, feeling like this strange woman wanted to usurp her position, his dad couldn't have been more pleased. The old man definitely enjoyed the eye candy.

"Binoculars?"

"Check."

"Camouflage?"

"Check."

"Mini cameras?"

"Check."

"Old sock?"

"Check—wait, what?" Eric looked up from where he was checking the supplies that had been neatly organized into his suitcase. "What do I need an old sock for?"

"You're a guy, ain't ya? That means you're going to be pleasuring yourself a lot. You know, basting the ham, arguing with Henry Longfellow, battling the purple-headed yogurt slinger, bludgeoning the beefsteak, flinging the phallus, frosting the maple bar, genital stimulation via phallengetic motion—"

"All right, all right, I think I get the picture here. Old sock, check."

"Good. Now, where were we… ah, yes! Scent killers?"

"Uh, I don't think I've got any of those…"

"Hmm. I see. Well, don't worry. I'll lend you some."

Eric and Heather went through his entire suitcase of supplies before they repacked each article. Once all the articles and items were stashed away in secret compartments, the clothes were put on top of them. It wouldn't be good if someone went through his luggage and found those supplies, though why anyone would go through his stuff was a mystery—better to be safe than sorry.

"Now then, my young apprentice. This week could very well be one of the most important in your life." Like the sergeant who paces before her troops, Heather paced back and forth in front of Eric. "While there will be many other critical moments within your life, this is the first of those moments. This is your foray into a new world of peeping!"

"Yes, Master!"

"We will be going to California, my young apprentice!" Heather clenched her left fist and raised it to her face, as if this was emotive of her determination and feelings. "California, home to sandy beaches and beautiful changing rooms!"

By this point, Eric was crying. "Yes, Master!"

"This is a most crucial first step into this new, wide world. What happens to you during this week will determine how your peeping career will go for the rest of your life. Do well, peep hard, don't be spotted, and you will accomplish all of the goals that you set in life!"

Eric now had snot coming out of his nose, he was crying so hard. Truly, his master was the best. "Yes, Master!"

"Now then! Let us wait for everyone else to arrive and create a plan of action. You will need one if you plan on getting a glimpse of your female friends' naked, nubile bodies."

"YES, MASTER!"

"Good man."

Just then, the sound of the doorbell ringing alerted them to the arrival of their friends.

The sound of the door opening let them know that someone had already answered the door.

"Ohohoho! Hello, pretty girls! Let me shower you with love and affection!"

And the loud shouting followed by the sound of clothes being ripped off let the two know that the person who answered the door was Eric's old man.

"DIE, DESPICABLE FIEND!!"

Christine's voice rang out. Eric listened to the sounds that could only come from a violent beat-down: fist hitting face, fist hitting stomach, foot stomping on face, and heel grinding against balls. Eric was well-acquainted with each one, so he knew what they sounded like.

In the stillness that followed, Heather turned to her apprentice.

"Are you ready, my young apprentice, for this new world of femdom?"

"Yes, Master!"

"Attaboy! Now, let's go!"

***

"Holy shit!"

Those were the first words Eric spoke after entering the bus.

"That's what she said."

"That was lame, Alex."

"You're lame!"

"If you two start fighting on my bus, I'm going to rip both of you a new asshole."

"Eep!"

"We'll be good."

"I agree with ruddy over there," Iris piped up from where she lounged on a chair, curled up like a lazy feline. Unlike the other girls who wore either shorts, pants, or long frilly dresses, Iris was wearing a very short skirt. With the way she curled up on the chair, her thighs almost pressing against her chest, Kevin could see her panties. "That was lame, firecrotch."

"F-firecrotch?"

"Ruddy?"

Alex's shoulders slumped at both the nickname and how Iris apparently agreed with his brother. Kevin felt a small pang of sympathy for his friend. It seemed today was just not his day.

"Holy. Shit."

"You already said that, Eric." Kevin rolled his eyes at his friend. He honestly couldn't blame the perverted sophomore for being more than a little stunned. The bus interior looked more like something you'd find in a luxury hotel than a bus, like an RV for royalty. It had a fifty-inch flat screen TV. Heck, it even had a bunkbed located in the back!

"Alright everyone, get your butts on board. We're leaving."

Eric stepped further into the bus, Heather trailing behind him… and then he stopped when his eyes landed on *her*. His gothic hottie. She was sitting on a couch on the opposite side of the room, looking like some dark, mysterious sex machine. The scowl on her face made his perverted desire soar. Her dress caused his pervy little insides to catch fire. He wanted her, and he knew that deep down, she wanted him as well.

He ran to claim her.

"Oh, my Goth Hottie!"

Christine stood up, her scowl growing.

Oh, yeah. She definitely wants me.

"How I've longed to grab your glorious ginger bottom and squeeze my face between those cheeks of love!"

Her fists clenched, knuckles turning white. No doubt she was overcome with emotion at seeing him. He understood how she felt. It wouldn't be long now.

"Come here you—GUAG!"

Everyone stared in shock at Lindsay, who stood over a prone, twitching, and groaning Eric, after rendering the idiot insensate via clotheslining him. The girl felt the stares upon her and looked around. Her cheeks took on a light flush as she realized what she'd just done.

"W-what?" she asked, trying to hide her embarrassment by crossing her arms over her chest. "He was being a pervert. I just did what any good friend would have done."

The group looked from Lindsay to the still twitching Eric, then back to Lindsay. Christine was the first to recover, and she placed a hand on Lindsay's shoulder, getting the girl to turn around and look at her.

"I didn't really need help dealing with that pervert," Christine said, and Lindsay's shoulders slumped a bit. "But, still, thank you." Lindsay looked back up in shock. "I'm glad to have a friend like you watching my back."

Upon seeing that small smile on Christine's face, the gratitude in her ice blue irises, Lindsay couldn't help but blush.

"Um, anytime."

***

With the advent of the most lecherous creature's existence, the journey to California began. Kiara drove the bus out of Eric's gated community, picking up speed as they exited the main streets and drove along the highway.

With their trip to California finally commencing, the group decided to begin this most auspicious occasion by the time-honored tradition of trying to beat the crap out of each other in *Street Fighter*.

"No, Ryu! Don't do a Hadoken! I wanted you to do a Shoryuken!"

"Ha! You think you can beat me! Check out my Lily-pad's giant phallus of doom AND DESPAIR!"

"It's just a spike cannon, Iris. It's not like I actually have some kind of random phallic weapon to use." A pause. "And I thought I told you to stop calling me that!"

"Lily, the game."

"Ah! Go, Cammy, go! Spiral Arrow!"

"No! I lost again! How can I keep losing to this girl?!"

"It's because your skills pale in comparison to my sister's, puny human! Mwahahahahahaha!"

"Ugh, please stop laughing like that, Iris."

Sitting on the couch farthest from the TV, where most of the other members of their troupe were centered around, was Kevin, Christine, and Lindsay. While Kevin's mate kicked everybody's butt in *Street Fighter*, these three made conversation.

"I'm really surprised you're not over there with the rest of the dweebs."

Kevin looked up from the manga he'd been reading, a story about a female ninja who wanted to become the leader of her village, and focused on Christine.

"I'm not really interested in playing video games right now."

"I bet you just don't want to play video games because Lilian keeps kicking your butt."

"Urk!" Kevin felt like someone had shoved an icy spear in his chest.

"I'm right, aren't I?" asked a grinning Lindsay. "You've probably gotten so sick of her constantly beating you in every game the two of you play that you're no longer interested in video games. You've probably lost all of your motivation to play."

"That is a gross understatement," Kevin muttered. He then spoke in a louder tone. "And Lilian doesn't beat me at everything, just the fighting games. I can still take her on in FPS games. Even when she gets her hands on a sniper rifle, she's still no match for me."

"I can't believe she actually likes playing those stupid things." Christine wrinkled her nose, as if the very notion of playing a video game made her want to vomit. "They're nothing but brain-corroding garbage that cause children to think violence is a perfectly acceptable way of solving problems."

"Don't you solve most of your problems with violence?" Kevin pointed out.

"DON'T TALK BACK TO ME!"

"... Ouch."

Lindsay giggled as Kevin sat back on the couch, nursing a new lump on his head. Kevin tossed her a mild glare, but it didn't really have any bite to it.

"By the way, Kevin, I forgot to ask this with all the excitement going on, but what's up with the cat?"

At the word "cat," a certain feline paused in her self-appointed task of making Kevin's lap the most comfortable pillow possible. The black-furred feline looked at the doe-eyed girl with an expression that seemed inquisitive.

"Nya?"

Lindsay blinked. Then she looked at Kevin. "Nya?" she mouthed.

Kevin ignored the looks he received from Christine and Lindsay.

"I found her after delivering newspapers this morning." He lifted the furry critter off his lap, eliciting a mewl of complaint from said feline, and presented her to Lindsay. "Isn't she adorable?"

Lindsay leaned back as the cat invaded her personal space. She found herself staring at big, yellow eyes that peered at her with a cat's curiosity.

"Um, yeah. R-really cute."

"I know, right?!"

Lindsay watched Kevin rub his cheeks against the cat's fur, wondering just where the heck his strange love for animals came from. And maybe it was just her, but that cat looked like she was enjoying herself way too much.

Christine just glared at the furry critter. She hated cats almost as much as she hated foxes!

While the trio of youngsters conversed, and Lilian kicked the butts of the other teens in a metaphorical sense, Kirihime tried to keep her mistress from destroying anything.

"P-please do not touch those bottles, My Lady! They're very easy to break."

"Hawa, so pretty."

"They're also expensive," Kiara piped in, walking up to the pair. "I would like to ask that you not touch them."

While Camellia just looked at the inu with a tilted head, Kirihime stiffened. While her childish mistress wasn't bothered by the presence of an inu, she still felt uneasy around the woman—regardless of the past that Kiara shared with her honorable sister. Like most kitsune, she didn't like dogs.

"Muu! Okay."

As a depressed Camellia slumped into a chair, Kiara sat down next to Kotohime. Setting a small glass on the counter, Kiara opened a bottle of brandy with a flick of her thumb, and poured herself a cup. Her foxy counterpart was drinking sake from a saucer.

"I don't think I've ever seen my bus this lively before," the woman commented, her business suit wrinkling as she turned about on her stool to study the youngsters playing around.

"Hm."

Dark brown eyes glanced at Kotohime. The kimono-wearing woman didn't seem to be paying much attention to anything going on around her. It took Kiara a moment, but she soon realized what had most of the four-tailed kitsune's attention—or rather, who had the woman's attention.

"You know, if you keep staring at my disciple like that, I'm gonna think you're…" Kiara trailed off. Dark eyes scrunched up in thought. "What's that word again? Shotacon? Yes, I think that's the one. Anyway, I'm gonna think you're a shotacon if you keep staring at Kevin like that."

"I am not a shotacon," Kotohime gave her compatriot a mild glare. "I have no interest in Kevin-sama, and certainly not in that way."

Kiara shrugged. "Never said you did. I just said you should stop staring at him before I begin thinking you might. Not that I can't see why you're so interested in him. He's an awful lot like—"

"Please do not go there, Kiara-san," Kotohime said, sighing. "I would rather we leave the past in the past."

"You know that you're going to have to confront your past eventually. You can't avoid it forever."

When Kotohime said nothing, Kiara looked back at Kevin. The young man was still sitting on the couch, his new feline companion lying in his lap, while he read one of those Japanese comics that he loved so much. He'd occasionally make an errant comment when either Christine or Lindsay addressed him, but was otherwise engrossed.

"You know, I always blamed myself for what happened back then," Kiara said softly. "I sometimes wonder about what would have happened if you and Corban hadn't gotten caught up in my fight. Would he have avoided the fate that awaited him? Would you and I be where we are now? Would we be living a better life? A happier life? I always ask myself these questions when I'm alone and have nothing to keep my mind occupied."

Kotohime slowly sipped her sake. "Thinking about the past is pointless, Kiara-san. It does not do to dwell on what ifs. Had Corban-kun not been caught in that attack meant for you, perhaps he and I would still be together. Then again, perhaps I would've gotten bored of him already and things would still be the same. He would be in his mid-forties by now, and you know that we kitsune tend to lose interest in those who are past their prime."

"I guess that's true. Heh, kinda makes me worry for the kid."

"Kevin-sama is lucky in this regard," Kotohime said. "As Lilian's first mate, she will not leave him over something like age. It is an unusual aspect of us kitsune, but our first mates are always our most important. She will remain by his side until he passes on, and even then, she will remember him and hold all other mates to the standard that he sets."

Kotohime thought about her first mate, the man she'd given herself to just a few years after gaining her third tail. He'd been a kitsune, much like herself, and one of the few who, like her, enjoyed fighting. It was that very enjoyment of combat that got him killed. She did not begrudge her mate for losing his life in combat, but a part of her still wished he'd not gone into that fight.

"By the way, Kiara-san. Who is driving?"

"Heather decided to drive." Kiara grinned. "I don't think she was comfortable with a one-armed person driving on the freeway."

"Indeed."

Back by the television, Lilian had just finished beating the two twin brothers again.

"Gah! I can't believe I lost again?! How many times does this make now?"

"Ufufufu, this is the sixteenth time I've kicked your butt."

"Damn it!"

Having grown bored with beating the fraternal twins at video games, Lilian made her way over to Kevin and plopped down on his lap. The poor cat who'd been occupying that very spot was forced to jump out of the way, as the beautiful vixen made herself comfortable. Her midnight fur bristling, the feline hissed angrily at Lilian, who merely stuck out her tongue and wrapped her arms around Kevin's neck, placing a kiss on his lips.

For some reason, that kiss seemed to make the cat hiss even more.

"Are you really picking a fight with a cat, Lilian?" asked a somewhat incredulous Kevin.

"Hey, whether it's defending my position from pretentious snow maidens and annoying twin sisters, or even defending it from a cat, this Lilian doesn't do things half-assed."

"P-pretentious?! Regret those words and repent, Boobzilla!"

"Ha! Boobzilla, that's a good one. I should use that one more often," Iris said, her body slinking up to the group, moving along on all fours. Alex and Andrew, who had the pleasure of being behind her, passed out from massive blood loss—the crimson ichor spraying out of their noses like fire hydrants to splatter along the ground.

"Damn it." Kiara sighed at the sight of the floor being covered in blood. "Look at that. Now I'm going to have to hire a professional to get those bloodstains out."

"Don't worry," Kotohime reassured the inu. "Bloodstains that come from a nosebleed are only temporary. They'll disappear in about an hour or so."

"Really?"

"Ufufufu, of course. I am not one to lie."

"And where did you come by this information?"

"Kotohime got it from the *100 Laws of Anime*," Lilian answered from Kevin's lap.

"This isn't an anime!" Christine shouted.

Iris continued crawling along the floor, placing one hand in front of the other in painfully slow feline-like motions. Her spine arched delightfully as she moved across the open space, and the act of putting her hands in front of her invariably caused her breasts to sway enticingly. With the dramatic plunge of her shirt, the group of four were gifted with the sight of the raven-haired vixen's ample cleavage.

"So, if Lily-pad is Boobzilla, what would that make me, hmm?" The fox-girl grinned at her stunned audience. Even Christine remained silent, her eyes following the arch of Iris's back, which inevitably led to her magnificent rear. "Maybe I could be Sex Fiend McGee, or perhaps you could call me—gyaa!"

The spell that had been seemingly cast over the group shattered when, without warning, the cat jumped on top of Iris and sank her claws into the vixen's back.

"Ouch! Inari's hairy ball sack, my back! That hurts! Damn you, you stupid cat!"

The group watched Iris as she rolled along on the ground, wrestling with the surprisingly ferocious feline. The battle was intense. The two rolled all over the floor, biting and scratching and clawing. It was, well, it was kinda hot actually, watching as the sexy girl fought against the black cat. Sure, it was also kind of pathetic, but none of the people there could deny that there was a strange sort of aesthetic appeal to the sight of Iris's clothes being torn to shreds by a furry feline.

Lilian reached in between her cleavage and pulled out a large bag of popcorn. She shifted her position so that she was sitting sideways on Kevin's lap, and grabbed a few pieces. After eating a few bites, she held the rest up to Kevin, who allowed her to feed him, all without taking his eyes away from the fight. Oddly enough, she didn't either.

Lindsay did look away, if only for a moment. She looked at Lilian's chest, and then looked down at her own chest. She pouted.

"I wish my Extra Dimensional Storage Space was that big."

"Sorry, can't help you there."

"So not fair…"

***

"Ngggg…"

A groan emitted from Eric, who'd remained unconscious for the past hour or so. His body stirred, eyelids fluttering open. He looked up at the ceiling, the lights overhead causing spots to appear in his vision.

"What… hit me…?"

His head felt fuzzy, addled and slow. There was a strange ringing in his ears, reminding him of those times he'd smacked his head against a gong for shits and giggles.

"Hawa! Hahaha! Singing, singing~"

That's when he heard it. The loveliest voice he'd heard since the last time he heard his gothic hottie speak. It was a voice of innocence and naivety, lovely and sweet, like the beautiful melody of a giggling child combined with the lyrical essence of a fully grown woman. He knew who that voice belonged to and his heart, mind, and soul—but mostly his libido—wanted to claim that voice for his own.

Like a zombie rising from the dead, Eric clambered to his feet, groaning.

"Boobies!"

Yes, boobies, not brains.

"Boobies—"

"Can it, ya god damn pervert!"

"Guag!"

Seconds later, Eric Corrompere fell into blissful catatonia again.

***

Two hours into the trip, Kiara switched places with Heather, allowing the woman a small break from driving. The blonde-haired female had taken one look at Eric, still unconscious after Christine had smashed his head in, then suggested they all sing karaoke.

Which was how the group found themselves singing, mic in hand, as lyrics appeared on the 50' inch screen.

"Totemo tsumetai sekaide wa!"

"Watashi wa anata no hikari ni narudarou!"

"Kagayaki ni daun kagayakimasu!"

"Watashi wa anata no hōhō o gaido shite mimashou!"

The first person to decide they wanted to sing was Lilian, and where Lilian went, everyone knew that Kevin wouldn't be far behind. Seconds after she volunteered to sing, he decided they should sing a duet. Lilian had agreed.

Everyone except Lilian was regretting that decision.

"Mada daremo yoru no naka"

"Ima wa tada"

"KOKORO no oku ni sawatte"

"Afureru atsusa subete"

"Sasagetai!"

They would trade verses constantly, the two of them, acting with perfect timing and synchronization. It should have sounded beautiful, enchanting even, but it didn't.

"Totemo tsumetai sekaide wa!"

"Watashi wa anata no hikari ni narudarou!"

"Kagayaki ni daun kagayakimasu!"

"Watashi wa anata no hōhō o gaido shite mimashou!"

The problem, of course, was that neither of them could sing. They sucked. They were horrible. The sound of their voices caused ears to bleed and brain matter to liquefy. It didn't help that they were trying to sing in Japanese, which neither of them knew how to speak.

"Ugh." Christine covered her ears with her hands, grimacing and wincing every single time Kevin opened his mouth. "Someone," she groaned, a pitiful whine that resonated with everyone else. "Please… make him stop."

Sitting beside her, Lindsay also had her hands pressed against her ears. "I'm surprised the windows haven't broken yet."

Christine saw her friend's mouth move, but couldn't hear a single word being said. "What?"

"I said—oh, never mind."

"Chikai no kotoba ga"

"Kiseki wo okosu yo"

"Takanaru mune habatake!"

"Tobitateru"

"Negai haruka takaku"

A little ways over, Camellia sat daintily on another couch, laughing and clapping. At least she seemed to enjoy the singing, even if no one else was.

"Hawa! So good!"

Standing beside her, Kirihime was twitching, her smile fixed.

"O-oh, dear. This is…"

"Asayake no mukou matteru mono ga aru"

"Akiramenai yakusoku sou kawashiatta yubi"

"Uchiomesaretemo hitoribocchi ja nai"

"Namae yobu sono koe ga CHIKARA wo kureru to"

Iris had buried her head under a pillow. Normally, the sight of her backside sticking in the air, revealing her panty-clad rump for all to see, was something that every male there would have given their left arm to witness. Too bad they were all busy trying to block out the horrible nails-on-chalkboard voice of their tone-deaf friend.

"Ng… oh, god, I think my brain's gonna pop…"

"Speak for yourself, idiot brother, mine's already burst."

Even Eric had woken up from his fist-to-the-head induced slumber. The poor pervert was rolling around on the ground, covering his bleeding ears, as he tried to block out the pain of a thousand tormented souls screaming in agony—which was about what Kevin's voice sounded like when singing.

The only people not affected by the singing were Kotohime and Heather. They had the forethought to carry earplugs on their person, just in case.

"I'm beginning to think this might have been a terrible, terrible idea."

Kotohime could not hear what Heather said—earplugs and all that. However, she could read lips.

She was quite amused.

"Ara, ara."

***

The music eventually stopped and, quite mercifully, so did the singing. Kevin's and Lilian's faces were flushed from their exertions. They were also smiling big, wide smiles that nearly caused their eyes to squint shut.

"That was really fun," Kevin admitted.

"Wasn't it?" Lilian agreed. "I had no idea singing could be so liberating."

"Though I do have to wonder why we were singing in Japanese. I don't even know Japanese!"

"I think the author was trying out a song in order to come up with an opening theme for us."

"Can we even have an opening theme?"

"Well, maybe… possibly?"

"B-but wouldn't there be formatting issues?"

"There would indeed," Kotohime said, taking her earplugs out. "However, that is not something that should be discussed in the presence of everyone else. They won't understand what you two are talking about."

"Right, right," Kevin agreed, then blinked. "What were we talking about again?"

"Nothing, Kevin." Lilian distracted her mate with a kiss. It worked, thankfully. "So, what should we sing next?"

At the words "sing next," everybody else quickly shouted them down, including a shrill hiss from the cat.

"NO MORE SINGING OUT OF YOU TWO!"

CHAPTER 4

The Obligatory Hot Spring Chapter

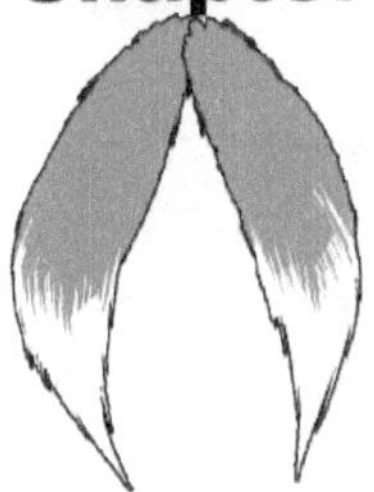

NOT COUNTING RESTROOM BREAKS, it took exactly six hours and thirty-eight minutes to travel from Phoenix to Los Angeles. Time seemed to fly by relatively quickly for the first few hours, but eventually, that time slowed to a crawl—at least for those who were still awake.

Having been the most rambunctious of the group, Kevin and Lilian conked out first. Lilian had pulled a sleeping bag from her Extra Dimensional Storage Space, and she and Kevin had crawled into it and passed out.

They lay on their side, the two of them. Lilian was snuggled against Kevin's chest, and the blond human had an arm around her waist, pulling her close. The others had to admit, however reluctantly, that the pair made for an unbearably adorable sight.

"Nya…"

The cat didn't seem to think so. It glared at the duo with something resembling irritation.

"Brother?"

"Yes?"

"Is it weird that I have this strange urge to squeal 'kawaii'?"

Alex glanced at what his brother was looking at... then shook his head. "That... I cannot answer."

"Hmm." Andrew pondered these words for a second. "What about wanting to wrap my hands around Kevin's throat and squeeze until his eyeballs pop out of his head and his tongue swells and thickens as he slowly suffocates to death?"

Alex took a moment to think up an answer. "... No, I think your feelings are perfectly acceptable, given the situation."

"Good."

"My Lord's greatness is unfathomable! I... I'm not even worthy of looking in the same direction as him! I'm not even worthy of standing in his presence!"

Eric cried inconsolably. His face was buried in his left forearm, tears and snot and gods-only-know what else gushing from his eyes and nose.

Lilian and Kevin were not the only ones sleeping. Camellia had long since dozed off as well. She lay on her back, on the couch, her head resting on Kirihime's lap as she snored away.

"Hawa-hawa-hawa-hawa...   zzzz...   hawa-hawa-hawa-hawa..."

A most unusual snore indeed.

Christine and Lindsay had also fallen asleep. The two remained on the other couch. Christine leaned her head on Lindsay's shoulder, lips parted as she breathed deeply and easily.

Sitting on a chair, Kotohime daintily cleaned her katana. It was a task that everyone else thought she did far too often. She didn't seem bothered by the stares she received, though, and she took great care in maintaining her blade.

She peered outside the window. What had at one point been a combination of desert and city had now become all city. Los Angeles was a sprawling metropolis. There didn't appear to be any rhyme or reason to the location of buildings; they seemed to have been thrown about at random, dotting the landscape with no discernible pattern.

Smog and pollution from millions of cars and hundreds of factories filled the air.

"It's a rather sickening, yet somehow beautiful city, isn't it?" Kiara asked. She was sitting next to Kotohime.

"Indeed. Even though it is a complete dissociation from nature, I still can't help but marvel at humanity's ingenuity."

Movement caught Kotohime's attention. She turned her head and frowned.

"Iris-sama, what are you doing?"

Iris grinned, but did not look up from her work. "I'm playing a prank. What's it look like I'm doing?"

"Yes, I can see that. What I meant was—never mind. I suppose I know why."

Kotohime said nothing after that, just watched in silence as Iris continued to draw on Christine's and Lindsay's faces. She could see what was shaping up to be the mushroom head of a particularly crude phallus on Christine's right cheek.

"We'll be at the hotel in about fifteen minutes," Heather called from the driver's seat. "You guys might want to wake everyone up."

Iris stopped drawing on Christine. She capped her marker and stood up. "I'll—"

"I shall wake Lilian-sama and Kevin-sama," Kotohime declared. Iris pouted, but she ignored the vixen. Standing smoothly to her feet, she went over to the slumbering couple, where she proceeded to shake them awake.

"Mmm… munya…"

It was almost amusing to watch the pair wake up. Lilian yawned while Kevin groaned. The two rose with almost deliberate synchronization, stretching their arms and legs as they sat up. Even their blinking was done in synch.

"Oh, Kotohime." Lilian's speech was halted by a loud yawn. "We there yet?" she asked. Meanwhile, Kevin stuck a hand under his shirt and scratched his chest.

He's gained a six-pack, Kotohime observed with a critical eye. *Impressive.*

"We shall be arriving at the hotel soon, so I suggest you get up," she said.

"M'kay."

Together, the two worked to roll up the sleeping bag and put it away. Kotohime was almost positive that Kevin's participation was just an excuse to fondle Lilian's breasts without anyone noticing, but she didn't say anything.

The lovebirds were not the only ones waking up. Camellia also awoke from her nap.

"Hawa…"

Her catchphrase: It could even be used as a yawn.

"Did you sleep well, My Lady?" asked Kirihime.

"Tee-hee, Camellia slept great."

Kirihime smiled gently at the woman's childish and innocent expression of joy. Over on the other side, Lindsay and Christine were just waking up to see the many crude and vulgar drawings on each other's faces.

"The hell happened to your face?"

"My face? You should check out your own face."

Christine turned towards the window, and then gaped at her reflection. She really couldn't be blamed. Drawn in big, black, bold marker were several penises: one on either side of her cheeks and pointed towards her mouth. On her forehead was an eyegina. And, as if to add insult to injury, the words "I'm a frigid bitch" were written on her chin and made to look like a beard.

Christine shivered in rage.

"IRIS!"

"Yes, oh cold and angry one?" Iris asked, a smile that was too innocent to be real plastered on her face. To Christine, it looked more like a wicked grin.

Christine hissed. "Explain this!"

"I think it's pretty self-explanatory," Iris said, observing the drawings with a keen eye, as if she had not been the one to draw them. "Someone obviously thought you could do with a cock or two." A shrug. "Maybe they thought having you suck dick would make you less of a bitch."

Christine lost it.

"Y-y-y-y-you fucking BITCH! I'LL KILL YOU!"

Christine's shout of outrage was only outdone by the chilling mist that expanded like fog rolling in from the sea. The air became bone-chilling. Everyone shivered as hoarfrost spread along the ground and crept up the walls.

"I-is it me, or has the temperature suddenly plummeted?" asked Alex.

"It is not just you. Damn, who the hell turned the air conditioning to zero?" his twin asked.

"And what the hell is up with this fog? Where did it come from?"

"If you two are going to fight, then get the hell off my bus before you start going at it," Kiara said. "Otherwise, I'm gonna get involved, and I doubt either of you wants that."

Iris squeaked while Christine reluctantly ceased using her powers. Neither of them had any desire to fight Kiara. Even if either of them was predisposed towards fighting, which they weren't, the idea of picking one with the inu was not pleasant. Despite having only a single arm to fight with, she still scared the crap out of them both.

"What the hell, Kiara? Why did you stop them?" Eric groaned.

"Because I'm not gonna have them mess up my bus," Kiara said.

"Aw, man!" Eric raised his hands as he bemoaned this most terrible loss. "And here I was hoping I would get to see a super awesome catfight!"

"What was that?!" Christine asked, her voice reminiscent of a hissing cat.

"I said I wanted to see you two start ripping each other's clothes off and—guag!"

All words from his mouth died when Christine punched him in the face.

"Die!"

***

The gigantic bus looked more than a little out of place among all of the tiny cars in the parking lot. Even the large pickup trucks were overshadowed by the mammoth vehicle. It certainly drew numerous looks, pointing, and whispers from the people parking their vehicles that evening.

Disembarking from the vehicle, the group of twelve walked into the open air. It was evening. The sun was going down, casting the city in glowing colors.

Iris peered around at everybody, a surprised frown on her face. "I think we're missing someone…"

At her words, the others looked around as well.

"We are missing someone," Kevin muttered, brow furrowing in thought. "Where's Justin?"

Now that he thought about it, his quiet and unobtrusive friend had been missing the entire bus ride. They'd not seen hide nor hair of him at all. How the heck did that happen? The bus only had one room.

His arms were full of cat. The small black feline looked up at him with a tilted head. She "nya'd" at him, as if asking, "Who is Justin?"

"How did we possibly miss the disappearance of someone in our group?" Alex questioned out loud. "It's not like we're that large a group to begin with."

"Well, it is Justin," Andrew added, nodding several times as if that answered all of their questions. "He's so quiet and tends to go off into his own little world. It's pretty easy to forget about him."

"Heh, true that."

"No, that's not it," Lilian declared. "I'm pretty sure the author just forgot to add him into the last couple of scenes."

Hey!

"I concur," Kotohime added, "Author-san is very absentminded. And he's not that smart."

Th-that's a rude thing to say.

"And he doesn't really think when he writes. Or at all. In fact, I'm pretty sure he never thinks period," Iris added mercilessly.

Y-you guys are so cruel!

"What the heck are you three talking about now?" asked a thoroughly confused Heather.

"Ufufufu, nothing that you need to concern yourself with," Kotohime said, hiding her smile behind the sleeve of her kimono. "In either event, we should probably call his cellphone to find out where Justin-san is. I can only hope we didn't leave him at one of the rest stops. It would not be pleasant if we had to drive back and search for him."

Many an eye widened, and several people fished for their cellphones to give Justin a call, when a voice spoke up behind them.

"No need... here..."

Everyone turned. Justin walked slowly down the stairs of the bus. His dull, half-lidded eyes peered at everything and nothing with his perpetually slow look. The entire group stared at Justin, who either didn't seem to realize, or was ignoring, the "WTF?" looks he received, as he stepped into the semicircle of people.

Kiara recovered first. "Since you're here, let's hurry up and get our hotel rooms. This place has a hot spring, and I wanna try it out before hitting the sack."

"A hot spring?" Lilian asked, her eyes widening.

Iris's eyes also widened. "Has it finally come?"

"Has what come?" asked Kevin.

"Don't be dull, Stud. Do you not realize what this is?"

"Um, no. What is this?"

Lilian and Iris stared at each other, then looked at Kevin.

"It's the legendary hot spring episode!" they said at the same time.

"The hot spring episode?" Eric's eyes also went wide. "You mean the episode in every anime where all the women get naked together, and the men try to unsuccessfully peep on them, which usually ends in a horrible, yet hilarious moment of perversion?"

"I see." Heather cupped her chin in thought. "So, it is that time already. Apprentice, we must convene later today, preferably before everyone goes into the hot spring."

"Yes, Master!"

Kevin stared at the group, then looked down at the cat. "I feel like I've just lost something important in all this," he told the feline.

"Nya?" the cat tilted her head.

"Never mind," Kevin sighed.

The hotel they'd booked rooms with appeared every bit the five-star resort. Built like a combination of a Mediterranean palace and Greek mansion, the Sobre el Natural Resort was an oasis in a jungle of glass and steel. An impressive structure of symmetrical facades, the resort towered over them at four stories in height. Corinthian columns lined the building. Fountains dotted the front and side entrances. Kevin could see a number of gazebos built within grassy fields and meandering trails.

They walked through the front entrance, marked by an extravagant archway. Pavement changed into tan marble tiles polished to a shine. An arched ceiling loomed above them. More columns stood as silent sentinels as they walked up to the front desk, where a lady dressed in a business suit stood ready to greet them with a smile.

"Hello, welcome to Sobre el Natural. How may I help you?" she asked.

"We have a seven-day reservation for thirteen," Kiara, having been the one to book the reservations, did the talking. "It should be under the name Kiara F. Kuyo."

The woman's eyes widened. She definitely recognized the name. Who wouldn't know the name of the woman who'd revolutionized the fitness world?

"Yes, yes, it's right here," the woman's voice became high-pitched and excited. Kevin could practically see the woman's thoughts as she stared at Kiara like the inu was the sole center of the universe. "Please wait just one moment and allow me to get your keys."

The woman practically tripped over herself to grab their key cards. When she returned, she handed them to Kiara.

"Here you are. As per your reservations, all rooms are in the same hall and located across from each other. Your rooms are on the third floor, west wing. That'll be down the hall and to your left. Just keep going until you reach a pair of elevators. You can't miss them."

"Right. Thank you."

"Oh, it's no trouble at all." The woman smiled before noticing the cat in Kevin's hands. "Now, I do need to tell you that while we have a pet-friendly policy, you are responsible for them, meaning that, should they make a mess of your room, you will be charged extra." She sent Kiara an apologetic and nervous smile. "I hope you don't mind?"

Kiara gave her a strained smile. "I don't mind at all."

"Good, good. If you need anything, please be sure to let me know. I'll do anything you ask of me."

Kiara's strained smile twitched. "I actually do need something from you."

A radiant smile was given in return. "How can I help you?"

"You can help me by letting go of my hand."

"Eh?" the woman blinked. Then she looked down at her hand. When she realized that, indeed, she was still holding Kiara's hand, the female attendant gave a "Kya!" and jerked back as if scalded. She then apologized profusely, bowing several times and begging for forgiveness.

Kiara sighed. "Come on, everyone. Let's go."

Kiara led the way. The group followed. They walked along a red-carpeted floor. Beige walls trapped them on either side, and a curved ceiling with evenly spaced lights lit their path. Kevin, the cat enjoying her place in his arms, hastened to match the brunette's pace.

"Is it always like that wherever you go?" he asked, making strange gestures with his head.

"Not always, but most places, yes, I receive a similar reception." If Kiara was bothered by this, she did not show it. Kevin figured she must have been used to such treatment.

They were led to their rooms and given their keys. They'd gotten three rooms: one for the adults, one for the girls, and one for the boys. The insides of the rooms were just as elaborate as everything else. With dark brown carpet and tan walls, each room was ornately furnished with beautifully burnished decorations made of rich wood that sparkled in the light. The beds, four in total, were all four-poster beds with their own curtained canopies. The light-colored blankets, satiny white sheets, and fluffy pillows fit the resort's regality with the conformity of a glove.

The black cat leapt out of Kevin's arms and walked further into the room. Kevin let it be in order to explore his new surroundings.

"Man, talk about ritzy."

Eric and the twins rushed into the room. Kevin and Justin held back as the three other boys each claimed a bed for themselves—or tried to.

"Hold up, you two," Kevin stopped Alex and Andrew before they could claim separate beds. "There are only four beds, and since you two are twins, you're going to be sharing one of them."

"WHAT?!" The shout came from them both.

"That's not fair," Alex whined.

"Yeah, why do I have to sleep with this idiot?"

"Don't act like you're the victim here. I'm the one who's gonna be stuck dealing with your antics, you damn bed-hogger."

Blink.

A vein throbbed on Andrew's head. "A bed-hogger, am I? Well, who's the one who's always stealing the sheets? Huh! Huh?!"

Blink. Blink.

"At least I don't still wet the bed!"

Massive blinking.

"You... you promised you'd never tell anyone that! And I haven't wet the bed in, uh, well... a while! Besides! Who was the one who left his bed a sopping mess the other day?!"

"Why you... that was a special moment! SPECIAL!"

Kevin, Eric, and Justin watched as the two fraternal twin brothers tackled each other to the ground. They rolled around on the floor, pushing and pulling and biting and hitting and clawing. It was like watching two dogs trying to chase each other's tails.

"Ne, Kevin, do you know what those two are talking about?" asked Eric.

"No." Kevin shook his head. "No, I don't." A pause. "And I don't think I want to know."

"... Hehehe..."

***

Lilian entered her room with the other two girls. Christine and Lindsay preceded her while Iris followed behind them. Her sandal-clad feet moved along soft carpet, while her emerald eyes surveyed the beige walls and illustrious decor.

If she was being honest with herself, the room bore too much of a resemblance to those she had seen in the mansions of rich, snooty noble kitsune clans for her taste. It made her feel confined, restricted, and like her freedoms had been taken away by the cold hand of her birthright.

Christine and Lindsay didn't seem to agree.

"This is so cool!"

Lindsay squealed like the teenage girl that she was. Her eyes panned across the room, then locked onto the bed. With a grin, she dropped her suitcase and jumped onto the sinfully soft mattress, bouncing several times before lying still on her back.

"This has to be the most incredible hotel room I've ever stayed in." Grinning, Lindsay rolled over onto her stomach and kicked her feet in the air. "I feel like royalty."

Although Christine's reaction was much more muted, Lilian could clearly tell that the yuki-onna held the same excitement as their friend.

"It is very nice." The pale-skinned girl set her own baggage down and crawled onto the bed. She moved up towards the headboard and lay against the pillows. She was smiling. "This is a lot more comfortable than my own bed, that's for sure."

Lilian set her stuff down and kicked off her sandals. She, like the other two, tried out the bed for herself.

"I think I like mine better," she declared.

Christine clicked her tongue. "You only like it better because Kevin sleeps with you."

"So? And who said that's the only reason? This bed is too soft for my taste. I feel like I'm sinking into the mattress rather than being supported by it."

"Excuses."

"I agree," a grinning Lindsay said. "I think you're just grumpy because you're not going to be sleeping with Kevin."

"If you'd like, I could keep you company, Lily-pad."

Iris, a salacious grin on her face, crawled onto Lilian's bed. The redhead would have said something, but found herself momentarily stunned as her sister "walked" towards her on all fours. Her feline-like grace, the arch of her spine, which curved into sensually swaying hips that encompassed a magnificent rear end, caused all of Lilian's brain-motor functions to cease.

"Ho? Are you thinking about it, my dear, sweet, Lily-pad?"

Iris's alluring crimson eyes gazed into innocent emeralds. Lilian took a slow, shuddering breath.

"No…" she managed. "I have no desire to let you sleep with me, especially since you can't seem to remember how much I hate that nickname."

"Oh, but it's all in good fun," Iris teased. "There's nothing wrong with a little bonding between siblings, is there?"

"It is when that sibling is obsessed with her twin sister."

"Aster and Azalea are lovers."

"They're also raging lesbians with several screws loose."

"Hmph. Fine, fine." Lilian breathed a sigh of relief when Iris backed off. "I suppose I'll let you sleep alone, for now." Getting off the bed, Iris stretched, ignoring the gawking Lindsay and the disgusted Christine. "Now, then, I think we should check out these hot springs I've heard so much about. You girls in?"

Christine, Lindsay, and Lilian looked at each other.

"We're in," Lindsay spoke for all of them, "I've always wanted to try out an authentic hot spring."

***

"All right, men! Today is the day we all step into the wide world of manhood!" Eric barked at his friends.

They were all sitting on their respective beds… except for Kevin. He'd gone off somewhere, which was why they were even having this discussion. There was no way they could let their friend know what they were plotting.

"Uh… what manhood are we talking about?" Alex asked, raising his hand like a kid in a classroom.

"I am glad you asked." Eric had a notoriously lecherous grin on his face. "I've received intelligence that the girls will be taking a bath in the hot springs—"

"And who gave you that intelligence?"

"—which means this will be the perfect opportunity for us to peep on them!"

"Seriously, how do we know this isn't a trap?"

"You all know what girls do in a hot spring, don't you?" Eric held a fist up to his face. His eyes ignited with the powers of perversion. His mind conjured images only a man of his salaciousness could conceive, and he had no problem sharing that imagery with his friend. "They get naked! They strip down and frolic through the hot, steam-filled room, their boobs bouncing, their butts wiggling. Hot, wet, naked, nubile flesh is waiting for us just around the corner, my friends!"

None of the people there—aside from Eric—could be described as perverted, but they were still men. While they probably would have told their friend to piss off on any other occasion, tonight, they found themselves caught up in Eric's depraved desire to see naked female flesh—that every female on this trip was drop-dead gorgeous certainly helped.

Eric pointed a finger at the ceiling. "Yes, today is the day. Today is our day! The day we all become men! The day we see those magnificent bouncing bazongas for ourselves! Men! Let us be off! To the land of tatas!"

"To the land of tatas!"

A great cheer went up.

"… Tatas…"

And then there was Justin.

"To me, men! Come! We must make haste!"

***

When Alex, Andrew, Justin, and Eric arrived on the male side of the hot springs, the place was mostly empty, save for one old man with a balding head and an odd green tint to his skin, like he'd been stuck in the ocean for too long and his skin had soaked in the sea's color. The group of hormonal teenage boys paid little attention to him, busy as they were drilling holes through the bamboo wall that separated the male section from the female section.

"Damn it, I can't see anything. Why can't I see anything?"

"Is it because of the fog? Maybe it's too thick?"

"No. If that were the case, I would at least see white. All I can see is gray."

"… Steel…"

"Eh?"

"He's saying the walls have a layer of steel between them."

"Dang it. Eric, what do you think we should do?"

…

"Eric?"

Upon receiving no response, Alex and Andrew looked around to see that Eric had vanished.

"Where did he—"

A hand clamped against Alex's and Andrew's mouths. The pair's eyes widened.

"Ah, ah, ah, ah. Don't scream. That wouldn't be good. Do you want the ladies on the other side to hear you?" Two head shakes. "Good. Now, I'm going to let go. Don't scream, alright?" Two nods.

The hands were removed. Alex and Andrew spun around to see who'd snuck up on them.

"M-Ms. Grant!"

"Shhh!" the woman held a hand to her lips.

"S-sorry," they apologized.

"What are you doing here? Uh, you know this is, um, the men's side, right?"

"I am well aware of that," the amused Heather Grant said, grinning. She was dressed in a bikini instead of buffing it. It had nothing to do with modesty. She had a job to do, and she couldn't do that if these boys were distracted.

"Um, then, may I ask why you're, ah, here?"

"You, ah, may, um, ask."

"Okay… so, why are you here?"

"I'm glad you asked!" Spreading her feet shoulder-width apart and placing her hands on her hips, Heather gave the group of boys a grin. "I am here because my peeping senses told me that a couple of young boys would need my help to learn the sacred and traditional art of peeping!"

…

Silence. Several crickets began chirping.

"That's right, boys! Today is your lucky day, for I, Heather Grant, Master Peeping Tom, am going to teach you how to peep with style!"

More silence. A crow cawed in the distance in a most annoying manner.

"By the way, where's Eric?" Heather asked.

***

"Hehehehe…"

Giggling, Eric hid behind one of the large boulders located on the women's side of the hot spring. Like a good deal of hot springs, this one tried to retain a more natural look, rather than the manmade look of a spa. The spring appeared as a placid pond. Smooth rocks covered much of the surface. Large boulders like the one he hid behind rose from the water, giant fingers stretched towards the sky.

There are so many perfect hiding places.

The doors slid open. Eric giggled some more. It was show-time!

"Kukuku, come to me, my pretties…"

"Hawa! Such a lovely hot spring!"

"Please be careful, My Lady. You wouldn't want to—"

"H-hawa!"

"… trip…"

"Ufufufu, it seems Camellia-sama never changes."

"Damn, she's clumsy."

"… Hawa…"

Peeking out from behind the rock, Eric was given a sight that made his daring, cunning, reckless, and downright stupid plan totally worth it. Four of the hottest women he'd ever seen walked into the hot spring. Their figures were covered by towels, but he didn't mind. They would lose them soon enough.

"Ku ku ku…"

"H-hawa… is something wrong, Kiara?"

"…No. Nothing's wrong."

Eric clamped a hand over his mouth to keep from laughing anymore. He kept his back to the rock, listening to the sounds of sloshing water, as the women waded into the steamy spring—

"Hawa! It's so hot! Look, Kirihime! Look! Steam! Hawa!"

—or in the case of Camellia, rushed into the water with reckless abandon.

"Hawa!"

"My Lady!"

And ended up tripping. Again.

She really is clumsy. Eric grinned. *But she's so hot I don't care!*

Peering around the hot spring again, Eric found a sight that would never leave him. His eyes devoured the sinful vision, delighting in the bouncing bosoms, becoming mesmerized by the nubile flesh, and thoroughly enjoying the gorgeous, naked bodies before him. So into the magnificence was he that Eric never even realized he'd been spotted, until a bright flash of silver created a graceful arc immediately in front of him.

"AAHH!"

Eric stumbled backwards in shock. The rock he'd been hiding behind had just been cut in half! Even now, he watched as the upper half of the rock slid off the lower half and fell into the water. The surface where the rock had been cut was perfectly smooth.

Standing on the opposite side of the rock was Kotohime. Her katana was out, the flat of the blade resting against her shoulder, the sheath in her left hand. She stared at Eric with her unfathomably dark eyes. They were like a storm brewing within a tumultuous black sea.

"Hello, Eric-san."

"Uh, um, h-hello."

Eric's heart pounded in his chest. What was this abominable fear? Why did he feel so cold? He was in a freaking hot spring!

"Are you enjoying the view?"

"Ack. U-u-um, y-yes?"

"Ufufufu, that is good. It is always nice to have one last good vision before being turned into a corpse."

"Gurk."

"Can I kill him?" asked an utterly insane-looking Kirihime. Gone was the appearance of a beautiful and demure young woman. In that person's place, was a woman whose widened eyes and dilated irises gleamed with the spark of insanity.

"No, no, not yet, Kirihime." Kotohime smiled. It was the smile of a woman about to unleash hell upon the hapless and foolish man who dared to peep on her. "Perverts like him must be made to suffer before they die."

"Gah."

Eric knew that he had to get away from here. Reluctant though he was, he couldn't afford to stay in this place, not if he valued his life, which he did. Even perverts had self-preservation instincts.

Unfortunately, when he turned around to try and run off, he found himself staring at a very unhappy Kiara.

"And just where do you think you're going?" the woman asked, cracking her knuckles. Eric backed away, but all that meant was that he'd traded one angry female for another—no, two others.

Kirihime's psychotically gleaming eyes caused his soul to quake, and the way Kotohime prepared her katana really didn't inspire much confidence in his survival. And where had Kirihime pulled those knives from?

"W-wait!" Eric raised his hands in a warding gesture. "C-can't we talk about this like civilized people?"

"Coming from a pervert such as yourself, I find such words almost amusing," Kotohime said. Her smile widened. "Almost."

The group of women closed in. Eric's girly screams soon echoed across the hotel.

***

"KYYYAAAA!!!"

Alex, Andrew, Justin, and Heather all looked at the wall, as if doing so would allow them to see through it.

"That scream was…"

"That was definitely Eric."

Heather pressed a palm to her face. "Really, Apprentice, trying to sneak into the women's side of the hot spring without being fully trained in the ways of peeping. What kind of idiot are you?"

"OH, MY GOD! PLEASE! STOOOOPPPPPP!"

While Eric's friends turned pale, Heather merely sighed. "That Eric, I keep telling him that he's not ready for this level of difficulty yet, but he never listens."

"I-is he going to be okay?" asked a worried Alex.

"They won't kill him, if that's what you're asking."

"OH, DEAR SWEET BABY JESUS! I'M GONNA DIE!"

"They'll just torture him until he wishes he were dead."

Alex and Andrew shuddered.

"That really doesn't inspire much confidence."

"MOMMY!!"

Eric's echoing screams of horrendous agony became hoarser and hoarser, until they eventually died down, leaving a stilted silence behind.

"So," Heather started, smiling as if nothing had happened, "who wants to peep first?"

All three boys shook their heads frantically. They were no longer interested in peeping. In fact, each one made a vow never to try and peep on a woman ever again.

It would be the best decision they'd ever made.

***

"Can someone please tell me why we're stripping?" Christine asked, even as she began the laborious process of undoing all the straps and laces of her Lolita outfit. "I mean, I'm pretty sure this isn't one of those hot springs where you can just wander around in the buff, and is that something we really want to do?"

On the opposite side of the changing room, Lilian slid her shorts down her long, beautiful legs.

"Aren't we doing this because that's how it's done in Japan?"

"Don't answer my question with another question! And this isn't Japan, damn it! It's America!"

Iris rolled her eyes, even as she pulled off her shirt, allowing her breasts to bounce free. "The reason we're doing this is because the author's an idiot who's obsessed with Japanese culture."

"Eh?"

"Yeah, he's got it in his head that in order to appease the fan base, he needs to have a hot spring episode."

"Huh?"

"You know, have the girls strip naked, show a little T&A, maybe get some random boob groping in there. It's like a staple in Japanese pop culture."

"What?"

Iris smirked. "You don't understand a single word I just said, do you?"

"I would understand if you didn't say such stupid stuff!" Christine snapped in response to Iris's taunting.

Lindsay, already bereft of clothing, grabbed a towel hanging from a nearby rack and wrapped it around her torso. "Could you two please not argue? We're here to enjoy ourselves, remember? So let's just do that, okay? Have a good time and relax, while taking a nice soak in the hot spring."

"W-whatever." Christine huffed and crossed her arms. "It's not like I care or anything."

"Uhuhu, don't be like that, chibi."

"Shut up, wench!"

As one, the group of females walked into the hot spring. It was already occupied by several familiar faces. Kiara, Kirihime, Kotohime, and Camellia lounged around in the steaming waters. None of them were wearing clothes either.

Christine and Lindsay both took one look at Kotohime's and Camellia's breasts, which appeared to have unusual buoyancy as they floated on the water's surface. Then they looked at their own breasts.

They suddenly weren't so eager to enter the hot springs anymore.

"Kotohime, Kirihime, Camellia!" Lilian greeted her vassals and her mother with a sunny smile as she stepped into the water, allowing her towel to fall by the wayside.

"Hawa! Lilian! Iris! Hullo!"

"Hello, Lilian-sama."

"Lady Lilian, Lady Iris, I hope you enjoy the water."

"Oh, sure, just ignore Kiara," a certain inu said, rolling her eyes. "Let's just pretend she's not here. Maybe then she'll go away."

Lilian stuck her tongue out at Kiara as she sat down next to her maid-slash-bodyguard.

Her breasts started to float.

So did Iris's.

"I'm suddenly feeling this intense urge to run back inside, get dressed, and pretend this never happened," Lindsay said. Christine agreed, even if she didn't say anything.

"Aw, don't be like that." Iris patted the spot next to her. "Come on, get in and relax. No one cares if you two are flatter than a billboard."

Christine snorted as she stepped in. There was no way she'd back down from this pretentious bitch.

She sat several feet away, followed closely by Lindsay. Neither of them discarded their towels. Unlike the kitsune, who lacked many of the nudity taboos that humans possessed, and Kiara, who just plain didn't care about such things, they were still very self-conscious about their bodies.

"You'll never find a man if you keep acting like that," Christine said to Iris's taunting.

"You'd think that, wouldn't you?" Smirking, Iris raised a single index finger, which she stuck into her mouth and lathered in oral secretions. Her eyes gleamed mischievously as she pulled out the saliva-coated finger and poked her own chest. "But I beg to differ, my frigid little friend."

Lindsay and Christine went beet red.

"There's a difference between being sexy and being a skank," Christine snapped, recovering with admirable swiftness.

"Which you clearly wouldn't know about," Iris returned fire.

Christine stood up in the water and glared. "What was that?"

"You heard me." Iris, also standing to her feet, smirked down at the other girl, who only came up to her chest—her obscenely large chest.

Christine saw red. "You wanna fight? If so, then just keep talking. I'll freeze your ass to this hot spring and let you stay out here all night!"

"Ho ho. Is that a challenge?" Iris chuckled. "Sorry, flatty, but I'm not really interested in fighting."

"F-f-flatty?!"

"There's only one thing that I care about."

Lilian only had enough time to notice the devious grin on Iris's face before the other vixen pounced.

"Kya! What are you—Iris, let go!"

"Uhuhuhu, have these gotten bigger since I last groped them? I think they have!"

"N-no! You can't touch these! Only Kevin—kya! Please stop! Let go of them!"

"Don't be such a prude and let me see how much my Lily-pad has grown."

"I'm not—iyahn! What are—ah! Ahn! Ah! Not there! —oh! Oh! Oh!"

"Uhuhu, they really have grown. You've become quite the big-breasted bimbo, haven't you?" Iris taunted, laughing in a frightening and creepy manner.

"Your breasts are just as big as mine!" Lilian wanted to scream. However, the way Iris roughly fondled and squeezed her breasts made doing anything besides screaming in a mixture of surprise and pain impossible.

Meanwhile, everyone else just watched as Lilian was molested by her own sister.

"Hey, Christine?" asked Lindsay, not looking away from the scene.

"What?" Christine, half-disgusted, half-aroused, found herself unable to disengage from the sight of Lilian being fondled.

"Is it wrong that I'm turned on by this?"

It took Christine a second to compute that sentence.

"What?"

When she looked over at Lindsay, it was to see the lithe blonde's eyes locked onto the struggling fox-girls with the sort of fascination one might expect from someone like Eric.

Her nose was bleeding.

Christine buried her hands in her face and bemoaned her fate. "Gods help me; I'm surrounded by perverts."

***

Kevin had decided not to join his friends in the hot springs. Tempting though it was, he had a lot to think about, and he didn't believe that relaxing in the hot waters with a bunch of other guys would help him. After taking a quick shower, he'd grabbed one of his manga, and found a quiet place to sit and contemplate the many important issues on his mind.

Sobre el Natural resort was home to more than just a hot spring. There were a number of places for people to lounge: three pools built to look like a lagoon, surrounded by comfortable chairs for sunbathing; verandas housing numerous tables; and a number of grass lawns with large, ornately-crafted gazebos that appeared to have been directly transported from Greece. Yes, there were a lot of places for someone who wanted to enjoy the peace and quiet.

Kevin passed a number of other guests in his quest for a place to relax. Some people were lounging by the pool, others dined on the verandas outside, various resort staff catering to their needs. Still more simply enjoyed the fresh outdoors, meandering along one of the many paved trails for people to walk through. Kevin found a small bench and sat down. He opened his manga and perused through the pages.

This particular manga was about a group of mages who were part of a guild. They took jobs and fought various bad guys. The main character, a young woman with blonde hair and boobs the size of Camellia's, could summon spirits with keys that opened the gates to another dimension.

"Fire Dragon's Iron Fist, huh?" Kevin looked at the image depicting a pink-haired mage smashing a fire-covered fist into an enemy's face. "That's such a cool name. I wish I could come up with a name like that, but I don't have any super cool powers that would be worthy of such a name." He sighed. "What I wouldn't give for the ability to use magic."

Kevin was a human, and as a human, he lacked the supernatural powers that Lilian and her family possessed. He wasn't jealous or anything. Still, sometimes being the only human among them made him feel a little inadequate.

As he continued looking at all of the awesome magic powers, something rubbed against his leg.

"Nya?"

Looking down, Kevin saw the cat that he'd brought with him. The feline stopped her rubbing to look up at him with her big, yellow eyes.

"Nya?"

"Hello there." Leaning down, Kevin scooped the cat up and deposited her onto his lap. "Maybe you can help me out with my problem." Fingers idly caressed the cat's back, the furry critter purring under his ministrations. "You see, I've been trying to come up with awesome names for my attacks, but I seem to be having trouble. None of my attacks have any magical abilities to them like fire or ice or what have you. They're just punches and kicks—not exactly conductive to kickass names, if you know what I mean?" He looked at the manga in his right hand, blue eyes narrowed in thought. "But I really, really want to think up some cool names, you know? So, would you mind being my sounding board?"

The cat just looked at him. Kevin couldn't read a cat's facial expressions, but he assumed she was giving him the go-ahead.

"So, for one of my attacks, I was thinking of calling it the Combustion Fist of Manly Souls Punch. What do you think?"

The cat stared.

"Okay, how about Iron Fist of the Heathen's Divine Fury?"

More staring.

"Um, then what about the Angry Fist of the Dragon Lord's Pantheon?"

The staring would not be stopping any time soon.

"Ugh, so not that one either, huh?" Kevin sighed. "Well, dang."

"Ara? Kevin-sama, what are you doing all the way out here?"

"Oh, Kotohime," Kevin greeted as the graceful katana-wielder approached him. "Did you enjoy the hot springs?"

"Ufufufu…" Something in that laugh caused the hairs on the back of Kevin's neck to rise in unpleasant ways. "I suppose you could say it was enjoyable, to a point."

"That's good… I think. Wait." He blinked. "To a point?"

"And what about you? Did you not partake in a dip within the hot springs?"

"Naw, I thought about it, but I'm a little too busy trying to think up cool names for my attacks."

"I thought all you could do was punch and kick."

"Ugh, don't remind me."

"Ufufufu." Kotohime sat down next to him. She set the katana in her lap. "Speaking of attacks, how goes your training with Kiara-san?"

Kevin winced as he thought of all the bruises and broken bones he'd received during his training sessions.

If it wasn't for Lilian's healing ability…

"Eh, it's going well, I guess. It's tough, but I've gotten a lot stronger, and I'm learning a lot, too. Kiara really knows her stuff."

"Indeed, the woman is most talented in the ways of unarmed combat, and she is an excellent instructor. Kiara-san's philosophy when teaching is that people learn best by experiencing combat first-hand. I suppose you could say that she believes in the 'trial by fire' philosophy."

Kevin felt a small trail of sweat trickle down the left side of his neck. "Yeah, I've kinda noticed that."

The two sat in silence, with only the gentle purring of the cat breaking it. A little ways away, an old man squatted down to admire some flowers. They were fire lilies, Kevin noted from their dark red petals.

"Ne, Kotohime, do you mind if I ask you a question?"

"Not at all." The woman responded by turning her body to face him more fully. "What did you wish to know?"

"I was kinda curious to know how you and your sister became vassals of the Pnéyma Clan." Kotohime's stunned expression darkened for an instant, and Kevin quickly amended his statement. "What I mean is, well, it's only if you want to tell me. You don't have to tell me if it makes you uncomfortable or anything. I just thought I'd ask."

Kotohime calmed Kevin down by raising a hand. "No, no. I do not mind telling you. It is just that I did not expect to be asked such a question." Her smile looked a tad bitter. "You caught me by surprise."

She looked out at the vast expanse of green, at the people wandering about. Some of those people stared at the two of them. They must have made an odd sight: a young man wearing faded jeans and a plain T-shirt, and a woman of clearly Japanese descent dressed in a dark blue kimono.

"My sister and I came from a small water clan. We were very few in number, less than two dozen, in fact, and therefore we didn't have much strength. It was no wonder, then, that our clan would eventually be destroyed."

Kevin was too stunned to say anything. Destroyed? How?

"Our village was attacked by a wandering group of raiders. They were a mixed bag of yōkai who were led by an, at the time, upstart yōkai called Nurarihyon."

"I think I've heard that name in one of my manga…"

"That does not surprise me. Many of the manga that you and Lilian-sama are so fond of are often based on facts that are steeped in legends and myths. Nurarihyon the Diplomat, as he is called in this day and age, is one of the most powerful yōkai in the world. He, along with The King of the Tengu Sōjōbō, and Shuten Dōji, the fierce king of oni, are yōkai considered to be on par with the three Kyūbi."

"Back then, Nurarihyon was not the great yōkai that he is now, but he was still exceedingly powerful. He and his legion of yōkai were trying to gain more power and followers by fighting yōkai clans that were strong, but not strong enough that he and his followers would be crushed."

"My clan happened to be one of those targeted. We put up a good fight, but two dozen River Kitsune were no match for several hundred yōkai. Our clan was defeated. However, Nurarihyon is an oddly honorable yōkai. After our defeat, he offered all of us a place among his group. Many accepted. I did not, and I took my sister, who had just gained her second tail at the time, and left."

Kevin remained silent, entranced by the story Kotohime wove like a master crafter spun threads to create a gorgeous tapestry.

"We wandered the world for many years after the destruction of my clan. During that time, I acted as a mercenary and made something of a name for myself. I eventually met Delphine Pnevma-denka, who was only an eight-tailed kitsune at the time. She'd told me that she was looking for someone with my unique talents, and so she offered me the position of a bodyguard for her clan. I accepted, and Pnevma-denka christened me with a new name—Kotohime."

"I've always wondered how you got your name, but I don't understand why someone would name you 'Thing Princess.'"

"Actually, depending on the kanji, 'Koto' can also refer to a Japanese musical instrument, of which I can play very well."

"I didn't know you could play a musical instrument." Kevin's eyes were wide and shone with an unusual luster. "Do you think I could hear you play sometime?"

Unable to resist, Kotohime ruffled his hair. Kevin pouted, but he was secretly pleased by the affectionate gesture. It had taken a lot of work, but the woman finally approved of and supported his position as Lilian's mate.

And just think, it only took me nearly being killed to earn that respect.

A hard bunch to please, these kitsune were.

"Maybe, sometime, I shall play for you. However, I have not played in many years. Not since…"

Kevin didn't need Kotohime to finish her sentence to know what she was talking about.

He decided to change the subject.

"So, what was your original name? If you don't mind my asking."

Kotohime stared at Kevin for quite a while, long enough to make him squirm in discomfort. He couldn't keep from feeling worried under that gaze. Had he asked something she didn't like? Well, of course he had. He'd probably brought up a bunch of bad memories with his question.

Dang it! How could I have been so careless and invasive?!

"Tsukihime."

"E-eh?"

"My name," Kotohime released a deep breath. "My original name was Tsukihime." She smiled, and Kevin thought that, even in its bitterness, her smile was beautiful. "I have not gone by that name for nearly two hundred years, though."

"Hmm…" Kevin paused. "I think Tsukihime fits you better."

"R-really?" Kotohime seemed surprised.

"Yeah!" Nodding, Kevin explained himself. "*Tsuki* means moon, right? The moon creates the tide, and it's really pretty to look at. Kinda like you." Kevin nodded to himself. "That's why I think Tsukihime is a much better name."

Kotohime was stunned, but only for a moment.

"Ufufufu, it seems you are still full of surprises, Kevin-sama." She ruffled his hair again, then smoothly stood up. "Now, then, I believe I shall go and see what my sister is doing. You should return to the others. I am sure they're wondering where you are. We'll also be having dinner together. You should let your friends know, in case they have not already been made aware of this."

"Right."

After he and Kotohime parted ways, Kevin arrived at the room he shared with his friends to a most unusual sight. Eric lay on the floor in their room, curled up in a fetal position, shivering and sniffling like a little girl who'd just seen *Saw*. Tears ran down his cheeks.

Kevin felt tempted to turn around and walk the other way. He was sure that he didn't want to know about whatever happened to his friend.

He sighed. Sometimes he hated being so nice.

"So what happened to him?"

Alex and Andrew looked at each other. Justin continued staring at Eric, poking him with a stick he'd gotten from somewhere.

"We don't know." Alex scratched the side of his head. "We lost him after going to the hot spring. When we came back to our room, he was here." He looked back at Eric. "He was already like this when we came in."

Kevin moved closer and knelt down next to Eric. The young man was mumbling something.

"... no way... refuse... not...he's not... oh, god! The boobies!"

"Uh..."

Kevin looked up at his equally confused friends. They both stared at him with the same look that he felt positive was reflected in his own features.

"Don't look at us. We've got no clue what he's saying either."

"Right, then." Kevin stood back up. "You guys might want to get ready for dinner. We'll be eating soon."

In an effort to bring some semblance of normality to the situation, Alex and Andrew went about preparing for dinner.

Justin continued to poke the insensate Eric with a stick.

***

Dinner that night was eaten outside.

There were no tables large enough to accommodate them, so they were forced to sit at separate tables. The groups intermixed. Kevin and Lilian sat together, naturally; there was no way they were gonna miss out on the opportunity to have a quasi-date. Kotohime, much to her consternation, sat beside them. She seemed to want to take up her normal position behind Lilian, however, neither Kevin nor her charge would let her.

"You're on vacation," they told her, "so act like you're on vacation."

Beneath the table, the cat Kevin had picked up drank milk from a bowl that he'd asked the waiters to set for her.

Bright and cheerful as always, Lilian's smile lit up the area. Several passing pedestrians had already been blinded. One couple even had to be removed on stretchers when they ran face-first into a pillar.

"I'm so excited about going to the beach tomorrow. Lindsay and I bought new bathing suits for just this occasion."

"I'm looking forward to seeing you in it," Kevin admitted.

Lilian's bright smile gained several extra levels of moé, as if pleased by the progress Kevin had made. Months ago, he would have passed out if she'd said that.

Several tables away, Eric fell off his seat.

"Oh, god! Her moé level is over nine thousand!"

"Shut up, idiot!"

"Eek! Why is it so cold all of a sudden?! And where did this ice spear come from?!"

Over at the table diametrically opposed to Lilian's and Kevin's, Iris sat next to Justin. The sexy vixen's carmine eyes glimmered in the light of several torches. Her smile reveled in the staring that she knew Justin tried not to reveal. Grinning, she stretched her arms behind her chair. Justin's eyes practically bulged when her large breasts practically popped out of her clothes.

"See something that pleases you?"

Justin turned his head.

"… No…"

"Uhuhu, someone isn't being honest with themselves, I see."

While Iris needled and teased Justin, Eric, after reclaiming his seat, hung onto every word his master told him.

"This is why I told you to wait before actually trying to sneak into the women's side of the hot spring, my young apprentice. Women, especially yōkai women, have very keen senses. They know when they're being peeped on. Only someone who has years of experience in practical application can accomplish what you tried this night. Do you understand what I'm telling you?"

"Yes, Master."

"Good. Then from now on, you are not to do anything without my say-so. Got it?"

"Yes, Master!"

"Glad to see you understand."

"I've never been to the beach before," Lindsay said as she and Christine sat with Alex and Andrew. "I can't wait. It's going to be so exciting. We'll be able to soak up the sun, play in the ocean, and maybe we can even play a game of volleyball. I've always wanted to play volleyball at the beach."

"I'm not much of a sports fan," Christine started to say.

"Please." Hands clasped in front of her face, Lindsay's eyes became large and teary. "Please, Christine, please say you'll play a game with me? At least one."

"All right. All right. Fine! Just stop making that disgusting face already."

Alex leaned in to whisper into his brother's ear. "Man, this girl is really tsundere."

"She's the tsunderist tsundere I've ever seen."

"I didn't know girls like this existed in real life until she came along."

"Would you two shut up! I am not a tsundere!"

Perhaps the oddest group there was Camellia and Kiara. They most certainly made for an unusual sight: The lithe and athletic woman with wild hair and a black business suit, and the tall, statuesque beauty with the large bust and innocent smile. On their own, they turned heads. Together, the dichotomy they presented could kill a man.

"Hawa…" Camellia peered at the unusual mix of food on their table: steamed fish and steak and chicken, along with several flour tortillas and a number of sides. "Camellia's never seen this kind of food before."

"It's called a fajita, My Lady," Kirihime said as she prepared one containing chicken for her.

Camellia took a bite, her eyes widening as she beamed at her maid. "It's really good."

"Would you like me to make some for you when we return home?" Kirihime asked, her face possessing a kind and gentle expression. "If you'd like, I can… ask the chef if he would be so kind as to part with the recipe."

"Um!" Camellia nodded enthusiastically and went back to eating.

Kiara watched the technically older female eat like a child who'd never been taught how to use a fork. Camellia had already made a mess of her face. "This woman…"

"Kevin-sama, you should add some vegetables to your dinner. You are a growing young man, after all. Here." Kotohime scooped up a few of her steamed vegetables and put them on his plate. "While meat is important, you need to maintain a balanced diet."

"You're right. Sorry." Scratching the back of his head, he gave the older woman a grin. "I didn't realize this dish wouldn't come with any." Kotohime returned the smile.

"You're acting like a responsible onee-chan, Kotohime," Lilian couldn't help but tease her maid. "Something you want to tell us?"

"Ah!" Kotohime only now seemed to realize what she'd done. Her eyes had gone quite round. "I-I was just making sure that Kevin-sama was eating a balanced and nutritious meal. It is my job as your maid to ensure his health."

"You've never done that for me."

Kotohime looked away. "You've never needed it."

"Uh-huh."

Lilian's tone and the look in her eyes told the other two that she did not believe the woman one bit.

A man strolled up to their table, dressed in the garb of a waiter. His blond hair was long and shiny, showing that he obviously took great care of it, probably more so than a man had any right to care for their hair. Light blue eyes were hidden beneath several strands of shimmering gold, and his pearly white teeth gleamed as he smiled.

Kevin nearly groaned. Great. This was just what they needed. A *bishie.*

"Good evening, ma'am, madam… sir." For reasons beyond Kevin, he felt like this man only added him at the last second as an afterthought. "Would either of you care for a refill?" he asked the two ladies at the table, though his eyes focused on Lilian. Kevin felt his blood boil.

"No thanks. I'm good here." Lilian dismissed the man without even looking at him. Vindication rushed through his veins when Kevin saw the pretty boy's right eye twitch. He apparently wasn't used to women ignoring him.

"I see." Kevin had to give the man credit. He kept his annoyance in check well. "And what about you, madam?" he addressed Kotohime. "Is the wine to your satisfaction?" He gave her his best smile.

"It's all right, I suppose." Kotohime took a sip of the wine that he spoke of, managing to hide her grimace. "Though I do wish that you were in possession of some sake instead."

Another twitch.

"I apologize that we could not accommodate you." He bowed. "I have, of course, already suggested that we begin working towards importing sake, however, these things do take time. It will probably be at least a year before we see anything done."

"A shame," Kotohime said, "I know that Kiara was most looking forward to trying some."

At the mention of Kiara, the man gripped the water pitcher in his hand hard enough that Kevin thought the handle would shatter. Did this man have a grudge against Kiara? He didn't think so, but then, who could say for sure. For all Kevin knew, this man could have asked Kiara out on a date, thinking his bishōnen good looks would make her swoon over him—and had then been disappointed when she told him that wimpy maggots who sparkled didn't do it for her. Kevin could totally see that happening.

"Yes, well, I am terribly sorry to disappoint a woman of her… esteemed position, but I am not in charge of imports, I'm afraid. I merely wait tables."

"Indeed."

"If you'll excuse me."

"Hold it."

The man turned around. Kevin almost smiled when the man aimed an evil glare at him. He raised his glass.

"I'd like a refill of water, please."

A twitch.

"Of course, sir."

The man refilled his glass. Kevin leaned in.

"If I ever see you stripping my girlfriend with your eyes again, I will rip your arms off and shove them so far up your ass that you'll need to have surgery done if you ever want to use the restroom again," he said, his tone and manner nonchalant.

"I have no idea what you're talking about," the man said, his smile fixed. "I am merely doing my job as your host."

"Yes." Kevin snorted. "I'm sure you are."

The man left. Kevin stared at his cup of water. He wasn't thirsty. Still, he grabbed the cup and took a sip.

Lilian rested her elbows on the table, chin atop her hands. "Have I ever told you that I really like it when you get possessive over me like that?"

"Once or twice."

Kevin held the glass of water to his mouth, still acting completely nonchalant. He felt so cool.

Too bad his moment of cool ended when something soft, long, and furry slipped into his pants and grabbed a certain part of his anatomy. Kevin did not spit take, but he did end up choking on the water. He also ended up falling backwards, banging the back of his head against the pavement, eyes crossing.

When everything swam back into focus, it was to see a worried Lilian staring at him.

"K-Kevin, are you okay?"

"Ugh… yeah, I'm fine." He blinked. Why were stars floating around his head? "Ngg… was… was that you?" When Lilian gave him a genuinely confused expression, he sighed. "Never mind."

He sat back up and resumed eating.

Meanwhile, the cat by his chair continued lapping up milk.

***

After dinner, the group split up. The adults went to their room a few doors down, the boys entered their room, and the girls went into the one across from the boys. Only Kevin and Lilian remained outside.

"This feels weird."

Lilian tilted her head.

"What does?"

"Just… this." Kevin gestured to the two doors, then themselves. "You and I sleeping in separate rooms. I've gotten so used to us sleeping together these past few months. It's going to feel weird not having you with me."

Lilian felt her heart swell until it threatened to burst from her chest. Her body tingled with the afterglow of his words, starting from her heart and spreading out to encompass the rest of her. The desire to pull her mate to her and kiss him until he couldn't stand almost overpowered her. She resisted by reminding herself that doing so would likely result in them never letting go of each other, but it still proved to be difficult.

"I know how you feel."

She caught Kevin's eyes and was unable to look away. Despite all the changes that her mate had gone through, both mentally and physically, she'd found that his eyes remained the same as when she first saw them during their first meeting.

I don't want to sleep in another room.

"Well…" Taking a deep breath, she pulled herself together. A smile was directed at Kevin, uncertain and awkward. "I… I should probably go to bed…"

"Yeah…"

Turning around, Lilian took a single step towards the girls' room. She stopped when a hand latched onto her wrist.

A shiver went through her body, a jolt, like the surging of electricity as it passed through a wire. It traveled up her arm and through the rest of her body, going from her head all the way to her toes.

Before she knew what was happening, Lilian found herself being spun about. She opened her mouth, though for what purpose even she didn't know: a yelp, a scream, a word? It didn't matter in the end, because her ability to release noise was soon hampered by another mouth.

Lilian all but melted as she and her mate shared a kiss. She resisted the temptation to rub her body against his, and instead contented herself with holding him close. Arms wrapped around her waist, strong and muscular from months of combat training and rigorous exercise. She reveled in their strength and the surety with which they held her. Truly, few things in this world could match being held by her mate.

Except taking a shower with her mate.

And being brought to multiple orgasms by her mate.

She imagined sex would trump being held, too, but she didn't have any experience with that yet. Damn it. What she wouldn't give to have Kevin tear her clothes off right now, push her up against the wall, and stick his long, thick…

"Whoo! Look at you two go! Maybe you should think about taking this to the bed. I certainly wouldn't mind watching, unless you'd like me to join in."

The kiss ended. Kevin jerked back as if scalded. Lilian turned to her sister, who'd interrupted them, and glared.

"IRIS!"

Iris grinned and bolted back into their room. Lilian chased after her.

It looked like this night wouldn't be ending on the high note that she'd hoped for.

CHAPTER 5

Trouble When the Clock Strikes Twelve

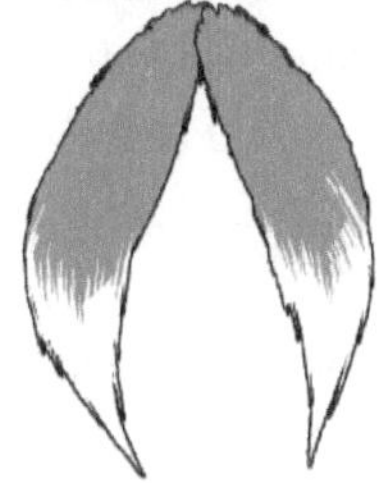

"WHY ARE WE DOING THIS AGAIN?" Christine asked as she, Lindsay, Lilian, and Iris sat in a semicircle on the floor of their room.

Night had yet to truly fall. The sky, still painted with an array of colors, shone through their window, a shimmering painting of delicate hues, saturations, and tones. It was a lot more vibrant than the sunsets in Arizona, but Kevin had informed Lilian that sunsets in California were caused by pollution and were not a natural phenomenon.

Since it was still too early for them to go to sleep, the group had decided to play a game.

"Because it's fun," said Lindsay. "And it's tradition. Haven't you ever been on a trip with your girlfriends before? This is something that all girls must play at least once when they go on vacation together."

A scowling Christine stubbornly crossed her arms. "I've never heard of this tradition before."

"That's because you've never had any friends before," Iris said with a wicked grin.

"You wanna say that again?!"

"Would you two stop fighting already?" Pouting, Lilian looked at the pair from where she sat cross-legged on the floor. While Christine had stood up to shake a menacing fist, Iris remained lounging on the carpet, her tails out and idly caressing her hips. "We're supposed to be having fun. How can we do that if you two are constantly arguing?"

"She started it!" Christine shouted.

"Don't look at me," Iris said at the same time. Christine cast her most hated enemy another glare while Iris just smiled condescendingly.

"Ha…" Lindsay released a large gust of breath. "Whatever, let's just start. Lilian!"

"Hai?"

A pause.

"… Hai?"

"Ah, um, uh, I mean, yes?"

Lindsay looked at her friend strangely but shrugged and got on with it. "Truth or dare?"

"… Truth."

Her feet kicking in the air, Lindsay held her face in her hands and asked, "How far have you and Kevin really gone?"

"Is it too late to say dare?"

"Yes."

"Hawa." Lindsay couldn't have asked a worse question. "I… can't tell you."

An eyebrow rose in response to her words. "Can't? Or won't?"

"Can't." Seeing the many looks directed her way, Lilian looked down at her hands, which she twiddled in her lap. "I promised Kevin that I wouldn't tell anybody about our private life, which includes our sex life."

"So, you two have had sex?"

"No, the most we've done is…" Lilian trailed off when she realized what she'd just been about to say. Her eyes narrowed at

Lindsay, and her cheeks swelled like balloons. "That wasn't very nice, trying to trick me like that."

Lindsay's smile was not apologetic in the least. "Sorry, sorry, but you can't blame a girl for trying. In any event, you can't not tell us now. You've got no choice in the matter now that you've selected truth."

"I could tell you all about what Lilian and her mate get up to," Iris said and was subsequently shot down by Lilian's tail. "… Ow."

"Be quiet you!" Lilian glared at Iris, who lay face-first on the floor, a large lump parting her hair, then she looked back at Lindsay and dithered. "I-I don't know…"

"Oh, come on," Lindsay urged her friend, "If you won't tell us, then I'm going to ask Iris."

Iris lifted her head, eyes lighting up like sadistic beacons. "I could definitely do that—"

"Not another word out of you!" Lilian growled, then sighed, her shoulders slumping. "All right, I'll tell you. Just… promise me you won't tell Kevin I told you this?"

"I really don't think Kevin will be upset, but if that's what it takes, then we promise not to tell him."

While Lindsay was the only one who vocalized it, Christine nodded as well. When Iris didn't say anything, Lilian glared at her. "Iris, your word. I want you to promise that you won't tell Kevin or anyone else."

Iris rolled her eyes. "Fine, fine. I swear on my life as a kitsune that I won't tell another living soul what you tell us here."

"Okay, well then, I guess I could tell you about the time we, uh…"

"Lilian."

"I know, I know, just… just let me think for a second, okay? I need to figure out which time I should tell you about."

Lindsay raised an eyebrow. "Do you really have to think about it? How many erotic moments can there be?"

"A lot," Iris butted in, her salacious grin growing. "Those two go at each other almost every night. I'm surprised they haven't—ouch!" Iris looked over at her sister with a mild glare. Another lump was added to her head. "Did you have to hit me again?"

"Yes," answered Lilian, her tail once again resting on her lap. "Okay, I suppose I could tell you about what we did for Christmas."

"Oh ho, going straight into the—gah!"

"Quiet you."

Lindsay leaned in, clearly eager to hear about Lilian's passionate tale of what she and Kevin had gotten up to on Christmas. Even Christine leaned forward, having long since given up on pretending that she wasn't interested in knowing how good Kevin was at pleasing women.

I'm only listening because I'm curious, Christine told herself.

We both knyow that's a lie. Nyou love him.

Be quiet! I do not!

Nya ha ha! Deny it all you want, but you can't fight your nature.

Christine growled and tried to block out the voice in her head. She was only mildly successful.

Licking her lips, Lilian began her tale. "It all started that morning, when Kevin decided to make me breakfast in bed…"

***

Lilian couldn't sleep. She tried. She really did. She'd kept her eyes closed and tried to empty her mind in order to let slumber take her. It didn't work. The covers were too thick, the pillows were too soft, the mattress made her feel like she was being swallowed by a marshmallow, and Kevin wasn't with her.

Unable to sleep, Lilian quietly snuck out of the room. After closing the door behind her, she sought the door on the opposite end of the hall. Kevin's room. The temptation to sneak in and snuggle up to her mate hit her worse than a psycho wielding a spear and shouting, "GAE BOLG!"

With a shake of her head, she dispelled the notion. Kevin wasn't alone in that room. Much as she didn't care about the others, she also knew that Kevin enjoyed keeping their love life private. Hugs and kisses and finding random spots to make out was fine, but sleeping together while a bunch of his friends slept in the same room? That was probably not a good idea.

Unsure of what to do, Lilian wandered the halls. Her bare feet padded along the soft carpet, and warm light from the lamps placed at even intervals illuminated her path.

She eventually took her wanderlust outside and found herself standing near a fountain. Small lights centered around the artfully crafted structure caused the water shooting from the many cupids near the top to sparkle in the starless night. Ripples in the surface at the bottom amalgamated together until miniature waves were formed. With a soft sigh, she sat down on the cool stone lip.

Lilian didn't know how long she sat there, staring up at the velvet sky, but it must have been a while. Footsteps eventually reached her, her ears twitching at the sound. She tilted her head to see lustrous raven hair wavering in a breeze and eyes of a most enchanting crimson gazing at her.

"Iris, what are you doing here?"

"Did you really think I wouldn't notice you slinking off in the middle of the night?"

Lilian had the decency to look embarrassed. Iris smiled, not her usual "I'm a sexy bitch and I know it" smile. This one appeared soft and tender, gentle almost—although the wicked gleam in her eyes did not instill any confidence in its sincerity. She sat down next to Lilian.

"I woke up when you got out of bed and left." She shrugged. "I was curious to know where you were going, so I decided to follow you."

"Oh…"

"Can't sleep?" Lilian shook her head. "I guess I can't blame you." Placing her hands on the fountain's lip behind her, Iris leaned back and looked at the sky. Lilian struggled not to stare at the way Iris's bosoms popped out of her somewhat translucent shirt. "Your mate's pretty warm. I imagine it's hard getting to sleep without that warmth, or his strong, hard body pressing against yours."

"Yeah, it is." Lilian nodded in agreement… and then she paused, her mind screeching to a halt. "Wait. How do you know my mate's warm? And how would you know what it feels like to have his body pressing against yours?"

"Isn't it obvious? I've been sneaking into your bed in the middle of the night." A devious grin pulled at the carmine-eyed vixen's lips. "I have to admit, I can see why you like him so much. He's got a nice body."

"Iris!" Lilian hissed, furious. "You… you… how could you? You know Beloved's not going to like that!"

"Oh, relax." Iris rolled her eyes. "I always left before either of you wake up." She paused, her expression thoughtful. "Well, there was that one time Kevin woke up before I could get out." The grin returned. "But I shoved Mom's panties in his mouth before he could scream."

That's not something to be proud of.

"Shut up. You obviously don't know what you're talking about."

"Stop talking to the author!" Lilian was still angry. "I can't believe you would do something like that. I thought I told you that we couldn't be anything. Kevin's not going to accept a relationship with you in it."

"Oh, relax. I was just sampling the goods. I needed to make sure he was worth your time and attention."

Iris tried to ruffle her hair, but Lilian stood up and began marching back to the resort's main building.

"Aw, come on!" Iris stood up as well. "I was just kidding! I—" Her eyes widened. "Lilian, look out!"

Upon hearing her sister's urgent shout, Lilian looked up.

She was just in time to see a shadowy figure descend upon her like an avenging angel.

***

Kevin woke up sometime around midnight, his troubled sleep interrupted by the need to use the restroom. Even after taking care of business and laying back down in bed, sleep remained elusive. He just couldn't bring himself to fall back into that restless slumber.

Unsure of what to do and unable to lie in bed any longer, he left the room and took to wandering the halls. His bare feet padded along the carpet. Black pajama pants with frolicking foxes (a Christmas gift from Kotohime) rustled and creased as he moved. He wore no shirt, so his chest was exposed to the cool night air.

He eventually made his way onto a veranda. This one meandered off for several yards before turning a corner. Columns lined the edge leading further outside, while evenly spaced windows situated in beige walls were on the opposite side.

The gray pavement felt cool against his feet as he walked to one of the columns. A soft breeze rustled his blond hair, bangs flowing over his face, strands swaying in front of his eyes. He couldn't see many stars out, but that didn't surprise him. With its many city lights and the ridiculous amounts of pollution, it was a wonder any stars were visible in Los Angeles' night sky.

It took Kevin a few minutes to realize that he wasn't alone. Sitting down on a cushioned chair, eyes lost in the distance, Lindsay also stared at the surrounding scenery.

"Hey," he greeted, walking up to her. "Couldn't sleep either?"

"Oh, hey, Kevin." She offered him a slight smile. "I guess you could say that. Actually, I was looking for Lilian. She wandered off somewhere, and I haven't seen her. Iris is gone too."

"Knowing them, Lilian probably couldn't sleep and decided to wander the resort. She has trouble sleeping at night unless she's snuggling with something." Like him. "Iris probably followed her." When an almost unnoticeable smirk appeared on Lindsay's face, Kevin gave her a look. "What?"

"Nothing." The blonde bangs of her pixie cut swayed as Lindsay shook her head, grinning. "I just can't help but marvel at how well you know Lilian."

"Ha…?" Kevin didn't get it.

"I mean that, from the way you talk about her, it's almost like you two are married."

"Marriage doesn't mean much to kitsune," Kevin informed his friend. "That's a human concept. And besides, if you really think about it, she and I kind of are married. I'm her mate."

"Yes, I know that. I was just…" she slowly trailed off when he continued giving her a confused look, her own face deadpanning. "Never mind."

"Okay."

Dismissing his friend's odd words easily enough, Kevin sat in the chair next to her.

Silence reigned for a time. It wasn't necessarily uncomfortable, but Lindsay didn't seem easy with it either. She glanced at him every so often, then looked away when he looked back. He frowned, but didn't say anything.

"You know, before you met Lilian, I sorta had a crush on you." Kevin nearly choked on his own spit. Gaping, he spun towards Lindsay, who refused to meet his eyes and instead looked at the moon. "I had always hoped that one day you would gather up enough courage to tell me that you liked me."

Kevin regained himself and closed his eyes. "Why are you telling me this?"

"I… I don't know," she said, shrugging. "Sort of like how you needed to confess to me in order to move on with your life, I guess I felt like I needed to be upfront with you for the same reason."

"I see." Kevin exhaled a slow, deep breath. When he looked at Lindsay again, his eyes were firm. "You know that nothing can happen between us, right? I made my choice. I belong to Lilian now, just as she belongs to me."

"Yeah, I know." Her smile, reassuring and friendly, put Kevin at ease. "Don't worry. I'm not trying to steal you from her or anything. I just wanted to tell you this."

"Fair enough."

"Still," her eyes danced, twinkling with enough luster that the moon was outshone, "I'm surprised to hear you speak with so much conviction. Don't you think you're a little young to make a claim like that?"

"Maybe if I was dating anyone else," Kevin admitted, "but I'm not dating just anyone. I'm dating Lilian. No." He shook his head. "I'm her mate. That's a lifelong commitment for a human. Lilian's not like human girls. When a kitsune chooses their first mate, it's more than just a passing interest. Take you, for example."

Lindsay raised an eyebrow. "Me?"

"Yes, you. When I confessed to you, you let me go."

Lindsay pouted. "You make it sound like I'm some kind of villainous fiend who used your feelings and let you go once I lost interest."

"Sorry, that wasn't my intention. I just wanted to point out that you let me go. Even though you liked me, you still let me go."

"I just wanted what's best for you." Lindsay blushed, just a bit. "You're my friend. I wanted you to be happy, and I knew that you were beginning to have feelings for Lilian, so…"

"Thank you. That means a lot to me." Kevin gave her a grateful smile. "Anyway, when you let me go, it hurt, right?" She nodded, her expression confused. "However, you eventually got over it. In fact, I'd say it probably took maybe a week at most before you were completely over our…" His nose scrunched up as he realized something. "We can't really call it a break-up, can we?"

Lindsay snickered. "Probably not."

"Well, whatever. My point is that you got over it quickly." He paused, reviewing all the information Kotohime had given him on kitsune. "Kitsune are different. They're not as willing to let their first mate go."

"Yeah, I kinda noticed that." Lindsay snickered. "What with the way Lilian is always clinging to you."

"Right." Kevin nodded. "A human girl will probably date several guys during high school and even more when she's in college. Kitsune don't. They stick with a single mate for many, many years. Even after they've parted ways, a kitsune will cross oceans if their mate is in trouble."

Kevin paused, and then released a sardonic chuckle.

"Of course, even though I say this, I am aware that kitsune are flighty creatures. Even if their loyalty is rock-steady, the only mate who really matters is their first one. Most mates after their first are usually just a passing interest, a way to satiate their desire to reproduce when they go into heat. It's the first mate that matters."

"You know an awful lot about kitsune, don't you?"

"Kotohime's been teaching me."

"I should have figured."

Lindsay shook her head, seemingly amused, but also impressed. No doubt, she still remembered a time when Kevin hadn't been as sure of himself, when he hadn't been able to speak like this. But that was then and this was now. He was different.

It is said that our experiences define who we are as people. If that was true, then Kevin could proudly say that he wasn't the same boy he'd been before meeting Lilian. The accumulation of events he'd experienced within the last eight months had changed him, turning him into a better person, a stronger person—or so he liked to think. Maybe he was just being arrogant, though he certainly hoped not.

Just then, several screams filled the night air.

"That voice…" Lindsay murmured.

Kevin jumped to his feet. "It's Lilian!"

"H-hold up, Kevin! W-wait!"

Lindsay watched as Kevin bolted off, traveling toward the screams at speeds that she could never match. Her outstretched arm fell to her side when he disappeared from sight. She stared for a few more seconds… and then rubbed her face.

"And there he goes. It's like he's got a one-track mind when it comes to Lilian."

Knowing that her friends needed help, Lindsay rushed back into the resort. She couldn't help them, but their chaperones could.

***

Blood pumped through her veins and youki surged through her body. With adrenaline raging through her, Lilian jumped back, avoiding the figure that tried to descend upon her like a fallen angel. A glint appeared within the blackness of their cloak. The figure, wreathed in darkness, raked their left hand out and slashed at the ground. Four long, deep gashes appeared in the grass. Lilian gulped.

If that attack had hit me…

"Lilian!" Iris rushed to her side. "Are you alright?"

"I'm fine," Lilian assured her sister, her eyes never leaving her attacker.

The cloaked individual climbed to their feet, their cloak swirling about them, covering their body and hiding much of it from view. However, while it was just a glimpse, Lilian could see the feminine curves, the swell of a prominent bust, and the flared-out hips of a woman.

"Who are you? Why are you attacking me?" she demanded.

Her attacker did not answer. She only hissed. Lilian barely had time to make a face at the odd sound before the woman bent her knees and shot forward quicker than a cannonball.

So fast!

Lilian and Iris moved in opposite directions, separating from each other to present two different targets. Unfortunately, no dilemma came to this woman's mind. She turned on a dime and continued her relentless pursuit of Lilian.

Her red hair whipped around her as she backpedaled. Lilian pumped as much youki through her body as she dared, reinforcing her legs to the maximum. It wasn't much—she lacked the capacity to truly make use of the reinforcement technique—but it was enough to keep her from being immediately overtaken.

"Kitsune Art: Orbs of an Evanescent Realm."

Six orbs of the purest gold appeared around Lilian's body, orbiting around her like planets around a celestial body. Each sphere hummed with otherworldly power. The light shining from deep within them created a blinding radiance that could not be looked at directly.

While Kiara often poked fun at her, claiming that she didn't train hard enough, the truth was that Lilian did train in her free time. It might not have been the kind of training that Kevin went through, but not all training involved getting your ass kicked on a daily basis. Lilian spent hours working on her specialized abilities, refining her techniques. It was difficult. She didn't have anyone to train her, but that made what she did accomplish all the more impressive.

These orbs were the results of her training. **Kitsune Art: Orbs of an Evanescent Realm** was the most powerful technique in her current arsenal. Celestial energy was compressed into tiny spheres that were controlled by her will.

"Go."

With naught but a movement of her tails, two of the six orbs sped off, barreling at the woman like homing missiles. The cloaked female leapt into the air. Smoothly, gracefully, her body began to spin, narrowing her profile and allowing her to slip between the spheres. She then flipped around and landed back on her feet, where she resumed her charge.

Behind her, the spheres quivered. Newtonian physics tried to keep the mass of energy moving forward, but Lilian's will, imposed upon the orbs, kept them from continuing on. They struggled against the natural order of the world, stilled, and then reversed course, back towards Lilian and, more importantly, the woman's back.

Lilian smirked. Game over.

It was not.

In a move that stunned her, the woman twisted in graceful, feline motions. She moved into a handstand and performed the splits. The first orb flew between her legs. Arms bending, the femme then lowered her body onto the back of her neck, and the second orb passed through where her crotch had been seconds prior. Then the woman leapt back onto her feet and shoved off the ground.

And then she was right in front of Lilian.

Eyes widening, Lilian sent all six orbs at this strange, elusive female. Surely, she couldn't dodge them all—not when they were so close and certainly not at the same time.

She could.

Body flowing like water, the woman twirled and spun, never staying still for more than a split second. She tilted her body to the side, at an angle that should have been humanly impossible, avoiding the sphere that came from her front. In that same instance, her body corkscrewed and she fell on all fours. An orb coming in from behind passed over her head. A leap forward let her dodge another orb, which struck the ground and exploded in a burst of celestial light particles.

Lilian gritted her teeth as she moved backwards. She commanded the orbs to surround and attack this mysterious woman, but it was all for naught. Like a contortionist, the cloaked female dodged and weaved through her attacks with ease and grace that was enviable. Several orbs dispersed when they hit the ground, and two more orbs were sliced to ribbons when the woman slashed at them with her bare hands.

That's when Lilian saw them. The woman's hands were clawed. Sharp nails at least three inches long gleamed in the moon's luminosity.

Realization struck her like a blaster bolt between the eyes.

She's a yōkai. Lilian's mind worked furiously, even as she moved her youki-enhanced body to avoid an incoming claw swipe. *But what kind is she?*

Knowing that she needed some answers, light emerged on the tips of Lilian's tails, coalescing into two small, but incredibly bright orbs.

"Kitsune Art: Divine Light."

The orbs exploded in a shower of light so bright that even Lilian had to cover her eyes. Another hiss escaped from the woman attacking her. The woman must have been blinded. Lilian couldn't see either, but she didn't need her eyesight to put space between them. She just needed to keep moving backwards.

When the light died down, it showed the woman hissing in pain, her hands covering her face. Lilian surmised that her corneas were probably burning from getting a full-on burst of intense celestial light.

The woman twitched and turned, facing Lilian. Her hands lowered. Lilian couldn't make out her face, but she could see the woman's eyes: two bright yellow orbs reminiscent of moons with black slits for pupils.

"That was an impressive distraction," the woman said, her first words since the beginning of the battle. Her voice had an odd purring quality to it. "I'm always amazed by the powers that you foxes possess."

Lilian glared at her attacker. "Who are you? What are you? Why are you attacking me?"

"It's nothing personal, nya," the woman said, though the way she bristled told Lilian otherwise. This was definitely personal. "It's just business."

The woman was about to attack again, when she was forced to dodge a small ball of black flames. It missed when she performed a back handspring and struck the ground several feet away. The flames dispersed almost immediately, but not fast enough to avoid damaging the ground. A black patch of nothing remained where the flames had struck.

"That was void fire," the woman said. She was then forced to dodge several smaller spheres of void fire, which came at her from the left. Lilian glanced that way and saw Iris rushing at the woman, flinging condensed balls of sentient darkness.

Her cloak swishing around her, the woman turned about, bending in ways that seemed impossible for even the most flexible of people. She dodged each attack sent at her. Lilian envied her flexibility.

"Are you alright, Lilian?" Iris asked. As a testament to how serious she was, her fraternal sister wasn't calling her by that gods-awful nickname.

"Yes, I'm fine." Lilian wiped a trickle of sweat off her brow before her eyes abruptly widened. "Iris... your eyes..."

Iris's eyes were no longer white. Her sclera, the white part surrounding her irises, had become encased in inky darkness, a void of incomprehensible malice.

"Don't worry too much," Iris tried to sound reassuring, but it was hard when her eyes looked like they belonged to a creature of unfathomable evil. "This has been happening recently whenever I reach into the Void. It's nothing to get worried over."

But Lilian was concerned. She knew that was not natural. She also knew that they did not have time to discuss it. Her attacker was still present, standing several yards away and eyeing them both, as if trying to decide who she should attack first.

"You there!" Iris pointed at the woman, and even in the low lighting provided by the moon, Lilian could see that her sister's nails were also covered in darkness. "Who the hell are you and what do you want with my sister? I warn you right now that if you're trying to kidnap her so you can have your devious way with her body, I am going to kill you. The only person allowed to take advantage of my lovely sister's bountiful harvest is me." A pause. Iris grimaced. "And the Stud, too, I guess."

"I-I-I-Iris!" Lilian hissed. She could feel her face burning. "Don't say something like that to an enemy! In fact, don't say that at all!"

But Iris just laughed. "Don't worry, Lily-pad. I won't let this woman have her wicked way with you."

"That's not what she's trying to do! And for the last time, don't call me Lily-pad!" She crossed her arms under her chest and pouted. "I hate it when you call me that."

The two were soon forced to leap away when something lashed at the air between them. A long, thin gash appeared along the ground, at least six yards in length. Something long and black retracted back into the woman's cloak.

"I hate to break up your comedy routine," the woman started, her purring voice casting shivers down Lilian's spine, "but I really must do my job. I'm afraid I'm going to have to ask you to die, Lilian Pnéyma."

Lilian's eyes widened. "W-what? How do you know my name?"

The cloaked woman didn't answer. She rushed forward, intent on ending this fight. Lilian and Iris also prepared their own techniques.

"Lilian! Iris!"

And that's when Kevin arrived on the scene.

"I-would-call-this-dynamic-entry-but-cannot-for-fear-of-copyright-laws-kick!"

His body spinning in midair, the young man lashed out at the woman with a kick from behind. She seemed to sense it, however, and managed to avoid getting her head rung like a bell. Her body smoothly rolled across the grassy ground, where she skipped back up to her feet. She turned around to face her newest attacker… and froze.

"K-Kevin?!"

Iris leaned over and whispered into Lilian's ear. "Do you know this chick?"

Lilian shook her head. "Never seen her before in my life."

"Then how does she know the Stud?"

"I… I don't know."

Kevin pointed at the woman with an accusing finger. "Listen up, lady! I don't know who you are, but don't think for one second that I'm going to let you keep attacking Lilian! That girl is my mate, and that means any attack against her is an attack against me! Keep trying to hurt her and I'll introduce my fist to your face!"

Iris facepalmed. "That was so lame."

"Kevin…" Lilian flushed. She didn't need his protection, but by Inari, if she didn't love it when he acted protective like that. It made her so hot and bothered.

The woman froze for all of one second. Then she placed her hands on her face and began wiggling about in a worrying manner. "Nya! Oh, no, Kevin's here! Nya!"

"Nya?" Kevin made a face. So did Lilian and Iris.

"Nya, nya, nya, he wasn't supposed to see me. Oh, cruel fate! Why must you torment me like this? Nya!"

"Okay, seriously, who are you, and what's up with the 'nya'?" asked Kevin. It was a good question, and something that Lilian and Iris wanted to know as well. Too bad the woman wasn't listening.

"Nya! I have to get out of here!"

"You're not going anywhere!"

Kevin rushed forward to attack the woman. Lilian and Iris also prepared to attack with their respective techniques. Light glowed along Lilian's tails and darkness wafted off Iris's. It was time to end this.

Before any of them could actually attack, the female assassin bent down and struck the ground. The area around her exploded with an expanding cloud of smoke and…

"Bubbles?"

Yes, bubbles. Dozens of bubbles ranging in size from no larger than a thumbnail to bigger than Kevin's head. Yet they didn't look like regular bubbles. Hazed in red, wavering like a flame, Lilian thought they looked like liquid fire, a thin film of lava that retained a spherical shape. They moved along invisible air currents, zephyrs floating on a summer breeze. After moving to a certain point, the spheres popped in a brilliant sparkle of fiery particles that forced the smoke to disperse, revealing an empty clearing.

The woman who had attacked Lilian was gone.

***

After the woman disappeared, Kiara, Kirihime, and Kotohime arrived, having been woken up by Lindsay. Lilian explained what happened with some help from Iris. Since Kevin only arrived minutes before the woman fled, he couldn't tell them much, so he just listened in silence.

In the end, Kotohime told them that they should all get some rest. She would stand guard while they slept for what remained of the night. It was already 1:43 a.m. by that point, and if they wanted to be fully rested for their time at the beach, they would need to sleep.

"Hey, Kevin, do you think I could sleep with you?" Lilian asked as the others went their separate ways. When Kevin looked at her, mouth open to respond, she continued. "Part of the reason I was up tonight was that I couldn't sleep without you."

"You mean you needed your hugging pillow," said an amused Kevin. He scratched the side of his head. "Ha… well, I guess we could sleep together, but—" He glanced at their respective hotel rooms. "—I don't know if that would be a good idea. I doubt the girls would appreciate me being in your room, and the guys, well…"

"I don't mind sleeping in the guys' room," Lilian said quickly, "I'll just wear my pajamas."

Kevin rubbed his face, even as his eyes wandered across her frame. Her pajamas were very modest for a kitsune—especially for a kitsune, he amended. Long red fleece pants covered her legs and shapely bottom. Her spaghetti strap shirt, red with pink strings, also covered her a good deal, though it still showed more cleavage than he was comfortable with his friends seeing. That she wasn't wearing a bra, noticeable by how her nipples poked through the fabric, made the idea of her sleeping in his room less than desirable.

He really, *really* didn't want his friends seeing any part of Lilian. Call him possessive, call him jealous, but he didn't like the thought of his friends ogling Lilian. He knew they'd already stripped her in their minds. He would be damned if he let them see her wearing something like this.

At the same time, Kevin just couldn't say no to her. Call him a sucker for a pretty face, call him a sentimental fool, call him a needy little boy, the facts remained the same. Kevin wanted to sleep with Lilian just as much as she wanted to sleep with him.

"All right," Kevin agreed, and Lilian's grin preluded a cheer, which he stopped before her shouting could wake everybody up. "Just be quiet, okay? I really don't want them waking up."

"Okay," Lilian whispered back.

Making their way inside the boys' hotel room, Lilian and Kevin moved along with the stealth of two ninjas.

They even made the weird hand signs.

The other boys were still asleep. Eric snored away on his bed, the sheets long since discarded, and his body was sprawled across the entire mattress with one leg hanging off the edge. Justin lay curled up underneath the blankets, seemingly dead to the world. On the last bed, Alex and Andrew looked like they were fighting over the sheets. It seemed like not even sleep could stop their lifelong arguing.

Kevin and Lilian crawled under the covers of his bed, which was mercifully located closest to the door. They rested on their sides: Lilian on her left and Kevin his right. He slid his right arm under the pillow, while his left went around Lilian's waist. She scooted closer until their bodies were touching, tucked her head underneath his chin, and threw her right leg over both of his.

Once they were comfortable, they fell asleep—eyes closing, breathing slowing, exhaustion hitting them like a sack of bricks.

***

Within the darkness of the night, a small black feline entered the room. Bright yellow eyes peered at the world around it before, with unusual grace, it leapt onto Kevin's bed.

It took one look at Kevin, and then it noticed Lilian snuggling with the boy. Hissing and spitting silently, it glared as it saw the happy smile that the redhead wore.

Knowing that nothing could be done about this situation, unenviable though it was, the cat curled up into a ball at the foot of the bed and went to sleep.

The young couple slept on, blissfully unaware of their bed's new occupant.

CHAPTER 6

Good Times at the Beach

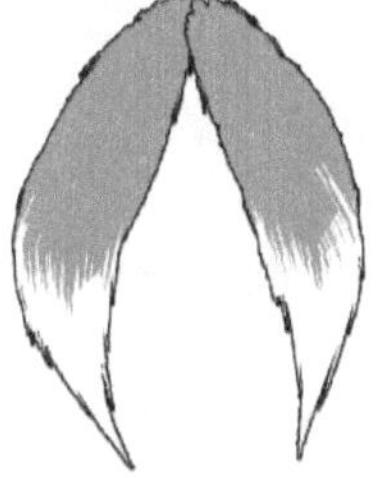

KEVIN SWIFT WOKE UP to a series of unusual sounds. The first, not to mention easiest, for him to identify was crying—no, not just crying. Sobbing. It was the sound of someone sobbing manly tears, though they did not sound sad. The second sound was, strangely enough, a word: *kawaii*. Just what the heck someone was doing speaking Japanese was beyond him. It was the third sound, however, that caused him to open his eyes—namely because it was right next to his ear.

"Nya."

Cracking a single eye open, Kevin first saw nothing but red. It was hair. Lilian's hair. A million strands of silk that tickled his nose. The familiar scent of strawberries and vanilla lulled his mind into a sense of contentment. He must have buried his face in her hair sometime during the night.

"Nya."

Something swatted at his ear, sharp and hard. It kind of hurt.

Unburying his face and turning his head, Kevin met the large yellow orbs of a black cat.

"Nya."

"Morning." He yawned.

"Nya."

"Did you sleep well?"

"Nya."

"Good to know."

"Nya."

"… You don't really say anything other than 'nya' do you? Shouldn't you be 'meowing' instead? You know, like a cat should?"

The cat tilted her head. "Nya?"

"… Never mind."

Snickering reached his ears—and sobbing, but the snickering was closer.

The snickers came from Alex and Andrew. Justin appeared to be snickering too, but he had his back turned, and Kevin could only see the shaking of his shoulders. He looked back at the twins and glared.

"What are you two laughing at?"

"You're talking to a cat," Alex said.

"So?"

"So…" Andrew's eyes glinted mirthfully. "You know that cats can't understand humans, right?"

The cat seemed to take offense to this. It hissed at Andrew, who backed away from the creature as its fur bristled.

"Nnnn… Kevin…" Lilian randomly moaned, rubbing against him and causing his already tight boxers to become increasingly uncomfortable. "Make me feel good… munya-munya… zzzz… I wanna feel real good…"

"Uh…"

The snickers stopped. Alex and Andrew glared at him. They were like a pair of laser pointers. If their eyes could actually shoot lasers, Kevin knew he would have been dead—or castrated, since it looked like they wanted to do that, too.

"You didn't hear that," he told them.

"No, no, I'm pretty sure we did," Alex insisted.

"No, you didn't," Kevin pressed.

Just then, Lilian spoke again. "We should get some... whipped cream... zzzz... lather it up and lick it off... munya-munya... zzz..."

More sobbing echoed around the room. That must have been Eric, Kevin realized. Alex and Andrew glared some more. The cat switched its glaring and hissing from the auburn-haired Andrew to Lilian.

"Munya-munya-munya... zzzz...."

All the while, Lilian slept on, oblivious to the goings-on around her.

***

It took Kevin a good deal of time, effort, and shaking to wake up Lilian. Every time he thought the girl was stirring awake, it was only so she could snuggle closer to him. It felt nice. Really nice. But she needed to wake up, and he was growing uncomfortable with the glaring and sobbing of his friends, especially the sobbing.

Thankfully, Lilian did eventually wake up. She stretched her body underneath the covers, rubbing against him in all sorts of delicious ways. Then she reached up with her right fist and cutely rubbed her sleepy green eyes. Only after she'd done all that did she grace him with a smile.

"Morning, Kevin."

She tilted her head up to kiss him on the lips. In spite of his embarrassment, Kevin found that he could do nothing more than kiss back.

Dang it. These lips should be considered illegal.

Hissing interrupted them.

Kevin could only watch in shock as the cat leapt at his girlfriend and attacked her with sharp claws.

Lilian squealed in pain as her face was scratched.

"KYA!"

She and the cat fell off the bed, hitting the floor with a dull thud, where they began to fight. They rolled all over the carpet, clawing and hissing and biting. Even Lilian got into the fight. She didn't even seem to realize that she was picking a fight with a cat.

"You stupid cat! Get off me!"

"NYA!"

"GYA! My face! This thing's scratching up my face!"

Kevin knew that he should stop this before it got ugly—uglier—but he wasn't sure how to do that. While trying to figure out the most efficient method of stopping this catfight, he noticed that Lilian's clothes were getting cut up by the cat's claws.

"Damn, that's hot," Alex said. Kevin twitched as blood dripped down his friend's nose.

"You said it," Andrew agreed. He was also suffering from massive combustion of the nasal cavities. "Who knew a catfight with an actual cat could be so sexy."

"Stop nosebleeding over my girlfriend!"

Several seconds later, Alex and Andrew were unconscious with two large bumps the size of Texas on their heads. Kevin stood over them, a vein throbbing on his forehead and the fists that he'd used to render his friends insensate shaking in rage.

"Stupid, dirty perverts." Snickering brought his attention to Justin. "You wanna have my fists in your face too?" Justin stopped laughing. He shook his head. "Then shut up."

He turned back to Lilian and the cat. "Ha… how am I supposed to make them stop? Eh?"

Sob.

Kevin twitched.

Sob, sob.

The sobbing continued. Kevin didn't know how long the pervert had been crying for, but Eric was huddling over in a corner, his face turned to the wall. His body was wracked with shaking as he bawled and sniffled like a baby whose toy had been taken away.

"Ha! Think you've got the upper hand on me, do you? Take this!"

Lilian grabbed ahold of the cat's tail and bit down. Hard.

"NYA! Nya! Nya, nya, nya!"

"Gya! My boob! You just scratched my boob!"

Sob, sob.

"What's your problem?" Kevin asked his friend.

"I… I've just realized…" Sob, sniffle, sob. "How… unworthy I am… to be in your presence…"

Kevin twitched some more. Lilian and the cat continued fighting. Eric continued crying. The twins were still unconscious. The only one of his friends acting even remotely normal was Justin, and he was supposed to be the most abnormal of them all.

He buried his face in his hands. He didn't cry like Eric, but he certainly felt like doing so.

"Where did my wonderfully normal life go?" Kevin asked no one in particular.

***

Kevin eventually forced Lilian and the cat to stop fighting. By the time he'd done it, both looked like they'd been through a dry tumbler. Lilian's hair was a mess, her body was littered with cuts and scratches, and her clothes were ruined. The cat looked more like a giant ball of fuzz than a cat.

After wrapping his girlfriend up in a blanket (because there was no way he would let her walk in front of people practically naked), they wandered into the girls' bedroom. Lilian had somehow managed to convince him to take a shower with her.

The girls were all still asleep. Miraculously. He thought the noise they'd made across the hall would have woken them. With Lilian's hand clasping his, the gorgeous kitsune pulled him into the small restroom.

Much like the restroom that he shared with the other boys, this one barely had enough room for three people to stand in together. A toilet sat opposite the door. The tub took up the entire wall to their left. A small sink on their right held the girls' toiletries, which Kevin noticed there was a lot more of than what he and his guy friends had. He shook his head.

Girls.

Only when the water was sufficiently hot and steam began expanding throughout the room did they step into the shower together.

A part of Kevin wondered how he could remain so calm while standing in the shower naked with an equally naked and absolutely stunning girl, rubbing and caressing and fondling her body with his soap-covered hands as she did the same to him. A part of him chalked it up to experience, but really, that couldn't be all there was to it, right?

"This is kind of exciting, don't you think?" Lilian asked as he washed her back.

"What?" Kevin blinked. "Oh, yeah, exciting. Right."

"Something's wrong." Lilian turned around and pouted at him. Her breasts smashed into his chest. "You're not even paying attention to me."

"O-of course I'm paying attention to you." Kevin tried to maintain eye contact, but it was so hard. His eyes kept dipping below her face, and every time they did, his lower body became stiffer.

A smile lit Lilian's face. It was such an innocent and happy expression that it looked out of place on her—well, it wouldn't have normally looked out of place, but she was currently naked. Innocents and nudity didn't go well together unless you were talking about a baby.

Kevin almost bit his tongue when Lilian wrapped her arms around him. He could feel her, all of her. It was electric.

"L-Lilian?"

"Thank you for going along with my selfish request," she murmured. "I know you're uncomfortable doing stuff like this when we're with our friends."

Kevin felt Lilian shaking against him, and he realized that she was still afraid of what happened last night. Calming down, he wrapped his arms around her waist and nuzzled her fox ears with his nose.

"Don't mention it. I'll always be here for you. You know that."

"I know. Thank you."

Lilian eventually broke away from him, and they finished washing off.

They had just stepped out of the shower and were drying off when the handle turned.

They looked at each other and froze.

They had forgotten to lock the door!

The door opened and in walked a bleary-eyed Christine. The girl's sleep ensemble was surprisingly fitting: black pajama bottoms, black oversized shirt, and black socks. She cutely rubbed her tired eyes with her left hand. Her other hand held the stuffed Umbreon that Kevin had gotten for her at the arcade. She opened her mouth in a wide yawn, and it soon became clear that she was not fully awake, which explained why she hadn't noticed their presence yet.

"Mmm…"

It wasn't until several seconds of standing in the bathroom, allowing her eyes to slowly pry themselves open, that the girl realized she was not alone.

She froze. The slow widening of her eyes expressed her sudden awareness at her situational altercation more than words ever could. She stared at Kevin and Lilian, the *naked* Kevin and Lilian, for several long, silent seconds.

"Um." Kevin tried to think of something he could say that would get them out of this predicament. "I'm sure you're wondering

about this, um, situation. However, let me assure you that there is a perfectly logical and non-sexual reason Lilian and I are like this."

"Really, Beloved? Do you honestly think she's going to buy that?"

Kevin shrugged. "It's worth a shot."

Christine's face froze over in a full-blown yuki-onna blush. Then she screamed.

"KYA!"

"Whoa!" the shout came from both Lilian and Kevin, as several dozen shards of ice tried to impale them.

"FUCKING PERVERTS! DIE!"

***

Lindsay was jerked awake by a scream.

"FUCKING PERVERTS! DIE!"

It wasn't the kind of scream one heard often. Sitting up, she turned to where she'd heard the scream come from. She was just in time to see a naked Kevin and Lilian fly out of the restroom like two bats out of hell. Several appliances chased after them, and more screaming came from inside of the bathroom.

"WHAT THE HELL WERE YOU TWO THINKING?! BUNCH OF FREAKING PERVERTS!"

"Hey, that's rude! I am not a pervert!" Lilian shouted—only to squeal and duck when a razor blade flew from the bathroom.

That's one of mine, Lindsay absentmindedly realized. She was still trying to process what she was seeing.

"GYYYAAAA!" came a scream from inside the bathroom.

"Holy crap!" Kevin shouted as he and Lilian suddenly ducked underneath...

And that's a kitchen sink...

Lindsay spent several more seconds watching the duo dodge everything from small household appliances to kitchen sinks and toilets. Then she lay back down, rolled over, and tried to go back to sleep.

It was way too early to deal with whatever was happening right now.

***

The walk to breakfast that morning was awkward, incredibly so. Kevin tried to ignore the stares at his back, the sobs coming from Eric, the chortles from Kotohime, the still shocked looks from Lindsay, and the eyes drilling a hole through his head from Christine. He attempted to pretend they didn't exist, but couldn't. How could he after everything that had happened?

Iris wasn't helping.

"So, let me see if I'm getting this right. After waking up, Lilian got in a fight with the furball here." Said furball hissed as she strode imperiously on all fours alongside Kevin. Despite having clearly spent a good deal of time and effort combing her fur coat, the black cat still looked like a ball of fluff. "You and Lily-pad—"

"Don't call me—oh, forget it!"

"—decided to take a shower together," Iris continued, "and you decided to use the girls' shower for your sexy shenanigans."

At the sight of her grin, Kevin could only blush. "I didn't want Eric and the others trying to peep on Lilian," he mumbled lowly.

"Okay, I can understand that," Iris conceded. "No one wants that pervert ogling Lilian, least of all me."

"Hey!" Said pervert sounded insulted.

"So, yeah, I guess I can understand. But…" Her grin widened. "… Did it never occur to you that you could've used the showers by the hot spring? Heck! You two could have gone into the hot springs together and had your sexy times there."

Kevin and Lilian looked at each other. Their stunned expressions were mirrored by the other. Why hadn't they thought of that?

"I... didn't think we were allowed." Lilian still seemed shocked by her sister's ingenious solution to this morning's problem. "The women's showers are separated from the men's showers, aren't they?"

"So?" Iris didn't see the problem. "It's not like anyone else is awake to use them at this time."

She had them there.

"She's got you there."

There you go. Thank you, Lindsay.

"... Shut up."

"Ufufufu."

"You too, Kotohime."

After taking the elevator down to the first floor, they entered a hallway, which eventually expanded into a large room. Four-seater tables were situated in the center. To their immediate left, a number of booths lay pressed against the wall. On the other side, a currently empty bar could be seen.

Kiara was already awake and sitting at one of the booths facing them, a cup of what Kevin presumed was coffee sitting in front of her. Heather was also awake, but she looked half-dead. As the one-armed woman spotted them, she waved the group over.

"Good to see all of you are awake. Kotohime, did you find out what all that noise was about?"

Hiding her lips behind the sleeve of her kimono, Kotohime chortled. "Ufufufu, indeed I did."

"But you're not gonna tell me, right?" When Kotohime merely maintained her smile, Kiara shook her head, seemingly amused. "I figured as much."

"What's up with Master?" asked Eric.

"Nggg..."

"She's not a morning person," Kiara answered simply.

Kevin and Lilian slid into the booth on the opposite side of the two adults, while Kotohime sat with Kiara. The others arranged themselves at various tables. The cat prowled around on the ground, rubbing itself against Kevin's legs.

"Scooch over, boya." Iris also made herself comfortable. Lilian and Kevin were squished together, which they didn't really mind, until the red-haired vixen's sister draped herself over Kevin.

"Iris…" Lilian's voice contained a hint of warning.

"Oh, relax, I'm not gonna do anything to him," Iris said, spreading herself out over the two of them. With her head in Lilian's lap, Iris grinned like a sexual deviant. "Hey, I can't see your face from down here."

Lilian twitched.

A waitress soon came to take their order. Kevin went with simple eggs, bacon, and hash browns. Kotohime ordered a breakfast burrito and Iris a yogurt parfait. Kiara decided to have the breakfast special, which consisted of enough food to fill up an elephant. Lilian…

"I want waffles!" The redhead declared. "And I want them to have blueberries, bananas, strawberries, whipped cream, powdered sugar, and a lot of syrup!"

"That girl…" Christine growled. "Listen to her. How can she eat something with so much sugar and not get fat?"

"It probably all goes to her chest," Lindsay lamented. She looked down at her modestly-sized chest and bemoaned her fate. "Some girls get all the luck… and the best genetics."

When the waitress left, Kiara put her elbow on the table and used her hand as a headrest. "So, I think we should keep our eyes on the lookout while we're at the beach, just in case."

"You suspect Lilian-sama's attacker from last night may try something again?" Kotohime wove a simple illusion around their table. It wouldn't do for the other humans they were with to overhear this conversation.

Kiara nodded. "The way you two—" She pointed at Iris and Lilian. "—described her reminds me of an assassin. Assassins never let their targets get away. She'll strike again for sure. We'll need to be ready for anything."

Kevin and Lilian shared a look. Neither of them was pleased with this assassin business, but they also wondered why an assassin would be after Lilian. While she was a member of the Pnéyma Clan, that didn't make her a high-profile target for assassins. If anything, Camellia should have been a more tempting target, since she had five tails. Then again, her mind had regressed to that of a child, so she didn't pose much of a threat.

"I'm still not sure I understand why this assassin is going after Lilian," Kevin said. "I mean, if they wanted to hurt the Pnéyma Clan, there are other targets they could go after that would be more damaging to them in the long run."

"Now that's just rude." Iris defended her lovely Lily-pad. "You make it sound like she's not an important target."

Lilian blinked her big green eyes. "But I'm not."

"Lilian!"

"From a purely objective standpoint, Lilian-sama and Kevin-sama are indeed correct, Iris-sama," Kotohime supplied. "In the grand scheme of things, Lilian-sama's importance to the Pnéyma Clan as a whole is minimal at best, especially as Lilian-sama's refusal to mate with Jiāoào-san has effectively nullified whatever political advantage she could have provided for the clan."

"Don't expect me to apologize," Lilian declared.

Kotohime smiled. "I would never expect you to apologize, Lilian-sama, not when you're in the right. I was merely stating the facts. Your most important role was to mate with Jiāoào-san, or another noble from the Shénshèng Clan, in order to build an alliance between the two great clans of Pnéyma and Shénshèng. Now that you have disgraced Jiāoào-san by refusing to mate with him and choosing a human instead, an alliance with the Shénshèng Clan, or any clan that has expressed an interest in you, has vanished."

"Do you think that's why she's being targeted?" theorized Kiara. "Maybe one of her siblings or the matriarch felt she was a liability and decided to make her disappear."

A heavy silence settled on the group. The idea of family hiring an assassin to go after their own kin was anathema to Kevin. However, with the idea implanted into his mind, the possibility suddenly seemed much more real.

Lilian shivered, which caused Kevin to wrap an arm around her shoulders and pull her close.

"Pnéyma-denka would never hire an assassin to dispose of someone from her own clan," Kotohime dismissed Kiara's theory. "It's not her style. Nor would she let a member of her clan hire an assassin to kill her granddaughter. If one of them did do this, it wouldn't matter how far up in the hierarchy they are, or how important they are to the clan, she would have them publicly executed for going against the orders of their matriarch."

The group breathed a collective sigh of relief. Worry was still clearly reflected in their eyes, but they all knew that Kotohime's words could be trusted.

Breakfast soon came and the group dug in with much gusto. It was only after their food was nearly gone that Eric, of all people, realized they were missing someone.

"Hey, where's the French maid hottie and the MILF?"

Kotohime and Lilian would have glared at Eric for the crass nicknames he gave their mom and sister respectively, but at that moment, loud crashes, bangs, and shouts came from above them.

"HAWAWAWAWA!"

Kevin, Lilian, and Iris all shared a collective sweat-drop. They knew who that was.

Crash!

"My Lady!" cried Kirihime.

"My luggage!" came the voice of some random guy none of them knew.

"Those two," Kiara muttered, facepalming.

"Oh, my," Kotohime added, rather unnecessarily in Kevin's humble opinion.

***

After breakfast, everyone traveled to the bus, which they used to drive to Long Island Beach.

Lilian was the first one out of the bus. She stepped onto the blacktop of the parking lot, which sat next to a small carnival. She would've been the second person out, but Camellia had tripped over her own two feet in her haste to be first.

"Hawa!"

"A-are you alright, My Lady?"

Iris chuckled as she followed Lilian and Kevin. "Don't worry, Kirihime. Her breasts softened her fall."

"Hawa…"

"What I wouldn't give to grab those giant tits and squeeze them… hehehe—GUH!"

"You're seriously beginning to disturb me," Christine said to the nearly unconscious Eric. Lindsay followed her friend, snickering. The others came out behind her. They gave Eric looks of pity as they passed—except for Heather, who stopped by his side and helped the young man up by slinging his arm over her shoulder.

"Come on, apprentice. Up you get."

"Ngg… Mommy? Mommy, is that you?" Eric's eyes focused on the decently-sized, milky-white breasts near his face as Heather half-carried, half-dragged him out of the bus. "Definitely not Mom's. Too pretty. And too large."

"Why, thank you."

Thwack.

"Ouch!"

"Now stop staring at your master. She can't teach you if you're busy gawking at her tits."

"H-hai…"

Thwack!

"Ow!"

"Don't speak Japanese either. It's not cool, and you're not Japanese."

"Ugh… yes, ma'am."

I can't believe we're at the beach!" Lilian grinned as she stared at the ocean. She'd seen it plenty of times back in Greece and Florida, but being with her mate made this experience so much more exciting.

Lilian hadn't gone with her usual outfit. She instead wore a lovely red two-piece bikini and black flip-flops. Kevin had chosen them for her several weeks ago when they were planning this trip, claiming that the red of the bikini complimented her hair and skin tone.

"Come on, Kevin! Let's go!"

As Lilian dragged him by the hand, Kevin tried to keep from tripping. "You act like you've never been to the beach before."

"I have," Lilian confessed, "but it's not like I ever had any fun. I never had any friends, so I always went alone—well, Kotohime was there, but that's not the same as being with your friends, you know? And I'm also here with you, which makes this whole experience a thousand times better. By the way, you look good in swim trunks."

Kevin was, indeed, wearing a pair of swim trunks. They were black with orange lines going down the left and right sides. He wasn't wearing a shirt, so Lilian also had an unfettered glimpse of his torso. With all the training that he'd been doing for the last five months, Kevin was rocking what several girls had once referred to as a Beach Body.

I wonder what that means? It's not like being at the beach has anything to do with his body.

It must have been a human expression, she concluded.

Heat rose to Kevin's cheeks. "Um, thanks."

"Slow down, you two! Damn it! Stop running!"

Iris tried to run after the pair. However, Kevin and Lilian swiftly outpaced her. Sure, she could have used reinforcement, but she'd never been the type who enjoyed exerting herself.

The only two who matched the couple's pace were Lindsay and Christine—and that was only because Lindsay was dragging Christine behind her as she ran.

"What are you doing? Let go of me! I can walk on my own just fine."

"But if I let go, you're going to take forever. Now quit complaining and come on!"

While the youngsters ran in the direction of the beach, eager to see the crashing waves and sandy shores, the adults hung back and moved at a more sedate pace. Camellia did try to run off, but after tripping several more times, Kirihime held her hand, forcing the woman to stay with her.

Kotohime frowned as she looked around the parking lot. There were a lot of cars, so many that it was a wonder they'd been able to find enough space for Kiara to park that giant bus of hers. There were also a lot of people, and she imagined there would be even more down by the beach.

"Something wrong?" Kiara asked.

"… No." Kotohime shook her head. "I'm just sensing the presence of a lot of yōkai."

Kiara nodded. "Yeah, California has a lot more yōkai than Arizona, so I'm not surprised. There are probably a couple dozen hiding out amongst the humans around here. Most of the yōkai here are ocean races, after all."

Kotohime narrowed her eyes, but didn't say anything as they continued walking across the parking lot.

Lilian, Kevin, Lindsay, and Christine reached the other side, where only a small wall separated them from the beach. It didn't take long before they glimpsed sandy white shores and blue ocean as far as the eye could see. To the far left, way off in the distance, Kevin could make out the end of the beach, marked by a large rock formation that protruded into the sea like a tiny peninsula. The other side stretched on for at least several miles before coming to an abrupt end as it ran into a harbor filled with pleasure yachts.

Kevin and Lilian stopped at the wall, allowing Iris to catch up.

"Ha… ha… did you two really have to sprint? Couldn't you just walk like the rest of us?"

"But we're at the beach, Iris! The beach!" Unlike Iris, who didn't seem to care where they were, Lilian's excitement could not be diminished. "Look around! White sand, blue ocean, clear sky, the sun over our heads, and we're with friends!" Lilian's eyes sparkled like two brilliant stars as she waved her free hand around. "Aren't you excited?"

"Not in the least."

"She's lying," Kevin determined. "You can tell she's excited just by looking at her."

Iris smirked at Kevin and, quite suddenly, the young man found his free arm being gently pressed between two soft breasts, which were barely covered by two very thin black triangles.

"Uhuhuhu… you seem to have figured me all out, Stud." A smirk, alluring and provocative, appeared on Iris's face. "You know me too well."

"I don't know what you're talking about." Kevin turned his head.

"Uhuhuhu… of course not."

She leaned in and gave his ear a delightfully slow lick—

—and then she found herself eating asphalt when something hard, long, and furry smacked her on the head.

"… Ow"

"Thank you," Kevin whispered to Lilian, whose tail retracted before anyone else could notice.

"I don't know why you're thanking me." Lilian's eyes were dazzling as she peered at him from beneath thick lashes. "I know that you're not interested in going the harem route."

"Uh…"

"Don't worry, Beloved!" Lilian clenched her hand into a fist. "So long as that remains your desire, this Lilian Pnéyma will make sure no other female touches you!"

"Uh…" Kevin didn't really know what to say to that. "Thank you?"

"You're welcome."

Lilian gave Kevin a quick peck on the lips. After pulling back, she and Kevin laced their hands together and stared into each other's eyes, as if nothing else existed in this world except for them.

Christine grimaced. "I hate it when those two act all lovey-dovey and crap."

"Now don't be jealous," Lindsay admonished. "Just let them be all lovey-dovey and come with me."

"C-c-c-c-c—ah! What are you saying?! What the hell is that supposed to mean?!"

"It means we need to beat them to the beach! Now come on!"

"Beat them to the—wait! Damn it, stop pulling me!"

Despite the early hour, the beach was crowded that day. They couldn't walk more than five feet without running into a group of people. Large umbrellas of all colors created a combination of swirling patterns that would have tripped out anyone with an aerial view. Dozens—no, hundreds of people had already set up their towels and were now lying on the sand, soaking up the UV rays in their never-ending quest for the perfect tan.

Half of these people wouldn't even look good with a tan. It was only after shaking the errant thought away that Kevin noticed something. The stares. He and his group were receiving numerous stares.

This no longer surprised him. It normally didn't bother him anymore, but his group seemed to be getting more looks than usual, which surprised him because they always received a lot of stares. He wondered why they were staring now.

Ah, well. I should just ignore them.

Walking through the crowd, they found their own slice of beach paradise—a small space of white sand warmed by the sun's rays. Beach chairs were soon unfolded and towels set on the sand. The bags were placed by the beach chair that Kotohime claimed as her own, and a large umbrella impaled the white shores.

As she sat on her beach chair, the traditional Japanese beauty, much like the other ladies, drew more than her fair share of stares. She wore a two-piece swimsuit with a modest skirt covering her lower half. Despite not showing off as much as Iris or even Lilian, her natural grace, porcelain skin, and voluptuous figure drew the eyes of many a male.

"Hawa... Kirikiri?"

"Yes, My Lady?"

"That outfit... are you really going to wear that in the water?"

Kirihime looked down at her swimsuit, which looked like a one-piece version of her maid outfit. The difference was that, instead of being made from silk and cotton, its composite material was polyester. It also had a larger dip in the front, exposing ample amounts of her generous cleavage.

Kirihime looked back up at her mistress. "Is there something wrong with my swimsuit?"

"Hawa, I guess not..."

Standing in front of the umbrella, Kiara looked out at the ocean with a large grin. The stump that made up her missing arm was completely visible. In contrast to her kitsune companions, she wore an all-black one-piece. She also received many stares, but most of them were disturbed looks from people gawking at the stump where her arm used to be. Several people turned green from the sight.

Kevin looked around at all of his friends. Lindsay had already discarded her skirt and shirt. She stood by Christine, showing off her cute, dark blue swimsuit. Christine was taking much longer to discard her Lolita clothing, which she'd worn despite knowing she'd have to lose it.

He had to admit, the yuki-onna looked very pretty in her white one-piece. Several frills around the hips helped draw attention away from her lack of chest, while still flattering her figure. Kevin really hoped there weren't any lolicons in the area—for their own sake as much as Christine's. She didn't take well to perverts, after all.

"Waa! My Goth Hottie looks so sexy! Come here, you—griglhurle!"

"Go die in the sand, you vulgar piece of shit!"

Kevin sighed as Eric was kicked in the face after attempting to grope Christine. When the girl proceeded to shove Eric's head face-first into the sand, no doubt attempting to asphyxiate the boy, Kevin turned away and looked around some more.

His eyes landed on Camellia. He really didn't know what to think of her white two-piece. The bikini was certainly modest enough, especially when he considered how kitsune normally dressed. But, still, those breasts, they were just so…

Boing.

"Hawa! Kevin-kyun!" Camellia noticed his eyes on her and gave him a wonderfully childish smile. "What do you think of my swimsuit?"

"Again with the 'kyun.'" Kevin sighed, but he still answered her question. "You look nice. It definitely suits you. The white goes well with your dark hair, and white is also a symbol of purity, so it kind of fits your personality."

"My mom's not pure, you know," Iris butt in. "She may be a useless mother—"

"H-hawa… Iris, so mean…"

"—but she's still mine and Lily-pad's mother."

Kevin rolled his eyes. "Yes, I'm well aware of that. I didn't mean pure as in 'never had sex.' I meant her personality."

"Ah, I see, I see." Iris fell silent for a second. "Yeah, I guess I can see that. Though I would say it's more of my mom just being as useless as a child than any sort of purity."

"Hawa…" Camellia's shoulders slumped in abject depression.

"L-Lady Iris, you shouldn't say such things about your mother," Kirihime admonished the dark-haired vixen with as stern a frown as she could muster.

"Oh, please, like you've never thought the same thing."

"I haven't."

"And you expect me to believe that?"

Shaking his head, Kevin left Iris and Kirihime to their bickering. He headed over to Lilian just as she was discarding her flip-flops. It was almost amusing to watch as she stuck her feet into the sand, clenching and unclenching her toes so as to feel the tiny grains between them. It was even more amusing when she took a stance, feet sliding until they were shoulder-width apart, left hand on her hip and right clenched into a fist near her face. Kevin knew she'd gotten that pose from an anime or a manga—probably several. It was a common pose, after all.

"All right! It's time to get wet!"

He facepalmed.

"That's really not something you should be saying in public."

He looked over at Justin, Alex, and Andrew, all of whom were lying on the ground, twitching. Blood squirted from their noses like oil from a broken gas line.

"Really not something you should say in public."

"What do you mean, Beloved?" Lilian asked, looking honestly confused.

Kevin opened his mouth to answer her, but Iris suddenly pounced on her sister before he could say anything.

"Kya! I-Iris, what are you doing?!"

"Aww! My Lily-pad is so adorable when she gets all Dungeons and Dragons on me! Come here you!"

Kevin had to hold his nose to keep the blood from spilling out. Iris had caught Lilian from behind. With their bodies pressed firmly together, and Iris's chest smooshing against Lilian's back, her breasts were practically spilling out of her extremely skimpy black bikini. It was more than most boys could handle. The only reason that Kevin didn't pass out was that this wasn't an uncommon occurrence for him. He'd become partially desensitized to the erotic acts that Iris committed upon her sister.

"Get off me! And stop calling me Lily-pad!"

"Hmm…" Iris, arms still wrapped lovingly around her sister's thin waist, absently rubbed her right leg along the redhead's perfectly-shaped right calf. Lilian shuddered. "I guess I could stop calling you Lily-pad. This joke is kind of running flat anyway. I've got it!" Her dark carmine orbs gained a dangerous glint. "How about I call you Lily-buns?"

"No!"

"Lily-cat?"

"I'm not a nekomata!"

"Lily-button?"

"Now you're not even trying!"

Deciding to ignore the two girls, Kevin began walking towards the ocean, when he was stopped. He looked at the woman whose hand rested on his shoulder. Her dark eyes gazed at him in mild concern and just a little exasperation, as if he'd done something wrong without realizing it.

"I apologize, Kevin-sama. However, I cannot allow you to go into the ocean just yet."

"Um, why not?"

"Because you have not put any sunblock on yet. Now, if you'd please come this way, I shall put sunblock on your back."

"Actually, Kotohime," Lilian interrupted, walking up to them. Kevin wondered how she'd gotten away from Iris, but then he looked behind her and saw the dark-haired twin lying face down in a crater. "I'm going to put sunblock on Beloved's back."

The yamato nadeshiko giggled. "Ufufufu, of course, Lilian-sama."

"Come on, Kevin."

Lilian dragged him over to a towel and bade him lie on his stomach. Once he'd done that, she straddled his legs and began spreading sunblock on his back. It felt nice. Lilian's soft, delicate hands roamed over the muscles of his back, massaging lotion into his skin. It was so soothing that he felt like he might fall asleep.

"Turn around, please."

Seeing nothing wrong with the request, Kevin did as told. It wasn't until she straddled his thighs and started to rub his chest that Kevin had a problem—two problems, actually.

"Lilian, I, uh, I don't really think this is…appropriate."

Lilian paused in her rubbing. Emerald gems blinked once, twice, thrice. She tilted her head, red hair shimmering like a layer of silk in the sunlight as it swayed around her face.

"Why not?"

"Because people are watching."

Kevin tried not to turn his head. He didn't need to. He could feel their eyes on him and Lilian. It usually didn't bother him anymore, but there were times when it did get to him, like when his overly affectionate girlfriend-slash-mate did something, well, sexy, in public. He especially disliked it when they stared at her.

"Oh…" Only after he'd spoken did Lilian seem to notice the stares. "Uh…" Her cheeks reddened. Lilian, for all her exquisite beauty and vivacious attitude, didn't realize that her appearance and actions generated a lot of male attention. Kevin thought it was endearing, but it was also kind of annoying. "I… guess I should get off, then."

"That would probably be a good idea."

"Wait." Lilian's eyes brightened. "I can just craft an illusion to make people think we're not here. Then I can finish putting sunblock on you!" Her normally bright eyes dimmed, becoming half-lidded and smoldering. "And then you can put suntan lotion on me."

The idea had merit. Kevin would admit that it appealed to him. However…

"They've already seen us. Wouldn't it be weird if we suddenly disappeared while they're still staring at us?"

"Uh, um, oh…" Lilian's shoulders slumped. "Right. I forgot about that."

Kevin chuckled. He'd never met someone who could be so blissfully ignorant about matters like this. Then again, Lilian was something of an abnormality, both among humans and yōkai. She was wholly unique.

Fortunately, matters were put to rest when he offered to rub lotion on her back. Lilian's mood improved as their situation was reversed, with him straddling her thighs, and his rough hands rubbing lotion onto her back. Kevin rather enjoyed the moment as well. His mate's skin was so soft and warm, and the soft moans that escaped from her parted lips were like listening to an angel's choir.

And then Lilian rolled over.

"Front now."

And Kevin facepalmed.

"Can't. People are watching, remember?"

"Oh… right."

***

For nearly an hour, the group of teens played in the water. Even Christine, who complained about the water being too cold, enjoyed splashing water at Lilian, Lindsay, and Iris.

"Ha! You think you can beat me in a water fight! I'm the master of water fights!"

"Oh, yeah? Take this!"

"Gya! My eyes! Saltwater in my eyes!"

"O-oops, sorry."

"Gotcha! Now we'll see who's boss!"

"Mmrrrggle!"

The water fight ended when Lindsay nearly choked after Christine got a little overly enthusiastic. The yuki-onna had dunked the poor blonde tomboy's head underwater, and then she wondered why Lindsay had stopped moving.

Kevin and his friends also tried their hand at bodysurfing.

"Okay. In order to catch a wave, you have to get the timing down. If you start too soon, you'll overtake the wave. If you start too late, the wave will pass you by."

"Shut up, Andrew. Don't try to sound like an expert here. This is the first time you've bodysurfed in your whole life."

"So what? This is the first time you've done it, too, jerkwad."

"And you don't see me trying to act like an expert when I'm clearly not, do you?"

"Just shut up!"

"Come on, you two. Let's not—buwaf!"

While Eric tried to make the two stop fighting and ended up embroiled in the battle royale after Alex and Andrew both sucker-punched him in the face, Iris teased Lindsay.

"Would you mind helping me catch a wave?" she asked. "Maybe you could hold me up while I kick my feet." Iris pouted, sticking out her lower lip as if daring the other girl to nibble on it. "It would be a really big help."

"Uh…" Lindsay seemed at a loss for words. Her face looked like it might explode. "… I-I, well, if you want me to…"

The poor girl nearly passed out when a pair of boobs pressed into her back, and a beautiful mouth nibbled on her ear. "Thank you so much. I would have asked the Stud and Lily-pad, but they're so busy being a lovey-dovey couple that I didn't want to interrupt them."

Blood trickled from Lindsay's nose as she struggled to remain conscious.

"U-uh… it's no problem…" she said with glazed-over eyes.

Kevin felt vindicated by the sight. "I'm glad to see that I'm not the only person she does that to."

Lilian just facepalmed. "Idiot sister, your true colors are showing."

After trying to bodysurf, the group decided to play with a beachball.

"Lilian."

Kevin bumped the ball with an underhand hit that sent it sailing towards the redhead standing opposite of him.

"Alex."

Lilian, in turn, hit the ball to Alex, who bumped it to Eric.

"Gothic Hottie!"

"Stop calling me that!"

Despite her *tsukkomi* act, Christine didn't miss a beat and hit the beach ball towards Andrew, who then bounced it at Iris.

"Snow Wench."

Christine gritted her teeth as Iris gleefully smacked the ball towards her harder than necessary.

"Fox Cunt."

In retaliation, Christine hit the ball twice as hard, not even bothering to hide that fact by lobbing it high like Iris had done.

"Bitch Tits."

Iris returned the retaliation by reinforcing her muscles and smacking the ball again. The ball ended up getting whacked so hard that it was a wonder the thing didn't pop.

"Go suck a dick, bitch!"

"Maybe later. And at least I can get a dick to suck. I'd be surprised if anyone wanted you touching theirs, flatty."

"I wouldn't mind if Gothic Hottie sucked my—"

"Not another word out of you, pervert!"

"BUAFF!"

And just like that, their game ended when Christine slammed the ball into Eric's face, not only causing it to burst, but also sending the perverted lech into blissful catatonia.

"What?" She glared at everyone as they stared at her.

"Way to go, Christy," Lindsay said. "You just popped our ball."

"I didn't mean to! It's all their fault anyways!"

As Christine pointed an accusing finger at them, Eric groaned and Iris smirked.

Since they could no longer play with the beachball, the group went back up to their umbrella. Kotohime and the other adults were all waiting for them… well, Kiara and Kotohime were waiting for them. Camellia was playing in the water, and Kirihime was trying to keep the infantile woman from tripping. She failed, of course, but Camellia didn't seem bothered.

Her breasts broke her fall.

"I'm glad all of you could join us. Would you like some snacks?"

Before coming to the beach, Kiara had convinced them to stop by a shop where they'd loaded up on food. There were all kinds of treats located inside of their bags: chips, sandwiches, salads, and various flavored drinks both carbonated and not.

All of it was store-bought, so it didn't taste as good as Kotohime's or Lilian's home cooking, which Kevin was quick to point out. His words earned him a kiss on the cheek from Lilian, and Kotohime ruffled his hair like an affectionate older sister.

"Ufufufu, this humble Kotohime does not deserve such kind words."

"Modesty doesn't suit you," Kevin shot back. "And do you ever stop laughing like that?"

Kotohime just hid her smile by placing her hands on her cheeks. "Ara, I don't know what you mean."

"… Right."

Munching on a sandwich, Kevin stared out at the vast ocean. Waves lapped against the shore with an almost gentle nature that belied the tide's strength. In some ways, the ocean reminded him of Kotohime, gentle at times and, well, decidedly *not* gentle at others.

As he gazed upon the water tenderly caressing the sandy shores, Kevin thought he saw several strange objects in the distance. He couldn't see them clearly, but they looked like streaks of blurring color moving at high speeds across the water's surface. He blinked once and they were gone.

I must be seeing things.

"Is something wrong, Beloved?" Lilian asked, sitting beside him and munching on a bag of chips.

"Naw." Kevin dismissed his worry with a grin. "I'm just surprised that a tentacle monster hasn't risen from the ocean and started randomly groping people."

A perfectly valid concern.

"Don't jinx it," Lilian warned him. "Knowing the author as I do, he might very well decide to do that now that you've mentioned it."

Also a perfectly valid concern.

Kevin's eyes widened. "You're right! With how cruel and sadistic he is, it wouldn't surprise me if people started getting tentacle-raped for no reason."

I take offense to that.

"Ugh," Kevin groaned, "I really shouldn't have opened my big mouth."

"What the hell are you two talking about?" asked Christine.

"We're talking about—" Kevin stopped talking. His eyes went through a series of rapid blinks, then he turned to Lilian. "What were we talking about again?"

"Ha…" Lilian sighed in disappointment. "It seems the power is still weak in you."

"That's because Kevin-sama is a human," Kotohime interjected herself into the conversation.

Kevin crossed his arms. "And what's that supposed to mean?"

"She's talking about your ability to break the fourth wall," Iris commented. She lay on her side, traces of sand clinging erotically to her still wet skin, which glistened in the sunlight.

Kevin shook his head. *How does she make everything look so freaking sexy?*

"Indeed." Kotohime nodded. "I suspect that the only reason Kevin-sama is even capable of doing this much is because of his exposure to kitsune."

Lilian tilted her head before nodding. "That makes sense. So, does that mean that Kevin would lose his ability to break the fourth wall if we stopped living with him?"

"Stop talking about me like I'm not even here!"

"Probably. After all, Kevin-sama is just a human."

"What's that supposed to mean?!"

"Ufufufu, nothing at all, Kevin-sama."

"Dang vixens," mumbling to himself, Kevin went back to his sandwich.

At least you won't make fun of me. He took a vicious bite out of his food.

***

After they finished eating, the group split up to do their own thing. Lindsay dragged Christine off somewhere, the twins wrestled in the crashing waves, and Eric and Heather were gone. Kevin assumed they were trying to peep. That worried him, but he told himself that what they did wasn't any of his business—unless they peeped on Lilian. Then there would be hell to pay.

Kiara was trying her hand at bodysurfing, and she was doing a lot better job than he and his friends had done. This was despite the fact that she only had one arm. Meanwhile, Kotohime was helping Kirihime keep an eye on Camellia, who splashed around in the water like a child having a field day.

He and Lilian meandered along the edge of the beach, hand in hand, water lapping at their feet. The suggestion to relax and travel along the shoreline had been Lilian's. She thought it would be romantic. Kevin felt the same way.

"I wish we could go over to the theme park."

Kevin looked at the park that Lilian spoke of. He wouldn't call it a theme park, for the term implied a large-scale park with roller coasters. This place didn't have a single roller coaster, though it did possess several rides that were often found at carnivals. He didn't bother correcting her.

"We could probably ask Kotohime to go with us," he suggested. "I'm sure she'd agree."

"She probably would, but I'd rather we go there alone, just the two of us. It wouldn't be the same if she came along."

"I'm sure she'd follow from a distance."

Despite his words, Kevin understood how she felt. Lilian wanted it to feel more like a date. It wouldn't feel like a real date if they knew Kotohime was hovering over their shoulders, even if she did keep her distance.

"Well, there's not much that we can do about that," Kevin mused. "With that assassin still out there, you're not allowed to go anywhere without either Kotohime or Kiara around. It's for your protection."

"I know, but it still sucks," Lilian muttered. Even though her ears and tails weren't visible right then, Kevin could imagine the way they would have drooped, as if mirroring their owner's despondency.

As they continued walking, Kevin noticed something odd happening to the sea.

Is the water swelling?

Indeed, all of the water near the shore was getting sucked back out to sea, towards a large swell that looked a lot like a wave—except it was far too big. And it continued growing larger with each passing second, until it towered over everything else, even some of the houses lining the street across from the beach. Kevin noticed that all of the water in the harbor where the yachts were parked had also been pulled away. The various boats now lay on the beach floor beneath the dock.

What the heck is happening?

"Lilian-sama! Kevin-sama!"

He and Lilian turned their heads towards Kotohime. She was rushing towards them, running quickly, body blurring; she must have been using reinforcement to reach those speeds. Her eyes looked panicked. They were wide, and the pupils were dilated. Kevin couldn't remember seeing her look so frightened.

"Lilian-sama! Kevin-sama! You two must get away from there! That's a—"

But Kevin couldn't hear anymore. All he could hear was the rushing sound of water. He looked back at the wave and saw that it was all crashing down.

Time seemed to slow as Kevin realized instinctively that he was going to die, crushed by several tons of water.

"Get down, Kevin!"

Something tackled him to the ground. A body pressed against him. He stared up at what should have been the sky, but all he could see was the giant wave descending upon them. Then the wave came crashing down and Kevin saw no more.

CHAPTER 7

Heartache

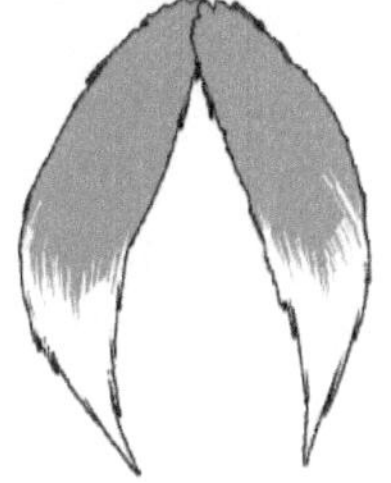

SECONDS BEFORE THE WAVE crashed on top of her, all Kotohime could think about was how she'd failed. All she could see was Lilian and Kevin as they were mercilessly crushed by several hundred tons of water. Her mind, her heart, even her body rebelled against this knowledge. Yet her eyes could not deny what they saw, and the weight of her failure should have crushed her.

But it didn't. She couldn't let it.

Acting with the quickness bred from years of experience, Kotohime's four tails sprang out from her tailbone, pushing aside her bikini bottom. Youki flowed through her tails like water rushing down a river. All of Lilian's and Kevin's friends were with her, which was fortunate. While she might've been too late to help Lilian and Kevin, she could at least protect the people they cared about.

Kitsune Art: The Water Temple's Ancient Realm was one of her most powerful techniques. It wasn't an attack. It couldn't inflict damage upon another. What it did was allow her perfect control over any body of water within a two-meter range. This technique could usually only be used by a kitsune with five tails or more, but her talent at wielding water meant that she could use it at four. Her sister could not use this technique, but she had no doubt that Kirihime still lived. She was inventive.

Kotohime barely paid attention to the others as they gazed at the dome that had trapped them, watching as the water swirled around them in all directions. She needed to concentrate to maintain the technique. Even the smallest slip in her mental discipline would cause it to come crashing down.

This was especially true since River Kitsune like herself couldn't manipulate saltwater. In order to use this technique, she'd been forced to draw moisture from the air and separate the salt with another technique that she'd created. She was essentially using two techniques at the same time.

"Whoa," Eric whispered. "What… how… what is this?"

"It's a kitsune technique," Heather told her apprentice. "If I had to guess, I would say that this is an ocean technique." She looked at Kotohime, as if to confirm that she was right. Kotohime said nothing.

"What's wrong with Alex, Andrew, and Justin?" asked Eric.

The three young men in question were lying unconscious in the center of the dome. They were completely still; however, the rise and fall of their chests showed that they were alive.

"Don't worry about them," Iris declared, biting her lip. The girl was trembling, and her eyes quivered with unshed tears. She'd clearly witnessed what happened to Kevin and Lilian, the same as Kotohime, and she was doing everything possible not to cry. "They've been placed under an illusion."

"A very well-cast illusion," Heather added, eyes flickering back to Kotohime. "I'm impressed. I'm no expert on kitsune abilities, but I imagine it takes a lot of effort to cast two techniques simultaneously."

Kotohime remained silent. It had not been two techniques. It was three, and it did take a lot of effort.

"You can't talk, can you?"

A head shake was Heather's answer.

"All right." Heather sat down, crossing her legs as she lowered herself to the floor. "In that case, I suppose there's nothing for us to do but wait."

"H-hold on!" Eric shouted rather obnoxiously. "I don't get it! What's going on? How do we get out of here?"

"You need to learn when to stop talking and start observing, Apprentice," Heather chided. "Right now, there is nothing that we can do, so do yourself, and us, a favor: sit down and keep your mouth shut. This technique is obviously taking a lot of effort to keep up. We don't want to break Kotohime's concentration and suddenly find ourselves drowning under several hundred tons of water, do we?"

Eric gulped. "N-no, I guess not."

"Good." Heather patted the spot beside her. "Now, pop a squat and sit tight. I think we're going to be here for a while."

***

While the people unlucky enough to be on the beach when the wave struck were annihilated in a single swoop, those who were on the streets did not find themselves crushed by several hundred tons of water.

Christine and Lindsay were among those lucky few. Lindsay had wanted to see the carnival, and she'd decided to drag Christine along with her. The two of them had waded through the crowds of people, sampling the cuisine and enjoying the festive atmosphere. Even Christine had fun, though she'd never admit it.

It had been while they were waiting in line to go on a ride that the wave had swept over them. A torrential flood of swiftly moving water had rushed through the carnival. Dozens of people were swept up by the raging tide. Some were fortunate enough to have been near cover, and the water flowed around them. Others had not been so fortunate.

Christine had been lucky. She'd sensed the rushing water and reacted quickly, erecting a strong wall of ice that curved around her and Lindsay like a half-dome. Even so, the sound of water slamming into the barrier raged in their ears, and they could still see the water from the other side as it rushed past their position.

They also saw several very unusual sights play out.

"Christine," Lindsay muttered as she pointed, "is that a man in a kayak?"

Indeed, moving through the waters was a man in a kayak. He looked like one of those extreme daredevils that pulled reckless stunts for fun. He soon swept past them, his kayak carried by the ravaging waters.

"Yes," she muttered, dazed by the sight. "Yes, it is."

"Okay," Lindsay said, nodding as if everything was normal.

The next sight that crossed their field of vision was two people on a surfboard. One was a man, the other a woman. They were both butt-naked, save for the whipped cream covering key parts of their bodies.

"Christine?"

"Yes?"

"I think I'm going to be sick."

Christine took one look at the naked couple and promptly turned green.

"Me too."

Several more unusual people flowed past them, including a pink-haired man riding a shark, a mini-sub with a window that had a strange man wearing large spectacles looking out of it, and a pair of children fishing as they sat in a washtub. Christine tried to ignore the stupidity of what she was seeing and focused on her friend instead.

"Are you okay, Lindsay?"

"Yeah... I'm fine." Lindsay gave her a smile that didn't fool Christine for a second. "I'm more worried about our friends."

Christine was also worried about the others. They'd been down by the beach. She squeezed her eyes shut as she imagined the wave crushing her friends. She was even worried about Iris, that annoying vixen who did such a good job of pissing her off. Christine hoped they were okay.

"They have Kotohime and Kirihime with them. I... I'm sure they're all right," she said, though part of her remained unconvinced.

"Yes... I'm sure they're just fine." Lindsay's smile said that she didn't believe what they were saying any more than Christine did, but she wanted to remain hopeful. Because sometimes, hope was all a person had.

During the time they spent waiting, Christine thought about this strange occurrence. While it was impossible to know what had caused the tidal wave, that did not mean that she had no hunches. Whatever had caused this improbable situation was not natural. It couldn't be. And if it wasn't a natural occurrence, then that meant it could have only been caused by one thing.

A yōkai, or several, had created this perilous phenomenon.

The thought sickened her. How could a yōkai, how could anyone, do something like this? Christine had no doubts that, even if Kevin and the others had survived, none of the normal humans had. They would have been crushed beneath the massive tidal wave, their bodies broken. What sort of monster could unleash a technique like this with innocent people around? She didn't know, and a part of her hoped that she would never have to find out.

"Christine," Lindsay grabbed her attention. "The water stopped."

Christine looked around to realize that her friend was right. Some water still remained in their area, but the water level was rapidly decreasing. Still, she waited for a few more seconds before letting the half-dome protecting them melt.

The levels had decreased to the point where only their feet got wet. However, the devastating after-effects of the raging waters remained. Signs were bent and twisted, their poles nothing more than lumps of metal that reminded her of half-formed pretzels. Park rides were destroyed, some were gone entirely, swept away by the water, while others had simply collapsed.

It wasn't just rides that had suffered. Many people looked to have been injured as well. A middle-aged man lay motionless on the ground, while a little girl—his daughter, she presumed—was shaking his shoulders as if trying to wake him up. Blood ran from a wound on the father's forehead, and the girl was crying incessantly, asking him why he wasn't waking up.

Those two weren't the only people who had suffered either. Everywhere she looked, someone was injured. Bodies of all shapes, sizes, ages, and genders lay strewn across the ground. Some were moaning in pain, while others were completely motionless.

"Oh…" Lindsay whispered, holding a hand to mouth, looking sick. "This… this is so horrible."

Christine agreed, but she didn't say anything. Nothing she said could make this situation better. Instead, she grabbed her friend's hand and led her down to the beach.

The wave had receded long before they arrived. The beach was mercifully clean of corpses, which Christine had expected to see in abundance. She could only assume that they had been washed out to sea. However, the contrast between now and several hours ago was startling. To think that this place, which had once been so lively mere minutes before, was now a graveyard—unsettling didn't even begin to describe it.

Luck finally seemed to be on their side as they located their friends. It was hard to miss them, since they were the only people left on the beach. They stood in a circle, crowded together. Kotohime and Kirihime looked exhausted, their bodies slouched as if they'd spent weeks awake without rest and were then forced to do strenuous labor. Alex, Andrew, and Justin seemed somewhat disoriented, but other than that, everyone else appeared to be fine.

"Guys! Hey, guys!" Lindsay waved at her friends as she and Christine ran over to the group. "I'm so glad you're all okay!"

However, while Lindsay smiled and cried tears of relief, and even Christine showed how happy she was to see them alive, the group they ran to remained surprisingly somber.

"Guys…?" Lindsay's voice trailed off. No one spoke. No one said a word. Not a *"I'm glad you two are safe,"* nor a *"I'm so relieved to see that you're alright."* Nothing. What was going on?

That's when they both noticed it. Two people were missing.

"Guys…" Lindsay's lower lip trembled. "Where are Kevin and Lilian?"

Kotohime opened her mouth, but no words came out. That's when Christine noticed that the maid was crying, and she wasn't the only one. Kirihime shed silent tears as she held Camellia to her chest while the five-tailed kitsune looked confused.

"Kirikiri, what was that wave? Do you know? What happened? Where are Kevin-kyun and Lilian?"

Her words made Kirihime stifle a sob. Kiara clenched her hands until her knuckles turned white. Even Iris, normally unrepentant in everything she did, had sunk to her knees, buried her face in her hands, and wept bitterly.

"No," Lindsay whispered, her voice wrenching with agonized shock. As she gazed at the faces of those around her, the blonde tomboy stumbled backwards as if she'd been physically slapped.

Christine held a hand to her chest, sinking to the ground as a sharp pain stabbed her heart. It felt like a hole had appeared in her chest, a gap in her heart where something had once existed. Images of Kevin flashed through her mind and the hole grew wider.

On that day, Christine lost the most important person in her life. Oddly enough, she couldn't seem to shed a single tear.

***

The trip back to the resort was a quiet one. Even Eric was silent, lost within his own mind, not even looking at the many beautiful females in bikinis that surrounded him. Camellia sat sniffling in a corner, tears still running down her cheeks from having learned the reason Kevin and Lilian weren't with them. Kirihime had done her best to comfort the woman, but it was hard when she herself was so distraught. Christine and Lindsay leaned on each other for support. Lindsay's eyes were red from crying, while Christine's were blank and dull and lifeless, like a doll's. Even the cat, which had stayed by the bus as they enjoyed the beach, had an aura of despondency surrounding her.

The only one who did not appear completely broken was Kiara. She remained stoic, a bastion of strength in a turbulent sea of crestfallen emotions. Sitting beside her, Kotohime remained dead to the world, eyes glassy and dull as her mind replayed her failure over and over again. If only she had been just a bit faster, she could have saved them. She had failed to protect someone important to her again. Was this her destiny? Doomed to be incapable of protecting the people who mattered most?

While Kotohime's heartache was powerful, it did not compare to the devastation that Iris felt. Lilian. Her dearest, most beloved sister was gone, and what had she, Iris, done to help her? Nothing. The only person that she had ever loved was dead, and she hadn't been able to save her.

She sat against a wall, knees drawn up to her chest, arms wrapped around her legs, and her face buried into her knees. She didn't cry. She had already run out of tears. Her eyes, red and swollen, remained shut. Her mind, wracked with guilt, became a receptacle for something sinister.

"It is the way of things."

The voices returned. Dozens of wretched voices, beings from beyond dimensions whispering a cacophony of sickening words that made her want to hurl.

"What has a beginning has an end. Everything that lives must eventually perish."

"Be quiet…"

They offered no platitudes. They didn't care. Nothing mattered to them but bringing this world to its final demise.

"All will eventually become one with the void. There is no way to stop oblivion from spreading."

"Stop it…"

Within the darkness of her own mind, Iris struggled against the incomprehensible whispers of creatures that defied time, space, and dimension. She pressed her face harder against her knees and tried to block out the voices to no avail.

"… Shut up…"

Iris never noticed the inky blackness coating her nails.

***

It was a desolate group that arrived back at Sobre el Natural. The difference between how they were that morning and how they were now was like night and day. Where before, everyone was laughing and having fun, now they were silent and despondent, their faces filled with grief and their hearts with despair.

They walked into the resort, ignoring the many people passing by, just as they, too, were ignored. These people didn't care about them, about their heartaches and their troubles. Like two strangers passing in a room. You might be curious about that person and their circumstances, but really, it wasn't any of your business, and so you just moved along.

The group split up after reaching the hotel. Iris entered the girls' bedroom and buried her face in her pillow. No one else went in. They left the young vixen alone to her grief.

Kotohime went off somewhere with Kiara. No one knew where they went, but they didn't try to find her. The traditional Japanese beauty had been about as distraught as Iris. They would let

Kiara deal with her. Kirihime had also escorted Camellia to their room, where the woman's loud bawling started up again.

"Come on, Apprentice." Heather placed an arm around her student's shoulders. "It's not good to keep all those feelings bottled up."

She drew Eric to her chest, holding him close and letting him rest his head on her bosoms. For once, Eric didn't think about how amazing her breasts felt against his cheek. For once, he didn't think about the fact that he was resting his head against a woman's breasts. For once, that didn't matter.

He wrapped his arms around Heather's waist and cried. Christine would have been shocked, but she supposed that even a pervert like Eric had more on his mind than perverted stuff.

She left the hallway, seeking comfort in solitude. She walked along one of the many paths that ran through the resort. Her already weak legs eventually lost the strength to support her, and she found a bench to sit on.

She stared out at the surrounding view, a panorama of greenery and natural beauty mixed with Mediterranean architecture. On any other occasion, Christine might have admired the beauty. That day, she saw none of it.

Unlike the others, who were all distraught, Christine felt nothing. She was empty, like a chalice that was once full, but the contents had been poured out. Kevin was gone. She hadn't been there to see it, but the evidence was undeniable. He was gone. How was she supposed to feel about that?

Kevin, the young man whom she'd confessed her feelings to and been subsequently rejected by. She still loved him despite his rejection. That was the curse of being who she was—no, of being what she was. It was unlikely that she'd ever find somebody else who could be to her what Kevin was. Even if he never loved her, Christine would never be able to love anyone else. It was only now, after he was gone, that this fact truly sunk in.

I'm so stupid. I know that I said we'd still be friends, but I... I should have tried harder to make him fall in love with me.

I'm sorry, the voice of her alter-ego said. *I knyow how much he meant to nyou. Thanks to nyour genetics, it will be impossible to find someone else who can—*

Shut up! Christine sniffled as she wiped at her eyes. *Just stop talking! It's not about that! I don't care about our genes! I just...*

I knyow. just want Kevin to love nyou the way nyou love him.

Christine remained silent. There was nothing she could say to that.

"I was wondering where you'd gone off to," a voice said next to her.

Christine looked up to see Lindsay looking down at her. The blonde looked about as good as Christine felt, which obviously meant she looked like shit.

"You look like shit."

Christine had no issues telling her this either.

"So do you," Lindsay fired back.

The blonde tomboy sat next to Christine, who watched her for several seconds before returning to gazing at nothing. Silence eclipsed them. Unable to scrounge up the desire to speak, Christine was loath to break it.

"It's hard, isn't it," Lindsay said, her voice so soft that Christine almost missed it. "Knowing that someone you love is... that they're not... not here anymore... I... it's weird. I feel like there's this gaping hole in my chest." As if to emphasize her point, Lindsay placed a hand over her heart and clutched at her shirt. "It hurts so much, like someone shoved a hand through my chest and tore my heart out."

Christine still said nothing, but her hands began to tremble. Lindsay turned to her.

"I don't know if that's what you're feeling, but I want you to know that I understand how much it hurts. I also know that you shouldn't keep these feelings bottled up."

"I'm not bottling anything up," Christine whispered, but the quaver in her voice betrayed her thoughts.

"You are." Lindsay's smile and bloodshot eyes were filled with equal amounts of sorrow and compassion. "I know you are. Throughout the entire trip here, you didn't cry. Not even once. You love Kevin even more than I do, and now he's gone. That has to hurt, but you don't have to keep that bottled up inside of you." Christine became stunned when Lindsay pulled her into a hug. "Let me shoulder some of this pain with you."

Christine's eyes blurred with tears. She tried to keep them in, but it was impossible. A sob wracked her body, shaking her frame. Pain unlike anything she'd ever felt filled her chest. She wanted to tear her own heart out, if only to stop herself from feeling this way.

She didn't know how long she cried. Her mind wasn't capable of telling time. She eventually became aware of a hand that had, at one point or another, began stroking her head. It was comforting. It helped soothe her frayed nerves. Cries turned into sniffles and sniffles soon stopped altogether. All that was left was a dull ache in her chest.

"Do you feel better?" Lindsay asked.

"A little bit," Christine confessed.

She pulled away to thank her friend, but appreciation turned into shock when she realized that Lindsay's entire front was covered in a thick layer of ice. The girl's light skin had also turned a startling, ghostly pale.

Because their bodies ran so cold, yuki-onna could not produce tears like humans did. Instead, they shed ice—even their sweat came out as sleet. While Christine was only half yuki-onna, that half of her was the dominant side.

Christine's eyes widened. "I-I'm sorry. I didn't mean to—"

"It's okay." Lindsay smiled and shrugged, even as she shivered. "I know you have trouble controlling your powers when you get emotional."

Christine blushed. She wanted to deny those words, but really, how could she deny something when the evidence was staring her in the face?

"Thanks," she mumbled.

"You don't need to thank me." Lindsay shook her head. "Whenever you need a shoulder to cry on, I'll always be here for you."

Christine wished she could have smiled. She was grateful to her friend, truly. Yet, even though she felt better, all she could think about was how her one chance at happiness was gone forever.

Her life would never be the same again, no matter how hard her friend tried to cheer her up.

***

Kotohime and Kiara walked down one of Los Angeles' many streets. The sidewalks were crowded with people who pushed, bumped, and shouted, all of them trying to arrive at their destination without delay. No one seemed to care for the two non-human women walking amongst them, though the one dressed in a kimono and carrying a katana did generate some stares.

"... And in other news, a most unusual occurrence happened this afternoon in Long Beach, California." Kotohime stopped in front of a small shop. A TV sat in a glass display, and the female news anchor on it was giving the latest news. "A large tidal wave crashed into the beach in what scientists are calling an anomalous and unprecedented disturbance in the ocean's tides. It is believed that the cause could possibly be related to global warming, however, no evidence has been given yet to suggest that this is indeed the case."

Snorting, Kotohime ignored the rest of the reporter's words and started walking again. That woman knew nothing.

"Global warming my left butt cheek," Kiara said, apparently agreeing with Kotohime. "We both know that was not caused by anything natural, or even by humans."

"Indeed," Kotohime's voice remained composed. "That wave was most definitely a yōkai technique. There are a number of water-faring yōkai who are capable of creating something like that. An Ocean Kitsune with at least five tails could have done so easily. It could have also been a particularly strong kappa, or even a group of kappa. Amabie are also capable of such feats, as are akamata."

Kiara stayed silent for several seconds before summing up her thoughts. "So in short, we have no clue as to who or what caused this."

"Not quite," Kotohime confessed. "While we were at the beach, I saw several figures in the distance. I could not see them clearly because they were too far away; however, I am now positive that they were locked in combat."

"So, there was a battle going on at the beach," Kiara mused. She hadn't seen anything, but that didn't surprise her. Like most dogs, she had an incredible sense of smell and powerful hearing, but her vision was lacking. "However, we don't know who was fighting or why."

"That's correct."

"In that case, we need to gather information," Kiara determined. "We're not going to be able to avenge Kevin and Lilian if we don't even know who did this." Her eyes flickered over to Kotohime. "I'm guessing that's why we're not at the resort?"

"Indeed. We're going to look for information."

Kitsune were creatures of impulse, of desire—including Kotohime. While she always presented a calm front for others, she was just like every other kitsune, and she'd just been hurt by the loss of a loved one. Like any sentient being, she wanted to take revenge on the people who'd killed Lilian and Kevin.

"Good idea, but, Kotohime?"

"Yes?"

"Do you even know where to find the information we're seeking?"

"..."

Kiara facepalmed. "I thought not."

***

Kevin awoke, not with the slow realization that came from regaining consciousness, nor with the startled gasp of a man having a nightmare, nor even the groan that was stereotypical of anime characters when they wake up—no, when Kevin woke up, it was to the feeling of a hand being shoved down his throat.

His eyes snapped wide open. However, he still couldn't see anything. His eyes perceived nothing beyond the amalgam of blurred colors, mixing and matching and morphing and changing, a sickening compendium that his mind couldn't comprehend. Images flashed past his vision. A walk on the beach. Red hair. A swell. A raging torrent, an infinite tide of water rising into the sky, cresting against the heavens. He tried to cough, to hack, to something, but it was no use. The hand remained shoved firmly down his throat.

And then it was gone.

Kevin gagged, and then coughed out what must have been several gallons of water. Each cough wracked his body with pain. Each breath caused his ribs to creak. Even the slightest movement hurt.

Something appeared in front of him. It was a blurry green object.

What... the... heck?

"I'm glad to see that you're awake," the shape said. Kevin blinked. "Tell me, how many fingers am I holding up?"

"Fingers…"

Was what he meant to say.

"Fssshrrsss…"

Was what he said.

"Hmm, it seems your eyesight is a bit unfocused. Here, let me fix that for you."

Kevin would have asked what this object—person? — meant, but he never got the chance—because something smacked him in the head. Hard.

"Ouch!"

Kevin covered his face with his hands. Gods that hurt! What the hell was he just hit with? A mallet?

"What the heck was that for, you crazy coot?!"

"Ho? Can you see me now? How many fingers am I holding up?"

Kevin was about to answer, but words fled when he realized who—no, what stood before him. Scaly green skin covered a small, squat body, clothed in a plain brown robe. This… thing stood with a stoop. It had a hunch of some kind, and Kevin was certain that the robe was covering something big attached to its back. A really long neck protruded from the robes, which was attached to a reptilian and very bald head. It was holding up three fingers. Mainly because it only had three fingers.

"Holy crap, it's a Ninja Turtle!"

The "Ninja Turtle" twitched.

"I am not a Ninja Turtle!" It shouted. "Don't confuse those sea turtle rejects with me!"

"Holy crap, it talks!"

More twitching.

"Of course I talk, you idiot!"

"Well, excuse me for having never seen a talking turtle before," Kevin snapped. "You think this is easy for me? Waking up to find out that some turtle has been shoving his hand down my throat? It's not, especially after I…" Kevin's mind screeched to a halt. His eyes widened. "Lilian! Where's Lilian?"

"If you are talking about the… kitsune who was with you, she is right over there."

If Kevin heard the way the turtle-person said kitsune with enough venom to slay an elephant, he didn't show it. He turned his head to follow the hand that was pointing at a bed several feet away. On that bed lay a familiar figure. Long red hair. Soft and smooth skin, unblemished and perfect. A white blanket covered her up to her chest, but he could see the swell of her breasts, the rise and fall she took with each breath.

"Lilian…" he said weakly. Wanting to go over to her side, Kevin made to get off the bed.

"Hold up, young man. You shouldn't try to stand up just yet. Your body is too—"

The turtle winced as Kevin crashed to the ground, his body toppling over like a broken doll.

"—weak," he finished. The turtle stared at Kevin, who stared at the ceiling, eyes blinking, not quite comprehending his situation.

"Why is the ceiling suddenly so high up?"

The turtle could only facepalm.

"… Idiot…"

***

It took about an hour before Kevin had enough strength to stand on his own. Fifteen minutes after that, the turtle-thing, which he'd learned was a kappa, checked him over and proclaimed that he was able to move without further embarrassment. They spoke while the turtle-doctor checked him over.

"So, you're a kappa?" Kevin asked, ignoring the small hammer tapping against his knees, testing his reflexes. "No joke?"

"What is that? Some kind of slang you brats use? Of course I'm a kappa. What the hell did you think I was?" The doctor's gruff response bothered Kevin. Actually, he just didn't like sitting there while Lilian was laid out on the bed next to him. He sat still, however, knowing that moving before this strange talking turtle said he was ready would result in him getting whacked over the head. It had already happened twice. "And if you say, 'Ninja Turtle,' this Taylor hammer is going down your throat."

Kevin snapped his mouth shut.

The rest of the checkup proceeded smoothly. Kevin remained quiet, mostly because he was trying to come to terms with the fact that he was standing—sitting—in the presence of an honest-to-gods kappa. He knew they existed. Kotohime had taught him that much. She'd said that all yōkai who appeared in manga and anime existed, along with several that hadn't appeared in Japan's most well-known forms of media.

It still shocked him, though. While he should have seen this coming, and a part of him was berating himself for having reacted the way he did, another part had never expected to meet one. Perhaps this was what it meant to be human. Maybe he would be shocked every time he met a new yōkai.

He certainly hoped not. His reaction upon waking up had been embarrassing.

"Okay." The kappa took the freezing cold metal cylinder off his chest, the task of checking his heartbeat finished. "You seem to be fine. In fact, you're unusually healthy and hearty for a boy your age."

Kevin dismissed the claim. "I work out a lot."

The kappa looked at him for a little longer… and then sighed. "Right. Anyway, you're free to move about, however—" dark eyes hardened into a glare "—you are not to leave this room. If you do, then I won't be able to guarantee your safety. Someone will come by later to give you some food."

With that, the kappa packed his medical bag and left. When the door closed with a soft click, Kevin scrambled over to Lilian's bed.

He sat down on the edge, the mattress giving way underneath him. Lilian's body shifted slightly as a result. Reaching out with his left hand, he tentatively let it come to rest on her cheek. Her skin was smooth and soft, but it also felt cold. Letting his thumb move without conscious thought, he slowly rubbed circles against her skin.

"Lilian…" he whispered, his voice cracking. "Please wake up."

She didn't. Not that Kevin had expected her to. She was clearly unconscious.

As he sat there, staring into a face that was too beautiful to be human, an idea slowly churned in his mind. It was, admittedly, an idea born of desperation, but he didn't think that made it any less viable. If it worked in *Sleeping Beauty*, then surely it would work in real life.

I must be stupid to think this is going to work.

He leaned down and pressed his lips to hers in a light kiss. A second passed, then he pulled back and waited—waited for a sign that she would wake up. A fluttering of lashes. A parting of lips. Something. Anything. What he got was silence.

Frowning, he tried again.

He pulled back and waited.

Still nothing.

Feeling more than a little desperate, he kissed her again and again and again and again. Each time he kissed her and didn't receive a response, he became more overwrought. Something was wrong. It had to be. Lilian never failed to wake up after the first kiss.

One last time. He kissed her one last time and pulled back. Nothing happened. Kevin was just about to panic, when he noticed something that he hadn't noticed before.

Lilian.

She was smiling.

Kevin deadpanned.

"All right, you can open your eyes now. I know you're awake."

A single green eye cracked open, lashes fluttering slowly as they unveiled the gem hidden behind them.

"You caught me," Lilian said, her smile turning just a tad sheepish. "I'm sorry for deceiving you, but it's been a really long time since I've played a prank on anyone."

"You're terrible," Kevin growled. "Do you know how worried I was when you wouldn't respond? I thought something might be wrong. You really… you had me so worried."

Lilian's eyes widened, then softened. Her smile became warm and caring, genuine. It was the smile that she reserved for him.

"I'm sorry."

"It's okay," he relented. He wasn't really angry, just worried. There was something else on his mind anyway. "You saved me. Back there when that wave came crashing down, you protected me."

It wasn't a question, but Lilian answered anyway. "I did. Right before the wave was about to hit us, I used a new technique that I've been working on. **Kitsune Art: The Barrier that Protects the Princess.** It's a defensive technique that creates a small layer of celestial youki around an area of my choosing. It's not complete yet, but it was enough that we survived having a large wave crash on top of us."

Kevin closed his eyes as a wave of self-loathing and disgust hit him. Once again, he'd proven to be useless, and Lilian had been forced to save him. All of the training that he'd gone through, all of the work he'd put in so that he could stand by her side, and it was nullified by something so far outside of his ability to deal with, it was almost laughable.

What have I been doing all this time? Am I really so weak? I've been training with Kiara so that I could help Lilian, not burden her! I really am a—

"Stop that," Lilian said, her voice adamant.

"W-what?" Kevin snapped out of his thoughts and sent her a startled glance.

Lilian's gaze was firm. "That, stop degrading yourself like that."

"I-I don't—"

"You do," Lilian interrupted. "You always make a face whenever something happens that you feel you should have been able to stop. You need to stop thinking like that. You're not useless. You never have been."

"I… you're right," Kevin said, shaking his head to dispel his negative thoughts.

Lilian beamed at him. "Of course I'm right."

He returned her smile. "Thank you, both for saving me and for now. I don't know what I'd do without you."

Lilian's smile turned somewhat devious. "You want to know how you can really thank me?"

Amused, Kevin allowed himself to fall into her trap. "How?"

"By giving me a kiss."

The feelings of self-loathing disappeared as her smile soothed his troubled mind. Kevin decided to give his mate exactly what she wanted. He leaned down and pressed his lips against hers.

All of the negative emotions that he'd been feeling vanished when their lips touched. Relief washed over him. The tension in his back eased. Even the hard knot of anxiety coiling in his stomach came undone. In that moment, nothing mattered to him except the girl whose breathtakingly soft lips were pressed against his.

Wanting more of this feeling, Kevin climbed onto the bed until he was straddling her waist. Even as he moved, his lips never left Lilian's. He took her lower lip between his teeth and gave it a gentle tug. Lilian moaned in response and squirmed underneath him. A pair of hands found purchase in his hair, nails scraping pleasantly against his scalp. In return, his hands pushed the covers down. He noticed, almost absently, that Lilian was wearing a shirt. Strange. She had not been wearing one at the beach.

He dismissed the thought a second later in favor of slipping his hands underneath her shirt and touching her directly. Her skin was warm, pleasant, and softer than silk. Kevin had always admired how soft her skin was. Even back when he'd been sure that he was in love with Lindsay, the feeling of Lilian's skin never failed to send his mind into a state of pleasure-driven delirium.

They broke away for a breath, but even then, they couldn't keep their hands or lips off each other. Their eager bodies kept the flames of their desire alive, rubbing and grinding in all sorts of delicious ways. The friction created was intense, even with the blanket and clothes keeping them from directly stimulating each other, the slightest trace of movement sent ripples through their bodies. Their lips, incapable of leaving each other alone, continued giving small pecks between breaths, stoking the flames of their passion.

The battle began again when Lilian's voracious tongue penetrated his mouth, bypassing his teeth and pushing against his own. Kevin responded as best he could, allowing her tongue to glide and dance across his. When he was sure that she wouldn't be able to escape, he closed his mouth around her tongue and suckled on it.

"Hfnnfnnn!"

Lewd slurping noises, Lilian's moans, and the rustling of fabric were the only sounds in the room. That sound was pierced by a loud, albeit muffled, moan when Kevin tweaked Lilian's right nipple. Like ripples in the water's surface after a stone sank to the bottom, the enchanting kitsune shuddered. Her body was on fire. Her desire for him became an overwhelming need, a hunger that could not be satisfied by anything less than taking that final step and becoming one.

"Kevin..." she panted. "I need... you so badly... please... now..."

While Kevin had done many things with Lilian, sex was not one of them. They'd done every form of foreplay imaginable, but he'd yet to take that final step. It wasn't because of his age. He was simply scared. How well would he perform? Would he be able to please Lilian? The last thing that Kevin wanted was to be one of those minute men who couldn't please their mate.

Should I do this? Is... is this really the right choice?

Kevin would never get to find out what might have happened if he'd been given more time to consider her offer.

"Ahem."

Because in that moment, reality chose to remind him of their situation. Another Teenage Mutant Kappa Turtle walked into the room, and this one actually fit the bill of a teenager. He couldn't have been much older than Kevin—at least, Kevin didn't think so. It was hard to judge age with yōkai.

"When I came in here, I didn't think I'd be getting dinner and a show," the kappa said.

"How long have you been there?"

"Several minutes now."

"You mean you were watching us?"

"Aw, don't get so upset. I couldn't see any of the goods because your fatass was blocking the way."

Kevin twitched as the kappa walked further into the room, a tray of food in his hands. This one's skin had a greenish-blue hue. Turquoise? No, cyan sounded more appropriate. Either way, this one, unlike the kappa who'd done his checkup, didn't walk with a stoop and didn't wear that bulky brown bathrobe. He walked straight, and his clothes were normal—mostly normal. He wore swim trunks and no shirt, which meant that the large shell on his back was visible.

"And just who the heck are you?" Kevin asked.

"The name's Kyle Colz, but you can just call me Kyle."

Kevin rolled his eyes. What a clichéd response. Still, he introduced himself. "I'm Kevin, and this is Lilian."

"Hello," Lilian greeted politely, though her eyes glared at the kappa who'd interrupted them, even as she did her best to hide underneath the covers

"I don't care who you are. Now here." The kappa set the tray down on the nightstand and turned to leave. "After you finish eating, I'll take you to our leader. He wants to talk to you."

Kevin and Lilian looked at each other as Kyle left, leaving the two alone. Holding a silent conversation, they decided that the best thing to do was learn more about their situation.

"Hey, Kevin?"

"Yeah?"

"Do you think… that our friends are okay?" Lilian twirled her spoon around in her food, a bowl of clam chowder, as she bit her lower lip.

Kevin put on a smile that he didn't quite feel. "They're with Kotohime, so I'm sure they're fine."

"Right." Lilian's smile was about as unconvincing as his.

"Are you two done eating yet?!" came the shout from outside.

"Don't be so impatient!" Kevin and Lilian shouted at the same time.

Kevin and Lilian finished eating quickly. Then they stood up, laced their hands together, and left the room.

Kyle was waiting for them outside. "You two ready? Good. Then follow me."

It didn't take long to realize that they were in some kind of resort. The room they'd just left held the appearance of a small hospital wing, and the hall they walked through reminded them a little of the Sobre el Natural, only less extravagant. Where the Sobre el Natural seemed like a place fit for kings, this building's interior appeared humbler. One thing that Kevin and Lilian noticed was the lack of guests.

They were led into an enclosed and somewhat small room with a knee-high table. Kevin recognized it as one of those tables often used in Japan. Just seeing such a thing being used in America made sweat trickle down his scalp.

Sitting at one end of the table was an old man… kappa… turtle… thing. His greenish skin had long since turned gray. Wrinkles covered much of the skin that could be seen, especially around his eyes and mouth. He wore a plain mauve kimono. Looking at this kappa, Kevin couldn't help but think of the Godfather for some reason. Well, a Japanese mutant turtle version of the Godfather.

"Ah, so both of our guests have finally woken up, aru."

"He's Chinese!" Lilian exclaimed in surprise.

"I am not Chinese, aru!"

"I don't know." Kevin looked at the man dubiously. "You certainly sound Chinese to me. Only Chinese people say 'aru' at the end of their sentences."

Lilian nodded in agreement. "That's right. Every Chinese person in anime and manga says 'aru' at the end of their sentences."

"They do not, aru!"

"You're not really convincing us you know."

"Just sit down and be quiet, aru!" Realizing that he was getting angry, the old kappa coughed into his hand. "There are very important things that we must discuss, aru."

"Really not helping your case."

"Just sit down already, aru!"

Lilian and Kevin sat at the table on the opposite side of the kappa. They sat side by side. Reaching out underneath the table, Kevin slid his hand into Lilian's, lacing their fingers together. She squeezed his hand reassuringly in return.

"Before we begin our discussion, I suppose I should introduce myself, aru."

Kevin leaned into Lilian, his mouth resting against her ear. "And he says he isn't Chinese," he said, not bothering to whisper despite leaning in.

"Stop that, aru!" the kappa grumbled about "young whipper-snappers" before speaking again. "My name is Shuǐ, aru."

"Isn't that a Chinese name?"

"Enough with the Chinese already, aru!" Shuǐ calmed down, but it was clear that he was still agitated. "I am the leader of this small yōkai clan, and I would like to apologize on behalf of my clan, aru." He performed a deep bow to the pair. "You were caught up in a technique that went out of control and almost ended up getting killed as a result. For that, you have my sincere apologies, daughter of the Pnéyma Clan, aru."

Out of his peripheral vision, Kevin saw Lilian tense. Using his thumb, he tenderly stroked the back of her hand. She relaxed under his ministrations.

"I suppose I can forgive you," Lilian said in a voice that was too formal to be real. It reminded Kevin of the time she'd been prepared to banish herself from the Pnéyma clan. "However, that's only on the condition that you tell us what's going on."

"Of course, however, before we get to that…" Kevin and Lilian tensed when Shuǐ reached underneath the table and pulled out… a game board? "Would you like to play a game of shogi while we talk, aru?"

The sound of Kevin's and Lilian's faces smacking against the table echoed down the hall.

***

Because Kotohime clearly had no clue where they needed to go in order to find the information they sought, Kiara ended up taking the lead. Having traveled to this city many times in the past—unlike her four-tailed friend—she knew of several areas within Los Angeles where yōkai gathered.

The Yōkai Café was located within a well-established part of the city. It looked just like any other café on the outside: a brick building with stained glass windows and a large sign over the door welcoming customers in. Nothing seemed out of place.

Upon stepping inside, the two were met with an atmosphere that nobody would have expected from a café established by yōkai. Warm lighting projected a friendly and inviting atmosphere. The wooden tiled floor, painted with a glossy finish, shone and sparkled under the lamps hanging overhead. Everywhere Kotohime looked, people sat at small round tables and booths with soft red cushions. Smiling faces greeted her vision. The friendly mien of the place stood in stark contrast to her own heartache.

Perhaps the most unusual part about this café was its maids. They were not human. Not only were they not human, but they didn't bother hiding their inhuman features. She could see several neko dressed in maid uniforms waiting tables, their tails swaying behind them and their cat ears twitching. A yuki-onna, obvious from the pale tone of her skin and dark hair, sat in one of the booths, putting the moves on a man who seemed inordinately pleased to have such a beauty showering him with attention. There were several other yōkai as well: kappa, tanuki, and tengu. She even saw a kijo—a female oni—moving past the window separating the café from the kitchen.

"Nya! Welcome home, Mistresses. Nya!" They were greeted by a young neko, a cute girl with blonde hair and amethyst eyes. Kotohime believed she was a bakeneko, seeing how she only had one tail. "Please, allow me to serve you."

They were directed to a seat and placed their orders. Kotohime simply asked for green tea, but Kiara asked for onigiri as well. Before the girl could leave, Kiara also asked if they could speak with "Kuroneko" and tell the "old cat" that Kiara needed a word. The young neko seemed to know who she was talking about, because her eyes widened, and she promised to let the woman in question know that they wished to speak with her right away.

"You look surprised," Kiara observed. Kotohime looked at her partner.

"I am," she admitted. "I know that we yōkai hide amongst humanity, and that many of us do what we can to make a living, however…" she trailed off, eyes straying to all the humans who lounged in the café, unbothered by the fact that they were surrounded by yōkai. "I've never seen anything like this."

"That's because you've spent too much time with the Pnéyma Clan and not enough time around humans." Kiara also observed the people around them. "Everyone knows that humanity is fascinated by creatures beyond their ability to understand. That's why stories about vampires and werewolves and elves are so popular. They like to imagine what it would be like if such otherworldly creatures existed."

"Very true," Kotohime conceded her point. "I suppose it was inevitable that something like this would happen. Still, I am surprised by this atmosphere. It reminds me of the maid cafés back in Japan."

Kiara leaned back in her seat and placed her only remaining hand on the table. "That's because it is. Everyone knows that Japan was the first country to discover the existence of yōkai. Almost all legends about us were first derived from there. You could almost say they have a monopoly on our mythos."

"And with the recent rise in the popularity of Japanese pop culture, it was only natural that someone would take advantage of America's new fascination for all things Japanese," Kotohime concluded.

Kiara nodded once. "Right."

"And this 'Kuroneko' is the one who did it?" she asked.

"You would be half-right," said a woman who walked up to them.

Unlike the other women around them, this one wore a loose-fitting kimono that revealed hints of her cleavage. She was also much older than the other yōkai. While still appearing young and beautiful, with long black hair and dark green eyes and a body to die for, anyone observant enough could see the wisdom behind her gaze. Only someone who'd lived for a long time could have eyes like that. She also had two tails, which occasionally popped out of her kimono.

A nekomata.

Nekomata was liberally translated as "Split-Tailed Cat," due to how their tail split into two. They were the most powerful of all cat-type yōkai. Bakeneko were the weakest, and while kasha were powerful, they could only use hellfire and minor illusions. Nekomata were capable of wielding more than just fire. While there were no nekomata that could match a Kyūbi in terms of sheer power, they were more than capable of fighting on par with an eight-tails.

Kotohime's body stiffened when something pushed down on her, a strange pressure, as if Earth's gravity had suddenly increased. It wasn't killing intent. It felt more like someone's soul was bearing down on hers, judging her, weighing her, determining her worth. This presence... it was almost like standing in front of the Pnéyma clan's matriarch!

Her hands gripped her kimono tightly. It was all she could do not to react to this incredible presence.

Kiara, apparently unbothered by this force of presence, grinned. "Kuroneko, you old cat. How've you been?

Kuroneko glanced at Kiara in mild disapproval. "I believe I told you to stop calling me old."

"And I believe I told you that the next time we met, I wouldn't be so easily cowed."

The pressure suddenly increased. Kotohime's teeth rattled. However, just as quickly as it had come, the pressure left.

"So you did," Kuroneko admitted. Then she smiled.

Kotohime watched, stunned, as Kiara and this nekomata, whose presence reminded her of the matriarch, shared a hug. How did her acquaintance know this woman?

Kiara sat down again. Kuroneko joined them.

"It's been quite a while since the last time we saw each other," Kuroneko said, her smile lazy and delighted, very much like a cat's. "How many years has it been. Ten? Twenty?"

"Try one hundred and fifty."

"That's right. One hundred and fifty years. My mind must be slipping. I remember, the last time we met, you were looking for a teacher to help you get stronger." Ancient eyes wise beyond compare studied the inu, analyzing her with a single glance. Kuroneko nodded. "It seems you found someone."

"That's right." Kiara smirked. "I did find someone who helped me get stronger. She might even be more powerful than you."

"Oh ho?" Kuroneko seemed more amused than anything. "I may have to meet this woman if she's as powerful as you claim. Although, I am not much of a fighter these days." She leaned back in her seat, her posture lazy. Kotohime felt a strong urge to correct it, but she resisted the impulse.

Her body went stiff when dark green eyes fell on her.

"And who is this? A young four-tails." Those eyes observed her in the same way they had done to Kiara. Kotohime felt naked in front of that gaze. "She's quite beautiful, and a *yamato nadeshiko* to boot." Kuroneko turned back to Kiara. "Where did you find this girl?"

Kotohime bristled at being called "girl." She was far from young. However, this woman, clearly ancient and powerful, was much older, so she refrained from responding inappropriately.

"My name is Kotohime." Since she was sitting, she couldn't bow. Instead, she nodded her head respectfully. "It is a pleasure to meet you."

"And so respectful too!" Kuroneko's amused, lazy smile widened. She glanced at Kiara. "I'm surprised you managed to find such a delicious catch. Who knew you had it in you?"

"I'm not a dyke," Kiara said, rolling her eyes, "and Kotohime is straight. Get your mind out of the gutter. We're on serious business today."

"Really?"

Leaning forward, her elbows resting on the table, fingers laced in front of her face, Kuroneko gave Kiara a curious look.

"What kind of business?" she asked with a fanged grin.

***

"So, you're telling me that a clan of Ocean Kitsune have invaded your territory and are trying to take over Los Angeles?" Kevin asked for clarification.

They were playing shogi, Lilian and Shuǐ. Kevin, unknowledgeable about the game, sat on the sidelines and watched as the two moved their pieces across the board.

"That is indeed correct, aru," Shuǐ said, studying the board. After analyzing the board, he grabbed one of his two gold general pieces and moved it, taking Lilian's rook. "They came to Los Angeles several months ago and slowly integrated themselves into the city. At first, we thought nothing of it. They came in slowly enough that we simply suspected they were a small clan seeking a place to live, and we don't really care if another group of yōkai wishes to share this land, aru."

Much of North America was free from the influence of yōkai clans. There were a few states that one clan or another had claimed as their territory, but only six of the fifty states had been claimed by a clan. Even then, those clans paid tribute to the Four Saints, who ruled over this land, for permission to make those states their territory.

California was not one of those six states.

Shuǐ observed as Lilian moved one of her pieces, claiming a knight and trapping his king. The girl was surprisingly good at shogi. It was too bad he didn't know that Kotohime had taught her to play when she was just a young vixen barely twenty years into her second tail. If he had, then she was sure he wouldn't have been so quick to play her.

"It wasn't until two months ago that we realized they intended to claim Los Angeles, if not the entire state, for themselves, aru. Several of our family members went missing. Our first thoughts were that they'd run into The Sons and Daughters of Humanity, a group of humans with anti-yōkai sentiments who've been getting more active recently—" Kevin and Lilian shared a startled look. Shuǐ made his move. "—we only realized a few days later, after one of our more powerful members came back near death, that this was not the case, aru."

Lilian studied the board, trying to determine her next move. Shuǐ had moved his king out of her bishop's path. After several seconds, she clicked her tongue and moved her knight into a position in front of Shuǐ's remaining lance. Now if he took her knight, she would be in a position to take his king.

"Hold on a second," Kevin said. "I'm confused. I thought kitsune disliked fighting?"

"They have not been fighting us!" Kyle spat. The younger kappa stood at the entrance, guarding the room, though Kevin could not determine from what. "They've been assassinating us, killing us from the shadows like cowards."

"Calm yourself, aru." Shuǐ admonished the boy lightly, even as he moved his lance away from Lilian's knight. "It does not do to get angry in a situation like this, aru."

"Easy for you to say." Kyle glared at nothing. "Your brother wasn't killed by those damn foxes."

Shuǐ sighed but didn't say anything.

"That is how most kitsune do things," Lilian said. She moved her lance again, closer to Shuǐ's king, though she didn't put it in check. "We don't much care for fighting. When we do, we normally use illusions to mask our attacks and keep the enemy from fighting back."

"Jiāoào didn't do that," Kevin pointed out. "Sure, he had that one illusion that made him invisible, but that was about it."

"Jiāoào was also an idiot, and a two-tails to boot." Lilian dismissed the other kitsune with a wave of her hand, her eyes never leaving the board. Shuǐ moved a pawn towards one of her silver generals. "Most two-tails lack the repertoire of older kitsune. It's not unusual for a kitsune with two tails to only have two, maybe three techniques total." She moved her gold general, hemming in Shuǐ's king. "You also have to remember that Jiāoào is young—even younger than me. He was only one hundred and thirty years old."

"Which explains why he looked like a kid." Kevin grimaced. "To think that I got my butt kicked by someone who was the physical equivalent of a fourteen-year-old brat."

"Jiāoào is still a kitsune." Lilian shrugged. "It's only natural that you would have a tough time fighting him. That you beat him at all is a feat worthy of praise." She sent him a glowing smile that made Kevin feel all warm and fuzzy inside.

Kyle looked shocked. "You defeated a kitsune?"

"Yep," Kevin said in his best, "*I know I'm awesome, but I don't want to sound arrogant,*" voice.

"But you're just a human!"

Kevin glared. "Just who the hell do you think I am? Don't underestimate me just because I'm a human. I might lack the supernatural powers that you yōkai have, but that doesn't mean I'm weak." He pointed an accusing finger at Kyle. "Listen up! I've trained hard to be able to match yōkai in combat! I've worked my butt off with my sadistic teacher every day for the past seven months! I may be human, but I'm not a pushover!"

While Kyle looked flabbergasted, Shuĭ chortled. "A most interesting human you've decided to mate with, Ms. Lilian, aru."

"Of course." Lilian puffed her chest out in pride. "My mate's the best."

Kyle stared at Kevin for a little while longer, then snorted dismissively. "Whatever. You might be okay in a fistfight, but you're still human. I would crush you in seconds. I wouldn't even have to lift a finger."

"Oh, yeah!" Kevin got up in Kyle's personal space. "That sounds like a challenge to me. Why don't you back up those words with some action?"

Kyle butted his head against Kevin's, glaring at the blond teen. "I would be more than happy to, except fighting against a powerless human isn't really my style."

"Sounds to me like someone's afraid of getting his butt handed to him by this lowly human."

"What was that?!"

"You heard me. If you want to prove your strength, then do so with your actions instead of your mouth, because all I see right now is a *Ninja Turtle* wannabe whose only talent is jabbering!"

"I'll show you *Ninja Turtle* wannabe when I blast you away with a Hydra Cannon!"

"Pfft! You won't get a chance to before I introduce my fist to your face!"

Shuĭ looked at the human and the kappa who were seconds away from fighting. He sighed. That youngster Kyle had always been a little too hot-headed for his own good.

"Checkmate!" Lilian declared with a happy smile.

"Eh?!" Shuĭ looked at the board in shock, then despair, when he noticed that, indeed, he'd been bested. "I can't believe I lost to a yōkai younger than I am, aru!"

Lilian just grinned as she held up her hand and formed the victory sign with her fingers.

***

Night had fallen. Nights in Los Angeles were never pretty. The lights were so bright that you couldn't see the stars. The sounds of constant traffic grated on the ears. Even further out of the main city, beyond where most of the activity took place, the mass of humanity overran everything.

Within one of those outlying districts, a group of kitsune had gathered. It was a small gathering. The main group had set up shop elsewhere. They'd been stationed there to keep an eye on things, to make sure the kappa didn't try to launch a surprise attack or something similar. None of them really understood the need. They'd been doing an excellent job of pushing the turtle yōkai back, but their matriarch didn't want to take any chances, and what the matriarch wanted the matriarch got.

There were only six of them. Four of those six only had two tails, like most of their clan, but two of them had four.

The group resided in what, to anyone not capable of seeing through illusions, appeared to be nothing more than an old, abandoned warehouse. In truth, it was actually a spacious compound that had been converted into a living space. Red bricks and a flat roof made up the exterior, while the interior had been decorated to look a little more like a home.

"How's that job of yours, Ken?" asked one of the four-tails. Short blue hair sat upon his head in a messy bed of spikes. Bangs framed a face that any human female would have fallen for. They hid light blue eyes behind them, giving him an aura of mystery.

The one called Ken leaned forward in his chair, resting his elbows on his thighs. His long blond hair fell over his shoulder, but he flicked it behind him again with a shake of his head.

"Meh, it's alright. I wouldn't call it a great job, but the pay is good, and I've met a lot of gorgeous women." His eyes lit up. "I did meet this one chick. She's fucking gorgeous. Long red hair, green eyes, and a body that I would happily mate with well into the night." The light dimmed, and his joy was replaced with a scowl. "Too bad the bitch has a boyfriend. Still…" He shrugged. "Gimme a few more days. I'll have her eating out of the palm of my hand, and her boyfriend will find himself somewhere in Canada."

"Why Canada?" one of the other two-tails asked.

"Why the hell not?"

"Good point."

"There is another problem that I ran into," Ken added, almost as an afterthought. "This group is traveling with an inu, a dog." The group wrinkled their noses in disgust. "They're with that bitch, Kiara."

"Fucking dogs," one of the four-tailed kitsune scowled. "They should all just do us a favor and die."

"This world would definitely be a better place without them."

Before the group could get going on their collective rant, the doors were blown wide open—along with a good portion of the wall itself. Despite their surprise, the group responded quickly, hopping to their feet and leaping away as the table between their chairs was crushed by a particularly large chunk of bricks.

"Sorry about that," a female voice said from beyond the dust created by the explosion. "I guess I don't know my own strength."

Two women walked into the room. One of them, a female with shaggy brown hair, dark eyes, and a feral appearance, clapped the dust off her hand by slapping her pants. Oddly enough, she was wearing a dark gray business suit. What startled the kitsune wasn't her attire, but the fact that she only had one arm.

The other woman was a kimono-clad femme: dark hair, pale skin, and a figure curvaceous enough to entrance all who gazed upon her. She came to a stop beside the one-armed woman. She was holding a sheathed katana in her left hand.

Both of them were clearly yōkai. The woman in the kimono had four tails and fox ears, and the one in the business suit possessed a single bushy tail and floppy dog ears.

"I know you two!" Ken shouted as he pointed at them. "You're that bitch Kiara, and you're one of the women who was with her. What the hell is a kitsune doing with an inu?!"

Kiara laughed as she stared at Ken, who flinched under her ferocious gaze, which seemed to promise violence. "I remember you. You're the punk who was trying to hit on my student's mate at Sobre el Natural. To think that you would be one of the little kitsune whose asses I'm going to kick."

Kiara's lips peeled back into a fanged grin. Ken took a step back.

"This is going to be fun."

CHAPTER 8

The Ocean Colored Red

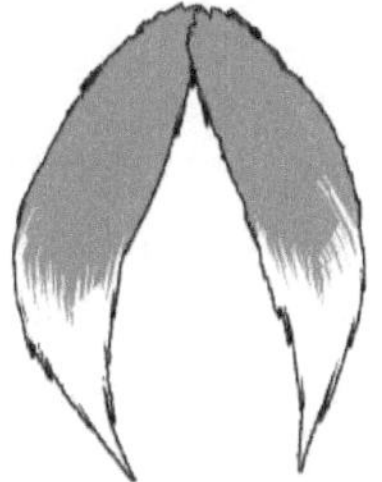

FOR ONE SOLITARY SECOND, no one moved. The two groups sized each other up. The group of kitsune seemed stunned that one of their own would work with an inu, while the other simply stood there as if they were expecting something to happen.

When nothing happened, Kotohime decided to make the first move.

A flicker of light was all the warning that the kitsune closest to her—a two-tails with brown hair and dark eyes—would get before Kotohime vanished and reappeared behind him, slowly sheathing her katana.

Click. The sound of her katana fully entering its sheath echoed almost ominously in the quiet room. Exactly one second later, blood gushed out of the severed stump that used to be where the two-tailed kitsune's head was. The body stood still for a second, crimson ichor spurting from its neck. Then it fell forward, first onto its knees, then toppling to the ground. It twitched once, twice, and then it was still.

Kotohime turned to face the other stunned kitsune.

"That's one down."

They kicked into action. The three other two-tails moved back, while the two four-tailed kitsune moved forward. One prepared for battle with Kotohime. The other found himself being pitted against Kiara. That one grimaced.

"Great, I'm fighting the one-armed dog."

"Now that's just rude," Kiara commented, seemingly not bothered by the insult. "This one-armed dog can still kick your ass."

The kitsune narrowed his eyes. "We'll see."

***

Kotohime moved with incredible grace as she crossed the distance between herself and her opponent. She slid her katana out of its sheath, the weapon arcing out in a slicing attack meant to bisect her target. Blade bit into flesh, carving through muscle and bone— or so she thought. It wasn't until a second later, when water spouted from the wound, that she realized what was happening.

She jumped back just in time to witness the water clone exploding. Unlike regular water, which would have sprayed everywhere, this water formed into several streamers that followed after her.

Like the swordswoman that she was, Kotohime remained calm. She moved with alacrity, cutting down each streamer in succession. Unfortunately, the streamers that she cut did not disperse. They simply turned into more streamers, which turned into more streamers. Before Kotohime knew it, she was surrounded by a dome composed entirely of swirling water.

"Hmmm… this is **Water Art: Water Prison.**"

Much like the name suggested, the technique created a prison composed entirely out of water. In some ways, it looked similar to her technique **The Water Temple's Ancient Realm**; however, the execution was far different. For starters, **Water Prison** did now allow for perfect control over all water in a given vicinity. It simply created a prison. Kotohime's technique could do that, but it could also accomplish so much more. Any three-tailed River or Ocean Kitsune could use this technique.

Kotohime didn't bother using a stance. Wielding her katana, she slashed at the dome, tearing the prison apart with ease. The water dispersed, unable to remain cohesive, and Kotohime found herself in the center of an empty room. She frowned. Something was wrong. What happened to Kiara? She should have still been fighting that other four-tailed kitsune. And what happened to her own opponent? He should… her eyes widened.

This is an illusion.

Realizing that she'd been caught within an illusion, Kotohime began the process of breaking it. Illusions were the byproduct of a yōkai injecting their own youki into you, then using it to control one or more of your five senses. To break it, all one had to do was expel the foreign youki.

The illusion vanished. The world returned to its original state. Kiara and her opponent were fighting. The inu smashed her fist into her opponent's face, sending him flying through a wall. She laughed as she chased after him. Kotohime almost shook her head. That woman was enjoying herself far too much.

A noise came from behind her. Kotohime spun around and swung her blade upwards. Her sword met a wave of water that appeared out of nowhere. The water split apart as she cut it, then began swirling around her, circling her almost like a shark did with its prey.

Holding her blade in front of her, Kotohime shifted into a very basic *kenjutsu* stance, one that offered balanced strength and stability. It was the best stance to use for what she planned on doing next.

Water rose up as massive pillars that surrounded her on all sides, almost reaching the ceiling. Kotohime knew this technique. **Water Art: Entrapment.** Contrary to its name, the technique didn't just trap a person like the **Water Prison** did. This technique trapped a person, and then the constantly spinning pillars would slowly migrate inwards, eroding whatever was stuck inside. The technique had some decent power, but it wasn't particularly tough to break.

"Ikken Hissatsu. Ougi."

Using her stance's stability, Kotohime swung her blade while twirling around in a full circle. A powerful shock wave of condensed air, generated from nothing more than the momentum of her swing, greeted the water pillars. Much like with the water prison technique, the pillars were sliced apart and dispersed.

Her opponent remained hidden.

"I suggest you stop sulking and come out to face me."

Kotohime turned around slowly to keep track of her surroundings. Her opponent could not be far. Those techniques he'd used required a direct line of sight to the person they were being used on. Without knowing the position of your opponent, you would never be able to trap them. That meant he was hiding underneath an illusion, or maybe a technique that used the moisture in the air to bend light.

"Now why would I do that?" a voice echoed around her.

Several spears composed of water materialized around her. They flew at her, and she struck them down with lightning-quick slices of her katana.

"I might have never seen you before, but I know who you are," the voice continued. "You're The Kitsune Swordswoman, The Blood Moon Princess, The Monster with Four Tails. I am well aware of your skills with a blade. They're legendary. I also don't much care for close-quarters combat, so I think I'll stick to striking from a distance."

As he said this, the puddles of water that littered the ground came alive. They moved along the floor, tentacles crawling and creeping at an impressive speed. The water tentacles latched onto Kotohime's legs, but they were cut down before they could do anything to her. It wasn't until she'd done this sixteen times that she realized that the tentacles were only a distraction.

Surrounding her on all sides, filling enough space that her vision appeared distorted and blurry, were thousands, possibly millions, of water needles.

"Do you like it? I call it **Water Art: Tide of One Million Water Needles**. I created this technique myself. Impressive, isn't it?"

"Hmm…" Kotohime eyed the surrounding needles warily. "This could pose a problem, yes."

The needles descended upon her like a swarm of locust, and Kotohime found that she had no more time to think.

***

"Come on, foxy! Why are you running away?!"

Kiara grinned as she chased after her foe. After the satisfaction of feeling his face cave in against her fist and watching him get blasted through a wall, she'd taken off after the kitsune in the hopes of finishing him off quickly. It turned out that the four-tails had a bit more fight in him than she gave him credit for. He had survived her initial attack with only a bit of bruising. She suspected he'd used reinforcement to protect himself.

Now she was chasing him through deserted side streets and back alleys. She wondered where he was going. Was he leading her into a trap? Perhaps he wanted to fight her in a more open space? She didn't really care either way. Her only desire was to fight, defeat, and make this fox suffer for the hand he'd played in killing her disciple.

The kitsune jumped onto the roof of a building, and Kiara did not hesitate to follow. The moment she touched down, however, several spears of water were launched at her left flank.

Grinning viciously, Kiara swiped at the spears, causing them to explode in a shower of water. She turned to look at the fox standing several feet away and raised an eyebrow.

"Is that it?" She clicked her tongue in disappointment. "I'm rather disappointed that you thought such a weak attack would do me in."

The kitsune smirked. "What makes you think that was my only attack?"

"What?" That was when Kiara noticed the water surrounding her, a thousand tiny droplets hovering in the air like celestial bodies. "Ho… what's this?"

"Water Art: Dance of Timeless Erosion."

The tiny droplets surrounding her began to spin, slowly at first, but quickly picking up speed. Soon they became nothing but a blur, then a streak, and then a continuous flash of never-ending streams of shimmering light. She'd been caught within a powerful maelstrom of youki-enhanced water, which began shrinking around her.

"I think I saw Kotohime use this attack during our spars once," Kiara commented. She wasn't worried, and the reason became clear when she unleashed a short but intense burst of youki. Water exploded in all directions, scattering on the wind. "Hmph. What a pathetic attack. Did you honestly think that—"

Kiara's eyes widened. A hand went to her throat as she found herself incapable of breathing. She tried to take a breath, to inhale a lungful of oxygen, but she couldn't. What was going on? This was…

An illusion?

She tried to dispel the illusion. She'd fought Kotohime enough times that she could break them easily. It didn't work. No matter how many times she tried to overpower the illusion with her own youki, she still couldn't breathe.

"It's not an illusion, *dog*." The kitsune sneered, staring down his nose at her with a sense of superiority. "It always amazes me to see how easily duped your kind is. I cannot possibly fathom why most kitsune are so afraid of your species." She glared at him, but considering she couldn't breathe, the glare didn't do much. "Now why don't you do me a favor and die?"

From her blurring peripheral vision, Kiara saw another kitsune standing a little ways off. It was one of the two-tailed ones. What was he doing here? Backup? No. Like most supernatural species, kitsune were exceedingly arrogant, and the one that she was fighting was definitely of the pompous ass variety. He wouldn't ask for help. So, why was that one standing there? What was…

Her eyes widened. Water gathered around her and formed into thirteen tridents, their tri-pronged tips gleaming with an evanescent sheen.

"Goodbye, dog," the kitsune said, gesturing with his hands.

The tridents flew forward, intent on impaling Kiara from every angle.

***

After finishing up their conversation, Shuĭ promised to have someone take them back to Sobre el Natural in the morning. It was late now. The sun had gone down several hours ago. Even though Kevin and Lilian wanted to leave right that instant, to go back to their friends and family, they agreed to leave in the morning.

It had nothing to do with the fact that Shuĭ offered them access to a private hot spring. Nothing at all.

Kevin sat in the steaming water, enjoying the jets as they pushed air against his back. It felt wonderful. He wondered if this was what he'd missed out on when he had turned down the chance to use the hot springs at Sobre el Natural.

Lilian sat next to him. She leaned into his side, using him as a pillow. His left arm was wrapped around her shoulders, pulling her into a half-hug. Like him, she was naked.

"Our friends are probably worried about us," Kevin mused.

"Yeah…"

"They might even think we're dead." The thought caused a tight ball of guilt to settle in his stomach. "We did get crushed by that water, after all. I doubt most people could have survived something like that. The only reason we're even alive is because you used that new technique of yours."

"The Barrier that Protects the Princess," Lilian murmured. She sounded drowsy.

"Right, your barrier technique." Kevin used his free hand to scratch the underside of his chin. "It's awfully convenient that you had a technique like that handy. I'm kind of surprised."

In response to his words, Lilian kissed his shoulder. "You shouldn't be. Back when I fought Kiara, I realized that I needed more defensive techniques in my arsenal—offensive ones, too, but I really needed something that could protect me from blunt force trauma. Half the reason Kiara's attacks hurt me so much is that I'm not very proficient at reinforcement. I can't do much about that, since I don't have enough youki to use it properly, so I decided to create a technique that I could use with my current reserves."

Like all yōkai, be they kitsune or otherwise, Lilian's techniques were fueled by youki, the mystical energy that yōkai were born with. Being only a two-tails, she didn't have much youki, which meant she needed to improvise when using techniques.

"And that technique is **The Barrier that Protects the Princess?**"

"Yep. It took me a while to create it, because I don't have anyone who can teach me celestial techniques. This is something that I had to come up with from scratch."

"No wonder it has such a horrible name."

"This coming from the guy who needs to use anime to name his attacks."

"Gurk."

"At least I can come up with something on my own, Mr. Stop-Ogling-My-Girlfriend-Kick."

"All right! All right! I get it. My naming skills suck. I see your point."

Lilian grinned. "As well you should."

"You're being awfully mean today." Kevin pouted. He would have crossed his arms for good measure, but one of them was currently full of beautiful girl. "First that mean prank on me after our near-death experience, and now you're making fun of my inability to name my attacks."

"I did apologize for that first one," Lilian pointed out, smiling brilliantly at him. "And you totally deserved that second one. Someone who has no talent at naming attacks has no right to make fun of me for what I name my attacks."

In the face of such flawless logic, Kevin could only pout.

"You're still being mean."

"Aw, I'm sorry."

Lilian slowly turned and climbed onto his lap. Kevin sucked in a deep breath as her thighs rested on either side of his legs. He twitched against her stomach as Lilian leaned in, her soft, feminine hands pressing against his chest, and a face that could make angels cry with envy coming so close their noses touched.

She wore a grin that was so Lilian it made his heart skip a beat—and made his erection twitch some more. It was a grin that said, *"I'm trying to look coy, but I don't really know what 'coy' looks like, so there."* Kevin loved how surprisingly innocent Lilian was, her desire to mate with him aside.

"How about I make it up to you?" she suggested.

Lilian's eyes were mesmerizing, half-lidded pools of liquid emeralds glimmering with an otherworldly light. Kevin stared into those eyes, through which so many emotions were reflected back at him. He didn't need to be an expert to read her gaze. She was an open book to him.

His eyes were inevitably drawn to her lips, which were light pink and glistening. The impulse to partake of those lips was so strong that he probably would have given in if he didn't know how to play the game.

Patience, he told himself. He couldn't just give in to his impulses. This was as much a game to see which of them cracked first as it was anything else. Kevin usually lost these battles, which was odd. You'd think that Lilian would have been the one who was overeager to get straight to the *ecchi* stuff, but no, more often than not, it was Kevin who couldn't hold himself back. This time would be different. He would make her make the first move.

"Kevin." He shivered at the earnestness in her voice. No one else he knew could suffuse such sweetness into their tone like Lilian could, especially in a situation like this. "Is there anything I can do to make up for being so mean? You know I'll do anything for you."

Those words made his body burn with intense hunger. He wanted her. Right. Now. It was almost frightening how much he craved this girl.

Kevin held back. He resisted. Two could play at this game.

"Anything, huh?"

Lilian gasped when a pair of hands grasped her rear end. The gasp became a low moan when those same hands kneaded the pliant flesh underneath their fingertips.

"Are you sure that's a wise thing to say? There are an awful lot of demands that I would like to make."

"If you asked me to, I would do anything for you," she said, and Kevin knew there was truth to her words. Lilian really would do anything he asked. It didn't matter how depraved, disgusting, or immoral it was, if he asked her to do something, she would do it.

It was frightening, the hold he had over her. He knew why. Lilian was a kitsune, a being that was fundamentally different from humans. They didn't have human morals. The things that his culture considered taboo meant nothing to a kitsune. He could have even asked her to let another girl join them in bed, and she probably would have allowed it. That fact made it all the more imperative to him that he not betray her trust.

"Kevin," Lilian whined, and he realized that her resolve was breaking. Just a little bit more, and he could chalk up a win on their imaginary scoreboard.

"Yes?" he asked. He tried to make his voice sound husky, but he wasn't very good at husky. It would've been probably lost on Lilian anyway.

Lilian was rocking back and forth now. Every time she did, her crotch would rub against him, though she was careful not to take things further than rubbing. She knew that he was reticent to have sex. She'd told him that she was willing to wait. Kevin wondered if Lilian knew how much that meant to him. Probably not, which made the fact that she was restraining herself all the more meaningful.

Eventually, I'll give Lilian exactly what she wants, he promised himself.

Despite them not going any further, the way her butt ground against his erection made him delirious. His hands moved of their own accord, squeezing her plentiful ass and causing her to groan. He could feel her nipples rubbing against his chest. He wanted to lean down, take one of them into his mouth, and suckle on it.

"I—" Lilian started.

Lilian was interrupted when the door suddenly burst open and Kyle rushed into the room.

"We've got a problem! I need you two to come with me!"

Kevin and Lilian froze. Despite being chest-deep in steaming water, it felt like someone had dumped several gallons of snow on them. Slowly, they craned their necks to look at the person who'd intruded upon their game. While they were in the hot spring. Naked.

Cue two indignant squawks.

"Don't you ever knock?!" they shouted in unison.

Kyle blinked. "Oh, were you two about to have sex? That's too bad. I need you both to get dressed and—"

"Shut up!" Kevin and Lilian shouted in sync. Lilian's tails extended and slammed into the kappa, launching him clean off his feet and out of the hot spring. Those same tails then grabbed the doors, pulled them shut, and locked them.

Silence descended upon the room. Kevin wondered what he should say in a situation like this. Should he lighten the mood with a joke? No, that would be in poor taste. Maybe he should try to get the mood going again, but… no. Kyle had killed the mood with all the subtlety of a Butt Monkey walking in on a group of girls while they were changing.

Great… now I'm going to have blue balls for the rest of the night.

"Kevin…"

Hearing his name being called, Kevin turned to face Lilian—

"Yes—whoa!"

—and then he had to brace himself as she pounced on him.

"L-Lilian! What are you doing?!"

"I'm starting back where we left off."

"Where we—w-wait! You can't do that! The mood's been ruined!"

"Ufufufu, not for me."

"Well, it has for—what are you doing with that tail? Wait! No! Stop stroking me, dang it!"

"I thought you liked it when I did this?"

"I do, but you need to at least give me time to emotionally prepare myself!"

"Sorry, Beloved, but my patience isn't going to let me wait anymore. Now, then, let's enjoy ourselves, ufufufu."

"Gya! Li—no! I'm not ready yet! Please! Lilian! Stop! Iyahn!"

Kevin's unmanly screams echoed down the hall.

***

Her blade was an extension of her arms. The constant shifting of her feet was a beautiful dance. Kotohime never stayed in one place for long, not even a tenth of a second. She was moving continuously, dancing an infinite dance within a storm of needles. Her blade lashed out against a countless barrage. A seemingly infinite number of attacks were defended against with an equally uncountable number of sword strokes.

The attacks suddenly ceased. Kotohime stood in an expanding puddle of water.

"H-how were you able to defend yourself against so many needles?!" a disembodied voice shouted.

She breathed in. Then she breathed out. The tension in her arms left. Kotohime looked around the room, her eyes sharper than the blade she wielded.

"While that attack was indeed troublesome, it has several major weaknesses. As someone whose body has been adapted to high-speed movements, defeating such a technique is well within my capabilities. That aside, you seem to have forgotten that I, too, am a kitsune capable of controlling water."

"That shouldn't matter! River Kitsune aren't able to control saltwater!"

Kotohime said nothing. She shifted her stance, sliding her right foot forward and bending it at the knee, and moving her left foot backwards. She raised her blade next to her head, the tip pointed at the wall in front of her. The blade was covered in water, which swirled along the gleaming surface, a tiny typhoon contained along the length of a silver edge.

"Now, it is my turn."

"Ougi."

"Water Art: Tsukuyomi's Typhoon."

Spinning on a dime, Kotohime made a full 360-degree rotation. Just as quickly as the spinning started, it stopped. She then thrust the blade forward, and from the tip, a powerful tornado of wind and water erupted.

There was a loud scream. Water flew everywhere, and a four-tailed kitsune appeared within the blast, flying backwards as her attack slammed into him. He crashed into the wall, which crumbled against her technique, throwing her opponent into the world outside as the tornado continued moving. It didn't disperse until the enemy kitsune struck the wall of a building on the other side of the street, which also crumbled underneath her technique's power, burying him in a pile of rubble.

Kotohime calmly stepped outside. She stopped several feet from the rubble and waited. One second passed. Then two. Nothing happened.

Her eyes narrowed. Was he truly dead, or was he playing possum? After several seconds of waiting and nothing happening, she shrugged and turned around.

"Water Art: Water Combustion."

Faster than quicksilver, Kotohime spun around and interposed her katana between herself and the explosion of water. The water made contact with her blade and was split in half, the two halves traveling behind her to strike the building she'd come from, demolishing more of the wall.

She looked around and spotted her quarry. The kitsune she'd nearly killed was limping away, trying to escape—a prudent course of action, but one that she was not willing to allow. This was one of the people who'd killed Lilian and Kevin. He would die this night.

"Water Art: Blade Extension."

The technique she used was simple. As the name suggested, it extended her katana's length by gathering moisture from the air and compressing the water along her katana, thereby extending the blade's length. If she wanted, she could extend that length indefinitely, provided she had enough youki.

The blade extended within seconds, piercing her opponent through the back, right where his heart was. The kitsune, skewered on her extended blade of water, died instantly—or so she thought.

Dark eyes widened when the kitsune on her blade dematerialized, and a vortex composed entirely of water appeared in the fox's place.

"That's—!"

She couldn't say any more as the tip of a blade composed entirely of water pierced her through the back, right where her heart was.

***

Neither kitsune could understand what happened. One second they had her. Kiara had been dead to rights. The next, an explosion of energy burst from her body, encasing her in youki so thick and potent that it bent the air and became visible. The tridents that had been heading towards her were destroyed, splattering against the ethereal red flames that covered her body.

Kiara stared at her foes.

She was grinning.

One of the kitsune took a frightened step back. "H-how…?"

"How did I break out of your little trap?" Kiara finished his question, her grin widening to reveal razor-sharp canines. "It's pretty simple, really. Once I saw the two-tails over there, I realized what was happening. You didn't cast an illusion to make me think I was being choked to death. It was a water technique, and you weren't even the one casting it." She pointed at the two-tailed kitsune who stood off to the side, gawking like an idiot. "He was."

The two kitsune were stunned. Kiara was on a roll.

"I'm guessing you led me to this place in order to trap me," she continued, enjoying the fear in their eyes. "You had the two-tails hide behind an illusion, and then you launched a standard attack, knowing that it wouldn't do much. That technique was actually done to set up the two-tailed kitsune's technique, which I'm guessing was to block my esophagus with water. After that, you decided to make extra sure I wouldn't survive by launching those tridents at me."

"How… huh… what…?"

The four-tails was pretty much struck dumb by this point.

"It was a good idea," Kiara admitted. "Had I been anyone else, it probably would have worked. Unfortunately for you, I've been sparring with a River Kitsune for a while now. The moment I saw your friend, I knew what was happening. It didn't take much to evaporate the water clogging my throat with my own youki. After that, it was just a matter of overpowering your technique with an even more powerful attack. Now, then…"

Kiara brought her only remaining hand into a standard Muay Thai guard position—at least, it would have been if she still had two hands.

"Let's begin this battle for real." Her vicious grin caused the two foxes to quake in fear. "This party's just getting started."

***

Kevin and Lilian were led to a garage by Kyle, where they were forced into a car, which was then driven out of the garage.

It had only been fifteen minutes since they started driving, and Kevin already wanted to get out. They were speeding down the street. Buildings, cars, and people passed by in blurs. The car skidded along the ground with every turn Kyle made. The kappa didn't even bother slowing down as he cranked on the wheel. Kevin was surprised they didn't have a horde of cops on their tail.

In an effort to take his mind off Kyle's reckless driving, Kevin tried to make conversation.

"So, Kyle the Kappa—"

"Don't call me that!"

"—How come you can drive?"

"What the hell is that supposed to mean?" Kyle nearly growled.

"Ah! No. I didn't mean anything by it." Kevin was quick to reassure the kappa that he wasn't trying to be insulting. "I'm just surprised that a kappa knows how to drive."

Obviously, he failed.

"Are you saying I'm too stupid to drive or something?"

"No, I'm just saying that I didn't think kappa would care for driving because you guys are, you know, yōkai."

Sure, Kiara drove, but he thought of that woman as a human who just so happened to have a tail. And floppy dog ears. And youki. And she could kill him with a flick of her fingers…

Right, so maybe he did see Kiara as a yōkai, but she owned the largest chain of fitness centers in the world. She needed to drive if she wanted to get anywhere.

"That's a very racist thing to say, Kevin," Lilian responded to her beloved's words before the kappa could. "A lot of yōkai live in human society. Naturally, yōkai like Kyle the Kappa and his clan have been forced to adapt to human ways in order to survive in this ever-changing world."

"Listen to your mate—and stop calling me that!"

"Get your eyes off my mate's boobs and I might."

"Tch!"

Lilian giggled and scooted closer to Kevin, both as a means of hiding her body from Kyle and because her mate's words pleased her.

"So, where are we going, exactly?" asked Kevin. He looked out the window but couldn't figure out where they were headed. Everything looked the same. The streets looked the same. The buildings looked the same. The lights looked the same. How Kyle drove with such surety was beyond him.

"We just received a report that a fight has broken out between two yōkai and those Ocean Kitsune," Kyle informed them.

"Gotcha." Kevin nodded, then asked, "and why are we going with you?"

"Because I was asked to take you two back to your resort after I check this out."

"Do you have a description of the two yōkai currently fighting the Ocean Kitsune?" Lilian asked before Kevin could respond.

Kyle nodded, even as he took a left-hand turn. The car skidded along the ground, tires squealing. Kevin's teeth rattled as he was nearly thrown from his seat. One of Lilian's tails, which had wrapped around him, kept his face from becoming a pancake on the car window.

"According to the report, the two yōkai fighting are another kitsune wearing a kimono and an inu with one-arm and wearing a business suit."

"That sounds like Kiara and Kotohime," Kevin said. Lilian nodded in agreement.

"I wonder why they're picking a fight with Ocean Kitsune," she mused.

Kevin shrugged. "Who knows?"

Kyle eventually stopped the car in a small alley, where it would hopefully go unnoticed. Kevin and Lilian exited the vehicle, grateful that they were no longer subject to Kyle's insane driving.

"Oh, ground, how I've missed thee!"

Lilian watched in amusement as her mate dropped to the ground and affectionately rubbed his cheek against the asphalt. Kyle twitched.

"My driving isn't that bad!"

"Yes, it is." Kevin didn't stop rubbing his face against the road. "You're a horrible driver, and coming from me, that says a lot about how crappy your driving is. I've ridden in a car with Kiara."

"You picking a fight?!"

"Now, now," Lilian decided to play the diplomat. "Kyle may suck at driving, but at least he got us here in one piece."

Lilian did not make a good diplomat.

Kyle growled. "Just follow me. The sooner we get this over with, the sooner I can be rid of you two."

"That's not a very nice thing to say, Kyle the Kappa."

"Seriously, stop that!"

***

Kevin and Lilian followed Kyle.

They were in a mostly abandoned part of town near the docks called Marina Del Rey. According to Kyle, this place had once been quite lively, but the kitsune who'd moved in had cast an area-wide illusion that caused humans to abandon it. The marina consisted of large buildings, parking lots, and empty docking stations.

Neither of them knew where he was leading them, but they trusted that he wasn't leading them astray. It wasn't like they had much of a choice anyway. They'd long since gotten lost in the maze of buildings, through the twists and turns that seemingly went on forever. It felt like they were traveling in circles.

It was an act of pure coincidence that they ran into someone else—a blond-haired kitsune with two tails. He turned a corner just as Kevin, Lilian, and Kyle were several feet from that same corner.

All four figures skidded to a halt. Three sets of eyes widened in recognition.

"You!" Kevin was the first to respond, pointing an accusing finger at the blond kitsune. "You're the fop who kept hitting on my mate!"

"And you're that human who thinks he's hot shit when he's really not!"

"Hey! That's rude!"

The kitsune deadpanned. "So is calling me a fop."

"Aw, whatever," Kevin dismissed the man. "You are a fop. I mean, just look at your hair."

A tick mark appeared on the kitsune's forehead. "What's wrong with my hair?"

"Nothing, nothing at all… if you're a girl, that is."

"Oh, that does it. I'm not usually one for fighting a human, but you've pissed me off, kid." The kitsune rolled up his imaginary sleeves… and then he paused. "Wait a minute. Did you say mate?"

That's when his eyes landed on Lilian in her hybrid form.

Kitsune are very vain creatures. They are naturally drawn to beauty. While what is and is not beautiful is subjective, there are some things that can be considered universally beautiful. Iris is a perfect example of this, and so is Lilian.

Kevin gained several throbbing veins on his forehead when he noticed the blond fox's lecherous gaze.

"Stop-ogling-my-mate-you-damn-pervert-kick!"

"Buaf!"

Ken was thrown backwards by Kevin's powerful double heel kick. Kevin, having used the kitsune as a springboard, flipped through the air and landed in a crouch. The two-tailed fox was not so lucky. After sailing through the air, he hit the ground. Hard.

"Urk!" Ken nearly swallowed his tongue as he slammed into the ground. He continued to tumble across the asphalt for several more feet before coming to a halt.

Kevin stood back up and clapped his hands several times, wearing an expression that epitomized satisfaction. He turned his head to look at his mate and the flabbergasted kappa.

"You just kicked a kitsune," Kyle stated the obvious.

"That I did." Kevin nodded, quite proud of himself. This was the first time he'd managed that kick without landing on his back. "You two should get going. I can handle things here."

"You sure?" Kyle appeared dubious. "You may have gotten the drop on him, but that guy is still a kitsune, and, well, you're just a human."

Two sets of cheeks puffed up simultaneously.

"Don't underestimate me! Who the hell do you think I am?" Kevin shouted, pointing at Kyle.

Don't underestimate my mate! Who the hell do you think he is?" Lilian also shouted. She was also pointing at Kyle.

The kappa looked at the two of them, his face slowly deadpanning. "You two just did that in synch."

Kevin and Lilian tilted their heads at the same time. Their expressions were almost identical. "We did?"

"Yes, you did."

The two might have responded to Kyle's words, but they were forced to scramble out of the way when a drill made of water crashed into the ground, which cracked underneath the intense pressure. They looked at the person who'd created it—Ken, once again on his feet, with blood trailing down his forehead, and his two tails writhing in furious agitation.

"Quit ignoring me!"

"Oh, right," Kevin muttered. "You're still here."

"Are you saying you forgot about me already?!"

"I'm sorry. You're just not that important."

"What?!" Ken gawked.

"That's what happens when you're a fop," Lilian added.

"Ugh."

"Yeah, nobody likes a fop," Kevin agreed.

"Gurk."

"Especially not pretty boy fops," even Kyle got in on the action.

"Shut up!" Ken growled, his cheeks almost neon red. "Shut up, shut up, shut up! I'll show you! I'll prove to all of you that I'm not a fop!"

"Only someone who's a fop would bother trying to prove that he's not a fop," Kevin chided.

"That does it!"

Water gathered in the air around Ken's left hand. Threads beaded together, congealing into a whip that extended along the ground for at least two meters.

"I'm going to kill you," he said, cracking the whip in Kevin's direction. Asphalt broke apart as it was struck. "And then I'm going to kill the kappa."

"I'd like to see you try," Kyle said, cracking his knuckles.

"Then once you're dead, I'm going to claim that girl for my own." Ken's eyes contained a gleam as he looked at Lilian and licked his lips. Lilian felt a sudden urge to bathe in lava. "I'll enjoy breaking her."

"That's not going to happen," Kevin declared. "I won't let you touch Lilian."

"What can you do?" Ken sneered. "You're just a human."

Kevin didn't bother defending human ingenuity and strength. Doing something like that would have been a waste of breath, and Ken clearly wasn't interested in listening. Instead, he set himself in his preferred fighting stance: body loose and knees slightly bent as he stood on the balls of his feet. His hands rose into a guard position that looked like a combination of boxing and karate.

Offering the kitsune a grin, Kevin goaded his soon-to-be-opponent. "Come on, then. Fight me and find out what this lowly human can do to a fop like you."

***

The four-tailed kitsune that Kotohime had been battling appeared several feet to her left, his form distorting as the water-based illusion that kept his body hidden from sight dispersed.

He walked toward the woman, smirking as she knelt on the ground, staring at the sword sticking out of her chest. It was the same water sword that she had used to try and stab him, a sword that was currently dripping with her… water?

He didn't have time to be shocked as Kotohime burst into a million crystalline droplets.

"What the…? Was that an illusion?" he asked, his eyes widening. "No, this is…"

"Water Art: Great Spear Pierces the Heavens."

Glittering like gems in the night, the ever-shifting droplets of water coalesced, merging, morphing, changing. The water became condensed, then it elongated into a spear exactly twelve feet in length. The spear, fully formed mere seconds after its creation, shot forth at supersonic speeds, impaling the four-tails in the chest—

—only for his form to evaporate like water on a scorching summer day. The weapon continued onwards, striking the ground with a ferocious roar, tearing the pavement asunder and sending chunks of rubble into the air.

Several dozen yards away, Kotohime and the man she'd been fighting reappeared.

"That was an impressive use of illusions," Kotohime complimented her adversary.

"How did you escape my technique?" the other four-tails demanded.

"You seem to forget that I, too, am a kitsune who wields water," Kotohime chided her foe. "I knew before I even extended my katana that the you that I was attacking was nothing more than an illusion. I am impressed by your skill, however. It takes a great deal of concentration to place an illusion over a technique to manipulate the space-time of water techniques like **Tsukuyomi**."

Tsukuyomi, a technique named after the moon god of Shinto religion. It worked by creating two vortexes of water that displaced the space-time continuum of other water techniques, essentially disrupting the concept of "continuity" and replacing it with the concept "water will pass through here and come out here." It wasn't a very powerful technique. It only worked against other water techniques whose youki consumption was not greater than that of the youki used to power **Tsukuyomi**. However, it still required a lot of concentration to use.

The other kitsune grimaced. Kotohime knew that she was wearing him down. She could see it in his heavy breathing and slouched posture.

That technique must have been his trump card, she reasoned.

"I suppose this is what I get for thinking something like that would work against the Blood Moon Princess."

"I do not particularly care for that title," Kotohime admitted coolly, settling herself into a basic kendo stance. "Now, since you have impressed me so much, may I know the name of the kitsune whose life I am going to take?"

The other Kitsune glared at her, but he still answered, "It's Kaine."

"Kaine," Kotohime tested the name, her nose scrunching cutely. "An odd name, but very well. Let us end this battle quickly, Kaine-san. I will be sure to make your death a painless one."

***

Blood flowed through Kiara's veins, pulsing in time to the pumping of her leg muscles. Her heart beat at an accelerated rate as adrenaline and the thrill of the hunt spurned her on.

After destroying their trap, the two kitsune had launched a simultaneous attack. She'd defeated it, of course, but that didn't matter to her two opponents. The techniques had served their purpose: a distraction that allowed them to escape. Now she was chasing them down, tracking them by scent and her acute hearing.

"Water Art: Water Spikes."

Several dozen spikes shot up from the ground, intent on impaling her. It was a localized attack, one that required precise timing and finely honed instincts to execute with accuracy. Impressive, but ultimately futile.

Kiara leapt into the air, avoiding the spikes. She channeled youki to her fist, encasing it in fiery red energy. When she reached the apex of her jump, she twisted around until her head was angled towards the ground, then she unleashed a barrage of punches. Massive bolts of energy were launched out of her fist, blasting the water spikes and much of the ground apart.

Landing back on the ground, knees bending to absorb the impact, Kiara slowly rose to her feet.

She was smirking.

"You're going to have to do better than that if you want to beat me!" she called out. Her floppy ears twitched as she tilted her head, listening. Eyes scanned their surroundings, observing the buildings that loomed over her. Her opponents were somewhere around here. All she needed was for them to make a single sound and—

There!

Kiara spun around. A large red ball of explosive energy was launched from her fist and struck the wall on the opposite side of the alley, blowing it apart. She narrowed her eyes at the blur that leapt away at the last second. Her ears twitched when the sound of feet striking pavement reached her. The sound came from her left.

She fired off two more blasts of youki at her enemies. Both were dodged. She knew this because there was no cry of pain. Her attacks struck a wall several meters away, blowing two large holes through it.

"Water Art: Transient Waterfall."

Instincts finely honed to a razor's edge warned her of impending danger. She spun around to see the incoming attack, a geyser of water barreling towards her. Kiara thrust her youki-covered hand at the technique. Red youki blitzed from her palm, taking the shape of a clawed hand that expanded to an incredible size, threatening to engulf the much smaller waterfall attack.

The waterfall passed right through her youki.

"What?!"

"Kitsune Art: Water Wave."

Her incredibly fast reaction time allowed Kiara to turn around, however, she had no time to do anything else as a rushing wave of turbulent water slammed into her and swept her off her feet.

***

After leaving Kevin to deal with the blond kitsune, Lilian followed Kyle as he turned corner after corner, past identical-looking buildings that she could have sworn she'd seen several seconds before. She was lost and worried, and she wasn't all that sure the turtle yōkai knew where he was going.

"Do you even know where you're going?" she asked.

"Of course I do," Kyle grunted, sounding insulted that she'd question his sense of direction. He turned another corner. Lilian followed. "I've been here hundreds of times before. This place used to belong to our family before the Ocean Kitsune stole it from us."

"So you say, but it seems to me like we're lost."

"We're not lost."

"We're going around in circles. How is that not lost?"

"We're not going around in circles! We're—"

Kyle said no more, not because he had no more to say, but because something slammed into him from above—a figure clad in a black cloak. Lilian stared in undisguised shock at the person who'd just landed on Kyle's head.

"You!"

"Nya, I knew you were alive," the woman's words were a sharp purr. It was an odd noise, to be sure, but Lilian didn't have time to dwell on it.

Lilian threw herself backwards, feet sliding along the asphalt. This allowed her to avoid having the woman's claws carve bloody furrows in her chest. Red hair whipped about her body as she moved, the woman following close on her heels.

She continued to move backwards. At the same time, two balls of light flared to life on the tips of her tails. They were not flung forward. The tails curved around her body, the tips touching in front of her chest. The orbs combined into a single large orb, which swelled to the size of a basketball before another layer of golden light encased it.

"Celestial Art: Celestial Cannon."

The **Celestial Cannon** was an attack of Lilian's own making. First, she created a large light sphere, then she encased the sphere within a shell made from a thin layer of youki. After that, she created an opening in the shell, through which the celestial energy shot out as a beam of destructive light. She'd created this technique based on the attack that she'd used to defeat Chris over half a year ago.

A beam of light the size of her fist burst from the sphere. As it was released, the beam expanded, growing larger at an exponential rate. Before long, it had become even larger than the woman it flew toward.

"Nya."

With feline-like grace, the cloaked woman moved, avoiding the beam, which slammed into a brick wall several yards away. The wall wasn't capable of withstanding the attack. It exploded and sent hundreds of fragments flying everywhere.

Lilian gritted her teeth. She knew that it was foolish to have expected her attack to hit. This woman was clearly a trained assassin. Avoiding an attack like **Celestial Cannon**, which could only move linearly, was easy for someone like that.

The cloaked woman looked at the damage that Lilian's attack had wrought, then whistled. "Nya, that was impressive." She turned back to Lilian. "It looks like I might have to actually take you seriously."

As the woman shifted into an unusually animalistic fighting stance, back hunched, knees bent, and claws positioned in front of her, Lilian slid her feet shoulder-width apart and tried not to show how nervous she felt. This was her first battle since Kiara, and it was against someone who clearly knew how to fight. It was not a good combination, as far as she was concerned.

Beloved, she thought as the cloaked woman launched herself at Lilian. *Please hurry up. I'm going to need your help.*

CHAPTER 9

Of Water, Illusions, and Light

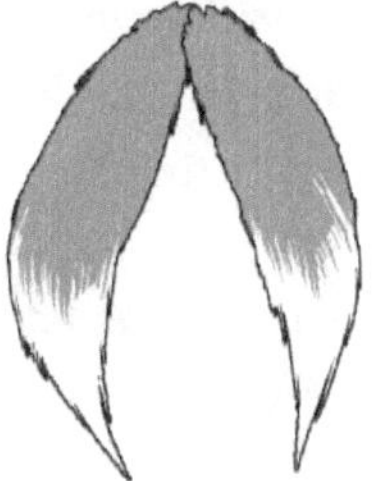

KIARA WAS HAVING PROBLEMS.

It had nothing to do with the strength of her opponents. Even together, they did not have the strength to match her. Four plus two did not equal six as far as kitsune power levels went. She had more youki, more strength, more power, and more experience than both of them combined. However, Kiara had forgotten something about kitsune and how they fought, something that had slipped her mind because of Kotohime's straightforward style of combat.

Kitsune specialized in illusions.

It was so simple, a fact of life, yet it was so easily forgettable. Kotohime never used illusions in combat. She relied mostly on her katana. When faced with something that her katana couldn't cut through, she used the specialized techniques granted to her by her River blood, and when those failed, she brought out the big guns. Illusions were not something that her friend used, and so, Kiara had no idea how to fight against someone who did use them.

"Water Art: Misty Land of Foxes."

Kiara glared into the thick fog that engulfed the area, billowing up from the ground, surrounding her on all sides. It was impossible to see through. She wondered if the kitsune she was fighting knew of her weakness.

Contrary to popular belief, dogs can, in fact, see in color. It's a common misconception that dogs can only see in black and white. However, their vision is limited and different than a human's.

A dog's vision is similar to a human with red-green color blindness, albeit there are some minor differences. Dogs are less sensitive to shades of gray than humans, and they're also only about half as sensitive to changes in brightness levels. Dogs are also nearsighted to boot.

It was the inability to distinguish between shades of gray that hampered her vision now. Her eyes simply couldn't perceive any shifts within this seemingly colorless void.

Fortunately, being an inu, she didn't need to rely on her eyes.

"Water Art: Fire Hydrant."

The roar of rushing water alerted her to an attack from behind. She swiped at the sound, her hair whipping around her as she spun about. Her timing was flawless. Her claw clashed with the water, which exploded on contact, spraying everywhere. Oddly enough, while water splattered all over the place with impunity, Kiara did not get wet. Even her clothing remained dry.

"Water Art: Kraken's Mouth."

Before Kiara could react, the water that had formed a puddle around her feet rose and morphed into six slithering tentacles, which wrapped around her legs and only remaining arm. The tentacles then constricted, pulling her body toward the ground as, all around her, water rose up like the jaws of some apex predator of the ocean.

"Don't think such a weak attack will be enough to defeat me!"

With little fanfare, Kiara's power burst free from its constraints. Unlike kitsune, who needed to channel youki through their tails and then shape it into a technique, inu had no such need—mainly because they did not have any techniques. All they had was power. Pure. Raw. Unfiltered power.

Her youki flared, the aura of her impressive energy becoming visible, bursting from her body with the vengeful wrath of a mighty storm, an unending, unbending tempest of unrestrained force. The tentacles that held her evaporated, and the watery jaws that sought to consume her were blown away. The power of Kiara's youki was such that even the cloying fog bowed before it, dispersing to the four winds.

She could only see one of them as the mist vanished. It was the younger kitsune, the one who'd tried to suffocate her with water. He stood there, his two tails swaying from side to side, lashing out in an agitated manner. His stunned expression caused her to grin.

"Let's see you escape from this!" she shouted before channeling youki to her mouth. There was no molding involved. She simply infused her youki into her mouth. Then she released it.

The gust that followed was much like the one that Lilian had nearly been caught in during their battle. It passed over the earth, tearing the ground apart. Large chunks of asphalt were ripped asunder, flying into the air, joining the maelstrom which eventually struck the hapless kitsune.

The kitsune became mist. The mist vanished. Kiara clicked her tongue.

"Another illusion."

That's what she hated about fighting against kitsune. Most of them preferred using stealth tactics. They'd bombard you with illusions and hit you with specialized techniques when you were distracted. It was a good strategy that worked well against stronger opponents, but damn if it didn't steal most of the fun out of fighting.

She searched for her opponents, but she could see nothing beyond buildings and road and rubble. Had they escaped? No, she could still smell them. They were near, but she couldn't pinpoint them. Their scent was everywhere. An illusion had probably been woven over their scent to confuse her.

She ignored her sense of smell and sight, and instead, she focused on her hearing. Her acute sense of hearing allowed her to pick up everything around her; the hum of generators within the buildings rumbled in her eardrums; the sounds of cars driving and honking in the distance provided a most annoying rhythm to the world around her; the sound of waves lapping against the dock would have been soothing under different circumstances. Now, where was…

There!

Footsteps echoed to her left.

Kiara turned, hyperextending her hand in a knife-edged strike. A crescent wave of youki shot from it, blasting across the street at breakneck speeds. There was a grunt of pain, followed by blood spattering against the ground. Something blurry appeared in front of her. Water sloshed off a figure, which revealed itself to be the four-tailed kitsune. A gaping hole could be seen in his chest.

The kitsune stumbled. He raised a hand to the hole. Disbelieving eyes stared at the wound as if he couldn't comprehend what had just happened. He looked up and met her gaze before his eyes glazed over, then he fell backwards with a dull thud, his head cracking against pavement.

Then his body turned into water.

It took Kiara several seconds to realize that she'd been duped by another illusion. The body was gone, the blood was gone, and all that remained was a puddle of water. She could no longer detect their presence. Even their scent had vanished.

Sighing, she lifted her only remaining hand and scratched the back of her neck.

"This is why I hate fighting against kitsune. Damn cowards."

***

Like most kitsune, Lilian had never been much of a fighter. She might love watching anime and reading manga, which usually featured people clashing in climactic battles of epic proportions, but that didn't mean she had a lot of fighting experience.

This fact became blatantly obvious as Lilian was forced into combat against her strange assailant. She'd tried everything in her arsenal, but none of it worked. Her celestial techniques were all avoided by limber and graceful movements. What's worse was that she knew this woman was just toying with her, like a cat toying with a mouse.

She'd dispelled her technique, **Celestial Art: Orbs of an Evanescent Realm**, when it became clear that it wasn't working. Most of the time, her spheres were dodged, and when her enemy couldn't dodge them, they were swatted away with contemptuous ease. More importantly, Lilian could only control three orbs at a time. She had neither the training nor the concentration required to control more.

As the six orbs surrounding her body were dispelled, the graceful assassin shot forward almost too quickly for her to track.

She's so fast!

Lilian pumped as much youki through her body as she dared and sent it into her legs. She sped backwards, avoiding the heel drop that would have pounded her into the ground. She eyed the indent left by the foot warily. Abrasions had appeared along the asphalt, proof of the woman's strength.

"Who are you?" Lilian demanded. "Why do you keep attacking me?"

Surprisingly, the woman answered her.

"Nya, like I said before, it's nothing personal…" She trailed off, then rescinded her previous statement. "Actually, I take that back. It wasn't personal, until you decided to be stupid and nearly got Kevin killed, nya."

"What does Kevin have to do with this?" The gears in Lilian's mind turned. "You… who are you?" she asked, subtly casting an illusion over the woman.

"Who I am doesn't matter, nya." The woman's solemn declaration was ruined by her strange catchphrase. "All that matters is that I've been contracted to kill you, so that's what I'm going to do." She paused. "And don't try to cast those pathetic illusions on me. They won't work."

"How did you…?" Lilian feigned surprised.

"I may not be a kitsune, and I may not be good at casting illusions, but I know how to dispel them." The woman set herself into a loose fighting stance. "Now, let's try this again, nya."

Gasping at the speed with which her opponent charged her, Lilian sidestepped to the left, her torso bending backwards as she dodged a viciously slashing claw. She created a bridge with her torso, her hands and feet firmly planted on the ground. She then pushed off with her feet, which forced her attacker back, lest the cloaked woman receive a kick to the chin.

Completing her maneuver, Lilian landed back on her feet and was just in time to be met with a flurry of swift punches. She moved as quickly as kitsune-ly possible, using the basic defensive style taught to her back when she'd still lived in the Pnéyma compound in Greece. Most of the mysterious woman's attacks consisted of jabs and claw swipes—an unusual combination, but undeniably effective. Lilian had no time to think, only react.

Lilian stumbled as the air in front of her was displaced by something moving at high speeds. She moved faster than she ever had before and was able to avoid the black blur that struck the ground. She tried to see what it was, but the object retracted into the woman's cloak too quickly for her eyes to follow.

Two short steps brought the mysterious woman into her guard. Lilian swiftly moved her left hand, even as she twisted her body to the right, deflecting a thrusting claw that would have stabbed her through the chest. Her feet slid across the asphalt, body spinning. Ducking underneath a claw swipe at the last second, Lilian grimaced when she felt several strands of hair get sliced off her scalp. She moved back to try and put some distance between them, but her foe clung to her doggedly, refusing to give her a space modicum.

Lilian's back was soon pressed against a wall as the woman thrust another clawed hand at her, too fast for her to dodge. All she could do was block. Lilian lifted an arm to defend against the clawed hand, but even reinforcing her skin as she was, the claws still penetrated her flesh.

"G-geh!" Lilian gasped as fire lit up her forearm. She could see them, the four claws that were firmly embedded into her arm. Blood leaked down her skin, running along her forearm and dripping onto the ground. Her attacker applied pressure to her arm. Lilian groaned and whimpered as she was forced to a knee.

"Nya, it looks like you managed to block my attack."

Lilian bit her lip, more to keep from crying out as the woman twisted her claws than for any other reason.

"Ha…" Her enemy, her face still hidden beneath the cowl of her hood, sighed. She sounded almost euphoric. "This is the end for you, nya."

"You'd think so, wouldn't you?"

"Eh?"

Bright yellow eyes widened as the girl in front of her, along with the blood on the ground, vanished. Those same eyes blinked when the cloaked woman realized that her hand was embedded deeply within a wall and not someone's flesh.

"Wha… an illusion? Impossible!"

"Celestial Art: Celestial Cannon."

Again, a large orb of golden youki appeared at the tips of Lilian's tails. A beam shot from the orb and engulfed the woman, the wall, and even the room beyond. Lilian shoved as much youki into the attack as she could, despite knowing that it would exhaust her. She wanted to make sure this assassin couldn't try to kill her anymore.

As the adrenaline left her system, Lilian slouched. Her raspy breathing grated harshly in her ears, and her tails hung limply, as if expressing that they were also tired from having released so much youki.

"There…" she gasped, sweat pouring down her face. "There's no way she could have survived that."

"You think so, nya?"

That voice…

Lilian froze. No. No, no, no, no, no, no! It couldn't be. There was no way… absolutely no way she could have survived that. Even a kitsune with three tails would have been annihilated by a technique of that caliber!

"You really surprised me with that last attack," the voice continued. Lilian shuddered, her mind trying to deny what her ears were registering. "I didn't think a kitsune with just two tails would be capable of an attack like that, nya. And to layer two illusions on top of each other without me even noticing it… clearly, I've underestimated you."

Lilian turned around, her breath catching in her throat. Before her stood a woman. Black hair had been woven into an artful series of braids that clung to the back of her head, held in place by a large pink ribbon. She wore a black latex bodysuit that clung to her like a second skin, conforming to her lithe yet voluptuous curves. Some of her clothing was gone, small patches had been burnt off by Lilian's **Celestial Cannon**, showing that she had not escaped the attack unscathed. Still, the fact that she was still alive sent shivers down Lilian's spine. Two long, thin black tails swayed behind her, and a pair of triangular ears twitched on her head.

"Nekomata…" Lilian breathed, struck by terror and despair.

"That's right." Bright yellow eyes stared at her, glinting like the edge of a razor blade. "I'm a nekomata, nya, and I've come to send your soul to the Shinigami."

***

Their fighting styles couldn't have been more different.

Kotohime realized this from the onset of their battle. Where she preferred close-range combat and sword techniques, her opponent had a predisposition towards illusions and long-range attacks. These he used to gain distance in order to weave his specialized techniques. He seemed to favor visual illusions rather than ones that messed with depth perception, hearing, or a person's coordination.

The pavement around her cracked and three geysers of water crested the air. The water undulated before each geyser morphed into something long and serpentine: dragons. The monsters stared down at her. Roars, mighty and powerful, erupted from their mouths before they descended upon her like ravenous beasts.

Kotohime sighed.

Then she dispelled the illusion. The dragons disappeared; the cracked ground became mostly pristine again, with only the pockmarks and furrows left from attacks made by her katana and her opponent's techniques showing.

"Kitsune Art: Hydro Cannon."

Kotohime turned around quickly. She slid her left foot forward and her right foot back, stabilizing her position. Her sheath remained in her left hand, the katana inside, and her right hand was on the hilt. In a classic use of battoujutsu, she smoothly slid the blade from its sheath, the hiss of steel inaudible over the sounds of rushing water, and sliced the water beam flying at her in half.

"Ikken Hissatsu. Ougi."

As if a tornado underneath her feet was driving her forward, Kotohime flew across the space that separated her from Kaine. Her katana, already released from its sheath, flashed once, twice, three times in quick succession—or so it seemed at first. It was only after nine silvery lines of light appeared on Kaine's body, crisscrossing along his skin and clothes, that it became obvious that the number of strikes she'd committed were three times the number of flashes seen.

Unfortunately, Kaine proved to be just another illusion, having replaced himself at the very last second after using the water variation of the speed technique: **Chiratsuki.**

"Your sense of timing is impeccable," Kotohime complimented as she regarded her surroundings. She could not sense any fluctuations in youki, nor could she sense any foreign youki in her body, meaning her opponent had not attacked her with an illusion after escaping from her blade.

"And your talents with a blade are just as unmatched as I've been led to believe. You truly earn your title of Blood Moon Princess."

Kotohime grimaced. She did not enjoy the title that kitsune and the other yōkai had given her.

"I really wish you wouldn't call me that."

"Why would I call you anything other than what you are?" the man asked, sounding almost condescending. "Everyone knows of what you've done, of the countless lives claimed by your blade. Blood Moon Princess is a name that suits you quite well. Or, perhaps you would like me to call you the Crimson Princess of the Ōnami Clan?"

Kotohime's lips became a flat line. "I suggest you cease speaking of things that you know nothing about."

"Oh, I know plenty. For example, I know that around one hundred years ago, you fell in love with a human."

"Stop it."

"And I also know that that human ended up getting killed when you—"

"I said stop it! **Gekido, Tsukiyomi-no-Mikoto!**"

It would have been inaccurate to say that Kotohime's blade moved, for the term implied that movement was visible, that it could be perceived. Similar in many ways to the question, "If a tree falls in a forest and nobody's around to hear it, does it make a sound?" As stated by the possibility of unperceived existence, the act of

Kotohime moving her blade from one position to another could have been stated as, "If a blade moves but no one sees it happening, does that mean the blade did not move at all?" While the idea sounded ludicrous, it was enough to give an idea of how fast she moved.

At the same time that Kotohime swung her katana, she spun around in a full rotation. When she stopped, her blade was in the same place it started before she began to spin, with the tip pointed at the ground in front of her feet. There was a moment of silence. Everything stood still, as if the world itself was waiting with bated breath.

Then it happened.

It was like something out of a natural disaster movie, like a documentary that showed the effects of devastating earthquakes and level five hurricanes. The ground around Kotohime exploded. The air around her reverberated as a powerful supersonic shock wave burst across the airspace. A ripple effect spread along the pavement, upheaving large chunks of asphalt, launching debris in every direction. The "ripple" spread at least one hundred yards outward from where Kotohime stood, and the large pieces of rubble flew even farther.

Several buildings in the immediate vicinity collapsed when the devastating shockwave crashed into them. The buildings wavered before literally falling in on themselves, like a stack of cards or a tower of Jenga blocks that were no longer capable of holding their own weight. The structures were shaken apart, until they were nothing but a pile of rubble.

This was Kotohime's second most devastating technique: **Gekido, Tsukiyomi-no-Mikoto. Wrath of the Moon God.**

When the technique ended, the vicinity in which Kotohime's battle took place looked less like a warzone and more like something out of an epic fantasy battle. She stood on a raised platform in the center of a massive crater at least fifty feet in circumference and twenty feet deep. The platform she stood on, a perfect circle with

completely smooth edges, was the only piece of flat land left in the vicinity. Everything else had been destroyed.

She took a deep breath, then released it. Looking around, Kotohime surveyed her damaged surroundings. She could not detect Kaine's youki anymore. Was he dead, or had he escaped?

Within the stillness caused by the aftermath of her devastating technique, Kotohime could only conclude that, whether her foe had died or not, this battle was over.

***

Kevin decided to start the battle cautiously. He knew nothing of his opponent, other than the fact that Blondie was an Ocean Kitsune.

Ocean Kitsune were kitsune who could only use saltwater for their techniques, which explained why they always chose to live near the ocean. Having never met an Ocean Kitsune before, Kevin didn't know much about them, but he'd been told enough by Kotohime to be wary.

Of course, most of Kevin's attention was focused not on trying to learn more about his opponent, but on dodging the whip that his enemy used. Fortunately, avoiding the incoming weapon was easy—too easy.

Kevin had become used to fighting people who beat the crap out of him on a daily basis. He'd spent over seven months sparring with people who were faster, stronger, more experienced, and just plain better than he was.

This person, this kitsune, was none of those. He moved slowly. Each swing of his whip was drawn back with obvious intent. Even if his swings hadn't been so ridiculously slow, Kevin would have still been able to dodge them with ease.

Because Kevin could see. He could see the minute twitching of muscles that told him where the attacks would land, and notice where the kitsune's blue eyes flickered to as he planned to attack. This fox just did not have the mentality of a fighter.

Kevin sidestepped an attack, going left, though his movements looked sluggish and awkward. The liquid weapon left an indent in the pavement. For something made of water, it was surprisingly strong.

"Hold still you!" Ken snarled.

"You can't honestly expect me to stay in one place and let you hit me, can you?" Kevin fired back, even as he clumsily danced away from the water whip. "That's just stupid. No one's going to stand around and let you beat them to death. Are you an idiot?"

"You're the idiot!"

Ken attacked with increasing fury. However, while this made his strikes stronger, it also made them sloppier. They were even easier to dodge.

Kevin had seen enough. His opponent was riled up good, and he knew plenty about how the fox moved. It was time to close the distance.

He stopped moving like a drunken sailor, then put on a burst of admittedly impressive speed and dashed straight at his opponent in a full-on frontal assault.

The two-tailed kitsune's eyes widened. The whip in his hand dissolved, and his tails curved around his body to point at Kevin. Water gathered at the tips, forming a sphere similar to Lilian's light spheres only, well, it was made of water.

It was only one sphere. Kevin remembered what Lilian had told him, about how most kitsune with two tails didn't have many specialized techniques. They lacked the youki and control necessary to use them. Lilian could use them, but that was because her celestial affinity was off the charts. This kitsune's affinity for water was unlikely to be anywhere near as high.

"Water Art: Water Sphere!"

Kevin threw himself into a shoulder roll, wincing as his shoulder was jarred against the ground. The attack flew over his head and splattered against the wall behind him. Another sphere formed on the tip of Ken's left-most tail. Kevin leapt back onto his feet and moved right, allowing the sphere to travel past him. Then he was within his opponent's guard.

His first attack consisted of a swift double-punch. The fox tried to block it, but he was clearly no fighter, and both fists slipped through his guard. Two jabs to the kitsune's solar plexus left the fox winded. While Ken was reeling backwards, Kevin set himself up for another attack.

When Kevin had told Kiara about the style that he wanted to create, she'd said that his fighting style was, *"reckless at worst and suicidal at best."* She'd then given him a thumbs-up, grinned, and said, *"I approve."*

Unfortunately, his fighting style was not complete yet. He'd been working on it for seven months, but it was still nowhere near ready. It was unlikely to be finished for another few years.

The style that he used in the meantime consisted of moving about like an awkward and clumsy fool, riling up his opponents so they wouldn't be able to think straight, then blitzing them with attacks that took them out of the fight before they could recover. It didn't work when fighting multiple opponents, or when facing someone with more experience, but against an inexperienced two-tails, it would do.

Kevin dashed again into his opponent's guard. Then he turned sideways, presenting his profile to the kitsune. Bending his knees as he brought up his hands, Kevin put his right fist into his left palm, then pointed his right elbow at his foe's stomach. He then used his new position to generate more force, shoving his elbow into Ken's gut.

The kitsune doubled over, the expulsion of air quite loud. Kevin saw that Ken's head was almost directly above his own.

Grinning, he leapt up, slamming the crown of his head into the blond's jaw.

"Gah!" a cry of pain escaped the surprised Ken's mouth. He stumbled backwards, blood dripping down his chin. A shaking hand rose to his mouth, which came away stained in crimson. "This is blood! My blood! I'm bleeding!"

Kevin would have rolled his eyes, but he was already preparing his next attack: a flurry of punches that knocked Ken for a loop. Straights, jabs, hooks, and curves were thrown with equal ferocity. Each fist that hit echoed loudly in the solitude of the night, sounding like the distant rumbling of thunder. Kevin's fox-eared opponent jerked back every time a fist slammed into him.

Noticing the way his opponent's eyes had glazed over, Kevin decided that it was time to finish this. He lowered his body until his knees were almost touching the floor, turning around at the same time to present his back to Ken. He placed his hands firmly against the ground, fingers splayed wide for better stability. Then he kicked his feet into the air, the muscles in his arms, chest, and shoulders straining to keep his lower half elevated. Folding his legs until his knees touched his chest, Kevin prepared for the only move in his arsenal that had a cool name.

"Double Helix Drive!"

The Double Helix Drive was nothing special. It was, in essence, a mule kick using the ground as a means of putting more power into his attack. Really, there were only two reasons this name worked and didn't sound like a child's presumptuous attempt at sounding cool.

First: the name really was a surprisingly good attempt for Kevin, whose aptitude for naming things sucked.

Second: Kevin's legs were really, REALLY strong.

It was like a shotgun going off at point-blank range. Ken's eyes went impossibly wide as his entire body was launched up and away from Kevin. The kitsune made an almost graceful parabolic arc as he soared at least fifteen feet into the air, mouth open in a silent scream of agony, right up until the point where he smashed into the ground with an almost sickening crack.

He didn't get back up.

Kevin climbed to his feet and walked over to the downed fox-man. A glance revealed that the blond's eyes were rolled up into the back of his head, and his mouth was still open, as if to emphasize the overwhelming pain he'd felt before being rendered unconscious.

"Huh?" Confused, Kevin reached up with his right hand to massage his left shoulder. It felt kind of stiff. "Is that it?"

Perhaps it was because the last time he'd fought a kitsune, he'd nearly died, but he somehow expected a more difficult fight. This had been almost like fighting against a human, albeit one who could control water to an extent.

This is... weird. I didn't think I'd lose, but I never expected to win so easily.

Shaking his head, Kevin decided not to look a gift horse in the mouth. He needed to meet back up with Lilian and Kyle.

As Kevin began moving, he stumbled and almost fell flat on his face when the earth started to shake.

"What the heck?!" he shouted, his voice lost as several buildings a dozen yards from his position collapsed.

***

From the moment she realized that the assassin was a nekomata, nothing had been going right for Lilian. Every attack sent her way came within a hairbreadth of killing her. Several times she'd nearly been skewered by the sharp claws of her opponent. The only reason that she hadn't died yet was because of all the times she'd watched Kevin spar.

It was almost strange, but watching Kevin spar had given her a slight edge in combat. With all of the fighting she'd seen, Lilian had picked up the ability to notice the ebb and flow of battle. While nowhere near as talented as her mate, her observative mind still managed to pick up the nuances about a person that most people would miss: The twitching of muscles that signified an attack, the shifting of eyes that let her know where the attack would be aimed at. It was this ability that kept her from being outright killed.

That, and her skill with illusions.

"Nya! Hold still!"

The nekomata hissed as she once again struck air. She ran straight through the image of what she'd assumed was Lilian, but what was, in actuality, a simple illusion.

Bending the light around her to render herself invisible and dancing away when the nekomata struck her illusion, Lilian panted for breath. Once she was a safe distance away, she let the two techniques, the illusion and her invisibility technique, **Chameleon Masquerade**, fade. While she would have preferred to keep them going, she needed to conserve her youki. Her reserves were already low.

She didn't try to attack the cat-woman, even though the other yōkai's back was turned. Lilian had learned her lesson the first time she'd attempted to launch a sneak attack from behind. Even now, the four claw marks on her arm, where she'd been hit by the woman's sharp claws, bled freely.

Her decision not to undertake another attempt at striking the woman from behind turned out to be a blessing. The nekomata's tail suddenly caught fire. It was not regular fire, or even kitsune fire. This was a dark purple flame. Hellfire. The fire that only those who have a connection to the underworld could use. Spirit Kitsune could conjure Hellfire, but Lilian was not a Spirit Kitsune.

Lilian had seen Hellfire several times in the past, while watching some of her cousins, aunts, and uncles train. Yet no matter how many times she saw it, the sight never failed to make her shiver in fear.

Those flames which screamed with the voices of a thousand tormented souls, they were conjured by plucking the lives of those who had perished and could not find their way to the *Sanzu River*. Those flames which stole the souls of those they engulfed, sending them to the underworld, they were cold, chilling those that touched them as opposed to burning them. While not as frightening as Void Fire, which erased one's very existence, Hellfire was still something to be feared.

As if the Hellfire had a mind of its own, it leapt from the nekomata's tail, and Lilian had no choice but to use a quick burst of reinforcement, pumping as much youki to her legs as she dared and running away. Times like these made her wish she knew **Celestial Transportation,** the speed technique of Celestial Kitsune—too bad that required at least four tails to use.

Using the strength granted to her through reinforcement, Lilian leapt onto the roof of the nearest building. The flames followed, not even bothered by the shift in elevation. Hellfire burst up in a pillar of colossal flames, a sweeping blaze of pure destruction, and not just from the side that she'd run up—no, the Hellfire surrounded the entire building, a wall of dark purple fire that trapped Lilian like a rat in a cage.

The flames descended upon her like a ravenous beast. Within the mighty conflagration, the faces of the lost souls that had been used to fuel it screamed in torment and rage, cursing the futility of their despair. Despite not wanting to show cowardice, Lilian clenched her eyes shut, unable to watch her death closing in.

"Water Art: Mighty Waterfall."

Over the roar of the flame came another sound: that of rushing water. Lilian looked up just in time to see an incredible sight. Hundreds of gallons of water hovered above the flames, swirling like a tornado. The water struck the Hellfire. Steam exploded everywhere, blinding her for a moment before her sight returned.

The fire was gone.

Lilian rushed over to the ledge where she found the kappa, Kyle, standing several feet from the building that she stood on, arms outstretched, gasping for breath. He must have been the one to save her, and it looked like he'd used a lot of youki to do so. That had been a big technique.

"Nya, so you woke up." The nekomata didn't seem pleased by this new development. She stood on another building adjacent to Lilian's. "I had hoped you would stay asleep. There's no profit in killing you."

Kyle clicked his tongue. "I'm the one who brought her and Kevin here, so that makes them both my responsibility. I can't let you kill one of them while they're under my watch."

"Nya, that's admirable and everything, but you really should think this through more carefully, nya." The cat pointed at him. "Look at you. You're obviously quite young, which explains why that technique took so much out of you. I doubt you have enough youki to do that again, nya." Dark purple flames suddenly flared to life on her tails. "I, however, am more than capable of conjuring more Hellfire, nya."

Lilian jumped off the building, knees bending to cushion her fall, and joined the kappa in confronting the nekomata assassin.

"It doesn't matter," Kyle said. "I can't just walk away from my responsibility, and this girl and her mate are my responsibility until I see them safely home."

"You see that, nya? That's why those kitsune you're fighting are winning. Your need to follow protocols and niceties keeps you from doing what needs to be done, nya."

"I don't wanna hear that from an assassin!" Kyle shouted.

A massive shockwave slammed into them before the nekomata could respond.

***

"Whoa!"

Kiara stumbled as the entire area was rocked to its foundations. She could see the fierce hurricane-like winds rising up in all directions, an omnidirectional maelstrom of cataclysmic energy generated by a shockwave. She knew that attack. She'd seen it before.

"Either Kotohime's opponent was more difficult to defeat than usual, or she's really pissed off," Kiara observed. "Well, at least now I know where she is."

Using her incredible leg strength, Kiara hopped from roof to roof. She needed to meet up with Kotohime so they could figure out what to do next.

***

Lilian was able to remain upright by spearing her reinforced tails into the ground. Kyle had fallen on his face, and the nekomata had been forced to leap off the building she'd been standing on, which collapsed upon itself as the shockwave slammed into it. Realizing that she had an opportunity to attack, Lilian took it.

"Kitsune Art: Orbs of an Evanescent Realm."

Half a dozen orbs of celestial energy burst to life on the tips of her tails. Upon their creation, Lilian immediately sent three of them at the nekomata, hoping to strike the woman down before she could regain her balance. Unfortunately, the foe that she was fighting was a cat-woman, and cat-women always landed on their feet.

While she had indeed stumbled, the nekomata turned her fall into a roll. Consequently, this allowed her to dodge Lilian's first orb. The second one she avoided by taking two steps to the left, then crossing over to the right in a zigzag pattern. Bending her knees, the neko hurled herself into the air, flipping like an acrobat as the last orb soared underneath her.

Lilian sent the other three at the woman. Gritting her teeth, she focused her will on the orbs and commanded them to attack the ferocious feline while she was still airborne. This proved to be a futile maneuver, as the raven-haired nekomata spun around by generating momentum with her arms and tails. All of the orbs except one were dodged, and that orb exploded into light particles when it met a clawed hand covered in Hellfire.

"Dang it! How does she keep destroying my attacks?"

"Maybe because she's stronger than you?"

"Not another word from the peanut gallery!"

"Who're you calling a peanut gallery?!"

Lilian and Kyle were forced to take evasive action when a wave of Hellfire was launched at them. They separated, moving away from each other and forcing the flames to decide who it should go after. While not exactly sentient, the flames were created by souls, and thus, they had a sort of sense, an ability to detect life and seek it out.

They went after Lilian.

"Oooh! Dang it!"

In an effort to escape, Lilian ran between buildings. Her reserves of youki were nearing empty, she was being chased by Hellfire, and she no longer knew where Kyle was. She also didn't know how to get rid of the flames nipping at her heels. Needless to say, things were looking grim.

"Lilian!"

Her heart began to soar.

"Kevin!"

Kevin stood several feet in front of her, his feet spread wide, a determined expression etched onto his face... and was that a hose in his hands?

"Duck!"

Lilian didn't waste any time. She dropped to the ground as he turned a knob on the large hose. From the nozzle came a massive spray of water, which struck the Hellfire. The flames, as if enraged by this new problem, cried out in anger and frustration as they were pushed back.

Unfortunately for the Hellfire, the ethereal flames had lost much of its potency during the chase. What was left was easily doused by the powerful spray of the fire hydrant-sized hose.

As the flames were quenched, Lilian stood back up. She looked at Kevin, who dropped the hose and grinned at her.

"Looks like I made it just in time to—oomph!"

Lilian did not give Kevin a chance to say anymore. She leapt at him, pulling his head down to hers and sealing his lips with a kiss. Kevin didn't bother resisting. She felt his strong arms wrap tightly around her waist, pulling her close, pressing them together. Lilian loved the feeling of being in his arms.

"Thank you," Lilian breathed after the kiss ended. "You saved me."

"That I did." Kevin's smile was so bright it nearly blinded her. "Now we're even."

"Even…"

Lilian didn't know what he meant by that, but she didn't care. She kissed him again.

Time lost meaning as she lost herself in his lips and the feel of his tongue playing with hers. She could've happily stayed there for all eternity, but alas, breathing became a necessity, and there were things they needed to do. Lilian reluctantly pulled back.

"Everything okay?" Kevin asked.

"Yes." Lilian, her cheeks flushed, beamed at him. "I've never been better."

Kevin looked uncertain, but he nodded anyway. "I'm glad to hear that. I was worried when I saw those flames chasing after you. Just what the heck was that anyway? I've never seen purple fire before."

He looked behind Lilian, and she followed his gaze. The flames were gone, but everything, from the ground to the walls, was blackened and burnt beyond recognition. Some sections of walls were even crumbling, as if they'd been a cake that had been stuck in an oven for too long and become extra crispy.

"That was Hellfire," Lilian answered. Kevin looked back at the girl in his arms. "It's a type of fire that only yōkai capable of using spirit techniques can do: Ghost Kitsune, nekomata, kasha, and certain types of oni can also use them."

"So, that was a spirit attack. Dang, that's impressive. I remember Kotohime telling me about them once, but I never realized they could be so powerful."

"Yes, spirit techniques are frightening," Lilian agreed. "Anyway, we should probably find Kyle and get out of here. That woman is still around, and I don't want to—"

"Nya!! Nya, nya, nya! Oh, no!"

Kevin and Lilian quickly realized that they weren't alone. Prancing around in a strange sort of dance was the woman who'd tried to kill Lilian. Kevin, having never laid eyes on her without her entire body being covered by a cloak, raised an eyebrow.

"Lilian?"

"Yes?"

"That girl… she has cat ears."

"Indeed she does."

"She has cat ears and a tail."

"Yep."

"… I didn't know there were cat-girls in this story."

Lilian's eyes sparkled. "Of course there are. We just haven't run into any until now. This story has every type of yōkai."

"Really? Are we gonna meet them all?"

"I doubt it. Could you imagine the word count a story like that would have? Not to mention the number of volumes. I don't have faith in the author's ability to write something that long."

Oi!

"Yeah, he is kind of a crappy writer, isn't he?"

Don't say that if you can't even talk to me, damn it!

While Kevin and Lilian turned the fourth wall into a heaping pile of rubble, the cat-girl—erm, woman, continued prancing around.

"Oh, dear, nya! What do I do? Kevin is here, nya! He's here! Right here in front of me! Nya, nya, nya! Should I keep fighting? No—I mean yes! I must keep fighting!" One hand clutched at her heart while the other went to her forehead. "Oh, cruel world, how could you make me fight while in the presence of my dear master? It's just too cruel, nya! But I must press on! There is no other choice. If I cannot do this, then I'll have failed my mission, and then Mistress Sarah will be mad at me! Nya, nya, nya!"

Kevin and Lilian finally turned back to the oddball on the roof. She was making an awful lot of racket.

"So, um, Lilian, who is that girl?"

"She's the assassin."

"You mean the one who tried to kill you?"

"Um." Lilian nodded. Kevin looked at her for a second, then he looked back at the woman who was mumbling to herself, prancing around like she was doing some strange voodoo dance or something.

"What is she doing?"

"I don't know."

"L-Lilian-sama? Kevin-sama?"

At the sound of a voice calling Lilian's and Kevin's names, the nekomata made one last "nya!" before fleeing. She disappeared before Kevin or Lilian could do anything—not that they would have. They were both frozen in shock. That voice. Could it be?

They turned around.

It was. It was her. It was them. They were both there.

Kiara and Kotohime.

***

Kotohime felt like her heart had stopped. She stared at the two figures, the two faces, which were so familiar to her that they might as well have been kin.

It was Lilian. There was no mistaking it. That red hair, those green eyes, and that innocent face, a vision of splendor and loveliness. She knew those features almost as well as her own.

And the person beside her. Kevin. It couldn't have been anyone else. Tousled blond hair fell about his face. Bangs swayed in front of eyes that contained a piece of the sky. It was her charge's mate. She'd only known him for seven months, but those seven months were enough for him to have earned her respect and affection.

They were both alive. They were both safe. They were both here.

***

They stood mere feet from each other. Kiara and Kotohime, their expressions disbelieving, stood on one side. Lilian and Kevin stood on the other side. Neither group knew what to say.

"Um," Kevin broke the silence. "Hey, you two, we're, uh, we're back."

He's always had a way with words, that Kevin.

"So… so you are," Kotohime sniffled. She raised a hand and wiped away a tear before it could fall. She looked back at the two youngsters, worry clear in her eyes. "Are… are you two well? You're not hurt, are you?"

"We're fine," Lilian assured her bodyguard. "We had a bit of a rough time when that wave fell on us, but someone saved us."

"I-I see. I shall have to give the people who saved you my gratitude." The raven-haired beauty's eyes began to water. "I… you don't know how glad I am to see you safe and sound, Lilian-sama."

Tears gathered in Lilian's eyes, but she still smiled. "Thank you, Kotohime. I'm truly blessed to have someone like you in my life, mother of my heart."

That seemed to be Kotohime's breaking point. Her eyes widened. Tears began to fall. She rushed up to Lilian, pulling the girl into a fierce embrace. The maid-slash-bodyguard buried her face into her charge's hair and cried tears of relief and joy. If Lilian was surprised by Kotohime's actions, she did not show it. She wrapped her arms around the older woman and pressed her face against the voluptuous vixen's bosoms.

Kiara walked up to Kevin, who stared at the scene with fond awkwardness. "This is a really beautiful scene."

"It is," Kiara agreed.

Kevin felt a self-deprecating smile appear on his face. "I feel like an intruder."

"People tend to feel that way during moments like this," Kiara informed him. "Best not worry about it. I doubt your mate does."

"Probably true."

"On a more important note." Kevin looked up when the woman's single hand landed on his left shoulder. "I'm glad to see that you and your mate are alive and unharmed."

"Ahahaha!" Kevin's nervous laugh was accompanied by him rubbing the back of his head. "Thanks! I'm pretty glad about that myself."

Lilian and Kotohime finally broke apart. Both were shedding tears. Both wore wide smiles.

"You will have to tell me about what happened, Lilian-sama. I would very much like to know what you have been up to since we were… separated."

"Okay," Lilian agreed, "but do you think we can do that after Kevin and I get some rest? We've been up for a long time now, and I just fought against a nekomata. I'm kinda tired."

"A nekomata?" Kotohime seemed alarmed, but she quickly regained her composure. "I see. That assassin must have found you after we got separated." Nodding, the kimono-clad katana-wielder made a decision. "Very well. We shall save this discussion for another time. We need to get back to the resort anyway. Your friends and family should know that you're alive."

"Right."

As they made their way out of the maze of buildings, Kevin had a strange inkling in the back of his mind. Something tickled the edge of his awareness.

"Is something wrong, Kevin?" asked Lilian.

"I don't know." Kevin looked at the redhead, frowning. "I can't help but feel like we're forgetting something."

***

Wandering through the darkness, with buildings looming over him like silent edifices, Kyle realized that he did not know where he was anymore. While he could usually figure out his location based on the taste of moisture in the air and certain landmarks, he was currently having trouble. Someone had done some major rearranging of the landscape.

"Hello!" He called out. His voice echoed back at him. "Is anybody there? Kevin? Lilian? Somebody? Anybody?" After several seconds passed and no one answered him, he crossed his arms and glared at nothing. "Damn it! Of all the times to get lost!"

Being a side character sucks sometimes.

***

It was late at night, or perhaps really early in the morning, that a small Bentley drove up to the front entrance of Sobre el Natural. Sitting in the driver's seat, looking none too pleased, Kyle grunted.

"Alright, we're here. Now, get the hell out of my car."

"Why are you being so rude, Kyle the Kappa?"

"I told you to stop calling me that!" Kyle glared at Kevin through the rearview mirror. "I need to talk to my clan leader, but I imagine I'll be coming by some time tomorrow, or maybe the day after. He'll most definitely want to talk to you two." They all knew that he was addressing Kiara and Kotohime, not Kevin and Lilian.

"And we will be looking forward to that meeting," Kotohime assured him.

Kevin, Kiara, Kotohime, and Lilian exited the Bentley, which drove off the moment they closed the doors.

"I get the feeling he doesn't like us very much," Lilian commented as the car raced down the road, the tires squealing.

"I can't imagine why," Kevin added.

"I know, right?"

After Kyle's car vanished, the group entered the resort. They wanted to see their friends, after all.

***

Lilian stared apprehensively at the door.

"Are you nervous?" Kevin asked.

"A little," Lilian admitted. "I don't know what I should say to them."

The people beyond this room were the first friends that Lilian had ever made. All she'd known before coming to Arizona was her family and the kitsune who tried to convince her matriarch to arrange a mating session with her. The people beyond this room were special, indispensable.

"I imagine you'll think of something." Kevin gave her a little push. "Now, go on. Let your friends know that you're alive."

"R-right."

Lilian took a deep breath. Grabbing onto the handle, she slowly opened the door and stepped inside. As she stood in the doorway, she immediately spotted the three people she'd come to see.

Lindsay and Christine lay on their beds. The blonde was lying on her back, her pixie hair a mess as she stared at the ceiling. Christine lay curled up on her side, her knees drawn to her chest. A little ways over from the two, Iris's dull eyes stared at nothing. They were listless, the eyes of someone who had nothing left to live for.

"U-um…" Lilian started, only to stop. She tried to speak again, but she didn't know what to say. What did you say to people who thought you were dead?

It turned out that she didn't need to say anything. Lindsay must have heard her. She was lying widthwise against the bed, and her head was almost falling off the edge. She tilted her head down, or rather, upside down, and blinked several times before her eyes widened.

"L-Lilian…?"

Christine, upon hearing Lindsay speak, uncurled herself and sat up. Turning to her friend, she revealed her puffy red eyes to Lilian, who realized that the yuki-onna must have been crying. Her eyes became the size of tennis balls when they landed on Lilian.

"No way…"

It wasn't until both Lindsay and Christine had already spoken that Iris responded to the noise. She looked around with her listless eyes, until they landed on the door. Gasping, her eyes grew wide and round.

"Lilian?" she whispered in a voice that made Lilian's insides squirm. It was the kind of voice people had when they wanted so fervently to believe something but couldn't bring themselves to hope.

"Iris…"

Sitting up on her hands and knees, Iris crawled to the edge of the bed. Her lips were trembling. "Lilian… is that… is that really you?"

"Um." Lilian nodded shyly. "It's me. Sorry for worrying you."

A moment of silence followed her words.

"LILIAN!"

The silence shattered when Iris pounced.

"W-wait! Iris—doof!"

Seconds after Iris's special move, otherwise known as the **Iris Pounce**, Lilian's back smacked against the floor. She would've said something, but her twin sister began bawling on top of her. Tears ran down Iris's face, soaking Lilian's shirt in salty liquid. She could say nothing as the vixen howled out all of her sorrow, anguish, and relief.

In a situation like this, Lilian did the only thing she could think to do: She hugged her sister. She pulled Iris into a tight embrace, whispering words of reassurance into her fraternal twin's ear.

"It's okay. I'm here now. I'm back, and everything's going to be okay."

Iris said nothing. She just continued crying into the chest of her most beloved sister.

*****

With his back against the wall, Kevin smiled sadly as he listened to the wails coming from the girls' bedroom. Hearing Iris bawling as she embraced her sister made him realize that Iris, despite her rudeness and annoying habits, really loved Lilian. It wasn't just the obsession of a siscon.

"Are you not going in there, Kevin-sama?" Kotohime asked as she, too, stood outside of the room.

"Naw." Kevin shook his head. "It wouldn't feel right if I intruded on them. I'll let Iris and Lilian have their time together. They deserve it."

"That is very kind of you."

"Hmm, you think so?"

"But of course." Kotohime affectionately ruffled his hair. "Kevin-sama is a very kind young man."

Kevin clicked his tongue in annoyance, but he didn't remove Kotohime's hand. "I have to see my friends anyway. I doubt they'll be as dramatic as Iris, but I'm sure they were worried about me. Of course, knowing my friends, they're probably going to hit me instead of hug me." Kevin eyed the busty swordswoman. "Keep an eye on things for me here."

"Of course, Kevin-sama."

Just as Kevin was about to head to his own room, loud thumping reached him from beyond the door to Lilian's room. The door swung open. Lindsay stood in the doorway.

She'd definitely seen better days. Her hair was a tangled mess, her eyes were swollen and rimmed with red, tear tracks ran down her face, and it looked like the last vestiges of snot were running down her nose. Her T-shirt was wrinkled and, judging by how he couldn't see anything covering her legs, he reasoned that she was probably only wearing panties.

A gasp came from behind her, and Kevin knew that Christine had seen him too.

Oh, dear. This is not good.

"Uh, hey," he greeted. Lindsay just stared at him. It made him very uncomfortable, being the recipient of that stare. "Is there, uh, something that I can help you with?"

"You can help me by telling me just where you think you're going."

"Uh…" Was this a trick question? "Back to my room?"

Lindsay narrowed her eyes and, before Kevin had a chance to say anything, she gripped his arm like a vice.

"You're not going anywhere."

The grip on his arm tightened. Kevin barely had time to let out an indignant squawk before he was unceremoniously pulled into the girls' room. The door slammed shut behind him. He would've complained, but then Lindsay had pinned him in place with a glare.

Oh, boy. She does not look happy. Come on, Kevin! Say something!

"Uh… Lindsay, I'm glad to see that you're, um, okay." His voice came out as a pitiful squeak when Lindsay's narrowed eyes turned into slits. By the anime gods, what was it about females and their glares that caused men to quake in terror?

"You…" Lindsay's teeth were clenched, and her face was twisted in a rather unsightly manner. Her hands were clenched hard enough that her knuckles turned white as her entire arm shook from the emotion she must have been feeling. "You… you idiot!"

"H-hey, now. There's no need to call me a—gah!"

Kevin winced when Lindsay slammed into him. It was only after a set of arms wrapped tightly around his waist, and his shirt became wet, that he realized what was happening.

"Stupid idiot," Lindsay choked out a sob, the arms tightening until her hug actually hurt. "Do you know how worried I was about you? Do you?"

"I can take a pretty good guess."

"I thought you were dead!"

Kevin's chest constricted, and it wasn't because Lindsay's arms were wrapped around him tightly enough to almost break his ribs. He felt guilty. There was a pit in his stomach, like a knot of remorse coiled around his intestines.

"Sorry." He placed a hand on her head, rubbing her hair with gentle strokes. "I didn't mean to worry you."

"I'll forgive you this once," Lindsay sniffled and rubbed her face against his shirt. Kevin really hoped those were tears and not snot that she was rubbing on his clothes. "Just don't do it again."

"I'll do my best."

Lindsay didn't say anything. As Kevin continued rubbing his friend's head, he looked around the room. Lilian was holding Iris, allowing the still distraught vixen to vent her emotions. He peeled his eyes away from the scene, feeling like an intruder, though he stopped when his eyes landed on Christine.

***

Christine looked away when Kevin's eyes focused on her.

She didn't know if she could handle seeing his gaze upon her. She was bursting with so many emotions—too many to figure out how she truly felt. To see him there, healthy and alive, it filled her with more relief than she could have imagined. Her lips trembled, her eyes moistened, and her cheeks gained a vivid flush. The temptation to rush over to him like Lindsay had done was there, but she didn't know if she should. He had, after all, turned her down.

"Um, Christine? Are you okay?" Kevin asked. "You seem, uh, conflicted."

She shuddered with pleasure and anguish. Why did he have to be so kind to her? Why did he have to act so damn cute? He was concerned about her when he should have been concerned about himself.

It's not fair.

"You… are you… okay?" Her voice was tremulous, hesitant, and feeble, like fragile autumn leaves caught in a powerful wind.

"Yeah, I'm fine. We had a pretty close call when that wave nearly crushed us, but we managed to get out alive," Kevin said as he continued rubbing Lindsay's head. Christine frowned. She wanted him to rub her head, too.

W-wait a minute! What am I thinking? I-I don't want him to rub my head at all!

It's nyot good to deny yourself what you want.

Shut up, cat!

"Really?" Christine knew that she was being silly, but even though Kevin was standing in front of her, she wanted to be reassured again. "Really, really? You're really alright?"

"Yeah, I'm really alright." Kevin's words had her sighing in relief. He gave her a soft look, one filled with gratitude and warmth. "You were worried about me? Thank you."

Critical hit.

"W-w-w-w-w-worried?! W-w-w-who—why would I—what makes you—no—I just—uh—I-I-I—what makes you possibly think I could be worried about an idiot like you!?" Her cheeks turned an icy shade of blue. "I-I-I wasn't worried at all! I just—Lindsay! It was because Lindsay was worried! I was only asking because she was worried about you! Don't look too deeply into this." She grabbed at the left sleeve of her dress with her right hand and tilted her head, refusing to look at him. "Idiot," she finished in a whisper.

She looked back up at him from beneath her bangs and gasped when he smiled. It was so bright! And wait. Were those tears in his eyes?

"Thank you, really." Kevin wiped at his eyes. "It makes me happy to know that you were worried about me."

He might as well have proposed to her on the spot.

"Chu!"

Christine trembled. Those eyes. How could anyone have such bright, warm eyes? They were like a beacon of warm emotions, filling her with fluffiness and flowers and all sorts of nice, pleasant feelings.

"I-i-i-i-idiot!" She tried to roar, but she was far too embarrassed. "D-don't look at me with such wonderful— disgusting! Don't look at me with such disgusting eyes!"

"Right, right. My bad." Chuckling, the young man held back a grin. "Tsundere indeed," he whispered. Lindsay giggled against his chest.

"What was that?!"

***

While Christine's tsundere protocols activated as Kevin unknowingly raised several of her flags, Iris sniffled as Lilian's tender hands gently ran through her hair. They were still lying on the floor. Iris refused to move, and Lilian didn't have the heart to make her move.

Iris looked up, resting her chin on her sister's chest. Dark eyes rimmed with red and bloodshot with tears stared into vibrant green.

"I was afraid that I had lost you." Ruby red lips trembled, as if she would start crying again at the slightest provocation. Lilian felt like she'd been slapped in the face. "You don't know how happy I am that you're alive."

Lilian's countenance softened. "I'm sorry for worrying you."

Iris shook her head. "It's not your fault. I know that there was nothing you could have done. Don't worry about it. Just..." she sighed, turning her head and resting her face against Lilian's chest. "Just let me stay like this for a while longer, kay?"

Lilian nodded as she rested her hands on Iris's back. "Okay."

As she stared at her sister, Lilian looked down at the hand gripping her shirt.

She gasped.

"I-Iris..."

"Hm?" Iris looked up.

"Your hand..."

Blinking several times, Iris looked down at her hand before she flinched. Her nails were black, and they had extended into a set of ugly-looking claws, but that wasn't all. The darkness was expanding, traveling across her fingers like inky tendrils.

Iris sat up and jerked her hand back as if she'd been scalded, but Lilian didn't let her get far. She grabbed the hand and pulled it to her, examining Iris's fingernails with horrified eyes.

"Lilian, this is—"

"When did this start happening?" Lilian asked softly.

Iris looked down. "S-since I found out that you had a mate."

That was nearly seven months ago. Lilian closed her eyes.

"Why didn't you say anything?"

"I... I didn't want to burden you with my problems."

"Iris, you're my sister. You could never be a burden."

"But you—"

"Just because I can't be with you in... that way doesn't mean that I don't love you."

Lilian brought her tails up to curl around Iris's hand. Her sister gasped as she channeled celestial youki through her tails and into Iris's hand. She waited for several seconds, then removed her tails to reveal that the hand was back to normal. However, just to be on the safe side, Lilian inspected the hand further, making sure that the blackness was completely gone.

"There," she said, nodding to herself. She gave Iris her hand back.

"Thank you," Iris whispered.

Shaking her head, Lilian smiled at her twin. "You don't have to thank me for that. Also, if something like this happens again, I want you to come to me."

"Okay." Iris nodded once, then closed the distance between them once again. "Thank you, Lily-pad."

Lilian decided to ignore her sister's use of the accursed pet name. She wrapped Iris in another hug.

Glancing around the room, Lilian saw that Kevin was still chatting with Christine and Lindsay. Lindsay was being a bit clingy, but considering what had happened, that didn't surprise her. Christine was also being her *tsundere* self, but again, she wasn't surprised.

She looked back at Iris, whose face was snuggled into her bosoms. It had been a long time since they'd been in this position. Of course, the last time they were in this position, both of them had been bereft of clothing, but that was beside the point. Lilian felt guilty for having neglected her sister for so long. She wished there was something that she could do for Iris, but no matter how much she wanted things to return to the way they had been, she knew that it wasn't possible.

I have a mate now.

Yes. She had a mate—a human mate. While Lilian was still learning about human culture, she knew enough to understand that polygamy and incest were frowned upon, never mind both at the same time. So, even though she felt bad for Iris, there was nothing she could do. She wondered if the shame she felt would ever fully fade.

Probably not, she concluded sadly.

***

They heard the rumbling of footsteps long before the door burst open.

"My Lord! You're alive!"

Like a hurricane of perversity, Eric swept into the room. He immediately sought out Kevin, who was still being hugged by a worried Lindsay. Brown eyes blinked once. Then blood dribbled down the boy's nose as he looked down at Lindsay's bare legs, which were toned and muscular from playing soccer.

"Eyes up, pervert!"

"Gao!"

Sweat trickled down Kevin's head as Christine drop-kicked Eric like a pro kickboxer. The power behind her attack must have been something else, because the poor kid was sent face-first to the floor.

Several other figures also entered: Alex, Andrew, and Justin. They stopped upon seeing him, if only to stare in shock before exploding into action.

"Kevin!"

"You're alright!"

"Are you okay?"

"You're not a ghost, are you?"

"… Hurt…?"

The questions came pouring in, a threnody of voices that barraged his ears with incessant amounts of noise. Kevin felt a headache brewing from just listening to them.

"I can't answer your questions if you don't even give me a chance to speak."

The group calmed down, and Kevin was able to explain that, yes, he was perfectly alright, and that, no, he wasn't a ghost. It took a while for the reassurances to sink in, especially because he couldn't tell them that the only reason he was alive was because his supernatural girlfriend used a celestial technique to protect them from the giant wave of doom.

"Man, you don't know how worried we were when we saw you get crushed by that wave," Andrew said. "We thought you were a goner." He shook his head. "Course, we don't remember much of what happened. The last thing I saw was that wave crushing you. Everything after that is completely blank."

From those words, Kevin inferred that either Kotohime or Kirihime had cast an illusion over his friends to keep them from seeing anything incriminating. While Eric and Lindsay were aware of the yōkai world due to Lilian's recklessness back when he'd been kidnapped, the others weren't.

I'd like to keep it that way, if I can.

The group eventually moved over to the beds. Kevin and Lilian sat down on her bed. Iris also chose that bed, sticking to her sister like they were glued together. The others arranged themselves wherever they wished. The twins sat on the floor, Justin leaned against a wall, and Christine and Lindsay sat on the bed right next to Lilian's—Iris's bed.

On a side note, Lindsay had put on a pair of pajama bottoms.

They spoke for some time. Kevin learned about what they'd done after the tidal wave struck the beach. It wasn't much. They'd been pretty listless after arriving back at the resort.

I don't think I'll ever be able to forgive myself after putting them through that.

During the time they conversed, Eric woke up. Now that the threat of nosebleed by a panty-clad female was no longer an issue, Eric could properly kneel before his liege.

"My Lord."

"Stop calling me that!"

"I am glad to see that you're unharmed. You had me very worried."

"Yeah, yeah. Sorry for worrying you."

The discussion continued, only with Eric's antics now involved. It was during this time that another group of people made their way into the room.

"Hawa! Lilian! Kevin-kyun!"

Neither Kevin nor Lilian could have prepared for what happened next. Camellia, her eyes streaming with tears and snot coming out of her nose, leapt at them, literally crashing into them like a battering ram. Their backs hitting the bed, the three youngsters—Kevin, Iris, and Lilian—could do nothing as the five-tailed kitsune bawled against them.

"HAWAWAWA!!"

Yes, that was bawling.

"Uh…"

Kevin shared a look with Lilian.

"Just let this run its course, Beloved," Lilian said, petting her mom's head, which they all knew the woman liked. "There's no stopping Mom when she gets like this."

"HAWAWAWA!"

"You mean this has happened before?"

"Only a couple of times."

"Gods help us."

Kevin looked down at the woman lying across him, Lilian, and Iris. She clung to them like a lifeline. His already wet shirt was becoming a sopping mess that clung to his frame.

She's totally getting snot all over me…

Trying to take his mind off how his shirt was becoming covered in Camellia's nasal excrement, Kevin looked up as a teary-eyed Kirihime stepped in front of them. She looked at them, hands clasped in front of her in a very maid-like sort of way.

"Lady Lilian, Lord Kevin, I…" The woman raised a hand and wiped away a tear. She then brought it back down and clasped her hands together. Her smile, so wide, compassionate, and lovely, trembled with the breadth and depth of her relief. "I am so glad to see that you two are alive and well."

"Thank you, Kirihime."

"Um, yeah, thanks."

"My Lord's power over women continues to astound me." Eric wiped tears from his eyes. These were not tears of relief, but of reverence. How could he not cry in the face of such amazing lady-killer prowess? "To think he's cuddling with a hot family of three like it was nothing! I'm so overcome with emotion!" Even though his eyes were flooding, a fire blazed within them. "My Lord, I shall strive to be like you in all things so that I, too, might one day gain my very own harem!"

"Dang it, Eric! Enough with the 'My Lord' crap already!" Kevin paused, but only long enough to take a deep breath. "And for the last time, I don't have a harem!"

***

She stared out of her bedroom window.

While the moon showered the earth with beams of light, she could not see the stars. Then again, what had she expected in a place like this? Los Angeles was a cesspool, a city of filth and decay. The stench of humanity was stronger here than anywhere else she'd ever been.

Ah, but that was what made this city so perfect for her plans. There were so many humans in this place, millions of them, and all of them were ripe for the plucking.

I'll have to thank Lord Shinkuro for suggesting that I come to this place.

A knock on the door caused her to turn away from the starless night. She looked around her room, noting with disgust how barren it was, then turned her attention to the door.

"What is it?"

"Lady Luna, Kaine, and Christian are here to see you. They said it's urgent that they speak with you," a male voice said from beyond the door.

"Do they now?" A frown marred her face. She'd sent those two, along with several others, to keep an eye on those troublesome kappa. "Very well, tell them that I shall speak with them in a moment."

"Of course, My Lady."

As she heard the sound of receding footsteps, Luna stood up, went over to her dresser, and began getting dressed. As she was putting on her panties, the lump lying on her bed stirred. A pair of furry ears poked out from beneath the sheets, which were soon followed by a sleepy face.

"Luna…" Droopy eyes the color of wine peered at her. "Who was that?"

"It was just Martaeux." Luna snapped on a black lace bra. "Apparently, Kaine and Christian have left their post because they wished to speak with me." Her eyes darkened. "They had better have a good reason for abandoning their station."

"Will you be coming back to bed afterward?"

Luna smiled and walked over to the bed. She sat down and let her hand travel behind her lover's head, wherein she pulled them into a kiss. The person underneath the mattress kissed back eagerly but submissively. Luna plundered her lover's mouth with her tongue. She could still taste herself on the three-tailed kitsune's lips.

"Go back to sleep," Luna urged her lover. "I'll be back soon enough."

Her lover nodded and, yawning widely, snuggled back into the covers and fell asleep. Luna finished getting dressed and left.

While her bedroom might have been insultingly spartan, she refused to let her appearance be the same. Her off-the-shoulder blue evening gown glimmered every time she moved, sparkling like a sea of stars. A slit on the left stopped at her thigh, not only allowing freedom of movement, but also revealing a wonderfully long, dusk-colored leg. The back of her dress plunged into a deep "v" that exposed her back, and black heels clicked against the tiled floor.

She found Christian and Kaine in her office, a modestly sized room with a couple of bookshelves and a desk. Once again, the lack of decorations had her scowling. It had been her own decision not to bring her favorite decor, but she still hated how barren this place was.

The two men bowed to her as she sat down. Looking them over, she could see that both were injured. Kaine's entire torso was wrapped in bandages that were stained red, and Christian's left shoulder bled from a large wound that was reminiscent of claws.

"I'll hear your report now," Luna stated, leaning back in her chair. At least her seat was comfortable, if not to her liking. "And it had better be good."

***

In the quiet and warm comfort of a relatively large room, four people slept.

These four were an odd group—really odd. Three of them were family: a mother and her two daughters. One of them was not family, but considering his relationship with one of the daughters, he might as well have been.

They were snuggled together, the teenage male in the middle, the two daughters on one side, and the mother just sort of sprawled out on top of them. It made for a highly unusual sight, as Kotohime and her sister could attest to.

"He looks uncomfortable," Kirihime said, worried. She was, of course, referring to Kevin, who lay in the middle of a bundle of prettiness. "Do you think we should get him out from there? Maybe we should put Lady Camellia and Lady Iris in a different bed."

Sitting in seiza beside the bed, Kotohime took a glance at the pile of sleeping bodies, then giggled. "Ufufufu, I believe they are fine where they are for now."

Kirihime did not seem convinced that letting the poor boy sweat and suffocate underneath a pile of females was a good idea, but she deferred to her sister.

"If you're sure."

"I am," Kotohime declared before changing the subject. "On a more important note, I need to fill you in on the most recent string of events."

Kirihime stood with her hands clasped in front of her, listening as her sister described the events that transpired after everyone arrived at the resort. By the end of the long and thorough explanation, her knuckles had turned white.

"I see. There was a battle going on several miles off the coast," Kirihime murmured. "Do those yōkai not realize what they've done? An attack of that magnitude going out of control..." Her hair antenna bounced as she shook her head. "They could have revealed our existence to the humans."

"Indeed they could have," Kotohime agreed. "They are very fortunate that their battle was so far away, and that the yōkai who have infiltrated this country's media networks managed to play the whole thing off as a natural disaster brought about by global warming."

Ever since the creation of photographs, the possibility of humans discovering the existence of yōkai had been a pressing concern. To combat this, various yōkai had banded together and infiltrated the many media networks and news stations around the globe. It was their job to cover up any incidents involving yōkai.

"Global warming?" Kirihime made an expression of adorable inquisitiveness. "The humans actually bought that?"

"It is not all that unusual, is it?" Kotohime asked rhetorically. "Humans fear what they cannot understand. The idea that creatures beyond their comprehension exist frightens them. Even now, after the creation of guns and nuclear weapons, the fear of the unknown terrifies them. It is better to deny that something has the power to wipe you off the face of the earth than confront it. I believe the human expression for this is, 'Ignorance is bliss.'"

"Not all humans are like that, though," Kirihime added.

"You are correct. Not all humans are like that," Kotohime agreed. She turned to Kevin, who was buried underneath three females whose breast circumference was twice as large as he was tall.

Kevin Swift was one of those humans who knew about yōkai and still accepted them. He treated yōkai like he would anyone else. Of course, Lindsay and Eric could also be included in this category, so it was not like he was special, but it was certainly a point in his favor.

While Kotohime tried not to see it at first, she could not deny that Kevin reminded her a lot of her last mate. Like Corban, he had been willing to accept and love a yōkai despite their differences.

Of course, Corban had learned of her status after they had become a couple. Kevin had discovered Lilian's inhuman origins before they were even friends. That actually made Kevin's acceptance all the more significant. That a human would welcome a yōkai into his life without any previous familiarity with the yōkai in question, or even knowledge of yōkai in general, showed his incredible capacity for acceptance.

Kotohime wondered: Was this the reason she felt such a strong familial affection for him? Because he reminded her of her previous mate? Or was it his ability to accept someone regardless of their species? Perhaps she would never know why she felt the way she did. Kitsune rarely focused on the hows and whys of their own feelings. The feelings were there, they existed, and that was all that mattered.

The door opened, disrupting her thoughts, and Kiara walked into the room.

"I've got Heather looking into this incident with Lilian and Kevin. Having worked for a secret organization before, she's pretty good at gathering intel, and we'll need to know more about this situation before making any judgment calls." She paused upon noticing the unusual silence. "Did I miss something?"

Kotohime shook her head. "No, we were merely discussing the past."

"The past, huh?"

Kiara walked further into the room and sat down on the floor with a grunt. Unlike Kotohime, who sat with her back straight and her calves folded underneath her thighs, Kiara sat cross-legged and with a slumped posture.

"Are you thinking about Corban?"

Kotohime sighed. "Yes."

"Mmm…" Kiara closed her eyes and leaned backwards, using her hands to support herself. "I remember the first time I met you and Corban, back when I was looking for someone to train me. I used to drag my little brother around everywhere, then I'd leave him to badger you for training." Her lips peeled back into a grin. "I don't think he ever forgave me for that."

"I never forgave you for the badgering."

"Ouch. Claws out tonight?"

"Only for you."

The smile that Kotohime gave Kiara was about as pleasant as the katana she wielded. Kiara chuckled.

"So, what are we gonna do about all this?" she asked, gesturing to Kevin and Lilian. Kotohime understood that she was not talking about how Kevin was buried underneath several women.

"Without knowing exactly what is happening, there is little that we can do," she admitted. "Of course, we could just pack up and leave, but I don't believe what happened today—yesterday—will happen again. It seems more to me like we simply became caught up in a power struggle between feuding yōkai."

"Yeah, I see your point." Kiara scratched the underside of her chin. "I'd hate to leave so soon after coming here anyway. The kid and his mate were really looking forward to this trip."

"B-but if we stay, something like this could happen again," Kirihime interjected. "Wouldn't it be better to leave before that happens?"

"That's only if it happens," Kotohime assured her sister. "The chances of something like this happening again are small, especially since we won't be going to the beach again."

"So, we stick around, protect the brats, talk to those kappa, and then decide from there?" Kiara asked for confirmation.

"I believe that is the best course of action."

Coming to an agreement, Kirihime, Kotohime, and Kiara left the room. Tomorrow, or rather, later this morning, it was going to be another full day. They wanted to be as well-rested as possible.

After all, there was no telling what else could happen come the morrow.

***

Luna felt a smile creeping on her face as she eyed the two four-tailed kitsune bowing submissively.

"So, Kotohime is here in California, is she? Who would have thought that I'd see her again after nearly one hundred years? You've done well to bring me this information. Go back to your post and put that woman out of your mind. I shall deal with her and the dog personally."

"Of course, My Lady," the two kitsune said in unison before leaving Luna to her thoughts.

Soon, I shall claim what is rightfully mine, Luna licked her lips.

CHAPTER 10

Revelations and Shopping

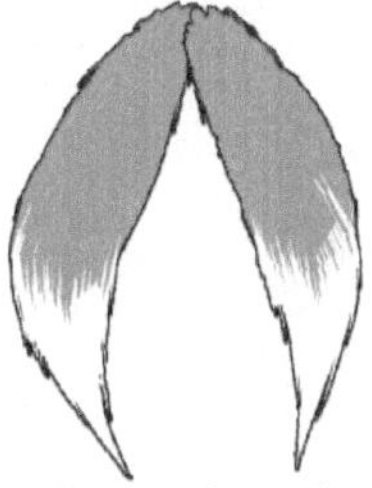

LUNA LAY IN BED with her lover of nearly a decade—the longest one she'd ever had. Her back rested against the headboard, and several pillows kept her nice and comfy. Her lover, a woman with a youthful appearance, snow-white hair, mocha-colored skin, and drooping red eyes, lay resting between her legs. The female moaned softly as Luna slowly drew circles along her hips. Both of them only had a single tail out, as having anymore while in bed would have been inconvenient.

"Taer," she said.

"Yes, Mistress?"

"I want you to do go out today and do some reconnaissance for me. An old acquaintance of mine is in town. I want you to follow her, learn what she's doing here, who she's with, and any potential weaknesses that I can exploit should a confrontation become necessary."

It pleased Luna greatly when Taer didn't even question her motives and simply responded with, "Yes, Mistress."

Really, she couldn't have asked for a better lover—unlike a certain someone who'd refused her advances one hundred years ago.

***

The hour was early. While the sun peeked into the room, casting soft rays of light on the beige carpet, it was still too early for anyone to be awake. Thus, the hotel room belonging to Camellia, Kiara, Kirihime, Kotohime, and Heather remained silent.

"Hawa… zzz… hawa… zzz…."

Except for Camellia's snores.

"Fumya-fumya-fumya… zzz… fumya-fumya-fumya… zzz…"

And Kirihime's snores.

"Ha! Think you can defeat me… Kael'thas… I'll show you… who's boss…"

And Kiara's sleep talking.

"Hehehe… look at all them pretty titties… huhuhu…"

And Heather's sleep talking.

Right, so maybe the room wasn't all that silent. Still, its occupants slept on, their expressions peaceful, untroubled by thoughts of evil plots or what the new day might bring.

"Kachu, kachu!"

Within this peaceful ambiance, Kotohime made several rather cute sneezing sounds. She mumbled a bit, then sunk further into her comfortable bed. The room became quiet once more.

"Hawa… zzz…"

Except for the snores.

***

The morning of Kevin's and Lilian's return promised to be a beautiful day. A bright, shining sun rose over the land, blessing it with warm rays. Birds sang a beautiful and uplifting tune, as if to offer praise to the gods who controlled the weather for granting them such a lovely day.

Iris woke up to the annoying racket that those birds made.

Incoherent groaning emerged from her ruby lips, sensual and soft, like silk touching the ear with the gentlest of caresses. Dark lashes fluttered open to reveal equally dark crimson eyes. Those carmine orbs flickered, taking in the sights before her. The room was dark, but not so dark that she couldn't see the people she was snuggling with.

Kevin and Lilian remained asleep, their eyes closed, their breathing even; they looked so peaceful. There must have been some shifting around during the night because Iris clearly remembered falling asleep spooning her sister. Now she lay on the other side of Kevin, away from her Lilian. Camellia was not there, but Iris assumed Kirihime had grabbed her sometime during the night and took the woman back to their room.

Christine and Lindsay's beds were empty. They were probably awake and already getting breakfast, or maybe they were simply waiting outside. She didn't know where they were, but it didn't matter anyway. All that meant was that she had the perfect opportunity for some fun.

She stared at the young man, trying to make a decision. Should she prank him for getting between her and her sister? The prospect was tempting. Messing with him always gave her a thrill of pleasure. He was such a good sport about it, too. Were she not so in love with Lilian, she might have fallen for him…

Pfft! As if I'd ever fall for an idiot like him!

As she continued to stare, her gaze going from Kevin to Lilian and back again, a beautiful, dangerous, and deadly smile caused her lips to curve in delightful artistry. A thought had occurred to her, and it sent a delicious ripple through her body.

Why have fun with one of them when I can have fun with them both?

***

Kevin woke up to a moan. It wasn't an unusual sound, as he was quite used to making Lilian moan, but the moan itself was unfamiliar; the pitch was too deep, the noise was too sexy. It was almost a purr as much as a moan. Lilian's moans turned his body into a furnace like no other, but even she couldn't make a noise like this.

He cracked an eye open to see the ceiling above him. Rustling to his left drew his attention elsewhere, and he soon turned his head to see what had caused him to wake up. He needed to blink several times, just to make sure he wasn't seeing things.

Oh. My. Gods.

Iris was straddling Lilian. She was wearing nothing, absolutely nothing. Her midnight black hair did little to cover her body. Beautiful pink nipples were displayed as Iris, her hands resting on her sister's stomach, squeezed her breasts together. Her lips were struck in a terrifyingly beautiful smile, and her eyes, locked onto Lilian, made her look every bit like the succubus that she was.

"Morning, Stud. I'm glad to see you're awake. This wouldn't be as much fun without you," Iris said, grinning at him. She then looked down. "And I see you're standing at attention too. I do so love it when men recognize my beauty."

Kevin didn't know what she was talking about—until he looked down and saw the blanket near his crotch rising to create a tent.

"Mmmph!" Lilian shouted, though her voice was muffled.

"Now, now, Lily-pad," Iris chided with a grin. "There's no need to be so impatient. I know how excited you are to have your mate watching us, but please show some restraint."

"Mmph hmm mpp mmmmm!"

Lilian was wide awake. It looked like she had been awake for some time. Unfortunately, it didn't look like she would be moving any time soon. Iris had wrapped her sister up in her tails in a sort of erotic furry bondage.

The tails kept Lilian's arms pinned to her side and her legs restrained. However, they also slithered over her body, particularly around her breasts, which were emphasized more than usual because of how the tails encircled them. His mate was moaning, her skin sweaty and flushed, visibly red even in the dark room.

Kevin wanted to help his mate, but he soon realized that he couldn't move, and the reason was because someone—all signs pointed towards Iris—had bound him in rope while he'd been sleeping.

He looked at Lilian's face. She was staring at him with wide eyes. She tried to speak, but her mouth was being gagged with…

"Is that…?"

"Yep. Mom's underwear," Iris said proudly.

"Mmmrrrgglle!"

"Don't be like that, Lily-pad." Chuckling, Iris gave her sister a smoldering look that made Lilian's entire body blush bright red. "It's been far too long since you and I have played together."

Kevin struggled to move, but all he could do was flop uselessly. "D-dang it. Why am I also tied up? And where did you get all this rope?"

Iris turned her head back to Kevin. She stared. After several seconds of this, Kevin looked away.

"Right. Stupid question."

"Uhuhu…" Kevin shivered. That laugh reminded him of a perverted old man. It was seriously creepy. "I wonder… what should I do to you first?"

Realizing that his mate's chastity was in danger, Kevin tried to break free. It was no use, however, as the ropes were a lot stronger than him.

"Don't touch my mate."

"Ho?" Iris leered at him. "Your mate happens to be my sister, and she was intimate with me long before you sank your fingers into her."

That made Kevin pause. He'd never bothered learning the extent of their relationship, but he did know that Iris had been Lilian's first kiss. Honestly, he'd assumed that it was something Lilian had done because she was curious about kissing.

But what if it wasn't?

What if Lilian had done it because she and Iris actually had that kind of relationship? He didn't know how to feel about that. Kevin had not been brought up in a religious home, but there were some things that were considered morally unacceptable by society. Incest was one of them.

"E-even if that's true, it doesn't change the fact that I'm her mate now."

Kevin decided to ignore whatever Lilian might have done in the past. It didn't matter. The past was the past and now was now, and right now, Lilian was his mate, not Iris's.

Iris nodded. "That is true, and I acknowledge you as my sister's mate. But, that doesn't mean I'm not going to have some fun with her from time to time. In fact, Lily-pad gave me explicit permission to have fun with her last night."

"HMPH MMRRRPPH!" Lilian screamed into her gag. Kevin didn't know what she was saying, but he hoped it was a denial.

"Now, then, it is time for you to be quiet." Before Kevin knew what was happening, Iris shoved something into his mouth. His yell was muffled by whatever it was. He sent Iris a venomous look, but she just grinned at him. "There's no need to look so angry, Stud. Just sit back and enjoy the show."

Lilian's eyes widened as one of Iris's tails pushed up her shirt. Her breasts sprang free with a bounce. Kevin's eyes bulged.

Then the room became engulfed in the sound of Lilian's muffled moans.

✳✳✳

Lilian used Kevin as a shield as they walked to breakfast. After what happened this morning, he couldn't blame her. Even now, she still had several bite marks on her skin.

"You seem displeased, Lily-pad." Iris looked smug. "Is something wrong?"

"Yes, something is wrong," Lilian practically spat. "You violated me!"

"You enjoyed it."

Lilian's cheeks gained a healthy blush. "Th-that is completely beside the point!"

"Wait. Did you really enjoy what Iris did?" Kevin asked.

Lilian froze. The blush on her cheeks spread to the rest of her face and traveled down her neck.

"W-well, I wouldn't say I enjoyed it per se. I mean, you know, it felt really good, but…" As Kevin and Iris continued staring at her, Lilian sank further into herself. Her skin, from her head to her toes, had gained the same red as her face. "I… I might have enjoyed it… just a little."

Kevin hesitated. "… Was she better than me?"

Lilian's guilty expression said it all.

"Ha!" Iris laughed. "It looks like I can chalk this point up to me! Don't worry, though, Stud. It's only natural that she would like what I do better. After all, I've known Lily-pad since she was born. You've only known her for a little over half a year."

Kevin didn't know how to feel. Lilian had all but admitted that Iris had done a better job of pleasing her than him. Her silence said as much.

Lilian glared at Iris, silently telling her to shut up, then switched her gaze back to him. Her consoling eyes made him feel ashamed, pathetic even.

"Don't let what Iris said bother you, Beloved." She took his arm and lovingly hugged it to herself. "I-it is true that Iris is… well, better than you are at making me feel good—"

"I knew it!" Iris cheered.

"Quiet you!" Lilian snapped, then coughed into her hand and continued. "But even if she's better than you are right now, it doesn't mean that will always be the case. Practice makes perfect, right? This just gives us an excuse to practice more."

"I'll help!" Iris offered.

"Shut up, Iris!"

Kevin didn't say anything as the two sisters bickered, lost as he was in his own thoughts. What Lilian said rang true, but at the same time, that wasn't his only concern.

Lilian and Iris were intimate before she met me.

Lilian and Iris were fraternal twins. The idea of them being intimate… well, he wouldn't lie and say that it didn't bother him. It did. At the same time, he didn't want to deny Lilian because of something like this. Regardless of what she'd done before him, he loved her.

They walked into the breakfast café inside of the resort. Everyone else was already present. Many of them were already eating breakfast. All of them stopped and turned the moment that he, Lilian, and Iris entered.

They stared.

"Nobody look at me." Lilian hid behind Kevin. "I feel so violated."

"A-are those…?" Lindsay couldn't help but stare in shock at the marks on Lilian's skin, most notably on her stomach and the swell of her breasts. Christine's face turned into an icicle as she froze in place, her eyes bulging.

"Those look like…" Alex's eyes widened.

"I believe they are…" Andrew stared in reverent awe.

"… Bruises…"

Everyone gave Justin an odd look.

Kevin and Lilian sat down at a booth. Iris tossed them one last wink, which elicited a glare from them both. She then sat next to an awed and embarrassed Lindsay and an angry and embarrassed Christine.

"Oh ho," Kiara laughed when she got an up-close look at Lilian.

"Whatever you're thinking, stop it," Lilian muttered harshly, hiding behind her menu.

"Ufufufu," Kotohime giggled demurely behind her hand. "It looks like Lilian-sama, Kevin-sama, and Iris-sama were having some fun this morning. Is that why you're so late?"

"I was not having fun!" Lilian hissed, her red cheeks revealing her true thoughts. "My sister practically raped me!"

"It isn't rape if you enjoy it."

"Shut up, Iris!"

"Kevin liked it!"

Lilian opened her mouth, then closed it just as quickly. She turned and gave Kevin an expectant stare. Kevin blushed.

"Ah." Awkwardly scratching his neck at the unexpected twist this conversation had taken, Kevin could do nothing but offer his honest opinion. "I... it was... kind of hot... I guess..."

Even if he thought it was wrong on so many levels, he wouldn't deny that it had aroused him. Throughout the entire incident, while Iris had been sucking and licking and nibbling on Lilian's skin, he'd been sporting a boner hard enough to cut diamonds.

"Well," Lilian mumbled, turning back to the menu, "so long as you liked it, I guess it's okay."

"In that case, wanna go again?"

"Don't push your luck!"

Heather stared at Eric as he turned away, sobbing. "How can such a great man exist in this world? He must be some kind of god! An earthborn god!" Seconds later, the young pervert raised a fist to the sky. "Oh, My Lord, your incredible way with women knows no—DOOF!"

Something hard and black smacked the back of Eric's head with a loud *thunk!* The boy crashed to the floor, unconscious long before he hit the ground.

"Shut the hell up, Eric!" Christine shouted, her face bluer than a frozen tundra.

Ignoring the insanity around him, Kevin hailed down the waiter and placed his order: oatmeal with a side of blueberries. The waiter nodded, writing down the order dutifully. However, when his eyes turned to Lilian, he started staring.

"Look at her with those lecherous eyes any longer and I'm going to rip them out of your sockets," Kevin threatened. The man squeaked and, after taking Lilian's order, he scurried off.

"Someone seems upset," Kiara whispered to Kotohime, who giggled. Kevin clicked his tongue, but he didn't say anything.

"K-Kevin," Lilian sounded surprisingly shy. "I-I really am sorry. I didn't... I mean, you know that Iris and I aren't..." She trailed off, as if she was unsure of how to finish that sentence.

Kevin, after taking a long look at her, sighed. "Yeah... I know... but that doesn't make me feel any better."

"Is there anything I can do to make it up to you?" Lilian asked earnestly. "You know I'll do anything for you."

And just like that, Kevin's mind went right down the gutter. Dozens of naughty images played in his mind. The scene from the bedroom repeated itself, except instead of Iris doing those things to Lilian, it was him.

"Kevin? Beloved? What are you—"

Everyone watched in mute shock as blood sprayed from Kevin's nose like a fire hydrant. His head slammed into the back of his seat. Because of Newtonian physics, his head came back down, and he slammed face-first into the table hard enough to leave a dent. He then slid off his seat and crumpled to the ground, clearly unconscious.

"Inari-blessed! Beloved!"

"Huh," Iris mumbled as she watched her frantic sister try to wake up her mate. "It's been a while since he's done that."

"Ufufufu, indeed," Kotohime said with a serene smile.

"Hawa…"

***

That day, the group's itinerary was Hollywood Boulevard, home to many different attractions and one of the most famous tourist destinations in Los Angeles. The bright morning sun bore down on the youngsters and their adult chaperones—plus Camellia. Hundreds of people walked alongside them, many of whom stopped when they saw the group. It was not hard to understand why.

"It looks like there are a lot of places to visit," Lilian said as she looked at the tourist guide brochure in her hands. "There's the Chinese Theatre, Dolby Theatre, Egyptian Theatre, El Capitan Theatre, Golden Age Theater—is it just me, or are there a lot of theaters here?"

"It's not just you," Lindsay confirmed.

"Oh, good. Anyway, there's also the Guinness Book of Records Museum. Hollywood and Highland sounds interesting. It supposedly has over three hundred and eighty-seven thousand square feet of retail space. It says there are a lot of restaurants, and nightclubs, and a bowling lounge, and a six-screen state-of-the-art cinema—that would be a great place to watch anime at." Lilian's eyes began to sparkle. "Could you imagine watching Natsumo Shinobi on one of those screens?"

"I know I could," Eric said, his eyes turning into pools of perviness. "Just imagining Natsumo being randomly stripped for no reason on the big screen, of her body put on display, and those luscious fun bags bouncing and jiggling and—Kuu!"

Eric Corrompore's face was planted into the ground with swift harshness, as a fist smashed into the back of his head with all the fury of a self-righteous angry female. After pounding his head in,

Christine showed that she must have some knowledge in wrestling. She straddled his back, grabbed his legs, then bent them until a loud *crack!* echoed across Hollywood Boulevard.

"Do you ever think about anything aside from tits?! Huh?! HUH?!"

"Gack! Of course I do—gurk! I also think of butts! Ah! Yours is very nice by the way—OH, GOD!"

"So, you've been looking at my butt, have you?! Damn, disgusting, dirty pervert! Scum of the earth!"

"Ack! That hurts! Mercy!"

"I don't even know what mercy is! Now die!"

"Maybe it's wrong of me, but I don't even feel bad for him anymore," Andrew commented as he watched Eric being tortured.

"Me neither," Alex said. "He totally deserves it."

"... Freeze..."

Once again, Justin received nothing but strange looks.

***

It took a while, but they eventually decided on their first destination.

Hollywood and Highland was a large complex. Surrounded on all sides by buildings that were packed so closely together there was no space between them, it looked as if they were all a single building instead of multiple buildings. Kevin and the others stood in front of the entrance, staring at the long set of steps leading up to a large archway: the entrance to the shopping center.

"Whoa..." Alex muttered.

Andrew nodded at his fraternal twin's words. "Whoa is right."

"This place is so big." Lilian spun around in an attempt to take everything in. "This mall is way bigger than the one back home."

"I'm not sure if this place can even be called a mall." Lindsay's own eyes were quite wide. "It looks more like a miniature city." Standing beside her, Christine could only nod in agreement.

"It's seeing things like this in my own country that reminds me there's still so much I haven't seen yet," Kevin admitted, though he wasn't quite as impressed as the others. Having traveled to several other countries, he was used to visiting magnificent architectures.

"That's right. I almost forgot that My Lord has traveled all over the world," Eric said, standing with a stooped posture. He looked like he hadn't recovered from Christine's beating yet.

"Seriously, could you stop—" Kevin stopped, then shook his head. "No, you know what. I'm not even going to bother anymore."

"Looks like Eric's wearing him down."

"Maybe we should start calling him 'My Lord' as well."

"Do that and I'll break my foot off in your, um, rear," Kevin tried to sound menacing, but it didn't work out too well.

"Looks like you still can't swear."

"What a prude."

"I'll show you prude!"

"Oh, wow." Iris snickered at him. "I knew you were innocent, but I had no clue you were *this* innocent. Ufufufu, how cute."

Kevin tried to ignore the way his face burned. "Sh-shut up."

"Don't worry, Beloved," Lilian reassured her mate. "I like that you don't feel the need to swear all the time. It makes you seem really mature."

Kevin stared at Lilian with large, hopeful eyes. "R-really?"

Lilian nodded, her own eyes glimmering like emerald stars. "Really."

"Oh, Lilian, you're such an amazing girlfriend."

"And you're an amazing boyfriend."

"Lilian."

"Kevin."

"Lilian!"

"Kevin!"

"I'll kill you both!" Christine shouted as the two embraced each other.

"I think we should do some shopping." Iris grabbed everyone's attention, especially the males, when she placed her arms behind her back and stretched, causing her chest to not-so-inadvertently pop out of her tight black T-shirt. "Look, it says here that this mall has a Louis Vuitton and Victoria's Secret." The vixen gave her sister a sly look. "Bet you want to go there, right? You and I can do some shopping and find something sexy for you to wear in front of your mate?"

"Hmph!" Lilian turned her head, looking away from her sister.

"Aw, come on! You're not still mad about this morning, are you?"

"Of course I am. Only Beloved is allowed to do *ecchi* things to me."

"Can we please not call them *ecchi*?" Kevin pleaded. "That makes it sound so naughty… and I don't think all of the readers will know what you're talking about."

"You bring up a fair point," Iris admitted. "Not everybody knows Japanese. Okay, then, let's call it kinky."

"Absolutely not!" Kevin and Lilian shouted at the same time.

"I'm really curious to know what those three got up to this morning," Alex said. Andrew and Justin nodded.

"Yeah, well, you can keep wondering," Kevin told them both. "You're never gonna find out."

"I don't mind giving you guys a little play-by-play," Iris said, a glint hidden within her carmine orbs. "Lily-pad and I—"

"Alright, that's enough!" Lilian, determined to shut her sister up, shoved a hand over Iris's mouth. "We don't need to hear—kya!" She retracted her hand and glared at her sister with a heavy blush on her cheeks. "You licked me!"

"I did indeed." Iris grinned and stuck out her tongue. "Would you like me to lick you again?"

"No thanks."

Kotohime stepped in front of the group and clapped her hands, getting everybody's attention. "All right, everyone! Because we have such a large group, we need to figure out how we're going to travel. Because there are nine of you and only five of us—"

"Are you including Camellia in that list?" asked Iris, raising an eyebrow.

"—Four of us," Kotohime corrected, getting a "hawa" from the woman they were talking about. "I would like to suggest that we split up into groups of two or three. We'll all go our separate ways to explore, then we'll meet up at the central courtyard."

"Christine and I will be a group!" Lindsay declared, grabbing her friend's hand.

"Eh?" Christine whined. "But I wanted to—" she stopped, looked at Kevin, then blushed bright blue from the roots of her hair down to her toes. "I-I mean, sure, I'll go with you."

"Uhuhu, did you want to go with someone else?" asked Iris, a leering grin on her face. "Maybe you wanted to go with a certain stud muffin?"

"Silence, skank!" Christine snapped.

They eventually decided to have the girls and boys go separate ways. Kiara and Heather would watch after the boys, while Kotohime and Kirihime kept an eye on the girls. It was only after the groups had been decided that Heather realized something.

"Hey, aren't we missing someone?"

Everyone looked at each other, mentally checking to see who was with them. A gasp from Kirihime caused everyone to stop their observations and turn to her.

"My Lady?! My Lady, where did you go?! My Lady!"

Everyone watched as the woman ran off in search of the missing woman-child, her frantic shouts echoing in the distance.

Kotohime slowly massaged her temples with her right hand. "Right, well, it looks like I shall be accompanying the girls myself."

With their decision made, the group split up and went their separate ways.

***

A young woman stared down at the group of humans and yōkai from atop a building. She observed the kitsune in the group: a beautiful woman with a busty figure dressed in a kimono, a gorgeous redhead with enchanting green eyes, and an almost ridiculously oversexed raven-haired girl with an erotic apollonian gaze.

"The one with the katana and wakizashi must be my target," she murmured to herself. "Then those other girls are… her charges, perhaps? Hmm…"

Wanting to know more, she looked at the others. Most were human and not worth her attention. She did spot a yuki-onna among them, which was odd and noteworthy, especially given the girl's clothes. What kind of snow maiden wore a black Lolita outfit? She also eyed the filthy and wild-looking dog with mild disgust, but Taer didn't focus on the horrid creature for too long.

"What an odd bunch," she murmured as the group walked through the arch that led into the courtyard. "I never expected to see yōkai cavorting with humans like this. I suppose it doesn't really matter, though."

That's right. She had a job to do. Mistress wanted her to spy on the busty woman and learn of any weaknesses. Nothing else mattered.

She stood up and began to move off. Unfortunately, she wasn't watching where she was going and ended up tripping on the lip of the building.

"Wah!"

She fell down and slammed face-first into the ground. Several people stared in shock as she pried her face off the now dented pavement.

"Um, e-excuse me, miss… a-are you alright?" a young woman asked hesitantly.

Taer sniffled as she sat on the ground, on her butt, holding in tears and rubbing her now sore nose. It was all red and swollen and it hurt really badly.

"Yeah," she said, "I'm fine."

"W-would you like some, um, help up?"

Taer looked at the hand offered to her and smiled before taking it. "Yes, I would appreciate that." She was pulled back to her feet, where she then proceeded to bow towards the young woman. "Thank you."

"Um… it's no problem." The woman seemed embarrassed by having someone give her such a formal bow. "Be, um, be careful from now on, okay?"

"Yes." Taer rose from her bow and smiled. "I will do my best."

What a nice woman. Taer watched the woman walk off. Several seconds passed. As everyone who'd been staring at her left, Taer frowned as she suddenly remembered something.

"Wasn't I supposed to be following someone?"

✳✳✳

The more time that passed, the more Christine began to realize how much of an outsider she was. She knew that shouldn't have been the case. Everyone seemed to accept her—even Iris, who she always argued with. Still, the feeling persisted. More often than not, she felt like someone who didn't belong, like something there was going on behind the scenes that everyone but her was privy to.

On a side note, Alex, Andrew, Justin, and Eric did not seem to be privy to whatever was happening either, but she didn't care about them.

She wasn't the only one who seemed to feel this way. Lindsay appeared to be of like mind. Unlike Christine, who felt annoyed at being out of the loop, her friend seemed to be perfectly accepting of it.

"Ah! I think this would look really cute on you!" Lilian declared passionately.

Lindsay stared at the object in her friend's hand. "Lilian… it's a bra."

"A sports bra," Lilian corrected.

"It's still a bra, and I'm not quite, um, how do you say 'well-endowed' enough for that."

"Don't be silly! You're so pretty! I have no doubt that you would look good in this!"

"Ah!" Lindsay flushed deeply at Lilian's words. Christine didn't know what the girl was so embarrassed about. "Th-thank you… i-in that case, I guess I can try it on."

"Mm! Mm! Try it on! I want to see you in it!"

"O-okay, then."

As Lindsay went to try on the sports bra that the bubbly redhead had picked out, the feeling of being an intruder increased.

After everyone had finished celebrating their friends' return, Lilian and Kevin had informed the group about what had happened to them. It had been a very basic explanation claiming they'd been rescued by a group of people who healed their injuries before taking them home. While her tomboyish friend didn't question it, Christine knew better. Something had happened last night that they weren't talking about, and she wanted to know what.

"Something on your mind, Frosty?"

Christine glared at Iris, who walked alongside her, hips swaying in a way that she—much to her disgust—could not help but admire. Everything this girl did filled her with a combination of admiration, revulsion, and envy. How could someone, anyone, make everything they did so damn sexy?

"Shouldn't you be hitting on your sister?"

Iris grinned, and Christine was sickened to know that even her grins looked abnormally hot.

"I've decided to give her some room for the moment. I might have gone a bit too far with my prank this morning, and now she's ignoring me."

This was the third time someone had alluded to what happened this morning. Christine was torn. She wanted to know about what happened, but at the same time, a part of her was sure that she would regret knowing.

"Tch. Whatever."

Christine looked back at Lindsay and Lilian. The tomboyish blonde was awkwardly posing for Lilian in the sports bra. If Lilian noticed how embarrassed the girl was, she did not show it.

"I knew that would look good on you! You look amazing!"

"D-do you really think so?"

"Of course! Now, let's look for some swimsuits! Will you help me pick out something?"

"Help you pick…"

"L-Lindsay! Your nose is bleeding!"

"What? Oh, crap!"

While Lindsay and Lilian freaked out over the tomboy's bleeding nose, Christine sighed and turned back to Iris. "Why are you bothering me?"

"I dunno." Iris raised her hands and placed them behind her head. The act caused that obscene bust of hers to pop out again. Was she doing that on purpose? "I suppose I could chat with Kotohime, but I felt it would be more fun to bother you."

"Great," Christine grunted, "this is just what I need, some skanky fox annoying me."

"There's no need to be rude," Iris said, walking diagonally until she was close enough to ensnare Christine's arm with her own. Christine would have yanked her arm out of the vixen's grasp, but Iris had leaned in close, lips right next to her ear, and whispered,

"Don't you wanna know what really happened to my sister and the stud last night?"

Christine bit her lip. She looked at Lilian, who was making crazy gesticulations with her arms and chatting excitably with Lindsay. Then she looked back at Iris.

"What happened last night?" she asked at last.

Iris grinned. Christine grimaced.

She already regretted letting her curiosity get the better of her.

***

"Okay, my young apprentice. I believe you are ready for the next stage of your training."

"What's the next stage, Master?"

"Learning how to determine a woman's three sizes from just a single glance," Heather said. She walked alongside her pervy little protégé, who hung off her every word. Alex and Andrew were listening intently as well. Even Justin seemed interested in what the blonde woman had to say.

Walking a little behind the group, Kevin and Kiara watched with disgust and amusement respectively.

"I can't believe there's someone out there who's as lecherous as Eric."

"That's because you haven't met enough people, boya," Kiara informed her disciple in the ways of asskickery. "It's a big, wide world, and there are a lot of different kinds of people out there. Don't think you've seen everything there is to see just because you've done some traveling. You'll understand this once you've met as many people as I have."

"Have you met a lot of people?"

"Boya, in the past one hundred years, I've traveled all over this globe. I've met all kinds of people, human and yōkai. You might think that Eric is the most lecherous young man in the world, and you'd probably be right in thinking that, but there are plenty of other people out there similar to him."

"I guess…"

Kevin looked at Eric, who had hearts in his eyes as he stared at Heather while she lectured him and the other boys.

"The key to figuring out bust sizes with a single glance is mostly a matter of experience. The more boobs you see, the easier it is to tell what their sizes are. For example, that woman over there in the Levi's and green shirt. Her breast size is seventy-five centimeters, or thirty-four B. And that woman over there has an eighty-five-centimeter bust circumference."

The woman with the supposedly eighty-five centimeters of bust must have heard Heather, because she covered her chest with her arms and glared at the blonde.

Eric stared at his master in awe. So did the other boys.

Kevin palmed his face. "I don't know why, but I feel like I just lost an irreparable piece of my soul by listening to this."

"Existential trauma," Kiara added, nodding.

***

Victoria's Secret was home to some of the sexiest lingerie around. They also sold a few swimsuits, apparently. This place brought back fond memories for Lilian, who recalled dragging Kevin to a Victoria's Secret store the first time he took her clothes shopping. In hindsight, that probably hadn't been a very good idea— at least not back then.

Would he still be against taking me here now that we're dating?

Surveying her surroundings with keen eyes, Lilian sought out her friends. Lindsay and Christine seemed to have disappeared somewhere. The last she saw of them, the blonde tomboy had been dragging the Lolita off to find a swimsuit. Her sister was checking out some of the sexier pieces of lingerie. After another moment of searching, she found Kotohime standing by a rack of plain-looking bras.

Weird. I didn't know Kotohime wore a bra.

Her eyes went back to the article in her hand. It was a cute shirt made of semi-translucent material. It would look really good with her green pajama pants. She wondered if Kevin would like it.

"Why didn't you tell me?"

"Kya!"

Lilian shrieked and spun around to discover Christine standing behind her, staring at her with equally wide eyes, as if she was shocked by her reaction. Feeling her heart rate slow, Lilian coughed into her hand and tried to hide the mild glow on her cheeks.

"When did you get here? I thought you were helping Lindsay pick out a swimsuit."

"She's in the changing room," Christine answered, still staring. "Now answer my question."

Lilian tilted her head to express her cluelessness. "I'm not sure what you're talking about."

"You weren't just rescued by those people after that tidal wave nearly killed you. You also fought against an assassin, and this wasn't the first time either." Her eyes narrowed. "You didn't tell me that an assassin was after you."

After getting over her shock, Lilian asked, "Who told you that?"

"Does it matter?"

"It was Iris, wasn't it?"

"…"

"I'm gonna get her for this. First she takes advantage of me this morning, and now she's telling you stuff like that? And she wonders why we're at odds with each other."

"I don't really care about your spat with your sister," Christine said. "I want to know why you didn't tell me about the assassin. Why are you leaving me out of the loop?"

"Honestly? I didn't think you'd care." When Christine glared at her, Lilian gave a helpless shrug. "We might get along now, but I didn't think you cared for me as a friend. I kind of assumed that the only reason you were in our group is because you like Kevin."

"K-K-Ke—why would I like that jerk?!"

"Your tsundere is showing."

"Sh-sh-shut up!" The pale-skinned young woman tried to hide her shamefully blue cheeks by getting back to their original topic. "A-anyway, from now on, I want you to tell me when stuff like this happens, got it?"

"Okay. Sorry I didn't say anything before."

"Well, now you know better, so don't let it happen again."

"Right."

While she didn't show it, Lilian was happy that Christine was concerned about her. It made her heart feel light and warmth spread through her body.

It's good to have friends.

"What are you smiling about?" Christine asked, giving her a stink eye.

Lilian merely replied with a mysterious smile.

***

Kevin and his group of would-be sex offenders found themselves in a video game store. Why? Because when teenage boys go to the mall, there are only a few places they go: arcades, video game stores, and sports stores. They didn't care about clothes—let the women worry about stuff like that—and there wasn't an arcade around, so video games it was.

"Hey, check it out. It's the latest *Call of Duty* game! *Call of Duty: Thug Life.*"

"Sounds like a poorly written crossover with *Grand Theft Auto.*"

"Whatever. I still want it."

"Oh. My. God. Master, look at this!"

"Le gasp! Is that *Desire Dungeon*? I didn't even know they sold this in America! Do they have any more? Damn it! If I knew America sold H-games, I would have started shopping at these places years ago!"

Once more, Kevin smacked his face with his palm as Eric and Heather drooled over the latest Japanese hentai game.

Those two are truly made for each other.

While all of his other friends moved around the store, Kevin stuck to one place. He didn't really feel like shopping for video games. Thanks to Lilian's love of games, he already had the latest RPGs, FPS, FTS, and just about every other game for his current systems. The fox-girl loved her video games.

Kiara stuck with Kevin.

"You really fought against a two-tailed kitsune and won? No joke?"

"You don't believe me?"

"Of course I do. I'm just a bit surprised. You didn't tell me you defeated a two-tails last night."

"There were more pressing matters at the time."

"Heh, true." Kiara scratched the underside of her chin. "So, how was it? Was the battle tough?"

"Not really." Frowning, Kevin stared at his right hand as he clenched and unclenched it. "Actually, it was kind of easy. I thought fighting against a kitsune, against any yōkai, would have been more, I don't know, difficult."

"Yeah, I can see why you would think that," Kiara nodded. "It's hard to imagine that a supernatural creature with powers most humans can only dream about would be defeated by a human. But that's what you've got to remember. If it's something that you find hard to believe, then it's inconceivable for a yōkai to believe."

Kevin looked at his combat instructor, but he didn't say anything.

"We yōkai tend to be an arrogant bunch. Even though you humans have come up with weapons that are so impressive that we've been forced into hiding, a lot of us still hold onto the belief that we are the superior race." Kiara paused for a moment, then shrugged. "It's easy to see where this belief comes from. Humans may have created weapons that can annihilate even the most powerful yōkai, but it's not something that you have inherently. It's not a power you were born with. In that way, yōkai are superior."

"It sounds like that very belief in yōkai superiority is a weakness," Kevin said.

Kiara's grin told him that he had hit the nail on the head. "Definitely. If you fought a two-tailed kitsune, and they fought you like they would any other yōkai, you'd probably lose unless you found a way around their illusions. The kitsune you fought didn't use any illusions, did he?"

"No." Kevin shook his head. "He didn't. Even if he had planned on using them, I don't think he would have. I had him so riled up, I doubt he was even thinking straight."

"I see." Kiara chuckled. "Going for the 'piss him off until he's seeing red' approach."

"More or less."

Kiara's grin was one of pride, and Kevin felt himself grinning with her. He didn't even mind when she ruffled his hair.

The grin left a second later.

"You know that strategy won't work for every yōkai you come across, right?" Kiara's serious expression caused Kevin to pay closer attention. "That might have worked on that two-tails, but he was obviously young and untrained. Anyone with more experience wouldn't have allowed themselves to get so angry in the midst of a battle. This is especially true for more war-like yōkai." She paused. "Except for Oni. Most Oni are simple-minded brutes, however, that works to their advantage. Their rage gives them power, so the angrier they are—"

"The stronger they become." Kevin nodded. "I follow you."

"Good. I'm glad to have a student who actually pays attention to my lectures," Kiara said before grumbling about a trio of idiots.

Kevin felt a drop of sweat trickle down his temple. "Right. So, how would I go about defeating someone who can cast illusions?"

"You know what an illusion is, right?" asked Kiara. Kevin nodded. "The key to beating an illusion is to dispel them by disrupting the foreign energy in your body by expelling your own energy, which isn't something that a human can do on their own. Or, you can inflict pain upon yourself. The pain will disrupt the energy, thereby dispelling the illusion. It's your best and only option."

Kevin shuddered. "I'm not sure I like the idea of inflicting pain on myself."

"Most people don't, but sometimes you don't have a choice. You do what you have to in order to survive. In other words, ask yourself this: would you rather hurt yourself but live to fight another day, or stay stuck in an illusion until the caster kills you in what's likely to be a painful and dramatic method?"

"Ugh," Kevin grimaced. "I see your point."

"That's good to hear. If you can remember that while you're in combat against a kitsune, or another illusionist, you'll be fine."

The group didn't linger in the video game store for long. None of them except for one person had enough money to buy anything, and she wasn't going to spend money on them.

Heather walked alongside the quartet of grumbling boys, humming to herself, a bag of H-games swinging in her hand. Unlike the other boys, who glowered at the woman for having money when they didn't, Kevin walked through the pavilion, his mind lost in thought—at least until the earth rumbled.

Kevin blinked when the loud rumbling echoed all around them. He stopped walking and immediately tried to discover the source, which turned out to be a pretty woman with white hair and mocha-colored skin. The voluminous sleeves of her kimono hid her hands from view, or they would have had the fabric not folded back as she pressed her hands against the glass display of a store. Blue jeans fit snugly on her hips, and Kevin could see the fabric conforming to her shapely butt.

The store that she was so fervently staring into was actually a restaurant. He could see numerous people beyond the glass panels lounging in booths and sitting at tables, eating and chatting away with friends. That reminded him, he and his group were supposed to meet Lilian and the girls in another hour or so.

The rumbling came again, and Kevin realized that the noise was coming from the woman's stomach. He hesitated for a moment before walking up to her.

"Excuse me, Miss?"

"Hmm?"

She turned, and Kevin found himself face-to-face with drooping eyes the color of wine. For a moment, he was struck speechless. While those eyes had nothing on Iris, the color was close enough to remind him of the events from this morning.

He shook his head and recovered his congeniality. "I'm sorry, but I couldn't stop from noticing that you seem, um, a little hungry."

Just then, her stomach rumbled again. While the woman's facial expression didn't really change, her cheeks did gain some color.

"Ah… yes." Kevin blinked. Even her voice sounded like she was half asleep. "I am a little hungry. I haven't eaten since breakfast." Her skin began to darken. "And I realized just a little while ago that I don't have any money to buy food with."

Well, you've gone up and spoken to a complete stranger. What are you going to do now, Kevin?

It was a bit troublesome, but Kevin couldn't very well turn his back on her now. No good sentient being would ignore a person who was hungry.

"Would you like to come with my group and me?" he asked. "My friends and I are going to meet up with another group and have lunch. You're welcome to join us. I'm sure we've got enough money to pay for your meal."

The woman's face moved into his personal space, causing Kevin to lean backwards.

"You would buy me food?"

"Um, yeah?"

She stared at him several seconds longer, long enough to creep Kevin out, before leaning back and smiling, just a bit. She bowed to him, a very formal bow with her hands clasped in front of her as she bent at the waist.

"Thank you very much. I would love to take you up on your offer."

Kevin recovered from his shock at this woman invading his personal space. "Then let's go. My friends shouldn't have gotten too far ahead of me."

***

After Kevin asked Taer if she wanted to come with him, he met up with the rest of his male friends.

It had been an… interesting experience.

Sob.

Like a man who'd just discovered life on Mars, Eric stared at Kevin and Taer, tears cascading down his face like two waterfalls. Kevin didn't know what was worse: the tears, or the fact that his salacious friend was staring at him as if he was the ultimate truth of the universe.

"It's like he makes girls fall from the sky!" Sob. "They just keep coming!" Sob, sob. "It's so beautiful!"

"Eric, what the heck are you—?!"

Kevin was stunned into silence when Eric lowered himself to his hands and knees and began kissing Kevin's shoes. The shock only lasted for a moment, however, before being replaced by embarrassment and outrage.

"Would you stop that?!"

Kevin shoved his right foot into Eric's face, trying to get the other teen off him. It didn't work. Eric just began kissing the bottom of his shoe. Kevin wrinkled his nose.

"That's disgusting! Get off right now! Get! Off—eh?"

While he'd been busy trying to get Eric to stop making a fool of himself, he'd failed to notice that his other friends were all following the perv's example. They didn't try kissing his shoes, thank the eight-million Shinto gods, but they did fall onto their knees in a strange form of abject worship.

"Master! Please teach us your ways!" they cried out in unison.

It was seriously beginning to freak him out. Why did this always happen to him?

It took a while, but he eventually shoved Eric off of him, and the others stopped making fools of themselves. Of course, after that he had to put up with Kiara and Heather teasing him about being a player, which he did not appreciate one bit. Their teasing lasted all the way until they met up with Lilian and her group. Fortunately, while Kotohime seemed willing to get on the "let's tease Kevin" bandwagon, the other girls were more interested in talking to the new female that Kevin had picked up.

"Oh, wow! Your hair is so pretty! Is that color natural?" Lindsay asked.

"Yes, it is."

"I love your outfit! It's so cute!" Lilian gushed. "Where did you buy it?"

"In my homeland."

"You had sex before coming here, didn't you?"

"Iris!"

"What? You two were asking her questions as well."

"I did," Taer admitted before either Lindsay or Christine could berate Iris.

"EH?!" the two girls shouted at the same time.

A few minutes later, they met up with Kirihime and Camellia, who appeared several minutes later from the opposite direction.

"Lilian!" Camellia shouted upon seeing her daughter.

"Mom!" Lilian shouted at nearly the same time.

The two met in the center and hugged each other, both of them giving simultaneous "hawas!"

"I'd never realized how similar Lilian was to her mom until this moment," Lindsay said, blinking.

"I think it's kind of cute," Christine admitted, until she received several stares. "I-I mean it's totally gross! Disgusting! Filthy!"

"That sister of mine," Iris sighed. "There are times when I love her, then there are moments like this."

"I still love her even during these moments," Kevin said, grinning smugly.

"Shut up, Stud."

With everyone present, they traveled to The Grill on Hollywood. Upon entering the expensive restaurant, they noted the pleasant but not over-the-top decorations. Dark lighting set the mood, creating a warm and inviting atmosphere. A hostess showed them to a private table on a balcony outside, promising to bring them an extra chair and tableware for Taer, who Kiara had not accounted for when she'd made reservations.

"You don't need to worry about finding an extra chair. I've got my seat right here," Lilian said before making herself comfortable on Kevin's lap. Kotohime, Heather, and Kiara all chuckled in amusement. Lindsay flushed a deep red, while Christine's face turned into an icicle. Alex, Andrew, and Eric began crying, but Justin merely stared at them with an unfathomable expression.

On a side note, the hostess seemed appalled by the redhead's blatantly shameless attitude.

Kevin gave his mate a dry look. "I have no problems with you sitting on my lap, but it's going to be really hard to eat like this."

Lilian turned sideways and faced him. Her smile, brilliant and dazzling in its stubbornness, told him all he needed to know before she even spoke. "Don't worry. I'll feed you."

"And who's gonna feed you?"

"You are."

Kevin snorted, amused. "Should've seen that coming."

"Indeed you should have."

Sob!

"Dang it, Eric! Stop crying!"

***

While everyone else conversed, Taer observed the strange group. Seeing them made her finally remember what she was supposed to be doing. These people, she was supposed to be spying on them, especially that elegant beauty with the incredible bust.

So she watched, and she observed, and she studied their habits. The human girl and the snow maiden sat next to each other, talking.

"I still think you'd really look good in that one-piece. The frills would go well with your cute figure."

"C-c-c-cute—don't say things like that!"

"What? Why not?"

"B-b-b-b-because you—a-ah! You just can't, okay?!"

They were obviously talking about swimwear. The yuki-onna seemed embarrassed by the blonde tomboy's praise. Taer wondered if that girl was what people called a *tsundere*.

"I think you'd look good in a one-piece as well," Kevin added. "I saw one in a store that we walked past. It was really cute, and it made me think of you."

Poof!

Taer blinked when steam burst from the yuki-onna's head.

The others chatted as well, conversing about a variety of topics that she knew nothing about, or had only heard of in passing: School, games, anime, manga, which girl in school was the hottest.

"I'm telling you, Iris is definitely the hottest chick in school. That girl is sex on legs," Alex said loudly.

"Why thank you." Iris winked at them.

Andrew blushed at the wink, but he still didn't look convinced. "Yeah, okay, I'll agree that she's eroticism in motion, but the hottest girl in school? No. That title definitely belongs to Lilian. She's got that innocent princess thing going for her—the way she talks about Kevin ravishing her notwithstanding."

"Don't talk about my girlfriend in front of me! In fact, don't talk about her at all! And for the love of God, stop talking about my sex life!"

Alex looked mockingly thoughtful. "Let me think about that. Nope. Nu-uh. Not happening. No way. You want me to stop talking about your sex life? Stop bringing it up in public."

"I don't bring it up in public!"

"You don't, but Lilian does."

Everyone stared at Lilian, sitting on Kevin's lap and smiling her innocent, enchanting smile. She noticed all of the looks being directed her way and, realizing they were about her, knocked her knuckles against her head and poked out her cute little tongue.

"Whoopsies."

"Ugh." Kevin buried his face in the crook of her neck. "This is all your fault, and I can't even be mad at you."

Lilian grinned, held up her left hand, and gave everyone the victory sign.

"So, you said that your name was Taer-san, correct?" Kotohime addressed her. Taer was startled, but she recovered admirably.

"Yes. My full name is Taerju Kumite." She bowed in Kotohime's direction. "It's a pleasure to meet you."

Kotohime returned her bow with a polite nod. "Likewise."

Mistress is interested in a strange group of people.

***

Much later that day, as the sun was beginning to set, the group arrived back at the resort.

Someone was waiting for them.

"It's Kyle the Kappa!"

"Stop calling me that!"

Kyle had indeed come back. Unlike the last time they'd met, the young kappa had changed his appearance to look more human. While his skin still had a greenish tint, Kevin could only tell when the light hit it in a certain way. His face also looked more human and not as turtle-y. He was even missing the shell that he'd been wearing before. Kevin wondered if his appearance was an illusion or a full transformation like what kitsune did.

He stood outside of the front entrance, leaning against his beat-up Bentley, arms crossed and a seriously annoyed expression on his face.

"Do you know how long I've been waiting for you guys to show up?" he asked. "Four hours! I've been waiting here for four damn hours for you people to make an appearance! Where the hell have you been? Did you forget that you were supposed to meet my leader today? How rude can you people be?"

"Who's this kid?" Alex whispered to Andrew, who shrugged.

"Beats me."

"… Turtle…"

"Have I told you that you're really weird?" Eric asked Justin, who gave him a blank look.

"Quiet down you four," Heather admonished them.

"Yes, Master," they said at the same time—except for Justin who lagged behind by a second before saying, "… Master…"

Kevin used Lilian's hand to facepalm.

I'm surrounded by perverted idiots.

Being the politest among them, Kotohime acted as their spokesperson. "We did not forget. However, we were not aware of when you planned on having us meet with your leader. We expected it to be later. If us not changing our schedule to accommodate you has upset you, then you have my sincere apologies."

Kyle mumbled incoherently to himself as Kotohime gave him a formal bow. Sighing, he returned the bow and said, "It's fine, I guess. We never did set up a time for our meeting."

"Hey, Kevin," Christine leaned in and whispered to him. "Who's the rude boy?"

"This is Kyle the Kappa." Kevin didn't bother whispering at all.

"Do you wanna die?!"

"If you'd like, we can leave right now," Kotohime diffused the potentially hazardous situation before anything could happen.

"Fine," Kyle grumbled before pointing at Kotohime and Kiara. "You two, come with me."

"What about us?" asked Kevin.

Kyle sneered at him. "Our leader hasn't requested your presence."

The two women entered the vehicle with Kyle. Kevin watched the Bentley speed off, pouting like a petulant child who'd been denied his favorite toy.

"What a rude person. He didn't even give me a chance to make a comeback."

Christine gave him a flat look. "You're upset because you couldn't make a comeback? Just who the hell was that anyway?"

"Didn't I already tell you? That's Kyle the Kappa."

"That joke only works when Kyle the Kappa is actually here, Beloved," Lilian chided him.

"Whatever."

"Okay, seriously you two, who is that guy?"

"I already told you. He's—"

"Don't give me that 'Kyle the Kappa' crap and tell me who he is!"

CHAPTER 11

The Turtle and the Bodyguard

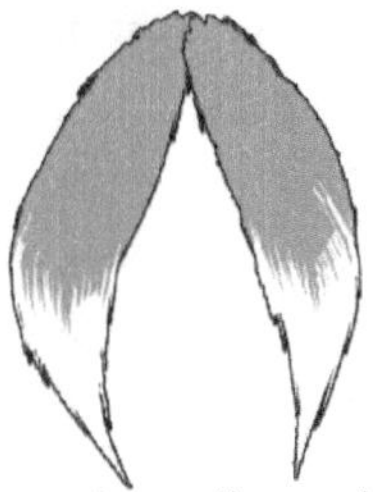

SITTING BEHIND HER DESK, Luna listened attentively as one of her underlings gave a report on their most recent business venture.

"We've managed to acquire ten more specimens through the usual means this past month."

"Have you taken the necessary precautions to ensure that we're not discovered?"

"Of course."

"Excellent. We cannot afford to have anybody find out about our operation, especially with Kuroneko of the Four Saints living here. We've managed to avoid her notice for the most part, and I would like to keep it that way."

"Yes, My Lady."

"And what of those annoying humans? The ones calling themselves the Sons and Daughters of Humanity?"

"They have been far more active as of late," her underling admitted. "They appear to have caught on to what we are doing and have stopped several transactions already, though they have not discovered our base of operations."

"Tch. Do you have any idea how they cottoned onto our operation in the first place?"

"I do have a theory. About a month ago, there were several missing people reports on various news sites. While this isn't unusual, I believe the fact that all of the disappearances were within a several-kilometer radius of each other must have tipped them off."

Luna felt the beginnings of a headache. All of the new technology that humans had been producing made accomplishing anything unnecessarily difficult. No longer could they remain in obscurity by enchanting someone to forget about them, or using an illusion to make them appear as someone else. Cameras were not fooled by illusions. Computer networks could not be tricked by enchantments. The world had changed, and kitsune needed to change with it if they wanted to survive.

This is why I despise humans.

"They haven't made contact with any of our agents, have they?"

"No, but it won't be long before something happens. We might want to consider discontinuing our operations for the time being, or at least changing our venue."

"You may be right," Luna mused to herself before shrugging. "Well, we shall cross that bridge when we get to it. Now, what of those kappa? Are they still putting up resistance?"

"They have been mostly quiet after our last battle at Long Beach," her underling reported. "We believe they are still licking their wounds. They suffered great casualties. We're unsure how many are left, but we know they lost about five of their people."

"Good." Luna was pleased. Kappa clans were not very large, usually consisting of fifteen to twenty members at the most. They couldn't have that many members left, since her clan had killed off six kappa before the battle at Long Beach. "We've already silenced the ones who made the mistake of stumbling onto our operation, and now that they have been weakened, we can deal with them swiftly. Have Kaine locate and destroy the rest of those accursed kappa."

"Won't that earn the attention of Kuroneko?"

"Doubtful. Kuroneko has adopted a policy of noninterference when it comes to yōkai affairs, unless it directly involves her, or jeopardizes the status quo between yōkai and humans. The kappa have no relations with her." She paused, then added, "Besides, getting rid of them will keep the Bodhisattva off our backs."

The Bodhisattva had been pressuring her clan into helping him get retribution on the Pnéyma clan. Luna had no desire to make war, but she also knew that it was only a matter of time before simple pressuring became an order. Much as she disliked the idea of fighting a war, she understood that, should the Celestial Kyūbi make it a command, her clan would have no choice but to join him when he made his bid to wipe out the Great Ghost Clan.

The creaking of the door caused Luna to look up from her introspection. Taer entered the room, closing the door behind her.

"Continue with our operation as planned," she addressed her underling. "Be sure to let me know if anything unexpected occurs."

"Of course, Mistress."

With one last bow, the three-tailed servant vacated the office, leaving Taer and Luna alone. Smiling, she stood up and moved around the desk, taking Taer into her arms and leaning down to press her lips against the other female kitsune's. Her lover didn't resist. Arms snaked around her waist, and a sensually lithe yet voluptuous body pressed into hers, as if trying to meld with her. The moan that escaped her mocha-skinned lover was like an aphrodisiac that spurred her on.

She would have loved to take things further, to shove the items and instruments off the desk, set this lovely young thing upon it, and ravish Taer until she screamed herself hoarse. Most unfortunately, there was still business to be done, and business came before pleasure.

"May I take your presence as a sign that you have accomplished the task I set for you?"

Taer nodded, cheeks flushed and voice breathless. "Yes, Mistress."

"Excellent." Luna smiled and guided the woman to a couch. "Come, sit and tell me what you have discovered."

***

The place that Kyle drove them to looked like a normal resort. While not extravagant by any means, The Surfing Turtle held its own unique charm. Painted in ocean colors, both the outside and the interior contained wave motifs that made everyone who resided there feel like they were at the beach. Palm trees and other plant life lived in the corners of every room, placed in pots that contained the same wave patterns as the walls and floor. The roof overhead had a mural that depicted a clear sunny day.

Kyle led them through a hallway lit with lamps at evenly spaced intervals. They eventually reached a room that reminded Kotohime of her old home back in Japan. Barren of all decorations except for the knee-high table, the only other object in the room was the ancient-looking kappa sitting at one end and the shogi board that lay on the table.

"Are these the two that you spoke of, aru?" the kappa asked upon noticing their arrival. "Please, do come in, aru."

He gestured toward the other end of the table. Kotohime chose to sit down as instructed. Kiara remained standing. The inu leaned against the wall, her business suit ruffling as she observed the proceedings.

"I assume you two are young Kevin and Lilian's chaperones, correct, aru?" the kappa, who Kotohime surmised must be Shuĭ, eyed the two of them with a look that had her instinctively wanting to pull out her katana. "I must admit, when young Kyle told me about you two, he failed to mention how beautiful you are, aru."

"Thank you." Kotohime kept her voice polite. "That is very kind of you to say."

"In fact, perhaps you would be willing to—"

"Discuss the matters of grave importance that Kyle-san mentioned," Kotohime interrupted with a smile. "We would love to. Or I could show you my katana. I am quite well-versed in the art of *iaijutsu*, you know?"

"Ah…" Shuĭ eyed the katana resting against the table with undisguised apprehension. He tore his gaze away from the weapon and tried to hide his fear behind a smile. "Perhaps it would be best if we focused on those important matters. I believe Kyle and your charges have told you about our problems, aru?"

"We did learn about some of what has been happening," Kotohime confirmed. "Lilian-sama and Kevin-sama have told us that a group of Ocean Kitsune have invaded your territory, and that they are attempting to get rid of you. I am actually surprised that a kitsune clan is making such an attempt."

Shuĭ nodded. "Indeed, we were as surprised as you, aru. It did not make sense to us at first. However, we have recently learned that there is some unrest among the kitsune clans, aru."

Kotohime's frown was very prominent. "Unrest?"

"Judging by your reaction, can I assume that you haven't heard of this?" When the swordswoman nodded, Shuĭ opened his mouth to speak, but he was interrupted by Kiara.

"Before we discuss the serious topics, can I ask something?"

"You can," Shuĭ said after a moment's thought.

"Why do you keep saying 'aru'? Are you Chinese?"

Shuĭ twitched.

✲✲✲

They were surrounded by beauty.

Fountains and greenery combined to create a scene out of a fairy tale. Flowers of all kinds covered the ground, blues and greens and reds and yellows, an amalgam of lovely, fresh-scented blossoms that spread their delicate petals outward. The variety of scents touched her nose, a gentle and fragrant combination, like the new coming of spring.

Christine paid attention to none of it. Not the beauty, not the smells, not the color, nothing. Her attention was focused solely on the two people before her.

True to Lilian's promise, the red-haired vixen had not left her out of the loop. Upon asking about the kappa that had driven off with Kiara and Kotohime, she and Kevin had brought her to this secluded section of the resort. Lilian had even gone so far as to cast one of her most powerful illusions on this area to keep the others from finding them.

"So, that's what's been going on…" Christine leaned back on the bench that she'd chosen as her seat, her mind awhirl. She'd just been informed of everything that had happened since the start of this trip, from the assassin to Kevin's fight with a two-tailed Ocean Kitsune. She should have been shocked, but the only feeling going through her in that moment was resignation. "You two are a magnet for trouble, aren't you?"

"That's not a very nice thing to say." Lilian pouted.

Kevin nodded in agreement. "Yeah, it's not like we going looking for trouble."

Faced with identical pouts, Christine came to the startling realization that these two were practically made for each other. It was almost odd, their relationship. They seemed to pull from each other's personalities. From Lilian, Kevin had gained courage and the ability to be outgoing. From Kevin, Lilian had learned restraint and modesty.

It made her wonder about her own designs towards Kevin. Did she love him as much as Lilian did? Could she love him like Lilian did?

Why are nyou questioning nyourself nyow? a voice with a feline-like purr asked her.

Lilian is everything that I'm not, Christine answered sullenly. *How am I supposed to compete with that, especially when she's already won?*

So, nyou are giving up? That's an awfully defeatist way of thinking.

I-it's not like I have much of a choice.

There is always a choice. Besides, nyou knyow that there's unlikely to be another person who's better matched for you—biologically speaking, I mean.

I know that... get off my back.

Have nyou thought of becoming his Mistress?

W-w-w-w-WHAT?! Why would I—you shut up! Shut your damn mouth, cat!

Nyahahaha!

"Christine?" Kevin interrupted her conversation with her other half. "Are you okay?"

"Huh? O-oh, yes!" Christine squeaked. "I-I'm fine! Of course I'm fine! Never better! Why would you even ask that?"

"Because you were spacing out, and your face has turned awfully blue," Lilian answered for Kevin, leaning down and placing her forehead against Christine's. "Really, though, are you sure everything's okay?"

"I-I'm fine!" Christine jerked back. She felt a little guilty when Lilian bit her lip, appearing hurt, but she brought them back to their original topic. "So, what do you two plan on doing about this?"

The young couple shared a look.

"We don't know," Kevin admitted.

"We're not exactly sure if there's anything we can do," Lilian added. "We don't know enough to make a decision. We know nothing about that assassin. We also don't know anything about those Ocean Kitsune and, honestly, neither of us wants to get mixed up in a battle that we have nothing to do with."

"Our life is hectic enough without us looking for trouble," Kevin reaffirmed.

Christine couldn't help but agree with them. "Makes sense. But, you do know that you're gonna have to do something. At the very least, you need to deal with that assassin. She's not going to go away just because you don't want her around."

"We know." Kevin grimaced. "But short of waiting for her to attack, there isn't anything we can do. We don't know where she is, how she found us, or even what her name is. We just know that she's a nekomata, and that she's been hired by some as of yet unknown benefactor to kill Lilian."

"You got me there." Christine worried her lower lip. "This is a really troublesome situation."

"It is, but Kevin and I have already talked about it at length," Lilian said. "We've decided that we're simply going to stay alert. We'll keep our eyes and ears open, and deal with her the next time she tries to kill me. That's about all we can do."

Looking back and forth between the two, Christine couldn't help but voice her thoughts. "You two are taking this awfully well. Aren't you worried? You've got an assassin after you!"

"Of course we're worried," Kevin said, running a hand through his hair. "But if we spent all of our time worrying, then we won't have any time left to create a plan to deal with this. Besides, with everything that I've already seen, heard, and done, having an assassin after me feels almost natural. I blame Lilian's poor taste in stalkers."

"Mou…" Dejected, the normally vibrant kitsune crouched down and drew circles on the ground with her right index finger. Christine blinked twice at the strange black cloud hovering over Lilian's head. "It's not my fault that idiot wanted me so badly."

"Yes, it is," Kevin retorted, eyes glittering with mirth. "It's totally your fault. If you weren't so pretty, none of this would have happened."

Lilian perked up. "You think I'm pretty?"

Kevin rolled his eyes. "I think you're gorgeous. Why else would I say something like that?"

"Oh, Kevin, you have no idea how much hearing you say that means to me." Lilian's eyes sparkled.

Kevin's eyes were also sparkling. "I'm only speaking the truth."

"Kevin."

"Lilian."

"Kevin!"

"Lilian!"

Kevin and Lilian embraced each other. Christine's right eye started to twitch.

"Stop hugging like that, damn it!"

***

The meeting seemed to have degraded, going from what should have been a discussion about why a clan of Ocean Kitsune were trying to kill off this group of kappa, to a shogi match between Shuĭ and Kotohime.

Kiara watched from her place against the wall. Her face was set in a frown as she wondered if her companion even noticed the passage of time. Kotohime seemed completely engrossed in her shogi game. Even now, watching the much older woman from afar, she could see the intense look of concentration; the furrowed brows and the black eyes that studied the shogi board with startling intensity. Kiara had never seen the four-tailed fox become so focused on a board game before.

"You're a very skilled shogi player, Ms. Kotohime, aru."

"As are you, Shuĭ-dono."

Shuĭ and Kotohime had been playing shogi for the past 30 minutes. Kiara was getting bored. How long did one game take?

She looked around the room, but there wasn't much to look at. The plain room didn't hold anything interesting. Really, couldn't they just finish their game already?

Fortunately for her peace of mind, the game came to an end when Kotohime trapped Shuĭ's king in checkmate.

"You are a very unpredictable opponent, aru," Shuĭ observed the board with the canny eyes of one who had seen much. "Rarely have I met a person whose unpredictably allows them to use the strategies and tactics that traditional players take for granted and create new moves so flawlessly, aru. You are incredibly talented."

"Thank you." Kotohime graciously accepted the praise. "You are also quite skilled. You had me on the ropes a number of times." She raised the left sleeve of her kimono to her mouth, hiding the delicate curve of her lips. "Your use of the Yagura Castle was quite admirable."

"Yet you broke it, aru."

"You sure you're not Chinese?" Kiara interrupted. She took a mild form of vindictive pleasure at seeing the kappa's face turn red.

"Enough with the Chinese already, aru!"

"Perhaps we should get down to business, then," Kotohime suggested smoothly, her polite tone calming the old-looking kappa. "You requested our presence due to the kitsune who have invaded your territory."

"Yes, that is correct, aru." Shuĭ coughed into his hand several times, then began his tale. "This is a most unusual situation, aru. You kitsune have never bothered other races unless it was to play pranks, and you usually prefer playing tricks on humans, aru. What makes the situation even more implausible is that these kitsune have invaded a state in North America, aru."

Kiara understood what the kappa was getting at. North America was often considered a free country among yōkai, a place where no one ruled over anyone else, where no yōkai factions or clans congregated and claimed territory for themselves.

Only one or two clans could claim to have any power here, and they'd been given express permission to claim a state as their own by the Four Saints—powerful yōkai who were charged with ensuring that humans did not find out about their existence.

Kitsune were no different in that regard. A few clans had estates here, but they were merely glorified vacation homes.

"I take it the reason for their appearance in this state has something to do with the unrest you spoke of?" asked Kotohime, her placid face gazing upon Shuǐ's wizened visage.

"We suspect that it does." Shuǐ nodded in her direction. "Tell me, aru, has the Pnéyma Clan contacted you recently?"

A disturbed expression crossed Kotohime's face. Kiara felt unease at seeing such a look on the face of a woman who normally appeared so calm.

"They have not," Kotohime replied, knitting her brows together. "The last message that Pnéyma-denka sent me was a request to stay in North America, and to remain constantly vigilant." A long pause followed. "Has something happened to the Pnéyma Clan?"

"We are unsure, aru," Shuǐ admitted. "You apparently do not know this, but our group has a deal with the Pnéyma Clan. To be more specific, we have a deal with the conglomerate known as Spirits Inc., aru."

"I see." Kotohime's eyes lit up in realization.

Spirits Inc. was a company owned and operated by the Pnéyma Clan. They were the tenth-largest company in the world, and they had their hands in many different businesses, including the importing and exporting of rare and valuable materials and artifacts.

"Yes." Shuǐ steepled his fingers together in front of his face. "Our group builds personalized luxury yachts. It is our largest and most important business. Over sixty percent of our income comes from it. The reason for that is due to our deal with Spirits Inc., whose exports include the rare and durable wood that we use in our yachts.

However, about five months ago, the shipments stopped coming, and we had no idea why."

The silence that followed this proclamation was profound. Even Kiara knew not to break it.

"About two months ago, we received information from Kuroneko, who'd been hearing rumors that there has been an altercation between the Pnéyma Clan and the Bodhisattva. We do not know what transpired. All we know is that the two clans are in a state of cold war."

Kiara and Kotohime shared an alarmed look. There was only one reason why the Bodhisattva and the Pnéyma clan would have a dispute: Jiāoào Shénshèng.

About four and a half months ago, Jiāoào, the son of Shinkuro Shénshèng, the Bodhisattva, had kidnapped Lilian. They, along with Kevin, had rescued her—and Kevin had utterly crushed Jiāoào, both physically and mentally. No doubt the cold war happening between the Pnéyma Clan and the Bodhisattva's Shénshèng Clan was due to that altercation.

"That would not normally affect shipments from Spirits Inc.," Kotohime pointed out, recovering from her shock.

Even if Spirits Inc. was a Pnéyma Clan company, the Bodhisattva knew better than to attack it. Spirit Inc. extended beyond the kitsune world. Humans and other yōkai clans also did business with it. An attack on Spirits Inc. could reveal the existence of yōkai to the humans, which was something to be avoided at all costs.

Shuǐ nodded as if he'd already expected that question and come up with a suitable answer. "You are correct. Kitsune affairs generally tend to stay kitsune affairs and rarely affect the rest of us. It does not change the fact that the materials we buy from Spirits Inc. have not been coming in, nor does it change that the Pnéyma Clan and the Bodhisattva are in conflict. We believe these two incidents are not unrelated."

"Do you have any proof?" asked Kiara.

The grayish, wizened head of the old kappa swiveled to look at her. Two dark eyes peered at her from underneath heavy brow ridges. "We do indeed. The clan of Ocean Kitsune who have been killing my people are members of the Mul Clan, one of the Twelve Great Kitsune Clans and, as of six months ago, allies of the Bodhisattva."

***

Kiara and Kotohime returned to the resort, shaken.

Kevin didn't know what they had learned. They had not told him, and he had not asked. Whatever knowledge they'd gleaned from the ancient-looking kappa, it was enough to have spooked them. In turn, that spooked him. Anything that could disturb the normally unflappable Kiara and the cool as ice Kotohime was something to be wary of. Still, he tried to put their expressions of shock out of his mind. If what they learned was important, they would have told him.

He lounged on one of the beach chairs that lined the pool, though to call the massive body of water a pool was a gross understatement. Pools were often tiny things. This was a gigantic body of water reminiscent of a lake or even the inlet of a bay. A "shore" near the chair that he rested on marked the start of the pool, which expanded until meeting its inexplicable end—a sharp drop that led into a basin down below.

His friends played in the pool. Eric laughed uproariously as Alex and Andrew quarreled about one thing or another, dunking each other's heads under the water with increasing violence. Justin did not join them. He, like Kevin, lounged on a beach chair, shades covering his eyes and earphones blocking out the world.

The girls were also having fun. Lilian and Lindsay were kicking water at each other and giggling. Even Camellia was having fun, jumping and bouncing around in the water, while Kirihime tried to keep the woman from tripping.

"Kirikiri! Play with me!"

"M-My Lady! Please be more—"

"Hawa!"

Splash!

"—Careful…"

Christine had chosen to not partake in the splash-a-thon. She sat on the shoreline, the water lapping at her porcelain thighs and bare feet. The yuki-onna watched the two more lively girls prance around, much to the joy of Eric, who Kevin realized had stopped laughing and was now staring at his mate.

Kevin felt a brief surge of irritation, but he buried it in the darkest corners of his mind. He couldn't blame his perverted friend for looking at Lilian's chest. That would have been hypocritical of him. Besides, if he got angry at every male who stared at his mate's breasts, then he would be Hulking 24/7. So long as they stuck to looking, he would not react with impending violence.

While his gaze encompassed the entire poolside, Kevin eventually realized that they were missing someone.

"Not gonna get all wet with your friends, Stud?"

Kevin looked down, blinking in a stupid manner as carmine eyes mere inches from his own stared at him. Iris knelt on his left, arms crossed over the beach chair, chin resting on them. The smirk on her lips, a delectable curve that made him realize how kissable those lips truly were, only added to her allure.

"When did you get here?" he asked.

"Oh, I've been here for a while now," Iris admitted.

"How come I didn't notice you?"

"Silly boy." Iris giggled, and it was all he could do to not shudder. That tone of voice, which could cause men to drown in lust, could be considered a weapon of mass destruction. "Avoiding the notice of a single human is easy for a kitsune."

She must have been using an illusion.

"Not quite," Iris told him when he mentioned as much. "Illusions are merely the act of tricking the mind into believing that something exists when it really doesn't. The image of a beautiful woman, the heady scent after a night of passion, the feel of skin against your body, of soft hands tenderly caressing you. Making people imagine that happening when it's not is an illusion. All I did was erase my presence, which is easy for a Void Kitsune like myself."

"Does everything that comes out of your mouth have to be sexual?"

"Embarrassed?" Iris shot him a teasing grin.

"Of course not," Kevin mumbled, looking at anything but the beautiful bikini-clad girl.

Iris chuckled as she rose from her crouch, her movement undeniably graceful. Lovely hands pressed against the bands of the chair, causing them to creak and bend. Hips canted and a knee rose onto the chair, joining the hands. This was followed by the other knee. Strands of midnight silk danced around her face, swaying as she crawled forward. Her firm butt moved with sensual elegance, timed to the movement of her slender shoulders.

Unbidden, Kevin's eyes moved to her front. Clad in nothing but a bikini, Iris's breasts were even more enticing than usual. The movement of her arms pushed them together, and Kevin struggled to ignore his rising libido.

I wish I could say she was using an enchantment on me, but she hasn't used one since the bathroom incident.

She sat down between his legs, her firm butt resting on the heels of her feet, hands in her lap. Kevin tore his gaze from her chest, which was no small feat as the perfectly rounded breasts were practically staring him in the face.

Calm down. It's just Iris.

"So, why aren't you playing with your friends or mate?" she asked, squishing her breasts together with her arms. This time, Kevin did not look, and Iris inclined her head, as if giving him a small amount of respect.

"I was just thinking."

"Ah, that must be why your face is all scrunched up like a pit bull." She chuckled when Kevin scowled at her. "All that thinking can't be good for you. It's gonna wrinkle that handsome face of yours."

"I don't know whether to take that as a compliment or not."

"Oh, it's definitely a compliment," Iris said eagerly. "I don't hand those out to people who aren't my Lilian very often, so you had better be grateful."

"Hn."

"So, then…" She leaned forward, and her face came so close to his that their noses touched. "What were you thinking about?"

He pushed her back, putting some distance between them. Iris offered him an unrepentant grin, but he ignored it. He knew her well enough by now to realize that she was doing this to get a rise out of him.

"If you must know, I was thinking about how a human would break out of a kitsune illusion without having to hurt themselves."

Iris blinked.

"Yeah, that's not possible," she declared. "Humans lack the ability to manipulate youki, which is the only way to break free of an illusion without hurting yourself. The only other way a human would be able to escape from an illusion is if a yōkai, kitsune or whatever, injected their own youki into the human in question, which would disrupt the illusion for them."

"So, basically, the only hope a human has of escaping an illusion without damaging themselves is to have a yōkai help them?" Kevin felt disappointed. He'd been hoping to find a way to break illusions without outside help.

"Why do you want to find a way around illusions?" Iris's lovely features morphed into an expression of honest curiosity.

"It was just something that Kiara and I were talking about. She mentioned that most kitsune fight using illusions, so if I ever get into a serious fight with one, then I need to know how to break them."

"And the only way to do that is to hurt yourself," Iris said, nodding. "Yeah, I can see why that would be a problem."

"It's more than just a problem. Do you know how distracting it would be to hurt yourself every time you got trapped in an illusion?" Kevin asked rhetorically. "Not to mention the possibility of all that accumulated damage taking its toll on your body. How many times can a human hurt themselves before the pain overwhelms them? How much blood can be lost before you succumb? Even the act of harming yourself is problematic because you have to take your attention off your opponent. Even a second on the battlefield can mean the difference between victory and defeat."

Contrary to what most people believe, combat is almost never a drawn-out affair. Most fights lasted around a minute, five tops. This is because the longer a battle goes on, the more strength the fighters lose, until they eventually run out of juice.

Of course, there are times when drawn-out battles happen. When forces are so equal that neither side can gain an advantage over the other, or when one side is simply so superior they let their arrogance get the best of them and play with their opponent.

It happened to Kevin when he fought against Jiāoào; the boy's arrogance had gotten the better of him. His belief in his own superiority had been his downfall. However, such instances were the exception, not the rule.

"You've been thinking about this a lot, haven't you?"

Kevin blinked. His mind snapped back into focus, and he sought out the girl sitting in front of him. Her inquisitive stare caused him to nod.

"Of course I have. Kotohime once told me that, between Lilian and myself, I am the weakest link, the chink in her armor. If someone captured me and used me as bait, then they'll have already won." Kevin looked down at his hands. Human hands. Hands that had no powers, no abilities to speak of. "I can't allow something like an illusion to beat me, and I can't afford to hurt myself every time I get trapped in one, so I need to find a way around that."

There it was again; respect hidden behind eyes that were wreathed in mocking amusement. The look in Iris's eyes lasted for but a second, then it vanished into the unfathomable depths of her dark irises.

"Uhuhu…"

Kevin's spine crawled at the sound of Iris's laughter. It was creepy and unusual, but undeniably sexy. Her voice was like a musical instrument, capable of emitting sounds more beautiful than a harp.

"You say some of the most interesting things, Stud."

"Would you please stop calling me that?"

"Hmm… nope!"

The cheerful reply, complete with a bright, smiling face, made him twitch.

"I rather like that nickname. I think it suits you." Once again, Kevin's ability to talk failed him as Iris leaned close enough that he could feel her breasts rubbing against his chest. Her finger trailed along his left arm, leaving goosebumps in its wake. "Don't you agree—gya!"

Fortunately for Kevin's quickly eroding teenage mind, his savior came in the form of a furry red tail. It smacked Iris in the temple before retracting just as quickly. His assailant fell off the chair and crashed to the ground, where she proceeded to lay splayed out, groaning in mild discomfort. Kevin turned his head when he realized that he was staring at her camel toe, and he discreetly readjusted himself.

"I'm still mad at you, Iris, so keep your sex-charged paws off my mate!"

This must be a case of the pot calling the kettle black.

"And you shut up!"

… Sorry.

***

Day turned to night. The sun passed down behind towering walls of steel and glass. The sky became dusk, a swirling mixture of reds, pinks, and purples that mixed together. This vibrant panorama only lasted for a few hours before twilight came upon them, perpetual darkness broken only by the light of the moon.

Kotohime and Kiara sat at a small table in their hotel room, along with Heather, who lounged in her seat more indulgently than the other two. Kirihime would have sat with them, but she was tenderly stroking her mistress's hair, gently lulling the child-like woman into a place of dreams.

There was a tension in the room, which none of them could ignore.

"Does anyone else feel like we're always getting caught up in problems that have nothing to do with us?" asked Heather.

"I wouldn't say that all of the problems we find ourselves in have nothing to do with us," Kotohime countered, tracing the lip of her teacup as steam wafted from the liquid contained within. "The people that you used to work for kidnapping Kevin-sama and using him as bait to capture Lilian-sama, that same group sending those unusual machines to kill you, and Lilian-sama being kidnapped by Jiāoào, all of it involved us." Raising the cup to her lips, Kotohime took a small sip before setting it back down. "Even what is happening right now has something to do with us, albeit inadvertently."

"What do you know about this Mul Clan?" asked Kiara. "My knowledge on kitsune clans is pretty lacking."

Kotohime sighed. "The Mul Clan are Ocean Kitsune. They have claimed both North and South Korea as their supernatural territory. They're not a very large clan. Last I remember, they only had about fifty members, though that was one hundred years ago."

"One hundred years…" Kiara muttered. "Then is this the clan that…?"

"Yes." Kotohime nodded. "It is."

"I see."

"Hard to believe they're a great clan with such small numbers," Heather said, either not seeing or ignoring the pensive expressions of her companions.

"Do not let their numbers fool you," Kotohime admonished the blonde. "That means very little in the kitsune world. The Pnéyma Clan is one of the smallest clans in the world, yet they are also one of the three most powerful. There are only about twenty direct descendants to Pnéyma-denka herself. Everyone else is loosely descended from the previous generations of leaders."

The swordswoman paused to allow Heather time to absorb that information before continuing.

"While the Mul Clan is not as powerful as the Pnéyma Clan, they are still the strongest clan of Ocean Kitsune currently. Many of their kitsune are highly skilled illusionists, and their ocean techniques are said to be unrivaled."

"No wonder I couldn't kill the one I fought." Kiara clicked her tongue, obviously irritated from being forced into a tie with her opponent. "He didn't seem to have a whole lot of power to him, but he was really slippery. Every time I thought I had him, he would turn out to be an illusion, and when I started bringing out the big guns, he fled."

Kotohime's elegant shrug said almost as much as her words. "That's a kitsune for you. Most of us aren't the fighting type. It's only natural that one of them would retreat after realizing he's been outclassed by a superior opponent."

"You're not like that."

"I didn't say all kitsune were like that," Kotohime pointed out. "Just most of us. The one that I fought was more combative than many other kitsune I've met. He was quite talented."

"I think we're getting off-topic here," Heather said. "What we need to be asking ourselves now is: what are we going to do about them?"

Kiara and Kotohime looked at each other.

"I do not know if there is much that we can do right now," Kotohime admitted after a poignant silence. "We have no clue where they're currently operating out of, nor do we know what their goals are. Without knowing where to find them, we can't do anything. Besides, this isn't really our problem."

"What I want to know is why they're targeting those kappa." Kiara tapped her index finger against the table. "I mean, it's not like disrupting those operations will put a dent in the Pnéyma Clan's coffers or anything. Isn't this just a minor side business?"

"It is," Kotohime confirmed. "I would even go so far as to say that it's not even that. There are no members of the Pnéyma Clan overseeing operations here, which means it's all being done by those kappa. This suggests that the operation is so far beneath Pnéyma-denka's notice that it wasn't worth sending a clansman over." Kotohime paused. "If I had to take a guess, I'd say Abercio-san is the one who cut this deal. Pnéyma-denka has placed him in charge of mundane operations that don't affect the clan, so it makes sense when you think about it."

"Then why would these Ocean Kitsune bother with this?" asked Kiara.

"There could be any number of reasons: Land, wealth, power, they could just want to claim this city as their supernatural territory and the kappa are in their way." Kotohime sighed. She was tired, but she wouldn't allow herself to show a lackadaisical attitude in front of others. "You know how kitsune can be when we want something.

We might not like to fight unless it's necessary, but that doesn't mean we're not above killing to acquire something that we desire."

"I've noticed. A lot of kitsune are pretty damn greedy," Kiara stated, amused. Kotohime didn't disagree. Neither did Kirihime, who joined them once Camellia was fully asleep. "I've got to admit, it makes you guys a tenacious bunch. Hell, from what I understand of your charge's relationship with my disciple, she practically wore him ragged for nearly two months before you even showed up."

Kotohime smiled at the mention of Lilian. "Lilian-sama is a very determined young woman. However, she is fundamentally different from most kitsune."

"How so?" asked Heather.

"Her innocence, for one. I don't think I need to tell you how innocent she can be."

Kiara snorted. "I don't think innocent is the right word for it."

"What other word would you use?"

"Naive, maybe?"

"It amounts to the same thing."

"No, it doesn't. Innocence implies moral purity. I've listened to some of the ideas that girl's got in her head, and believe me when I say that there is nothing pure or innocent about her."

"I was not implying pure thoughts," Kotohime defended her charge. "I am speaking of her attitude towards life. She is a very free spirit and doesn't want to be caged. That is the entire reason that she first ran away from home in the first place."

Warmth coalesced in Kotohime's chest as she thought of her charge. It permeated her being, spreading to her limbs, engulfing her entire body. It was a wonderful feeling.

"She always looks at the world as if she's seeing it for the first time. Every day is bright and sunny and new. She has a love for life that I have never seen in another person, be they kitsune or otherwise."

"Okay, I'll give you that," Kiara conceded. "She's a pretty cheery girl. You don't find enthusiasm like that every day."

"Hey," Heather interrupted before they could say anything else. "I was just wondering. This Mul Clan… they're allies of that Bodhi-whatever, right?"

"The Bodhisattva, yes."

"Right. And this Body-guy, he's like, not really pleased with the Pnéyma Clan for what happened to his son, right?"

"Yes," Kotohime said slowly, wondering where Heather was taking this.

"Do you think that maybe the reason these kitsune are in this city is because they know that Lilian is here as well?" Heather dropped the bomb. "Maybe they came here on orders from that Body-guy to kill her as revenge for what happened to his son?"

Kotohime was startled for a moment, but she quickly shook her head. "I doubt it. They have been here for several months already, and there's no way they could have known that Lilian-sama was coming that long in advance. That means their reasons for being here are different."

"Fair enough," Heather conceded.

"Well…" Kiara stood up and groaned, stretching her arm above her head. "I don't know about you gals, but I'm gonna hit the hot springs. It's been a long day, and I'd like to relax."

"I shall accompany you," Kotohime said, standing up as well.

Heather followed suit. "Heh… if you two are going, then I guess I'll go, too."

As one, the group turned to Kirihime.

"I think I'll stay here," Kirihime said, her smile polite and demure as always. "Someone must remain behind to watch Lady Camellia, after all."

"Suit yourself." Kiara shrugged. "Come on, ladies. The hot spring awaits."

***

The first clue Kyle had that something was wrong was the silence. The halls were too quiet, the rooms dead of life. Graves were noisier than this.

He walked down the hall toward the entrance, his footsteps echoing ominously loud in his ears. Ever since those kitsune began their extermination of his clan, he and the others had begun posting guards at the door. With only five members left, that meant four shifts, one for each member—except for their boss, who was too old to stand guard. It was the start of Kyle's shift.

The second clue he had that something was wrong was the lack of a guard at the front.

Ever since opening their luxury yacht business, they'd taken up residence in a hotel that would have been demolished had they not bought it. The old tiles creaked as he turned around in a circle. The service desk remained, a remnant from when this place used to house people seeking a warm bed. However, that was the only thing he could see. The guard who should have been there was absent.

"Nick?" He called out, frowning when no one answered him. "Come on, man, this isn't funny."

As he walked further into the room, something wet dripped onto his head. Water? Reaching up with his left hand, he wiped at the liquid. His confusion increased when he felt how warm it was.

This is not water.

He brought his hand back down and looked at it. Shock rippled through him. It was blood.

Another drop fell onto his head. Kyle looked up. His breathing quickened. His heart pounded against his chest. Fear, rage, and horror coursed through him like a massive tidal wave.

More blood dripped onto his face, splashing against his cheek. Hanging from the ceiling, strung to the rafters, was Nick. Holes perforated Nick's body, making him look like grated cheese. Blood leaked from these holes as his arms and legs dangled limply. His body was tangled in thick metal wires.

He was unequivocally dead.

Kyle stared for several more seconds before he realized something important. If his friend was dead, then it meant someone had killed him, and if someone had killed him, then that person must still be here. This meant that someone had infiltrated their home, killed his friend, and was now lurking around somewhere.

Oh, no…

"Boss!"

Kyle rushed towards the chamber where his boss slept. He ignored everything else. He didn't care about anything else. All that mattered was making sure his boss was safe. He burst through the door to his boss's room and entered without ceremony.

He froze.

"No…"

Shuǐ lay in bed. He looked peaceful—except he couldn't have been peacefully sleeping because blood was soaking his sheets, expanding like ink on paper. There was a large hole in his chest, as if a spear had impaled him. Water mixed with blood soaked the floor underneath the bed.

Kyle took a step forward.

"B-boss—ugh!"

His vision went white as pain overrode his nerves. It returned seconds later as numbness spread through his body. He looked down and saw something sticking out of his chest. A sword? No, a sword made of water. Swirling liquid hardened and sharpened into a blade. Blood mixed with the water, turning the blade red.

"O-oh…"

His vision blurred. The blade was pulled out, causing him to stumble forward. His legs wobbled as they turned to jelly. Unable to hold up his own weight, he toppled over onto his hands and knees. His arms gave out soon after, and he fell face-first to the floor.

He tried to move, tried to get up. He couldn't afford to die. He didn't want to die. But his strength was ebbing. His body felt cold. Numb. Why couldn't he feel anything? Why? Why…

Darkness.

***

"It's done. The entire clan of kappa has been wiped out."

Luna smiled as she listened to the voice on the other end of the phone. She did so love it when a good plan came together.

"Wonderful. Head back home and get some rest. I'll have another assignment for you soon."

"Yes, Mistress."

She ended the call and set her cellphone on the nightstand. "Hmm." She eyed the object appreciatively. "Sleek, sophisticated, and lovely. If there is one thing that humans did right, it was creating cellphones. They're such useful devices."

"Was Kaine's mission a success, Mistress?"

Luna peered down to see a naked Taer snuggling against her equally naked body. White hair framed wine-red eyes that stared at her inquisitively.

"It was," she confirmed. Fingers dancing against flawless skin, Luna enjoyed her lover's warmth. "Kaine has finally rooted out the last of those pesky kappa. I really must thank Tsuki-chan for leading me to them when we meet. Truly, her appearance was a blessing in disguise. Not only can I continue my operations without worrying about them inadvertently exposing my business, but this should serve to placate the Bodhisattva."

"Then you're really planning on seeing her?"

"Are you worried?" A smile curled her lips at the look on Taer's face. That expression was just too cute. "Do not fret, Love." She placed a finger under Taer's delicate chin, tilting the woman's head so that she could place a kiss on those sweet lips. "You needn't worry about me trying to claim that woman. She has already spurned me once. She even had the audacity to flaunt her human mate in front of me. She's been tainted by both man and human. I'll never let someone like her have the honor of bedding me."

Taer smiled in relief before snuggling her face into Luna's bare bosoms. Luna gazed fondly at the younger kitsune resting between her thighs.

Such a sweet girl, this one.

Luna closed her eyes and felt herself fall into slumber.

Soon, she promised herself. *Soon, I will make you regret spurning my love, Tsuki-chan.*

CHAPTER 12

Cats Love a Good Tale

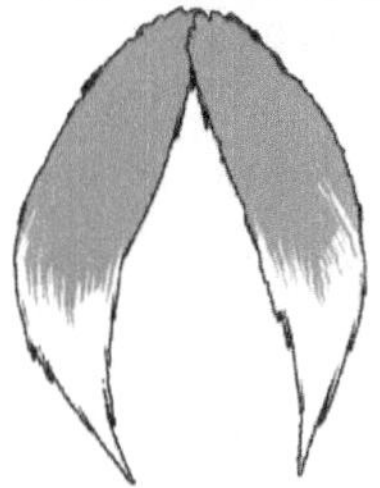

KOTOHIME SAT IN ONE of the booths at the Yōkai Café. She sat alone this time. She would have invited Kiara, but she didn't feel comfortable having Kirihime and Heather watch the children alone, not after everything that had transpired on this trip.

"Here… you go," a burly voice said. She looked at the speaker. Dark red skin hid behind a maid outfit complete with an apron. A jutting lower jaw filled with razor-sharp teeth and two horns protruded from a head full of thick black hair marked this woman as an oni.

Oni were a violent race that rarely communicated with others. While they could talk, most preferred to let their fists talk for them. Only a few ever rose above their violent nature to make something of themselves; Shuten Dōji being the prime example.

Due to an incident that had happened a decade before Lilian gained her second tail, Kotohime had acquired a strong aversion to oni. However, she tried to hide her unease behind a polite smile.

"Thank you."

"You are… welcome," the oni spoke in a halting voice, as if she wasn't quite used to speaking. "Kuroneko will… see you shortly."

"I see. Thank you again."

While she waited for the infamous Saint to arrive, Kotohime observed her surroundings some more. All around her, humans sat while being served by various yōkai. It still amazed her that something like this existed. At the same time, she was surprised that no one else had thought of doing something similar.

"Well, now. I didn't expect to see you again," a purring voice reached her ears. Kotohime turned her head to see yellow eyes dancing mischievously as Kuroneko slid into the booth with the sensual elegance of a cat. "I see that Kiara isn't with you. That's too bad. You two were in such a hurry the other day that we didn't get to catch up."

"I apologize—" Kotohime started, only to stop when Kuroneko raised a hand.

"If you really want to apologize, how about telling me how you two met? I'm most interested in hearing that particular story."

"I… suppose I could tell you that."

Kuroneko eyed her speculatively.

"You don't want to, though." It wasn't a question.

"I dislike thinking about that particular point in my past."

"Hmm… well, I'm not one to pry into someone else's unwanted past. We all have skeletons in our closet, so I suppose I could let it go." Kotohime sighed in relief. Kuroneko leaned back and gestured at her. "So, then, what exactly are you here for?"

"Information."

"Ho?" Dancing eyes glowed with the brilliance of two moons. "I certainly have plenty of information to give. However, information isn't cheap."

Kotohime felt something push her down. It was that pressure again. It felt lighter this time, but no less potent.

Sweat trickled down Kotohime's forehead. She clenched her hands, clutching the fabric of her kimono. Heart pounding in her chest, breath catching in her throat, she almost decided to forget about asking for help.

Almost.

"What do you want in exchange?" Kotohime asked.

The smile on Kuroneko's face was reminiscent of a cat who'd been given a bowl of cream. "A story," she said simply.

***

Lilian didn't know what to think. Her day had started off so well. She and her friends had taken a tour around the city. They'd gone to several stores and done some window shopping, and she and Kevin had even found a store that sold anime and manga.

Kotohime had been waiting for them when they arrived back at the hotel. She didn't know where the woman had gone, but she hadn't thought much of it, until her maid-slash-bodyguard invited her, Kevin, and Iris to her hotel room. There, she sat the three of them down and dropped a bombshell.

"We're leaving California. Right now. Pack your belongings and tell the others to do the same."

"W-what? You can't be serious!" Lilian said, aghast. The other two were also gawking at the woman like she'd sprouted five more tails.

"I am being completely serious, Lilian-sama."

"You can't demand that we just leave like this!"

"That is where you are wrong," Kotohime spoke, her voice calm. "I can, in fact, do this. While Kiara-san is the one who planned this excursion and rented these hotel rooms, I am the one who is in charge of yours and everybody else's safety. That safety is currently being threatened by a vindictive woman, and trust me when I say that this woman is as dangerous as they come."

Lilian stared at Kotohime in shock. She couldn't believe this was happening. Her maid wanted to take them home after all this planning, after she and Kevin bought those tickets and found their costumes, because of something like a woman with a grudge?

"Who's this woman you're talking about?" asked Kevin.

"Her name is Luna Mul," Kotohime sighed. "Back when I first met her, she was a member of the Mul Clan's branch family. I've recently learned that she has somehow managed to become the clan's matriarch. She is currently here in Los Angeles."

"How do you know this Luna chick?" asked a curious Iris.

"We met around one hundred years ago. This was before I became a servant of the Pnéyma Clan. Back then, I had a mate."

"I didn't like him very much," Kirihime admitted from where she sat on the bed, pampering Camellia with some head petting.

"Hawa…" the blissful mother of two muttered, oblivious to everything around her.

Kotohime nodded. "That is true. You were not fond of Corban, as I recall."

"I tried to kill him several times."

"You tried to what?" Kevin and Lilian asked at the same time.

"Getting back to the story," Kotohime continued, "it was during this that I met Luna-san. She became somewhat… attached to me after our first meeting."

"Attached?" Kevin asked.

"I believe you would call it an obsession." Upon seeing Kevin's incredulous expression, Kotohime grimaced. "She wanted me to become her lover. I already had a mate, and aside from that, I am straight. I told her no." Kotohime gave him a very bitter smile. "She didn't take the rejection well. She kidnapped Kirihime to get revenge. We mounted a rescue mission, but Kiara got caught in the crossfire, and my mate died trying to protect her."

"Wait. How does Kiara fit into all this?" Lilian wondered out loud.

The question, while directed at Kotohime, was answered by Kiara, who leaned against the wall.

"I had been traveling with my brother in search of a teacher to help me get stronger, for reasons that are my own. During that time, I met Kotohime, saw how strong she was, and tried to make her teach me." Kiara's faint smile spoke of amusement. "I don't think she liked me very much."

"With good reason. You're a dog."

"How is that a good reason?"

"The only reason you and I get along now is because I promised Corban that I wouldn't allow the inborn hatred of my race to cloud my judgment towards you." While Kiara gave her a very mild pout, Kotohime continued. "In either event, that is why we cannot stay in this state any longer. Doing so puts the lives of you and your friends in jeopardy."

A long silence ensued among those present. No one seemed to know what to say. Kevin stood next to Lilian, his expression contemplative. Iris also seemed to be contemplating something.

"So, you don't go for tacos?"

Iris's contemplation apparently had nothing to do with the fact that they were in imminent danger.

Kotohime's expression was that of someone who'd been slapped in the face with a dead fish.

"Of course not," she blustered, her cheeks surprisingly red.

"Huh, I didn't know that."

Kotohime twitched. "You thought I was into women?"

"Course I did," Iris declared. "You've gone through, what, one hundred heats since your last mate died? And you haven't once sought out a man to fuck? How can I not think you went for tacos over hot dogs? I thought you and your sister were doing the nasty together because, really, there's no one else you could've used to satiate your desires with—except for Mom, but that would just be weird."

"L-Lady Iris!" Kirihime looked mortified. "H-how could you—I-I mean, I would never—to do such a thing—and with my own sister!"

"Hawa?" Camellia looked up as Kirihime waved her hands frantically in front of her face. "Kirikiri, why did you stop?"

"Ah! S-sorry, My Lady." Kirihime quickly placed a hand on Camellia's head and recommenced her petting.

"Hawa…" Camellia experienced heaven.

"Iris-sama, please remember to be respectful of this humble Kotohime and her sister." Kotohime smiled a glorious, beautiful smile. "After all, I am the one with the katana."

"Urk."

"And I would hate for that katana to slip out of its sheath."

"Ugh."

"Why, who knows where it might swing?"

"Gurk."

"It might even end up biting into Iris-sama's flesh, slicing through her throat with ease, spilling her warm blood onto the carpet." Kotohime took on an expression of mock concern. "And that would just be awful. I would hate to be the cause of Iris-sama's death, so please, do keep your opinions to yourself."

Iris's mouth couldn't close fast enough.

"Don't use me as a shield!" Kevin shouted when Iris hid behind him. He moved out of the way. Iris grimaced.

"Come on, Stud. You heard her. She might kill me."

"If she does kill you, then you probably deserve it."

"Ouch. You're so harsh."

"I'll show you harsh!"

"This isn't fair," Lilian whispered. Dialogue ceased as the others directed their attention towards her. "You're telling me that we can't go to Comic-Con because some woman you knew in the past may or may not try to hurt us? How does that make sense?"

Kotohime withheld a sigh. "Lilian-sama, please understand. This woman is incredibly dangerous and—"

"But there's no guarantee that she even knows we're here!" Lilian argued. "Wouldn't she have already done something if she knew that you were in the same place as her?"

"You do not know this woman like I do," Kotohime said. "Luna Mul is a cunning and vindictive woman. She's not the type to instigate a direct confrontation without covering all of her bases first."

"I notice that you didn't say anything about whether or not she knew about us," Kevin pointed out.

Grimacing, Kotohime admitted, "There is a small chance that we have slipped underneath her radar. However, considering the kitsune that Kiara and I fought escaped, that chance is very slim."

"But there's still a chance, right?" Lilian said, her gaze imploring. "Please, Kotohime, don't make us leave just yet. This was going to be my first Comic-Con with Kevin. We've spent so much time planning what we would do and getting our costumes ready. This was supposed to be special. Please don't take this away from me, from us!"

"Lilian-sama—"

"One day," Lilian interrupted, holding up her right hand, a quivering index finger extended. "Please, give us just one day. Let us stay here tomorrow and go to Comic-Con. We don't even have to stay for the whole day. We can leave immediately after the costume contest."

"Lilian-sama…"

She stared at her maid, watching the woman slowly yield under her begging. Just one more push. "Please, Kotohime? I just want to have fun with my mate doing something that we both love…"

Kotohime's shoulders slumped, and her face became the definition of defeated. She breathed a heavy sigh.

"Very well. We shall stay." Before Lilian could cheer, Kotohime gave her a stern glare. "However, we're only going to stay at this convention for five hours and no longer. After that, we're leaving."

Lilian nodded enthusiastically. "Got it. Thank you, Kotohime."

Kotohime sighed again. She closed her eyes and pinched the bridge of her nose. Seeing this, Lilian grinned at Iris and Kevin as he held up her hand and gave them the victory sign.

****

The door closed behind Lilian, Kevin, and Iris.

As they left, Kiara glanced at Kotohime, a small smirk touching her lips. "Man, that girl has got you wrapped around her finger, doesn't she?"

Kotohime gave her a mild glare. "Please do me a favor and remain quiet, Kiara-san."

"Okay. Okay," Kiara chuckled before heading into the restroom.

Kotohime took one last look at the door. While the chances of Luna doing something to them at the comic convention were slim, given that it was a highly public venue, she still had a bad feeling about attending. But, still, she didn't want to take this moment away from Lilian, who'd been looking forward to this convention for the past several months.

Kiara-san is right. Kotohime sighed. *I really am wrapped around Lilian-sama's finger.*

****

"Yes, we'll be leaving tomorrow after the comic convention. I know you planned on waiting until the last day to extract me, but it seems you'll need to speed up your plan."

"..."

"We don't really have much of a choice—unless you're saying that you don't want to extract me."

"..."

"Then expedite your plan. There isn't anything I can do to change their minds. Something's got Kotohime spooked."

"..."

"Don't know. I didn't manage to catch their conversation."

"…"

"Very well. Until tomorrow."

Justin hung up his phone and placed it back in his pocket. Things were coming to a head, and it wouldn't be long before he left his friends and returned to where he belonged. It was kind of sad, but that was how life went.

Just one more day…

"Justin? What are you doing out here?" a voice asked, startling him.

Turning around, he addressed Kevin with the same bland expression that he always wore. "… Sunset…"

Kevin paused for a second before speaking. "I didn't know you watched sunsets."

He didn't, but Kevin didn't need to know that. "… Colors…"

"Yeah, I guess the colors sunsets have are pretty." He watched as Kevin looked at the sunset. "Sometimes, Lilian and I will watch the sunset together—well, we try to at least." Kevin turned back to him, his smile sardonic. "Iris has a bad habit of interrupting us whenever we try to do something even remotely romantic together."

It was almost amazing, the change that overcame Kevin's face as he spoke of Lilian. The strange softness of his eyes, the gentle smile on his face, all of it would have looked out of place seven months ago, but now it came naturally.

"You know, I'm kind of surprised you're not in the hot spring with the others."

"… Boring…" He paused and sent his friend a questioning look. "… You?"

Kevin chuckled. "I'm not really into bathing with other men. I know it's a big thing in Japan, and some places in Europe do it, but I never understood how a bunch of dudes bathing together equated to bonding. Girls I can understand. They go to the bathroom together all the time, but guys? I just don't get it."

Justin studied Kevin keenly. This confidence, while not totally new, seemed a lot more natural now than it had been several months ago. Even the way Kevin stood radiated a relaxed confidence that came from definitive life experience.

"… Changed…"

"Everybody keeps telling me that." Kevin rubbed the back of his neck, a self-conscious gesture, Justin knew. His friend did it a lot.

"… Truth…"

"You think so, huh?" Kevin looked back at the sunset. Light played across his face, casting shadows and making him look older than he was. "I guess I have changed a little. A lot's happened, things I never imagined possible, meeting new people…"

"… Lilian…?"

"Not just Lilian. I've met a lot of people." Kevin tossed Justin a grin. "Though I will admit that Lilian is definitely the most important. I really have to thank her for everything she's done for me. I doubt she even realizes it, but all of the changes I've gone through are because of her."

There was that look again. It was that strange warmth, a glimmer of tender feelings that only someone who shared in that intimate concept known as love possessed. This was the biggest change that Kevin had undergone. Before meeting Lilian, that look had never existed on his face, not even when he'd been crushing on Lindsay.

"A-anyway…" Kevin coughed into his hand, a mild blush on his cheeks. "Sorry for going off on a tangent like that."

"… Fine…"

Kevin patted Justin on the back. "Heh, thanks. You've always been a good friend… even if you are a little weird."

Justin would have pouted, but it wasn't in his nature. He instead watched Kevin walk away, wondering if the young teen would still think that after tomorrow.

Tomorrow, the day he would betray the people he called friends.

∗∗∗

A certain nekomata stood on the roof of Sobre el Natural. Arms crossed under her bust, she watched Kevin disappear into the resort. When he vanished, she sighed and crouched down, much like a cat.

Seeing Kevin again after so many years had made her job infinitely harder. Had her target not been so close to him, she was sure—no, she knew that the young kitsune would have died the night she first attacked. He made things difficult, not just because he interfered every time she tried to do her job, but also because his very presence made her feel funny.

"He's grown well, nya."

How old had he been when they first met? Four? Five? Something like that. She still remembered the day they met:

She was cold, tired, alone, and hungry. Lying in a dumpster, she tried to ignore the winter's chill. It was impossible. There was nothing she could use to warm herself up, not even a blanket. Her ears were cold, her fur was frosty, and her tail felt like it was frozen in a block of ice.

"Nya..."

Her stomach made a horrible rumble. She hadn't eaten anything in several days, her village had kicked her out, and her current job wasn't very lucrative at the moment. If things kept up like this, she'd die of malnutrition—if the cold didn't get her first.

"Ah!"

A gasp came from above her. Judging by the timber and pitch, it came from a boy—a very young boy, if she had to guess. Looking up, she was introduced to beautiful blue eyes surrounded by a frame of messy golden locks.

"It's a kitty! Come here, kitty."

Hands reached out and lifted her out of the dumpster. She shivered from the cold, but she soon became engulfed in warmth. The boy had wrapped her in his jacket and was holding her close, using his body heat to keep her warm.

Growl. Her stomach rumbled.

"Your stomach's growling. You hungry?"

"Nya..."

The boy grinned. "Don't worry, I'll make you some food. I'm pretty good at cooking."

As the boy carried her off, she couldn't keep herself from snuggling into his chest.

What a nice boy, *she thought as sleep slowly claimed her.*

That had been the first time that she met Kevin. He'd been nothing but a young and adorable little boy back then. His innocence had moved her, and his love for animals had warmed her heart. He'd taken care of her for nearly two months after that: feeding her and letting her sleep with him. Life had been bliss for those two months.

Then it had all come crashing down. She scowled upon recalling how the landlord had discovered her. He'd been livid and had tried to force Kevin to throw her out. The young boy had fought with the landlord, but then his mom had come into the picture, and Kevin had been forced to send her to an animal shelter.

Allowing the memories to evaporate, she looked back down at where Kevin had disappeared to.

In yōkai terms, their meeting hadn't been very long ago, but yōkai and humans were worlds apart. Kevin had grown up; she hadn't aged a day.

"He would make perfect mate material now," she mused before scowling. "Or he would if that damn fox hadn't gotten to him, nya." Emotions burned hotter than a furnace inside of her. "I can't let this stand, nya. Tomorrow, I'll make that stupid fox regret messing with my master." She nodded to herself. "It all ends tomorrow, nya."

***

Ken stood behind Kaine and Christian. They were in Luna's office, listening to the woman as she gave out orders. By Inari's left nutsack, he hated receiving orders from this bitch. Women weren't meant to order people around. They were meant to make babies. He held in his distaste, however, as no one else agreed with his beliefs, and he couldn't afford to let them know.

"Taer has informed me that tomorrow, Kotohime and her companions will be going to Comic-Con," Luna said, her voice flowing smoothly through his ears. She had a very pleasant voice, but really, he'd much rather listen to her screaming his name than giving him orders. "That is when you'll attack."

"Pardon for asking, Mistress," Christian started, stepping forward, "but why do we need to attack these people at all? Sure, they attacked us, but it hasn't interrupted our operations. It almost seems like they attacked us by mistake."

"A fair enough question," Luna admitted, nodding several times. "I do not doubt that you know at least two of those people: Kiara F. Kuyo…" At the mention of that hated name, all three male kitsune scowled. "… and Kotohime. What you do not know is that they are with three very high-profile targets. Lilian, Iris, and Camellia Pnéyma—three members of the Great Ghost Clan. The Bodhisattva has offered a reward to anyone who can bring him their heads."

Ken thought about that beautiful redhead and her sexy raven-haired sister. So, they were members of the Pnéyma Clan? He'd not known that.

"And you intend to collect that reward?" Kaine asked.

"The reward is merely a side benefit to what we stand to gain," Luna told them. "Thus far, the Bodhisattva has merely requested our aid; however, I do not doubt that his requests will eventually become an order. By presenting the corpses of those three to Lord Shinkuro, we can get him off our backs."

The Bodhisattva, Lord Shinkuro Shénshèng, was a Kyūbi. With power that was on par with many minor gods, Kyūbi were often considered divine entities themselves. One did not dismiss an order from a Kyūbi, for they reigned supreme over all kitsune. Luna's decision was probably the best course of action.

"Now, then, you three understand the plan, correct?" Luna asked.

"Yes, Mistress," they said in unison.

The smile on her lips made Ken nearly growl. Those lips would have been better off wrapped around his cock.

"Good. I'll be counting on you boys. Do a good job and I'll reward you."

He could think of plenty of things she could do to reward him. All of them involved her naked and tied to a bed.

Luna dismissed them. Ken followed Kaine and Christian, not really listening to their conversation. He instead focused on something more significant.

"You! You're the fop who kept hitting on my mate!"

"Aw, whatever. You are a fop. I mean, just look at your hair."

"Nothing, nothing at all... if you're a girl, that is."

Ken clenched his hands. He would show that damn human his place. He was going to enjoy torturing that boy until he was nothing but an empty shell, a husk devoid of life. Then Ken would find Lilian and take her.

He wanted to at least get a few fucks in before disposing of her and handing off her corpse to the Bodhisattva.

CHAPTER 13

The Los Angeles Comic-Con

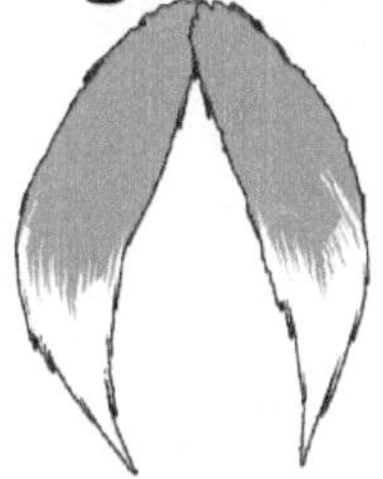

JUSTIN LOOKED AT HIMSELF IN THE MIRROR. A one-piece suit darker than his hair adorned his frame, stretching across his body. He really hated the feel of the spandex, but it was a necessary part of his uniform. Fitted over the spandex was a Kevlar vest, dark brown, with several pouches where smoke grenades and flashbangs were stored. Strapped across his thigh was a holster, which held his Beretta—a standard 9mm pistol. His outfit was finished off with a pair of dark gray boots.

As he looked himself over in the mirror, he felt a little bit of sadness. This would be the last day that he spent with the people he called friends. They were an amusing bunch. Few people were as entertaining as they were, especially after Lilian had entered the picture. He was going to miss that entertainment.

Ah, well. Such was life, he supposed.

During his walk to the entrance hall, he allowed his mind to drift. Christine and Lindsay probably wouldn't be wearing cosplay. Neither of them was really the type. Alex and Andrew might, but he didn't know if they had a costume to wear. He suspected that Eric would, and Kevin and Lilian would definitely be decked out in something. Those two were crazy about stuff like this. He still remembered their cosplay costumes for the Halloween party that Desert Cactus High School had hosted.

His theories were mostly confirmed when he entered the entrance hall. Christine and Lindsay were not wearing costumes. The blonde was dressed in jeans and a T-shirt, and the yuki-onna was decked out in a Lolita dress. Most people would probably think that the snow maiden was cosplaying anyway, but that was neither here nor there. Alex and Andrew had also not deigned to dress up.

Justin then turned to Eric.

"… Jabidaya…"

Indeed, Eric had dressed up as his favorite anime character, the perverted teacher of Natsumo Uzukami: Jabidaya. Waist-length white hair ran down his back like a lion's mane. A headband with a metal plate that had a dildo etched onto the center wrapped around his forehead, allowing two spiky locks from his wig to descend on either side of his face like a pair of testicles. A red jacket worn over a green long-sleeved shirt went down to his knees. Green pants and wooden geta sandals made up the rest of his ensemble. Judging from the quality of the outfit, it was one of those cheap ones that people bought online.

"Holy shit!" Eric pointed at him. The others were gaping, too. "You… what… where… how the hell did you get a costume like that?"

"… Parents…"

"I didn't know your parents could afford something like that!"

"… Saved up…"

"Who? You or your parents?"

"… Both?"

"Don't answer my questions with another question! And what do you mean both?"

Justin was saved from answering by the arrival of Lilian and Kevin… and the cat. Justin frowned for a moment, wondering when the feline had reappeared, but he shrugged the thought off. The costumes were more interesting.

"Oh, dear," Lindsay giggled nervously as she eyed Kevin's and Lilian's costumes with an expression that could best be described as, *"What the hell are those two wearing?"*

Christine just facepalmed. Iris seemed more interested in staring at Kevin's chest with undisguised interest.

"Holy flying fuck! What the hell are you two wearing?!" Eric shouted, pointing at the pair.

"Our costumes." Lilian beamed at them. "They're pretty awesome, right?"

"Awesome is not the word I'd use to describe those monstrosities," Alex said.

Justin had to agree. Lilian and Kevin were wearing the most hideous clothing that he had ever seen. Both of them wore a one-piece green spandex suit and orange leg warmers. That would have been disturbing enough, but they also had the largest, thickest, furriest eyebrows that he'd ever seen, which Justin almost mistook for caterpillars. There was one other thing he noticed, which disturbed him even more…

Kevin had breasts. Really big breasts.

Poke. Poke.

"Are those things real?" Iris asked, poking Kevin's boobs.

"Of course they're not real." Kevin swatted her hand away. "They're made of silicone."

"Hm…" Iris hummed as she studied Kevin's new assets some more. "Not bad. These are almost as big as Kotohime's. What are they? One hundred and eight centimeters?"

Poke. Poke.

"I don't know—and stop touching them!"

"Wha-wha-wha…"

"Look, Beloved." Lilian pointed at Andrew. "I think we broke him."

Kevin looked as well. "It certainly looks that way, doesn't it? Not that I blame them. They were probably blinded by our incredible cosplay."

"No," Alex mumbled. "Incredible isn't the word I would use."

"Hey! Answer my question, damn it!" Eric shouted.

"I thought that would be obvious." Kevin frowned. "We're—"

"I know who you are!" Eric snapped. He quickly calmed down and tried a different approach. "I mean—My Lord, surely, you don't intend to wear *that* to Comic-Con?"

"Of course we do," Kevin answered swiftly. "Why else would we bother putting these on?"

"But those are—"

"Awesome?"

"Um, no. They're—"

"Ridiculously awesome."

"Yeah, they're—no! No, they're not! And enough with the awesome already!"

"You don't think these are the coolest costumes ever?" Kevin shook his head at his friend. "I knew you were a pervert, but I didn't think you were also a heathen."

"Don't call me a heathen when you're wearing something like that! I thought you two were going dressed as Natsumo and Satsuki!" the young pervert said, his voice desperate.

"Why would we do that?" asked Lilian.

"So you can dress as the most famous yuri couple in the entire world!" Eric's eyes lit up like flames. "Why else would you dress up like them?"

Kevin gave him a look. "Okay… let me put this in a way that you can understand. Why would we do that?"

Eric's shoulders slumped. "You guys suck."

With Eric no longer dissing their downright frightening cosplay, Kevin and Lilian then turned to Justin. After eying him up and down, they both whistled appreciatively.

"Whoa," Lilian mumbled, "It's like someone combined Solid Snake with those stupid spandex agents."

Justin twitched. He would not get angry at her for that comment.

Lilian grimaced. "Man, that's just tacky."

He would not get angry. He would not get angry. He would not get angry. He would not—

"I have to agree." Kevin nodded. "That spandex is just ugly."

"Don't insult my costume when you're the ones wearing green spandex!"

Everyone stared at Justin in shock. It took him a moment to realize that he'd lost his composure, then another moment to realize that his friends were gaping at him. Seconds after that, he noticed that his finger was pointed at Kevin and Lilian. He slowly brought his hand back down and tried not to blush.

"I think that's the first time I've ever heard him say more than three words in a sentence," Eric mumbled.

"I think that's the first time I've ever heard him speak a full sentence period," added Kevin.

Finding himself under the most intense scrutiny ever, the only thing that Justin could do was try to hide inside of his jacket.

***

A clear blue sky marked the beginning of the day. The sun shone overhead, bright and warm, casting its rays of ardent sunlight upon the earth. A slight breeze caused trees and bushes to sway. It also served to cool off the procession that was vacating the large bus situated in the crowded parking lot.

Lilian was beaming as she stepped off the bus. She took in the sights and sounds around her. Hundreds, maybe even thousands, of people milled about. Most of them were in costumes. There were a few that she recognized and quite a few that she didn't. All of them were traveling in the same direction.

A figure stepped up beside her. Lilian turned her head. She had to admit, Kevin looked kind of silly wearing green spandex, orange leg warmers, long black hair, caterpillar-like eyebrows, and sporting gigantic breasts. But then, that was the whole point of these costumes: To have fun while looking silly. She probably looked just as goofy anyway.

"All right, everyone! I want all of you sticking together," Kotohime called out to them as the group disembarked, taking charge of the situation much like a mother with her children. "Don't separate into groups until after we've arrived and have picked out the time and place we'll be meeting for lunch."

Everyone agreed and off they went. They made for quite the sight: a group of people composed of mostly beautiful females. Aside from Alex, Andrew, Eric, Kevin, and Justin, the large gathering of fourteen people were downright gorgeous women. There was something for everyone within their group: The sexy succubus with raven locks and bewitching carmine eyes; the Lolita-dressed girl who looked like a porcelain doll; the chatty tomboy with blonde hair; the French maid; the innocent woman showing off ridiculous amounts of cleavage with her flimsy *Mahou Shoujo* costume; the kimono-clad femme carrying a katana; the feral beauty with wild brown hair, slitted eyes, and a predatory grace; … and then there was Lilian.

For the first time since entering the human world, the looks that Lilian received had nothing to do with her inhuman beauty. Absolutely nothing. Instead, everyone was gawking at her choice of attire—or her super large eyebrows, which looked like they might crawl off her face at any second.

"Look at all the costumes! Look, Beloved! Look!" An excited Lilian pointed out several people who were dressed in costumes that she recognized. "It's Ichika from *White Out*! And that's Vagino from *Dragon Warriors X*! Oh, oh, and that's Naruto Uzumaki!"

"Who?" Kevin asked, frowning in confusion.

"Eh?" Lilian blinked several times, her mind going over what she said. "Ah! I mean that's Natsumo Uzukami!"

Rubbing the back of her head, Lilian laughed awkwardly while everyone else stared at her. Feeling her cheeks heat up, she wrapped her arms around her mate's left arm and tried to ignore the looks being directed at her.

"Man, Lilian is hot, but sometimes she says the weirdest things," Eric declared.

Lilian pouted. "That's not very nice…"

"She's definitely an oddball, that's for sure," Andrew agreed.

"O-oi…"

"You won't find many girls weirder than Lilian," Alex added.

"Mu!" Lilian puffed up her cheeks. "You guys are mean."

"Don't worry about them, Lilian." Kevin smiled at her. "There's absolutely nothing weird about you. And even if there was, I would still love you."

Lilian sniffled. She stared at Kevin with her big green eyes, which sparkled with a brilliant and hopeful luster. "Really?"

"Really."

"Thanks, Kevin." Lilian's eyes became pools of adoration. "I love you, too."

"Lilian."

"Kevin."

"Lilian!"

"Kevin!"

Christine saw the two hugging and immediately began shouting, "I'll kill you both!"

Truly, this girl has embraced her role as the *tsukkomi*.

***

Getting access to Comic-Con was a simple process. Kevin and Lilian had already bought passes via the internet. All they needed to do was head into the large reception room, wait in line for a register to open, and then hand over the email confirmation of their purchase. After that, the group received their passes.

"Man, I can't believe we're actually going to the biggest Comic-Con in America," Eric said, sounding more than just a little shocked, as if it was just now hitting him. He looked at Kevin. "This must have cost a fortune. How the hell did you pay for so many passes?"

Kevin shrugged. "Found them on Groupon."

"Groupon? Really? They have deals for Comic-Con? For fourteen people?"

"I suspect this was a plot device myself," Kevin confessed.

Eric blinked. "What?"

Kevin frowned. "What do you mean what?"

Lilian's laugh interrupted the two before they could really go off. "Let's not try to damage the fourth wall any more than we already have, okay, Beloved?"

Eric and Kevin both blinked. "What?"

Lilian sighed. "… Never mind."

They made their way to the convention building. Large did not even begin to describe the structure's size. Monstrous might have been more accurate. It towered over them, a dome-like construction that could have probably fit several football fields inside. Lilian couldn't tell how many floors the building had, but there must have been at least five. Large windows sparkled in the sun. Gleaming metal glinted in the light. Banners hung everywhere, including one large banner that read *Los Angeles Comic-Con* in big, bold letters, surrounded by various comic, video game, and anime characters that she knew on sight.

The inside was no less stunning than the outside. Everywhere she looked, Lilian saw banners and images and statues and all sorts of paraphernalia. There were booths where Comic-Con goers could get their pictures taken, and she immediately zeroed in on one.

"We have to get our picture taken!" she declared. "Come on everyone! Let's—kya!"

Lilian squeaked when her sister hugged her from behind. That wouldn't have been so bad, except that Iris apparently had a case of wandering hands that day. Lilian tried not to moan as her sister shamelessly fondled her breasts in public.

"Aw!! You're so adorable when you get excited like this! Even if you are wearing the most hideous costume I've ever seen."

"Don't make fun of my awesome cosplay! And stop groping me! Only Beloved can do that!"

"There's no need to be like that, my dear sister. He can join us." Iris looked at Lilian and licked her lips. "I don't mind."

"We do mind!" Kevin and Lilian shouted at the same time.

"Ufufufu," Kotohime chuckled, "A dual *tsukkomi*. How cute."

"Simply adorable," Kiara agreed.

Christine clicked her tongue. "Just looking at them pisses me off."

Lindsay just giggled.

"My Lord!" Eric cried. "Even when wearing ugly cosplay, you still manage to make girls fall for you! I am so moved!"

"Shut up already, Eric!" Kevin shouted.

The group walked over to the photographer, paid the man, and stood in front of the green screen to get their photos taken. They could apparently have a background chosen, so they'd decided that, in the spirit of Kevin's and Lilian's costumes, they should have a *Natsumo Shinobi* background.

Unfortunately, problems occurred when they tried to take a group photo. It came in the form of Alex and Andrew.

"Get your elbow out of my side, idiot!"

"If you don't want me elbowing you, then maybe you should move your fat ass out of my way! You're bustin' my personal bubble here!"

"I can't move! I wouldn't be in the picture if I did!"

"Good! No one wants to see your ugly mug in a photograph! They'd die of a heart attack!"

"Oh, that does it! I'mma show you who's da boss around here!"

"It certainly isn't you!"

"Oi! Stop fighting, you damn ingrates!" Christine glared at the fraternal twins who were getting into fisticuffs. She tried to break them up, but she ended up getting beaned in the head by an errant fist. "Oh, that does it!" she growled, cracking her knuckles.

Several seconds later, Alex and Andrew were lying face-first on the ground, their butts sticking up in the air, and hoarfrost-covered lumps the size of Alaska on their noggins. The group ended up taking the picture without them. They were very disappointed upon waking up.

"Okay, everyone!" Kotohime clapped her hands together, getting their attention again. "I know you all want to go off and do your own thing; however, we need to determine groups."

"I'll take these four," Heather declared, pointing at Alex, Andrew, Eric, and Justin.

"Very well." Kotohime acquiesced to her request. "I shall be accompanying Lilian-sama and Kevin-sama."

"Where Lilian goes, I go," Iris declared, grabbing her sister's arm.

Kotohime gave her a placating smile. "Of course, Iris-sama."

"H-hawa," Camellia managed to finally focus on the conversation instead of the enormous amount of people and decorations. "I-I would also like to go with my daughters and Kevin-kyun!"

"Again with the 'kyun,'" Kevin sighed.

"In that case, I would also like to accompany you." Kirihime bowed before Kevin and Lilian. "If that is alright with you, Lady Lilian, Lord Kevin."

"I don't mind," Lilian said. "Kevin?"

"I'm fine with you two coming along," Kevin agreed.

Kirihime gave them a radiant smile. "Thank you."

"We'll be going with you guys, too." Everyone looked at Christine who, after noticing the eyes on her, suddenly realized that she'd spoken out loud. Her face then proceeded to spontaneously freeze over. "N-not that I actually want to be with you guys! D-don't look too into this! I'm only going with you because I don't wanna be alone with these two."

As Christine pointed at her and Kiara, Lindsay crouched down and hugged her knees to her chest. She then drew circles on the floor. A large black storm cloud also randomly appeared over her head like a physical manifestation of her depression.

"She didn't have to say it like that," Lindsay mumbled. "She makes it sound like spending time with me is worse than getting a venereal disease."

"There, there," Kiara muttered in a bored tone of voice that did little to console the depressed girl. She even patted Lindsay's head for good measure. "I'm sure she didn't mean it like that."

Kevin and Lilian stared at Christine for several long, awkward seconds. The snow maiden glared right back, arms crossed and cheeks blue, daring them to contradict her. When, after several more seconds of silence, neither of them said anything, the Lolita girl began to look uncomfortable.

"W-what the hell are you two staring at?"

As one, Kevin and Lilian slowly raised their left and right hand respectively—

—and gave Christine a thumbs-up.

"Nice *tsundere* act," they said in unison.

Christine's face could've frozen over hell. "Sh-shut up!"

***

The two groups broke off; Kevin's and Lilian's group went one way, and Heather's went another. Since Kotohime and Kirihime were going with the larger group, Kiara decided to travel with Heather.

Kevin and Lilian wore the widest grins ever as they rushed to the first booth that caught their interest. It was one of several booths that featured massive amounts of anime fan art. Hanging from the makeshift wall that separated the booths were posters featuring characters from various anime and video game fandoms. Camellia followed behind them as they discussed the displays.

"Um, I don't think it's bad, but the artwork is too stylized to be true fan art," Lilian mumbled, frowning.

"But isn't that what makes it fan art?" Kevin asked.

"No." Lilian was not of a similar opinion. "When creating fan art, artists should remain true to the original style. Even when taking artistic liberties, an artist should still try to illustrate canonical characters as close to the original artist's concept as possible. If I can't even tell who the characters are, then it's not good."

While the person whose art Lilian criticized took great offense to her words, Kevin shook his head and smiled. "You're really critical of art. Maybe you should think of becoming a mangaka or something."

"Hm…" Lilian actually appeared to ponder the suggestion, though she didn't say anything.

Some distance away from Kevin and Lilian, Kirihime and Kotohime, one wearing a placid smile and the other looking more than just a little amused, shared a glance between each other.

"Those two…" Christine stared at the couple with something resembling disgust. "They are way too enthusiastic about this."

"I think it's sweet," Lindsay defended the pair, who were even now making complete fools of themselves by drooling over several *doujinshi* that they had discovered at another booth—much to the mangaka's dismay.

"Would you two lean back a little? You're slobbering all over my artwork!"

Christine listened to the man complain about how Lilian and Kevin were getting saliva on his manga, then gave Lindsay a deadpanned stare.

"Okay," a sheepish Lindsay admitted, "maybe they are a little weird. I still think it's sweet."

"Whatever. Weirdo."

Lindsay's face took on a glum appearance. "That's not very nice."

***

"Apprentice!" Heather barked.

Eric jumped to attention, along with Alex, Andrew, and Justin. "Yes, Master."

The group stopped in the middle of the space between booths at Heather's prompting. The woman looked at the group of youngsters, a grin on her pretty face. Alex and Andrew both flushed red, while Eric had stars in his eyes. Justin's face remained mostly expressionless.

"I have a very important lesson to teach you today, my young apprentice... s." She paused, frowned, and then decided to just go with it. "I'm going to teach you how to grope a woman's butt... without getting caught."

With her left hand clenched into a diabolical fist, Heather grinned at the group of impressionable teens, all of whom gazed at her like she'd just given them the answer to life itself.

"Look around you, my young apprentices. You see all these people? You see all these women? Tens of thousands of people go to Comic-Con every year. Of those tens of thousands of people, at least half of them are female. These women wade through crowds of people, hundreds of bodies pressing together; bumping, rubbing, and touching. It's impossible for someone to walk two feet without accidentally enacting skin-on-skin contact with someone. With so many bodies being pushed together, it is very easy to grope a woman without them knowing who's responsible for it. I shall teach you, my young apprentices, how to grab, squeeze, and caress female flesh without them being any the wiser."

She looked down at the four teenagers standing before her. They were staring at her, their expressions one of awe. Eric was crying, his face leaking at least two different kinds of fluid. He stared at her as if he was in the presence of the truth of the universe. Nothing else seemed to matter to him but the wisdom that she had to offer.

"So, my young apprentices." She extended a hand. "Would you like to learn how to grope butts without getting caught?"

In the face of such an extravagant offer, Eric and the others could do nothing more than accept the invitation. "Yes, Master!"

Several feet away, paying just enough attention to them so that she knew where they were, Kiara flipped through the pages of a manga that had caught her interest.

"Iron Reaver Soul Stealer, huh?" she murmured, flipping through another page and reading about a certain half-human, half-dog yōkai as he fought against his older brother. "What an interesting move. I wonder if I can add it to my repertoire somehow?"

***

"Look, Belove—I mean, Sensei! It's Natsumo and Satsuki! We have to get a picture with them!"

Kevin looked at where Lilian was pointing. Indeed, standing not several feet away were the two titular characters of the *Natsumo Shinobi* series. If the obnoxious orange jumpsuit that Natsumo wore so often wasn't enough to confirm this, then the hairstyle shaped like a duck's rear end that Satsuki was known for having did.

"Yosh!" Kevin, still in the character of Mito Gay, the flamboyant martial arts master, grinned at his mate, who was currently dressed as his apprentice, Mook Lee. "Come, Lee, let us ask that youthful couple if they would like to take a picture with us."

"Yes, Beloved—I mean, yes, Sensei!"

"They're not even paying attention to us anymore, are they?" asked Lindsay.

"Do I really need to answer that question?" Christine replied dryly. Lindsay shook her head.

Like a whirling hurricane, Kevin and Lilian appeared before the two dressed in Natsumo cosplay. They wore matching grins, and their teeth sparkled in the light as they stood in front of the now freaked-out Comic-Con goers.

"Yosh! Good evening, my two youthful friends!" Kevin said in a booming voice. "Would you two care to take a picture with us?"

The two dressed as Natsumo and Satsuki took several steps back. Sweat dripped down their foreheads.

"Uh, um," the one dressed as Natsumo stuttered, "w-we're sorry, really, but we, uh, we have to, ah…"

"We have places to be!" Satsuki interrupted, grabbing her friend by the hand and pulling the other female away. "Sorry!"

Kevin and Lilian watched the two push their way through the throng of people, shoving and kicking and punching everyone who stood in their path.

"Ow! What the hell was that for?"

"Gya! Someone just poked me in the eye!"

"SQUEEE!" came the squeal of someone who was hit right in the daddy button.

Soon, the two cosplayers had completely disappeared from sight.

"They ran away," Lilian said, pouting. Crossing her arms under her breasts, which looked amazing even when covered by hideous green spandex, Lilian had the appearance of someone who was utterly dissatisfied. "How rude."

"They were most unyouthful," Kevin agreed.

Lilian grinned at her mate. "You're really getting into this, aren't you?"

Kevin's grin matched Lilian's. "I've never had so much fun at Comic-Con before."

Several feet away from the grinning pair, Lindsay, Christine, Camellia, Kotohime, and Kirihime watched Kevin and Lilian with a variety of different expressions.

"Oh, my."

"Ufufufu, Lilian-sama and Kevin-sama are so adorable, getting into their little comedy routine."

"I'm… not sure that was a comedy routine," Kirihime mumbled.

"Of course it is," Kotohime said, "no one can act that ridiculous and actually be serious."

"Hawa… Camellia wants to get her picture taken, too."

"I am ashamed to know those two," Christine declared in outright disgust.

"At least they're having fun," Lindsay tried to defend her friends. Christine gave her friend a look. The look lasted for several seconds before Lindsay turned her head. "Okay, so it's kind of creepy. I still think it's nice that they're having fun."

"Then maybe you should join them."

"I… think I'll pass."

"Hawa…"

***

Kevin and Lilian eventually split off from their group and went to register for the cosplay contest. Kotohime came with them, while her sister stayed with Camellia, Christine, and Lindsay. Camellia had tried to go with them as well, but Kirihime had used her tried and true head petting method to keep the woman from following them.

"That head petting of Kirihime's, it could almost be considered its own technique," Kevin mused.

"I know!" Lilian replied enthusiastically. "I was actually thinking of giving it a name… maybe something like **Kirihime Secret Technique: Head Petting.**"

"The first part's fine, but I think the last part needs to have a bit more panache. What about **Kirihime Secret Technique: Diligent Maid?**"

"Hmm." Lilian considered the name before shaking her head. "It's not bad, but I can't help but feel like it's missing something…"

The two tried to come up with a name for Kirihime's method of petting Camellia's head, at least until they located the place where they could sign up for the cosplay competition. The registration table wasn't in the main room with all of the booths, but rather, in a separate room located in one of several adjacent hallways.

There was a line to register, which meandered its way down the hall, extending well beyond their line of sight as it turned a corner. All of the people standing around, waiting and chatting, were dressed up in cosplay.

"Is this the line for the cosplay competition?" Lilian appeared startled to see such a long line. Kevin didn't blame her.

"Looks like it."

"Oh… that's a lot of people."

As she looked at the many different costumes, Lilian felt more than just a little intimidated. There were a lot of costumes, and a lot of those costumes were really good. While she loved the ones that she and Kevin wore, mostly because they had made these costumes themselves, many of the other costumes looked professionally made.

What if our costumes aren't good enough?

Some of those other costumes looked phenomenal. That Master Beef costume looked almost like it was made from real beef! How could they compete with that?

Warmth engulfed her hand. Lilian looked down to see the masculine hand that held her own. She looked up at Kevin, who sent her a confident smile, as if to say *"Let's win this!"* The silent support that he offered made her own lips curl in delight. She laced her fingers through his, and together they proceeded to the back of the line.

Kotohime followed after the two, looking beyond amused.

"Ufufufu, how precious," she muttered to herself.

***

Wearing a thoughtful frown, Christine studied the two items that had grabbed her attention.

She and Lindsay had wandered around the convention for what felt like an hour, checking the stalls and engaging in conversation. Christine had secretly wanted to look at some of the shojo manga that were being sold, but unlike Kevin and Lilian, she didn't want to be labeled as an anime freak, so she kept the desire in check.

That being said, she'd finally found a booth that no one would criticize her for, though it was that same booth that caused her current dilemma. The booth sold Lolita clothing and a variety of accouterments for Lolita clothing. Being a paramour of Lolita fashion, no one would give her strange looks for being there.

I wanted to pick up the latest volume of Kamisama Kiss, *but this is good too.*

She looked at the item to her left, then at the item on her right. The frown that she'd been wearing grew more prominent.

"Hey, Christine!"

Lindsay came up to her, wearing the largest grin she'd seen on the girl yet. She paid minimal attention to her friend, however, as her current dilemma consumed most of her focus.

"Lindsay…"

"Don't tell Kevin or Lilian I told you this, but this Comic-Con isn't half bad," the blonde admitted. "I thought this place would be filled with geeks and nerds like, well, like Kevin and Lilian, but they've actually got a lot of cool stuff here. Check it out! They've got Meow Meow Kitty keychains!" After saying this, Lindsay dangled a keychain of a white cat with an abnormally large head in front of Christine.

Meow Meow Kitty was a popular item from Japan. It had picked up massive popularity in America for whatever reason. Christine didn't really get it, but she had her own cat to deal with, so she didn't feel like having another one.

That's nyot very nyice.

Quiet you.

"That's nice," Christine said absently, eyes still locked on her dilemma.

Lindsay pouted. "You're not even paying attention to me, are you?"

In response to her words, Christine grabbed the two items sitting on the table and held them up for Lindsay to see. "Which one of these do you think would look better with my clothes?"

Lindsay deadpanned. "You're totally not paying attention to me."

"Just answer the question."

Lindsay looked from one item to the other. Held within Christine's left hand was what appeared to be a top hat, except it was smaller and thinner. Its heart-shaped rim also denoted it as something other than a top hat. The other object appeared to be a bonnet, the kind that wouldn't have looked out of place on someone like Little Bo Peep, but it was black and covered in lace.

"Uh…" Lindsay, clearly out of her element, tried to help her friend out. "Um, I don't really think either of them would go with your outfit." She didn't do a very good job. "Sorry."

"You're not sorry at all," Christine said with a sigh, though she put both objects back on their racks.

"So, do you want to check out those comics you were looking at next?" Lindsay asked as they walked off.

"They're manga," Christine replied automatically—and then she paused. "I-I mean… what are you talking about?! Why would I—"

"But you were looking at those… manga, right?" Lindsay asked, the word "manga" sounding foreign on her tongue. "I saw you looking at that romance com—manga, the one with the fox-man."

"W-w-wha—you don't know what you're talking about! Why would I want to read a story about a stupid fox—kya!"

Lindsay apparently decided to not listen to Christine. She grabbed the girl's hand and dragged her off.

"Come on, let's go check out that manga that you were so interested in."

"It's manga—I mean, no! Unhand me! I'm not interested in them! I'm not!"

Christine's protests went ignored by her friend. Naturally.

***

Kevin and Lilian continued to stand in line, which had grown since they'd joined the queue. He was very glad they'd decided to sign up when they did, or they'd have been waiting in line even longer.

"Mou… how long does it take for people to sign up for this thing?"

Lilian did not look terribly pleased to have been stuck in the same spot for several minutes. Her pouting face would have normally looked adorable—except she currently had some of the bushiest eyebrows known to man. Kevin thought their costumes were well-made, and they were having fun wearing them, but at that moment, Lilian didn't look all that cute. Goofy might have been a better word to describe her appearance.

"Don't know," Kevin said, shrugging. "This is the first time I've ever done something like this. I do know that the contest starts in about an hour, so I imagine it won't take more than half an hour for us to register, I think."

"You have no idea how long it's going to take, do you?" Lilian asked.

Kevin's shoulders slumped. "No."

Lilian's frown made Kevin sigh. His mate was the kind of person who was always on the move. She loved doing things. Standing still was anathema to her. Kevin didn't blame Lilian. As much as he loved spending time with her, even he would grow bored if all they did was stand in line for half an hour. They needed to think of a way to kill time while the line crawled forward.

"I've got it!"

Lilian's loud exclamation caused several people to look her way. They sent an appreciative glance towards her spandex-clad bottom and breasts. Unfortunately, when they got to her face, their own faces turned green upon seeing how bushy her eyebrows were.

"Beloved! —I mean, Sensei!"

Lilian gave him a dead serious look, one that forced Kevin to pay attention to her.

"Yes?"

"Let's have sex."

Whatever Kevin had been expecting, it wasn't that.

"We're not having sex. And we're definitely not doing it in public. We've been over this already, and you promised you'd stop bringing it up, remember?"

"Ha… right, right. I remember."

Kevin rubbed his forehead. While he understood Lilian's desire to have sex, and he would even admit that he wanted to do it too, he still wasn't sure if they should. It was odd, but despite how far he and Lilian had gone, he feared taking that final step.

Although if that kappa hadn't interrupted us when we were bathing in the hot spring, I might have entered adulthood right then.

"Lilian," Kevin said to get the girl's attention, "do you want to maybe…"

He trailed off when he looked over at Lilian. He deadpanned.

"Lilian… you're drooling."

Startled out of what must have been X-rated thoughts about them doing the nasty, the redhead quickly wiped the drool from her mouth and looked back at her mate.

"Okay, so no sex," Lilian said, feeling just a little bit disappointed. She perked up a second later. "How about we make out?"

"Nope."

"What? Come on. You know you want to."

"Not in public."

"We've done it in public before," she pointed out, giving him a look that made him turn his head, lest he be taken in by those beautiful big eyes and gorgeous lips.

"We have," he confessed. "And every time we have, I've been thoroughly embarrassed afterward."

"That's not my fault. You're too focused on what other people think."

"And you're not? Who's the one who started hiding behind me whenever we walk through the mall? Or even while we're at school?"

Lilian blushed. It was true. Where before, Lilian had been completely oblivious to anyone whose name wasn't Kevin Swift, recently, she'd become a lot more conscious of the effect that she had on people. Whenever she realized people were ogling her, Lilian would use him as a human shield. Thankfully, she still tended to remain oblivious until someone pointed it out.

"W-what? I do not."

Kevin stared at her. Lilian looked away.

"Oh, look," she said, changing the subject. "The line is moving! Come on, Be... Sensei!"

Kevin shared an amused grin with Kotohime before allowing Lilian to drag him off.

***

Christine and Lindsay walked through the crowd, wondering where to go next.

Thus far they'd visited several booths, and Christine had even abandoned her denial about liking manga. She now had several volumes of *Kamisama Kiss*, which swung by her side in a plastic bag.

"So, we got your... manga," Lindsay said. "Where do you want to go next?"

Christine blushed at the mention of her manga. There was no need for her friend to bring that up. It wasn't like she was a big fan of the stuff. She just liked this particular series.

"I... maybe we could check out some of the clothing?" Christine suggested. "I saw a few places that had some really nice accessories."

Lindsay appeared to think about it for a moment. "Sure, we can do that."

As the two went off in search of one of the booths selling clothing, a voice behind them said, "E-excuse me..."

Christine and Lindsay turned around to see a young man. Long greasy hair framed an acne-covered face. Large spectacles hid muddy brown eyes. His loose clothing hung from his lanky frame, and an expensive-looking camera with a large lens and a scope was attached to a strap. He stared at them with an eager expression that made Christine wrinkle her nose.

"Can I take a picture of you?" he asked.

Christine reeled. Lindsay blinked. "You wanna take a picture of us?"

"Not you." The nerd scowled at Lindsay, then turned back to Christine. Hearts appeared in his eyes. "You! Please let me take a picture of you!"

Christine stared at the boy in shock… and horror, but mostly shock. This nerdy, gross-looking person wanted to take a picture of her?

"Come on, let me take a picture of you!"

The man took a step forward. Christine took a step back.

"Please. I must have your picture."

Another step forward. Another step back.

"That lustrous dark hair. Those feminine curves. Your amazing outfit!" The nerdy boy held up his camera. "I must immortalize your form with my camera! Please… ha… let me… take… your picture…"

By this point, the young man was practically salivating. His breathing had become heavy, and his cheeks were stained red. Christine felt sick and terrified. She shuddered and took several steps away from the boy, but he followed her without skipping a beat. Panic began to set in.

This boy… he's even creepier than Eric!!

Eric was annoying but mostly harmless. This boy actually freaked her out. She couldn't even attack him because she was afraid of what would happen if she got too close.

Fortunately for her peace of mind, she just so happened to be with someone who didn't have the same fear that she did.

"I do not believe Ms. Christine is interested in having her photo taken," Kirihime stated from behind the boy, her voice surprisingly cold.

Everyone present stared in shock at the normally demure and unassuming woman. They hadn't even seen her move! Christine had to blink several times, just to make sure she wasn't hallucinating. It was only after taking nearly ten whole seconds to gawk that she noticed something shocking.

Kirihime was holding two knives. The one in her left hand was almost tenderly caressing the nerd's jugular. The one in her right was next to his baby-maker.

"Wha-what…" The nerdy boy who wanted to take Christine's picture was even more confused, not to mention frightened out of his wits. His legs shook—in fact, his entire body was shaking worse than a leaf caught in a hurricane. The kid looked like he was about to piss his pants.

"Did you not hear what I said?" Kirihime whispered, her voice so unlike what Christine had grown used to. Where before her voice possessed a kind and compassionate demeanor, now it contained darkness, madness, lust, and a desire to kill. It honestly freaked Christine out.

Holy shit! She might be scarier than Kotohime!

"I-I didn't—"

"I don't care about that," Kirihime interrupted. The boy shuddered. "What you did and did not mean to do has little bearing on the harm that your actions have caused. You made Ms. Christine uncomfortable. As she is one of Lady Iris's friends, I cannot let this go unpunished."

While the boy could not see it, Christine could—the sickening grin on Kirihime's face. It made her insides churn.

"I wonder… what do you think I should do first? Should I slit your throat?" The boy whimpered. "Or maybe I should start with dismemberment."

"P-please don't," the boy squeaked. "I'm sorry."

"No. No, you're not, but don't worry," Kirihime stated with certainty, "you will be soon enough. Now, then, what should I start chopping off first? An ear? No, that's much too clichéd, and not important enough to get my point across. Your dick?" The boy squeaked. "Maybe not. That threat is done too often in anime. Hum. I know! Why don't I start by de-legging you?"

"De-legging?" Lindsay made a face. Christine shook her head. She didn't want to know.

By this point, the kid was bawling. Tears ran from his eyes and snot dripped from his nose. He looked seconds away from releasing his bowels. Christine was actually beginning to feel sorry for him.

"Oh, God! Please stop! I'm sorry! Let me go! Please!"

"Hey, um, Christine?"

"Yeah?"

"Do you think we should, like, stop her or something?"

Despite her fear and nausea, Christine still managed to give her friend a flat look. "Do you really want to get between that?"

Lindsay looked at Kirihime as she continued whispering her torture plan to the nerdy-looking kid. She looked back at Christine.

"No, I don't. It's just—"

"Just what?"

"Well, security is coming. I think they might try to arrest Kirihime if we don't stop her."

Christine looked at where Lindsay's head was turned. She was right. There were indeed two security guards pushing their way through the crowd. Damn. It looked like she'd actually have to intervene. Fortunately, she had a plan.

"Oi! Kirihime!"

"Oro?" Kirihime stopped spouting death threats.

"Camellia's run off again."

"Eh?" Kirihime looked around to notice that, indeed, Camellia was nowhere in sight. "Ah! M-My Lady? My Lady?! Where did you go?!"

The nerdy-looking kid slumped to his knees in relief. He was so relieved, in fact, that a large puddle of not-water expanded from underneath him. Christine wrinkled her nose as the smell of urine invaded her nostrils.

"Ugh, gross."

"You can't really blame him," Lindsay pointed out.

"I know that. It doesn't make it any less disgusting."

"True. So, what should we do now? I mean, we're sort of on our own since Kirihime ran off."

Christine looked around, frowning. What could they do? They'd already checked out a lot of the booths, and there wasn't much else to do outside of admiring the artwork. While Christine wouldn't mind looking at some *Kamisama* fanart, she didn't think Lindsay would be as interested.

"WAAAAHHHH!"

Upon hearing a loud, obnoxious, and familiar scream, the two turned their heads to see Eric running from a horde of malicious women. Tears streamed from his eyes as he screamed his head off. Several unfortunate people who were in the way ended up being flung into the air when The Horde crashed into them.

"Oh, boy. I wonder what Eric did this time?" Lindsay pondered out loud.

Christine clicked her tongue. "Do you even have to ask?"

"Guess not."

Eric spotted them and suddenly changed directions, making a beeline for them.

"GOTHIC HOTTIE! HELP ME—BUAG!!"

Before the boy even had time to blink, Christine was upon him. She stuck out her left arm, and Eric, his forward momentum too great to stop, could do nothing as he crashed neck-first into the arm. It was a picture-perfect clothesline.

Everyone watched in muted awe as Eric spun through the air. He made an almost perfect parabolic arc before landing headfirst on the ground. Several people winced at the sickening *crack!* that echoed across the area. His neck was bent at an awkward angle, though he was still alive and kicking, obvious by the fact that he was still breathing.

Christine glared down at the boy, her cheeks blue and her eyes furious.

"Gothic hottie that, asshole!"

"Guu—GYYYAAA!"

As if the act of getting clotheslined wasn't bad enough, The Horde chose that moment to descend upon Eric with all the wrathful fury of a pantheon of angry goddesses.

His cries of pain echoed across the convention for all to hear.

***

After being ditched by Kevin and Lilian, Iris had decided to slip away from the others.

She'd taken to wandering around the many booths, seeing what the place had to offer. While she wasn't an anime and manga fanatic like her sister, she could appreciate the artwork being put on display. Seriously. Half-naked elf-girls? Nekomimi maids? These humans knew how to create some seriously sexy drawings.

As she walked around, heads swiveled and eyes tracked her. No one actually had the courage to speak to her, though, and they all seemed content with simple ogling. While she adored attention and loved having people recognize and admire her beauty, the fact that none of these people had the guts to even walk up to her was annoying. It was boring if she didn't even have to put any effort into becoming everybody's wet dream.

"Maybe I should have stuck with the stud and my sister," Iris sighed to herself, absently gazing at the people around her. One man caught her eye. She tossed him a wink, and the man was suddenly propelled backwards by a geyser of blood erupting from his nostrils. He bowled over several people before slamming into a booth, knocking over the table and scattering artwork everywhere.

Iris didn't wait to see if he would get back up. Growling at the response she received, she continued to prowl. Surely, there was someone in this place who would actually require her to work a little.

"What do you mean you can't make it?"

Iris paused. Had her ears been out, they would have undoubtedly twitched.

"You've come down with a fever? Damn it." A sigh. "All right, I understand. I hope you feel better."

Looking around, Iris saw a relatively plain-looking man with a vacant, tired expression on his face. The man pocketed his cellphone and ran a hand through his short brown hair.

"Great, now what am I going to do?" he asked himself. "Samantha was the only person I had who could fit into this outfit." Iris perked up. Outfit? "Now who I am going to get to wear it? Ugh, do I even know anyone who can…"

The man stopped talking, his mouth snapping shut and his eyes going wide as Iris walked up to him. Her predatory gaze held the man in place, and her smile had him shuddering in something that vaguely resembled post-orgasmic bliss.

Too easy. This man is too easy. But, still, he might prove useful.

Grinning, Iris pinioned him with her gaze and said, "What's this I hear about you needing someone to wear a costume?"

***

It took a long time, too long in Kevin's opinion, but their patience had finally paid off.

They stood in front of the registration table for the cosplay competition. A man sat behind it. He didn't look like anything particularly special. Spiky blue hair, light blue eyes. He was handsome, to be sure, but not like that idiot Ken, whose bishōnen appearance made him look more like a, well, like a Ken doll instead of an actual sentient creature.

"Hi!" Lilian grinned down at the blue-haired man behind the registration table. "We'd like to register for the cosplay competition."

The man looked up. His eyes locked onto Lilian, traveling up and down her body. He looked like he didn't know whether he should appreciate her shapely figure or be appalled by her bushy eyebrows. Fortunately, he also seemed smart enough to keep from saying anything insulting.

"Isn't that why everyone is here?"

Okay, so he kept from saying anything too insulting.

"I'm guessing you two are registering for the couples' competition?"

"Of course!" Lilian beamed. "We're going to win that competition!"

"I'm sure. Sign your names here, please."

They both signed their names on a sheet of paper. While they did that, the man sitting behind the table spoke in a tone dryer than parchment.

"There are a few things you should know about the competition you're entering. First, you are not allowed to change costumes during the competition. What you're wearing now is what you'll be wearing for the entire competition. Second, there are prizes for the top three cosplay couples, including one grand prize. If you win first place, you'll need to have your ID, address, and passport ready. All other prizes do not require any of that and will be given to you upon the competition ending."

Kevin and Lilian barely listened to the man as he droned on. They signed their names on the dotted line and slid the paper back to the man, who looked it over and nodded.

"You're all ready to go. Good luck."

"Thanks!" Lilian said in her cheery voice. "Come on, Sensei! Let's win that competition!"

"Right!" Kevin said as, hand in hand, he and Lilian left the registration table.

The contest was going to start soon, and they wanted to arrive early to scope out the competition.

***

There must have been something wrong with her. Men were admiring her sexy figure as she was dressed to the nines in some of the most sinful cosplay ever. She should have been ecstatic. People were practically orgasming at the mere sight of her! Yet for some inane reason, she felt absolutely nothing. No joy. No Happiness. Not even satisfaction.

It was just too easy. There was no challenge in it. She stood there, she posed, she moved around, and people loved her—well, they loved looking at her. It amounted to the same thing. Either way, she just didn't feel anything at the knowledge that these people were enamored by her beauty. It was just. Too. Easy.

"I'm done," Iris said.

"Eh?" The man she'd convinced to let her wear the costume looked startled. "Y-you're what? Done? You can't be done! I have to be here for another hour!"

"Not my problem."

Iris started walking away from the booth without looking back.

"What about my costume?! At least give that back!"

Iris turned to the man, looking into his eyes, her own irises glowing a vibrant crimson. The man's eyes glazed over.

"You don't need this costume back."

"… I don't need this costume back…"

"You gave it to me as a gift."

"… I gave it to you… it's a gift."

"You want to thank me for all of my hard work."

"… Thank you for all your hard work…"

"See ya later."

"… Bye…"

Iris walked away, this time unhindered. The crowd parted before her like the Red Sea. Iris felt a small flicker of disgust at these people, so simple-minded, so dull.

The stud would have resisted me and fought back... Speaking of him... *Aren't he and my Lily-pad doing a cosplay competition?* She smiled. *I think I'll go watch them.*

She began walking to where the competition was, but someone bumped into her just as she was turning around, causing Iris to fall onto her backside.

"Ouch! Hey, watch where you're going!" Iris glared up at the woman she'd bumped into. She only felt a tad insecure when she noticed the other female's large assets, sensual curves, and seductive yellow eyes.

I'm still hotter than her, Iris reassured herself.

"My bad, nya." The woman held out a hand. Iris eyed it with some distaste before eventually taking it, allowing the other woman to pull her up. "Sorry about that, nya. But you should be a little more careful yourself."

"I'm not the one who ran into someone," Iris bit back; however, it became clear that the other woman wasn't listening to her when she turned around. "Hey, don't walk away from someone when they're talking to you!"

"Sorry, but I've got places to be, nya."

The woman didn't even turn around. She simply raised her left hand into the air and gave Iris an almost dismissive wave.

Iris glared some more, but she eventually turned away when the slightly older-looking woman disappeared into the crowd.

"Tch. Whatever. Now, to find out where that competition is taking place."

She started walking again, traveling to where the cosplay competition was taking place, when something odd struck her about that woman's speech.

She stopped, her face twisting in confusion. "Wait. Did that woman just say 'nya'?"

A chime sounded out and a voice talking over the speaker system interrupted her thought process. "*Attention everyone, the cosplay competition will be taking place in room B206. I repeat, the cosplay competition will be taking place in room B206."*

"Room B206, huh? All right, I'm there."

Promptly forgetting about the woman she'd run into, Iris made her way to room B206—only to stop again and scratch her head in confusion.

"… Where's room B206, exactly?"

***

Lindsay and Christine eventually found room B206. It was a large room with what appeared to be thousands of people bunched together. There was a stage sitting against the back, complete with curtains and a runway.

Seeing how they didn't have anything better to do, they had decided to support their friends in their competition. Sure, they didn't think the two would win, but that didn't mean they couldn't at least console them after they lost. Upon arriving, they saw that both Heather's group and Iris had also managed to find their way there.

Kirihime and Camellia were conspicuously absent. Lindsay concluded that they were lost somewhere in the building.

"Where have you been?" Lindsay asked upon walking up to Iris. The girl in question gave her a shrug.

"Around."

"And where did you get that costume?"

"Oh, this old thing?" Iris grinned. "You like it?"

"Well… maybe a little."

"Heh… I noticed there was a suspicious pause in your words there."

"I-I don't know what you're talking about." Lindsay blushed. "So, who gave you that outfit?"

"A friend."

Christine deadpanned. "You mean you tricked someone into giving it to you."

"Don't ask and I won't tell."

"You're not going to tell us anymore, are you?" Lindsay asked as Christine wrinkled her nose.

"Course not." Iris winked.

Lindsay rolled her eyes. That was a typical Iris answer. She didn't even know why she bothered. This girl didn't seem to care about anyone other than her sister.

"Bitch," Christine muttered under her breath.

"Takes one to know one," Iris shot back, smirking. Even though the look wasn't directed at her, Lindsay felt her cheeks flush, just a little. Iris might have a horrid personality, but she was hot enough to make straight women turn into lesbians.

A woman walked onto the stage, and the noise generated by the crowd slowly died down. Lindsay almost wrinkled her nose at the woman's outfit. Garish didn't even begin to cover it. A short—very short—dark blue skirt covered a small portion of her upper thighs. The rest of her legs lay bare: mocha-colored skin visible for everyone to see before ending in a pair of unusual-looking boots. White with light blue lining the hem, skin-tight and fitting her like a glove, the shirt that the woman wore reminded Lindsay of a cartoon she'd seen about a magical moon princess. She believed it was a sailor uniform of some kind.

"Hey, doesn't that woman look kinda familiar?" asked Christine. Lindsay frowned.

"You think so?"

"Yeah, I could have sworn I've seen her before."

"Hmmm…"

"How is everyone doing today?!" The woman said into a microphone.

The crowd cheered. Lindsay frowned. That voice did sound familiar, albeit it was far too cheerful. She could've sworn she'd heard it before.

"Are you having fun?!" The crowd cheered louder. "I'm glad to hear that. Now, I'm sure you've all been waiting anxiously to see what cosplay people have come up with this year, and I certainly wouldn't want to keep you waiting. So, let's get down to business. How does that sound?" The crowd sent up in another earth-shattering roar. "All right! In that case, let's bring out our first contestant!"

***

Behind the stage, near the back of a decently-sized gathering of people, Kevin and Lilian stood side by side.

Kotohime had situated herself several feet behind them, katana clutched in her left hand. Her eyes were closed, but neither of them was fooled into thinking that she was anything but perfectly aware of her surroundings.

"Next up is Christophe dressed as Alucard! Let's give him a round of applause, people!"

A cheer went up as a man dressed in a charcoal-colored suit, leather riding boots, and a flamboyant and intricately knotted red cravat covered by a frock overcoat with a cape walked onto the stage. His wide-brimmed fedora bounced as he moved, and his orange-tinted goggles glinted in the lamplight. The crowd went wild when he pulled out two large handguns and struck a pose.

"Sounds like people really love his outfit," Kevin commented, all the while rubbing his chin thoughtfully. He looked over at Lilian when she didn't answer. "Nervous?"

Lilian smiled, but he could sense the anxiety beneath her visage. "A little. This is our first competition and, well…"

"You don't really like other people looking at you."

"Right."

Kevin slid his hand into hers. "You'll do fine. I'm here, so don't worry." Getting back into character, he gave her a brilliant grin complete with a thumbs-up. "I've got your back."

In response to his words, Lilian kissed him on the cheek. "Thanks."

"Not a problem."

"All right! Now that we've shown you all of the singles' cosplay, it's time for us to show you the couples' cosplay!" the lady announcer said.

As another cheer went up, Kevin and Lilian shared a look.

"Is it just me, or does that voice sound really familiar?" Kevin asked.

Lilian cocked her head to the side. "You know something? It does sound familiar."

Kevin and Lilian stared at each other for several more seconds, then they shrugged simultaneously. "Weird."

***

Despite not showing interest in the beginning, Iris had to admit that some of the costumes were really incredible. Artistic. Well-made. Stylish. She didn't know if they were homemade or if they were bought, but she couldn't deny their aesthetic appeal.

I'd look good in some of those.

Of course, a few of the costumes sucked, but that was neither here nor there. It wasn't like she cared anyway. She was just here for her Lily-pad.

"All right! Now that we've shown you all of the singles, it's time for us to show you the couples' cosplay!"

Iris frowned as she looked at the woman standing on the stage. She recognized her. How could she not? It was the woman that she and the others had met when they went shopping at that giant mall.

What is she doing here?

"Let's bring out the first cosplay couple!"

The crowd roared as the first couple was brought out, and then the next couple came onto the stage. One after the other they came. Iris saw several costumes that she recognized from the times when Lilian had forced her to watch anime with her. She recognized Natsu and Lucy, Natsumo and Satsuki, and Yusuke and Keiko. There were many others that she did not recognize, however. Her Lily-pad probably knew who they were, but she wasn't a Japanophile like her sister.

"Next up, we're bringing out a rather… unusual couple. Please give a round of applause for Lilian and Kevin, who've come dressed as… Mito Gay and… Mook Lee…"

The entire room went silent as Kevin and Lilian stepped onto the stage. Dressed in green spandex, orange leg warmers, and the bushiest eyebrows anyone would ever see, the pair made for quite the sight, especially Kevin, who was currently sporting a chest almost as large as Kotohime's.

Iris tried really hard not to laugh.

She failed.

***

"Beloved… they're not saying anything."

"They're not clapping either."

"What do we do?"

Kevin looked at the crowd of people. An unsettling silence had fallen over the audience. They stared. They gawked. They did everything except what they were supposed to do: cheer and clap. It was unnerving.

"No choice," Kevin mumbled under his breath. Lilian looked at him.

"Huh?"

Kevin turned to the redhead. "It looks like we have no choice. We're going to have to do… *that*."

412

Lilian's eyes widened. "Are you sure you want to do… *that*? Don't you think that's going a little too far?"

Kevin put his hands on Lilian's shoulders. His visage showed nothing but the utmost seriousness, causing Lilian's own face to become solemn. "I don't think we have much of a choice. We must do *that*."

Lilian turned and stared at the crowd. Their silence unsettled her. It was like they were frozen in time, unable to move, incapable of speech, mere statues caught within a kitsune's powerful illusion.

She looked back at Kevin. "Right. It looks like we have no choice. We have to do… *that*."

"That's right… Lee…"

"Gay…"

"Lee."

"Gay."

"Lee!"

"Gay!"

With tears in their eyes, the two met in a passionate embrace— and opened up Pandora's Box.

***

The world deteriorated. The stage vanished, dematerializing into particles of light. The walls, the ceiling, the ground, all of it disappeared. An alpine prairie replaced marble floors, spreading out as far as the eye could see. Blooming flowers dotted the landscape, and perfectly groomed grass sprouted underneath everyone's feet. A clear sky hung overhead, cloudless and bright, with a sun shining down upon the earth, kissing the land with gentle rays of sunlight.

Chaos reigned.

"What the hell is this?!"

"Oh, God! My eyes! They're bleeding!!"

"I don't wanna see anymore! Please! MAKE IT STOP!!"

As they were inundated by the sight, many of the people present fell onto the grass. Some covered their faces with their hands to block out the horrendous scene. Others clawed at their eyes, raking nails across closed lids. However, most seemed content to simply roll around on the ground, yelling and screaming themselves hoarse as they decried the horror that had appeared before them.

In the middle of this chaotic scene, standing within this beautiful alpine prairie, Kevin and Lilian continued to hug.

***

"W-what the hell is this?" Christine cried out as she stared at the scene in shock. Iris didn't blame her. Even she was surprised by this unusual illusion.

Lindsay also looked suitably horrified. "I… I don't know."

"What is My Lord doing?!" Eric, rolling along the ground with the other boys, squealed like a pig being gutted with a butcher knife. "Why would he subject me, his most loyal servant, to such horrendous torture?!"

"Oh, shut up!" Christine kicked Eric in the gut. "It's not that bad. Get a hold of yourself."

Unlike everyone else, who reacted violently to the chaotic illusion that Lilian had created, Iris simply stood there and waited for it to die down. She didn't have to wait long, as the illusion eventually disappeared. Looking at her sister and the stud, Iris could only shake her head when she noticed how confused they looked, as if they couldn't understand why the crowd was rolling on the floor, looking ready to gouge their own eyes out.

The woman, who Iris recognized as Taer, walked up to the bemused Kevin and Lilian. "Um, excuse me?"

The pair turned to her. Kevin blinked. "Aren't you Taer?"

"Um, yes," Taer said. "It's a pleasure to see you two again."

"Wow." Lilian blinked. "You sound a lot more emotive than you did when we first met."

"W-well, I'm currently doing a job, so…" Taer trailed off, shook her head, then started again. "Anyway, could you please move off stage so we can restart the competition?"

"Sure, we can do that," Kevin muttered.

Iris snickered as Kevin and Lilian left the stage. She couldn't even be mad at Kevin for stealing her sister anymore, not after that. Those two truly were a riot.

I'm going to have so much fun with them both.

"Okay… well… that was a, uh, an interesting last performance," Taer said. Iris held back a snort. "So, um, I guess… now that the contestants have all been shown, it's time to cast the votes and pick the winners."

Taer tried to get everyone's enthusiasm up again, but the sheer *"WTF"* that people felt from the past few seconds had caused too much existential trauma for that. The room remained quiet, still. Disturbed. No one spoke, thus, leaving it up to her to try and bring this whole event back on track.

Iris felt sorry for the woman.

"It looks like the votes have been cast, so now it's time to announce the winners!" Taer exclaimed, though no one clapped or cheered, leading her to cough into her hand and continue. "In third place for the singles competition, we've got Helena Trace, who dressed up as Tifa Lockhart."

No one cheered as someone dressed in short black shorts, a white shirt that exposed plenty of midriff, and coveralls, walked onto the stage. She received a medal, then left via the backstage again. This went on two more times, with the grand prize winner also receiving an all-expense paid vacation to Japan.

"In third place for the couple's competition, we have Jannice and Ulric, who dressed up as Natsu and Lucy!" Taer announced as two people dressed as a certain pair of fairies walked onto the stage amidst a silent crowd.

And that was how it went. The last two couples came up to claim their prizes, with the first-place couple pairing also receiving an all-expense-paid vacation to Japan. Iris just knew that Lilian was probably crying her eyes out right now. Kevin, too, for that matter.

It happened just after the winners for the couples' cosplay were announced. A strange shift in the atmosphere caused the hairs on the back of Iris's neck to stand on end. Something was wrong; a heavy presence existed where before there had been nothing. She recognized it, and that recognition sent a shockwave rippling through her body.

This is youki!

Seconds after this realization, Iris saw snowflakes, pristine and white, falling from the sky. They drifted down, landing on the people in the room, though no one seemed to notice them, which made sense, seeing how they weren't real snowflakes.

Eyes grew heavy. People stumbled, slumping over as if exhausted. Consciousness was soon lost. More than half the people succumbed to slumber within seconds. Her sister's friends had already fallen. They lay crumpled on the ground, all except for the snow maiden, who struggled to remain conscious. Yet even she was beginning to look heavy-lidded.

"An illusion..." Iris muttered. Cursing, she expelled the foreign youki from her body, breaking the illusion and clearing the fog clouding her mind. She went over to Christine, slumped next to Lindsay, who lay sleeping on the ground.

"What... are you—?"

Iris brought out her tails before she placed one against Christine's head and the other against Lindsay's. The two jerked, Lindsay more than Christine, as Iris flooded their bodies with youki, dispelling the illusion.

"Huh? Wha-what?" Lindsay looked around, her eyes wide and startled as she tried to reorient herself. A few seconds later brought her face-to-face with Christine, who blinked and tilted her head as the tomboy stared at her.

"Is something wrong?"

"Ah, no." Lindsay blushed. "Nothing's wrong."

"Really? Because you're looking at me strangely."

"S-sorry. I just…"

"Just what?"

Lindsay's cheeks grew redder. Christine looked even more confused. Iris sighed.

"I'm all for a little lesbian action, but you two might want to do that some other time," Iris interrupted them.

Upon hearing her, Lindsay leapt to her feet while Christine glowered at Iris as she slowly stood up. "What are you talking about, fox skank?"

"Nothing to concern yourself with," Iris said dismissively. "We don't have time for that anyway. We need to grab the others and get out of here."

"Get out of here?" Christine's frown became ever more prominent. "What's going on?"

"I don't know, but someone cast an illusion on us, which means trouble's afoot. Now, come on. Help me wake up the idiots and let's get going."

"Hold on! We're not going anywhere until—"

Christine started to say something, but Iris was not in the mood.

"Look, you two just fell under a kitsune illusion," Iris enunciated each word clearly, hoping that it would help them understand their situation better. "That means that there is at least one kitsune here who can cast a large-scale illusion on an entire group of people. Whoever this person is, they're strong—too strong for us to even think of fighting. That's why I need you two to help me get everyone out of here." When the two still hesitated, Iris lost it. "Now!"

"All right, all right. Geez! No need to flip." Iris actually glared at Christine, getting the yuki-onna to hold her hands up in surrender. "We're going. Keep your panties on, skank."

"Tch."

Iris watched the two move over to their friends and begin waking them up. Now that Christine knew about the illusion, she could dispel it. Iris frowned when she noticed that Justin was missing, but she put him out of her mind. He wasn't important anyway. The most important thing for her was getting to Lilian and Kevin. Kotohime was with them, and she would know what to do.

Before she or her friends could actually do anything else, however, two things happened near simultaneously. Several people stood up, showing that they hadn't been affected by the illusion. These people soon proved themselves to be kitsune when tails sprouted from their tailbones and their human ears became long and furry as they shifted on their heads.

At the same time, several windows and the doors suddenly exploded, and dozens of individuals dressed in black spandex stormed the room. They carried guns at their sides and had rifles slung over their shoulders, which they didn't hesitate to bring to bear.

The soldiers opened fire on the kitsune, who responded by launching techniques of their own. Explosions soon rocked the building, causing Christine, Lindsay, and the others who'd woken up to scream.

In a situation such as this, Iris could only think of one thing to say.

"Well, this escalated quickly."

CHAPTER 14

Crimson Convention

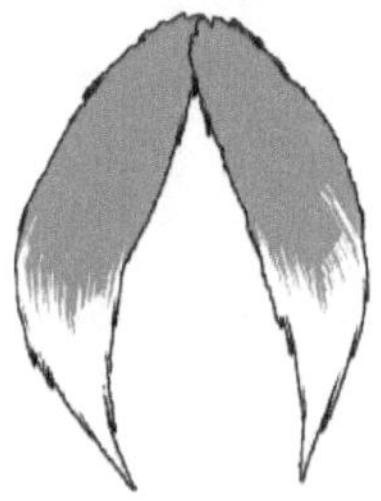

KEVIN DIDN'T KNOW WHAT HAD HAPPENED. One minute, he and Lilian were being consoled by Kotohime, and the next, his head was resting on a familiar chest while a pair of tails caressed his temples. He also felt drowsy, as if he'd gone on a twenty-four-hour anime binge.

"Lilian…" he mumbled into his mate's bosoms. In response, a pair of hands tenderly ran through his hair. He sighed and pressed his face deeper into Lilian's chest.

"How are you feeling, Beloved?"

"Tired… what happened?"

Lilian made a sound in the back of her throat. "It was an illusion. **Kitsune Art: Snowflakes**. It's an Ocean Kitsune technique."

"Ocean Kitsune…" It took Kevin several seconds to catalog this information and understand what it meant. "If an Ocean Kitsune is the cause of this, then…"

"It means that we have trouble on our hands," Kotohime interrupted. The woman seemed agitated. "I told you this would happen, Lilian-sama. Now do you see why I wanted us to leave right away?"

"… I'm sorry," Lilian muttered, her tone terribly contrite.

Kotohime sighed. "Well, what's done is done. We can't change anything now. All we can do is try our best to escape from this situation."

Kevin blinked several times, trying to bring his eyes back into focus. They were still behind the stage, though they were the only ones present—or so it seemed at first. It took a moment, but he soon realized that everybody else had fallen asleep and lay sprawled out on the floor.

"Are you sure you're well enough to stand?" Lilian asked as Kevin moved away from her.

"Yes, I'm fine." Kevin pressed a hand to his face. It felt like there were cobwebs clinging to his mind. "I just need to regain my bearings is all."

Just then, a sound thundered around them. Kevin recognized the noise. It was the roar of gunfire.

"What's going on out there?" he wondered out loud.

Before anyone could answer, Iris burst through the curtains and rushed up to them. "We've got problems!"

"So we've noticed," Kotohime said, her tone dryer than a desert.

Iris ignored her. "There's Ocean Kitsune out there, and they're battling against these spandex-wearing freaks with guns."

Lilian and Kevin shared expressions of alarm. Spandex freaks with guns? That sounded terrifyingly familiar.

"The Sons and Daughters of Humanity," he said.

"Well, this situation has escalated quickly," Lilian added.

"I already said that, Lily-pad."

"Shut up, Iris."

***

It was chaos everywhere.

Christine had thought that it was just happening inside of that one room, but no, wherever they went, kitsune were fighting against humans. Oddly enough, the kitsune seemed surprised at having to fight a group of armed humans. Several had gone down in the initial assault, and the rest were struggling to fight back.

"What the fuck is going on?! Is this some kind of dream?!" Alex shouted, his voice several octaves higher than normal.

Andrew held his hands over his head as he screamed, "If it was, I'm pretty sure we would've woken up by now!"

All of them were hiding behind an upturned booth that had been pressed against a wall. Alex and Andrew were flipping out, and she couldn't blame them—unlike Eric and Lindsay, they had no knowledge of yōkai, but they were now caught in the middle of a battle between yōkai and humans.

Though it's not like I'm in a better position than them.

The sounds of gunfire rang out. Screams resounded around the room. Several meters away, Christine saw a person clad in spandex fall like wheat before a scythe after getting impaled by several stakes made of water. Having seen the same thing, Lindsay whimpered.

"Christine, what should we do?" Lindsay huddled next to her.

"Why are you asking me?" Christine grimaced.

"I-I thought you might know what to do because, well…"

"I might be a yōkai, but that doesn't mean I'm used to situations like this. I've been living like a human my whole life, in case you haven't realized that yet."

"S-sorry."

"It's fine," she muttered.

As they remained huddled behind the table, several long tendrils of water seeped out of the ground around another soldier. The uniformed man shot at the tendrils with his pistol, but they quickly reformed. Then they suddenly constricted around the soldier. The man screamed. A sickening *crack!* was heard, the sound of bones being crushed, before the soldier went limp. The tendrils dropped him to the ground.

Lindsay looked away, her eyes closed and her body shaking. The others weren't looking good either. Alex and Andrew had stopped yelling, and Eric was abnormally quiet.

"W-what are we going to do?" Alex asked in a high-pitched voice.

"Th-this is… are we going to die here?" Andrew wondered.

"I think you guys are forgetting something important here," Heather said, causing everyone to look at her. There was an almost mocking smirk on her face.

Christine raised an eyebrow. "Oh, yeah? What's that?"

"That I was once a member of the Sons and Daughters of Humanity."

After saying this, Heather darted out from behind the booth and launched herself across the space between her and a fallen soldier. Several bullets of water splashed around her. None of the projectiles hit, however, and Heather rolled across the ground, snatched up the gun, and took up a crouched firing position. The gun rang out five times. Christine heard a scream of pain from the other side of the booth, which was followed by silence.

"W-what's happening out there?" asked Lindsay.

"I don't know," Christine said. "I don't know if I want to know."

"Would someone please tell me what the hell is going on?!" Alex screamed.

"Shut up, Alex. We don't have time to explain things right now," Eric snapped, surprising everyone. The young man then ran out from behind the booth and over to Heather. "Please let me help you out, Master!"

Heather sighed as she gave the boy a wan smile. "You can help me by getting back behind that booth. Kitsune aren't the only enemies that we need to worry about, you know."

"Eh?"

Hidden behind the table as she was, Christine comprehended Heather's words before Eric. The two of them were surrounded by, not only kitsune but also the spandex-clad soldiers. They just happened to have been lucky enough to find a spot where most of the soldiers couldn't see them. Now Eric and Heather were out in the open, and several guns had been trained on them.

"Do you think they'll let us go if we tell them we're not with the kitsune?" Eric asked, his voice strangely calm in the face of danger.

Heather eyed the soldiers surrounding them. "Somehow… I don't think so."

"… Well, shit."

***

Several hours before the battle between the kitsune and the Sons and Daughters of Humanity began, Camellia had wandered off on her own. She'd been so distracted by the colorful decorations and pretty costumes that it took her almost an hour to notice that she'd been separated from the others.

"HAWAAAAANNN!"

Since then, she'd been wandering the halls, bawling her eyes out like a child who'd gotten lost.

It was this very loud and obnoxious crying that eventually led to her being surrounded by several men wearing black spandex and carrying firearms. The men all looked baffled. Camellia was just as confused, and she stared at them with her large, innocent eyes.

"Hawa…?"

"Damn," one of them swore. "This chick is stacked."

"I never thought I'd meet someone this sexy in person," another agreed.

"Cut the unnecessary chatter, you two!"

"Yes, Captain!"

"What should we do with her?" asked one soldier.

The captain shrugged. "Why are you asking me? I don't have a clue."

"She's a civilian, right?" a soldier wearing a beret asked. "Doesn't that mean we should, like, protect her or something?"

Camellia, who was fortunate enough to not have her tails out—even she knew that kitsune weren't supposed to reveal themselves to humans—realized that these people didn't intend to harm her. She grabbed one of them by the arm and clung to him desperately, tears gathering in her eyes.

"H-hawa… please help me. I need to find my daughters."

Though her mind had been reverted to that of a child, she knew that her daughters were in danger. She might not have been much of a mother, but she still cherished both Iris and Lilian. Beyond the jumbled mind that had been devastated by circumstance lay the love of a mother who wanted to protect her progeny.

The soldiers melted at the sight of her gaze. There was no way they could resist those eyes, or that face, which was so beautiful and innocent that it made angels look devilish and…

… Hold on.

"Did she just say daughters?"

The group of soldiers looked at each other in shock.

"Damn."

"Damn is right. Who could have guessed that we'd run into a total MILF on this assignment?"

Camellia, who had absolutely no clue what they were talking about, just did what she did best. She tilted her head and looked cute.

"Hawa?"

***

Kirihime was worried.

Strange men in spandex were fighting against a group of kitsune. It was clear to her that both groups had been lying in wait. The kitsune, she guessed, were from the Mul Clan. They were probably here for her group. The soldiers were another matter entirely. She had no clue why they were present, but she supposed it didn't matter. All that mattered was that they represented a danger to the people that she was sworn to protect.

That meant they had to die.

She moved through them like a storm, slashing at her foes with the two knives that she kept hidden in her French maid outfit, slitting throats and lopping off limbs. She could not use any water techniques, but with her muscles reinforced by youki, decimating her opposition was easy.

The soldiers panicked.

"How can this woman move so fast?!"

"Damn it, I thought kitsune used illusions! We haven't been trained to fight someone like this!"

"Fuck! We need backup!"

One of the soldiers appeared in front of her. The pistol in his hands shook. He was afraid. That was good.

Feeling the grin on her face widening, Kirihime blitzed him. Gunfire met her advance, but she dodged each bullet with ease by tracking the soldier's muscle movements and predicting the pistol's firing trajectory. Left. Right. Duck. The gun clicked empty. She was in his guard.

A scream erupted from the man's throat as she slashed at the tendons in his legs. Unable to hold himself up, the soldier toppled over. Kirihime let him fall past her, twirling around gracefully to the left, and then slashing out with the knife in her right hand. Steel met skin and muscle and bone. Steel won out. Kirihime didn't bother watching the man's head fall from his shoulders and moved on to her next target.

It was just after she finished slaying the last soldier that her instincts warned her of danger. Her body moved before her mind could register the threat, leaping into the air just in time to avoid impalement via six spikes of water that shot up from the ground. The water proceeded to follow her, curving in its attempts to stab her.

Acting quickly, she slashed at the spikes, her reinforced limbs blurring. Unable to remain cohesive after she'd sliced them apart, the water splashed harmlessly to the ground. Kirihime landed on her feet and turned to see who had attacked her.

Her eyes widened. "You!"

Standing before her with unerring calmness was Taer.

***

The moment she noticed what was happening, Kiara had taken up arms and fought.

Unlike the others, who needed a moment to gather their wits, she did not. It didn't matter how unprepared she was, her mind, her body, the core of what made Kiara who she was would not allow her to stand idle. She attacked before anyone realized that she was there.

It was only after several minutes of frantic battling that Kiara realized she'd left the young ones behind with Heather. While a part of her was worried, another just shrugged. Heather was a capable woman. She could protect the kids, and Kiara could do a better job protecting the group by drawing as much attention to herself as possible. Thus, she continued to fight.

While Kirihime moved through her opponents like a whirlwind of blades, Kiara straight-up mowed them down, plowing into them with the force of a freight train. Her fists pounded skulls with ease. Each hit sounded like a thunderclap. Each strike was a kill shot. Humans, no matter how much protection they wore, couldn't stand up to the force that her strength could generate. Bones broke. Skulls fractured. Bodies were sent flying, smacking into walls, cracking booths, and skidding along the floor like ragdolls thrown by an angry child. No matter what they tried, it was all useless.

"Shoot her, men! Shoot!"

"I can't track her movements! She's too fast!"

"D-damn it! Why can't I—gurk!"

"Kenny!"

Bull-rushing one of the soldiers, Kiara slammed her fist into his face. She felt it cave underneath her attack as warm blood splashed across her knuckles. She could smell it, the coppery scent of ichor. The soldier was dead before her punch sent him flying into a wall, the concrete denting as abrasions spread from the point of impact.

Darting away, Kiara avoided several bullets and locked onto her next target. The young woman she aimed for panicked and fired off several rounds, but each shot went wide. It took less than two seconds for Kiara to get into the soldier's guard. Soon after, she slammed her fist into the woman's chest, which caved in as the punch launched the soldier into the air.

An eventual lull in combat allowed her to assess the situation. The area around her was mostly clear of enemies. Some soldiers were fighting against a three-tailed kitsune who was dual-wielding water whips to her right. The whips struck several soldiers, tearing through their Kevlar vests like a katana through parchment.

One of the dying soldiers managed to get a lucky shot in before his life was expended. Three shots rang out and slammed into the kitsune, who spun around, blood spraying from the open wounds, before the body hit the floor.

Several meters to her left, a familiar-looking fox trapped his opponents in an illusion. The men and women screamed at the top of their lungs, clawing at their faces like something hideous was crawling on them. Their lives were then extinguished by spears of water that perforated their bodies.

Kiara felt a grin split her face. Without any prompting, she dashed toward the four-tailed kitsune who, judging by the widening of his eyes, had not only spotted her but also recognized her.

"Kitsune Art: World of Transitory Perceptions."

She had to give the fox credit. He acted with admirable quickness. The world around Kiara distorted, flipping upside down and turning inside out. Colors inverted and lines wavered like ramen noodles after they've been boiled in water. It only lasted for an instant, the time it took Kiara to break the illusion, then the world reverted back to its natural state.

"That won't work on me anymore!" Kiara roared. She tucked her fist into her torso, then launched it forward, slamming it into the kitsune's face quicker than lightning.

Kiara frowned when the face burst into droplets of water. Glistening beautifully as the light was refracted off of the many glittering surfaces, the tiny drops acted as a multitude of prisms that caused a plethora of colors to burn her retinas. The lights shifted constantly, forcing her eyes to continuously adjust themselves to the new change in perspective. It was so distracting that only Kiara's enviable spatial awareness allowed her to sense the danger that she was in.

She flared her youki, which erupted from her body as a bright red flame. She was just in time. Not even a second after her aura appeared, something splattered against the protective flames encasing her.

Grinning, she spun around and extended her fist in a lightning-quick jab. A bright red bolt of youki burst from her fist. The energy crashed into a booth, sending splinters of wood and shards of plastic flying everywhere.

A figure shot out from behind the booth, landing several feet away. Kiara grinned at the frustrated expression on the kitsune's face.

"Your tricks aren't going to work on me this time," she declared. "I might have been unprepared to fight a kitsune the last time we tangoed, but I'm more than ready for you now."

"Is that so?" the kitsune scowled. "In that case, it seems I will need to get serious."

"So we're taking this up a notch, eh?" Kiara's grin threatened to split her face. "That's good. That's what I've been waiting for." She set herself into a southpaw stance. "Before we begin, do you think I could get your name?"

The four-tails frowned, but he answered nonetheless. "It's Christian."

"Christian, eh?" Kiara chuckled. "Well, then, Christian, here's to hoping you can give me a good fight."

There was no more need to talk. Kiara rushed forward as her opponent began weaving a specialized kitsune technique.

The battle had begun, and Kiara was looking forward to this rematch.

***

Kotohime led Kevin, Lilian, and Iris down one of the many hallways.

After leaving the backstage, they had discovered that the fighting wasn't just localized to one area. It was happening everywhere. No matter where they looked, kitsune and soldiers were fighting.

The humans clearly outnumbered the yōkai, and Kevin had realized that almost everyone who'd been at the Comic-Con was, in fact, a member of the anti-yōkai terrorist group. He only spotted a few pedestrians sleeping here and there, far away from where the fights were taking place.

Someone must have moved all of the civilians out of harm's way.

Thanks to an illusion that Kotohime had woven over them, they were all but invisible, allowing them to watch the battles taking place without being sucked in.

About three meters away, a kitsune went down in a hail of gunfire. To their right, several humans were killed when a dozen spikes of water pierced their bodies, soaking the ground with water and blood.

"How are you feeling, Kevin?" Lilian asked. Much like him, she looked slightly sick, but she was more worried about him than she was herself. Kevin was touched, and the nausea that he'd been feeling backed off a bit.

"I'm fine."

"You look like you're about to vomit," Iris interjected.

Kevin glared at her, but he didn't deny the accusation.

"By the way," she continued, "why are you still carrying those?"

Kevin looked at the fake boobs in his hands. He'd pulled them out of his shirt a while back because they'd been getting in the way of his running.

He looked back at Iris. "Because they might come in handy."

"How would they come in handy? They're silicone tits."

Kevin opened his mouth to answer, but Kotohime cut him off. "Now is not the time for that. Please remain silent and follow me."

They continued to move down the hall, keeping as far from the centers of combat as possible. Kotohime occasionally needed to take out someone who strayed too close. Kevin could admit that he felt sick watching their maid butcher people, but he held it in.

"Where are we going, Kotohime?" Iris asked. The girl appeared almost at ease among the violence, like she barely noticed her fellow kitsune being shot, or the humans being mowed down by supernatural techniques.

"We need to find our companions," Kotohime determined, moving with grace and confidence, her sheathed katana in her left hand and her right hand on the hilt. "I believe you mentioned that our companions were making their way out of the convention, in which case, we must travel to the exit and locate them. They have a head start, so I assume they're already outside."

"You mean if they haven't been killed," Iris pointed out.

"Iris!" Lilian said, aghast that her sister would suggest such a thing.

"What?" Iris looked at the redhead, whose narrowed eyes stared fiercely into her own. "You know it's a possibility."

Lilian frowned at her sister. "You still shouldn't say things like that."

"Yeah, fine. Let's all just ignore the reality of the situation."

"We're not ignoring anything," Kevin cut in. "We just don't want to think like that."

Lilian nodded effusively, causing Iris to sigh. "Alright, fine. I'll pretend there's a chance that the others are alive. Happy, now?"

"Not really."

"Whatever."

As they exited one hall and entered another, two large cyclones of water appeared out of nowhere and tried to drill through them. The group was forced to dodge—all except Kotohime, who unsheathed her blade and cut the cyclones in half with a well-timed slash.

Kotohime turned, and Kevin followed her gaze. Several meters away, walking through a door that led into the main convention room, was a kitsune with four tails.

***

"Now this is a problem," Kotohime mumbled, turning her head to the three youngsters. "I suggest you three continue on without me. This is not a foe that we can afford to leave at our backs."

Kevin, Lilian, and Iris looked at each other, then back at Kotohime.

"We'll leave this to you," Kevin said before all three of them rushed off, leaving Kotohime alone with Kaine, who made no move to stop them.

He's definitely smart. He knows that attacking those three would give me all the opening I need to kill him.

"I take it you're ready to finish our battle from before?" Kotohime asked, resheathing her blade and entering a classic *iaidō* stance. Kaine frowned as water coalesced around his forearms and hands, forming a pair of amorphous-looking claws.

"It seems I do not have much choice," he said, settling himself into an orthodox fighting stance. "I was told not to let you leave until Mistress Luna arrives."

Kotohime frowned. Then her face relaxed. "I understand. However, since I have no interest in meeting your matriarch again, it looks like I'm going to have to cut you down before she arrives." Her normally placid smile turned cold. "Do forgive me."

***

Kevin, Lilian, and Iris ran down the hall.

Without Kotohime there to protect them, they needed to be extra cautious. Lilian had used a technique that bent light to render them invisible, but because Iris was a Void Kitsune, there was a chance that the illusion would break.

As they ran toward the exit, they happened upon many scenes that were similar to what they'd seen already. In most cases, it was four or five humans battling against a kitsune with two tails, but every now and then, there would be a three-tailed kitsune combating seven or eight humans.

The humans fired their guns, while the kitsune wielded water like extensions of themselves. Shields blocked bullets. Whips lashed out. Swords sliced humans apart. Spears pierced flesh. Bullets penetrated skulls. Kevin even saw one kitsune turn water into chakrams, which he tossed at his foes, causing them to scatter.

They were almost to the escalator that would lead to the entrance hall, when they were forced to stop. Standing in front of the escalator was a familiar kitsune with blond hair, blue eyes, and a pretty boy appearance. The technique around them vanished as Lilian lost her concentration.

"It's the fop!" Kevin shouted, pointing at Ken.

Ken snarled. "I'm not a fop!"

"I don't know… you certainly look like a fop to me," Iris said.

"Ugh." Ken lurched forward as if he'd been physically struck.

Lilian nodded in agreement. "You're totally foppish."

"Urk."

"You're the foppiest fop I've ever seen," Kevin added.

Ken growled. "Shut up! Shut up, shut up, shut up! I'm not a fop! I'm not!"

"Denial is an ugly thing," Kevin said.

"Isn't it also a river in Egypt?" Iris asked.

"No, no." Lilian waved her hand dismissively. "That's The Nile, not denial. Denial is when—"

"I know what denial is." Iris twitched. "I was trying to make a joke."

"It was a lame joke," Lilian said.

"Totally lame," Kevin agreed.

Iris grumbled. "Whatever. You two just don't appreciate my humor."

"Stop ignoring me!" Ken shouted.

The trio turned back to Ken, who pointed at Kevin. "I'm here to settle the score with you, and this time, I won't hold back!"

"That's fine by me," Kevin said, stepping in front of Iris and Lilian. "I'd been thinking that my battle with you had been too easy and anti-climactic. I hope you can give me a better fight this time." He turned his head and looked at his companions. "There's another escalator on the opposite end of the hallway. Use that to reach the entrance."

"Okay." Lilian stared at him with an expression that all but demanded him to be careful. "Don't you dare lose."

Kevin smiled. "Don't worry. I've got this."

Lilian grabbed Iris by the hand and pulled her away.

"Don't think I'm going to let you leave!" Ken shouted as water coalesced around him. Before he could use a technique, Kevin threw his fake boobs, which smacked Ken in the face. The water dispersed.

"Your opponent is me, not them," Kevin said to Ken, who stared at the silicone mammaries in his hands like he wasn't sure what to make of them.

Throwing the fake breasts away, the blond fox glared at him. "Fine! If that's how you want to play, then I'll kill you first!"

"Bring it on, foppy," Kevin said, raising his hand and giving Ken a "bring it on" gesture. It was time to prove that being a human didn't mean he was weak.

***

As Kevin and Ken grew more distant, Iris turned to Lilian. "Are you sure we should leave the stud to fend for himself? I know he's got some sweet moves, but he's still fighting a kitsune."

Lilian understood why her sister was concerned, and she would be lying if she said that she wasn't worried. Kevin was fighting a creature that was more powerful than him.

However, Lilian understood something that her sister didn't. Faith. If she couldn't place her faith in Kevin, then she wasn't worthy of being his mate.

"Kevin will be fine," Lilian assured her. "He's really strong. Besides, he wouldn't forgive me if I intervened in his battle. Kevin has something to prove, and I would be a terrible mate if I tried to stop him because I was worried over his safety."

Iris raised an eyebrow. "And what is he trying to prove?"

Lilian smiled at her sister. "That even a human can defeat a yōkai."

***

Reacting quicker than anyone thought possible, Heather shoved Eric to the ground before she rolled along the floor. The airspace where they'd been standing became filled with bullets. Using her own talent with guns, Heather took aim from her prone position and fired off multiple rounds. Several men were forced to stop firing as they were hit. They stumbled but didn't go down, their Kevlar vests protecting them.

Realizing that Heather and Eric were in trouble, Christine leapt out from behind the table and, placing her hands on the ground, activated her powers. Ice quickly spread across the floor. Before the soldiers knew what was happening, they were all covered in a layer of ice, though they were still alive and capable of speech—or they would have been, had Christine not filled their mouths with slush.

"Whoa." Lindsay looked at Christine in awe. "That was really cool."

Christine blushed.

"Oh, my wonderful Goth Hottie, you're so amazing!" Crying tears of joy, Eric rushed toward Christine, his arms spread wide as if to engulf her in a hug. "I knew you loved me! Now come here and let me shove my face into those tiny lumps of—"

"Can it, pervert!"

"—GUAG!"

Everyone winced as Christine's foot met Eric's face. A brutal *crunch!* echoed across the room, and everyone thought they could actually see Eric's face caving in. He then went flying, crashing into an adjacent booth, the table shattering as he struck it with the force of a battering ram. The boy lay on the floor for several seconds, blinking up at the ceiling.

"Ow…" he muttered to himself.

***

Lilian and Iris didn't even get halfway to the escalators before they ran into trouble.

A shadow fell over them, forcing them to split apart. Iris went left and Lilian moved right. A figure landed where they'd been

435

standing, their heels plowing into the floor and causing it to crack. The person then stood up, her long midnight hair swaying, framing a pair of yellow eyes and a Cheshire-like smile.

Lilian growled. "Not you again!"

"Nya, that's not a nice thing to say," the nekomata said, her two tails curling behind her. "Especially after I came all this way to kill you."

"And that's supposed to make me happy?!"

"Nya!"

"Whoa!"

Lilian threw herself backwards as a claw tore through the space where she'd been standing. Several wisps of blackish-blue fire created streaks in the air, and she realized that the nekomata had coated her fingernails in Hellfire.

This is not good. I hadn't expected to run into her so soon!

"Extension."

The nekomata leapt into the air as two black tails tried to strike her. They struck the ground instead. She landed several feet away… and then fell to a knee as Lilian channeled her youki into an illusion.

"Celestial Art: Light Wave Distortion."

"Ny—ugh. What the…?"

The world around Lilian's foe became distorted. Objects that were far away looked much closer, and objects that should have been closer looked further away. Lines melded together and colors blurred. This was one of Lilian's new techniques, which she hadn't been able to use the last time because there hadn't been enough light, and she lacked the youki capacity to create sustainable illumination.

"An illusion, nya."

The nekomata flared her youki. Lilian clicked her tongue when she felt the illusion shatter, but she didn't let her disappointment stop her from flinging two light spheres at her foe.

"Nya!"

Lilian's enemy twisted around as she dodged the spheres. One almost grazed her nose while the other went under her leg. They continued on, striking a wall several meters away and leaving two perfect black circles.

Lilian scowled at how her surprise attack had failed, and she channeled more youki through her tails, weaving another illusion.

"Celestial Art: Light Inversion."

Light Inversion was a basic illusion that reduced a person's vision to mere black and white. Objects, walls, the floor, and the ceiling, everything was one of these two colors—or lack of colors. It even blocked out shades, so all someone would see was either pure black or pure white.

The nekomata broke this illusion, too, but Lilian had already prepared her next technique.

"Celestial Art: Orbs of an Evanescent Realm."

Six orbs swarmed the nekomata, attacking from all directions. Lilian watched as her enemy used her considerable speed and flexibility to avoid getting struck. Two orbs came from the left and one from the right. They were dodged when the nekomata spun around like a ballerina doing a pirouette. Another came in from behind, but it was likewise avoided. Then two more tried to attack from above. The nekomata moved backwards. The spheres missed, but they paused before striking the ground, quivered, and then chased after her.

Scowling, Lilian's opponent appeared to have grown sick of constantly dodging and, with Hellfire coating her claws, she tried to rake her sharp nails across the orbs. Lilian wasn't going to allow that. She directed the orbs to dodge, then she made them come in at different directions and angles.

"Nya! Hold still, you!"

Sweat trickled down Lilian's brow as she continued directing the orbs, infuriating the feline, who looked very much like a cat trying to smack several balls of sentient yarn. She'd never tried controlling all six at once, and the mental focus required made her body tremble.

"Hurry up, Iris," she grunted.

"Yeah, yeah, just hold on. This is harder than it looks."

Iris also appeared to be struggling. Her two tails had curled in front of her, their tips touching. Hovering above the two tips was a writhing black flame so dark it seemed to absorb light. Lilian shivered at the feeling that came from it: the all-encompassing desire to consume everything. It was an unnatural fire, even more so than their opponent's Hellfire.

Lilian clicked her tongue, but she didn't let go of her concentration. She sent an orb at the nekomata from behind. The nekomata whirled around and tried to strike it, but Lilian forced her to retract her hand by launching two more spheres at her arm. She launched three more orbs at her foe. One came from below and two fell from above. The nekomata attempted to hit them as well, but Lilian moved them around her strikes, causing the woman to hiss.

"This is getting annoying, nya!"

"Alright, Lily! It's ready!"

All at once, Lilian let the orbs disperse. At the same time, Iris released her technique. The black flame, writhing with an almost sentient hunger, shot forward and struck the area that the nekomata was standing on.

"Void Art: Void Fire."

The convention hallway was consumed by the Void.

***

Christine and the others made it outside—only to discover another problem.

"What the hell is that?!" Eric shouted the question that everyone else wanted to know.

The world had been cast in a haze. The light around them looked distorted, tinted like they were looking through glass colored in shades of blue. It was a beautiful sight, but it was marred by what was causing this scenic vision.

A giant blue dome appeared to have surrounded them. The dome undulated and warped at random intervals, as if the entire thing was made of jello. It looked like water, albeit very distorted water that was currently defying the laws of physics.

"This is a barrier," Heather observed. "It was probably set up by those kitsune to keep everyone not already inside of the convention building out. Knowing their specialty for illusions, it's likely been placed under one of those as well. People on the outside probably can't see anything out of the ordinary."

"All right! That's it! You people!" Alex pointed an accusing finger at everyone sans Andrew. "Explain all this to me. What the hell is going on?"

Heather looked at the teens who were already in the know. Eric was looking at the dome, Lindsay appeared to be staring at her shoes, and Christine had crossed her arms and looked away.

She sighed. "Okay, you two, I'll tell you what's happening. You deserve to know. I just hope you don't regret it."

With that, she began to explain what she knew about yōkai and the dangerous world they had found themselves in.

***

From the moment the battle had started, Kevin knew that something was wrong.

For starters, Ken was wielding not one, two, or even three whips, but one whip for each finger—except for his thumbs.

I thought two whips were his limit—

"Whoa!"

Two whips composed of water lashed at him. Kevin stumbled backwards. A large crack appeared where he'd been standing.

"Don't think you can just keep dodging me!"

Six more whips struck out at him, two from the left, two from the right, and two straight down the center. Kevin moved quicker than he ever had before. He shuffled and slid along the floor, his body moving without conscious thought. The air around him whistled as it was cut. Oddly enough, he couldn't feel the air as it was displaced, but he believed that was due to the water's composition.

Kevin continued weaving. Sweat broke out on his forehead, small rivulets that dripped down his face, stinging his eyes. He didn't dare rub his eyes or blink, however, lest he get hit by those abnormally durable water whips.

Something wrapped around his leg. Startled, Kevin looked down to see a whip encircling his calf. Another quick glance showed him that the water whip had come from behind him.

"Well," Kevin started, "this isn't good."

He let out a wordless scream as he was jerked off his feet. His back hit the ground. The air was driven from his lungs in a loud *whoosh!* He felt the urge to curl up in the fetal position, but he rolled sideways instead, which proved to be a good idea. Less than a second after he moved, a whip crashed into the floor.

Using his upper body strength, Kevin launched himself into the air, and then on his feet. He had to dodge a whip aimed at his face seconds later. Ducking under the blow, he… didn't feel the whip passing by overhead?

What's going on? I should at least feel the whip rustling my hair.

He wasn't given time to think on this development as, not even a second later, several lances coalesced into existence around him.

"Let's see you dodge this," Ken said, smiling widely. "**Water Art: Numerous Spears.**"

"And people say I'm horrible at naming things—eek!"

Ten lances were launched at him. He dodged the first and ducked underneath the second. His duck turned into a roll, allowing him to avoid the third and fourth lances, and then he shifted his body into a rotation while shuffling right, thereby avoiding the possibility of getting skewered by the fifth lance.

Back step. Move left. Two more lances were avoided.

The eighth lance came screaming in out of his peripheral vision. He turned around, then sidestepped. The lance shot past him and penetrated a wall several meters away.

The last two lances came in at the same time from opposite directions. Kevin moved along the ground, shuffling across the carpet as he turned his body, presenting his profile to the spears. The ninth spear glided past him, and the tenth one flew over his left shoulder. With the threat of impalement avoided, Kevin turned to Ken.

He took one step forward.

And then he stumbled.

Fire flooded Kevin's nerves as something pierced his back. He looked down to see the watery tip of a spear poking out of his belly. Placing a hand over the wound, feeling blood seeping between his fingers, he fell to his knees, and then onto his side. He felt something hard underneath him, but he couldn't figure out what it was. His vision was swimming. Everything looked fuzzy. Even the dead soldier that lay not a foot from his face appeared blurry.

Ken's grinning visage appeared in front of him. "Tell me, human trash, how does it feel to be beaten by simple illusions?"

"Illusions?" Kevin coughed. Blood splattered on the floor and trailed down his mouth.

"That's right. Everything you just saw was an illusion—a trick of the eye," Ken confirmed.

Kevin grimaced as he realized what had happened. Ken had created eight whips, but only one or two had been real. The others had been illusions designed to keep him distracted from the real whip. It was the same with the spears. They had been illusions that kept him from seeing the real threat coming at him from behind.

"D-dang it."

To think he'd been defeated by illusions and simple deception. How pathetic was that?

"It must be uncomfortable having something stuck in your body like that. Let me get it out for you." The spear in his stomach disappeared and blood began pouring from the open wound in earnest. Ken's grin widened as Kevin whimpered. "Ah, that's much better, don't you think?"

Kevin gritted his teeth as his consciousness started to fade. He could feel his body shutting down. Was he going into shock?

"Not looking so tough now, huh?" Ken mocked. "I wonder where all that confidence of yours has gone—not that you have any right to be confident. Your kind are a plague, a bunch of pathetic cockroaches scurrying underneath those who stand above you." A cruel smile tugged at Ken's mouth. "Now, I think I'll go see how that redhead is doing. She was quite sexy."

Lilian...

Kevin forced the darkness to recede. He looked up, and his eyes burned as he glared at Ken, who merely chuckled condescendingly.

"I think I'll let you live out the last remaining seconds of your life. That way you can imagine all the ways I plan on fucking your mate—sorry, I meant your former mate."

Ken turned and walked in the direction that Lilian and her sister had taken off in. Kevin struggled to think of something, anything that he could do to protect his mate from that disgusting kitsune.

The object underneath Kevin poked him as he shifted. He grunted as he reached down and grasped it, pulling it out from underneath him. It was a gun, a pistol of some kind, just like the ones he'd seen in *Call of Duty*.

Feeling the fires of determination light up within him, Kevin struggled to stand. He couldn't—standing proved to be impossible,

but he at least managed to sit up. With his left hand underneath him, acting as support, he aimed the gun with his right hand.

Eyes looking down the crosshairs, he bracketed the blond kitsune within his sights.

The sound of several gunshots rang out.

***

Kirihime recognized the woman before her. She was still wearing her dark blue skirt, schoolgirl sailor shirt, and magical girl boots. Three fox tails whiter than snow trailed along the floor behind her and ears of the same color drooped low on her head.

"You are… Taer, yes?" she asked.

"That is correct," Taer said.

"Um, forgive me, but why are you here, if I may ask?"

"I am here because my mistress would like to settle a dispute between herself and your sister."

"So I see," Kirihime muttered softly, her eyes growing dark and hooded. "Then you're here to stall us until Luna arrives." She looked out the window to see the barrier surrounding the building. "I imagine that barrier is also your doing?"

"That is correct. We do not want any of you escaping before Mistress Luna has had the chance to… meet with Tsukihime."

"She doesn't go by that name anymore," Kirihime said.

"So I've heard, but what name your sister goes by matters little to me. I am merely here to keep you away from your sister while she and Mistress Luna have their reunion."

"Then I have no choice." Kirihime readied her blades. "In order to protect my sister, I must go through you first."

"Indeed, you must." Taer readied herself for combat as well.

"In that case, I am terribly sorry, but you're going to have to die."

Kirihime did not give Taer a chance to respond before she attacked. Unlike her venerable sister, Kirihime had not mastered the art of removing salt from the atmosphere. She could not use water techniques. So, she used close quarters combat instead.

Her blades sought to penetrate Taer's body. She attacked the woman's weak points: collarbone, armpits, carotid artery, and solar plexus. However, despite her droopy eyes, Taer was not lackadaisical by any means. She moved swiftly, avoiding Kirihime's strikes with ease.

Danger. Kirihime sensed the movement before the strike. She moved her head back. Taer's clawed hand flew upwards as if to slice her face from chin to forehead.

"Water Art: Hidden Blade."

Kirihime felt searing pain along her chin. Stumbling back, she raised a hand to her face as something warm and wet dripped down her skin. She looked at her hand. It was stained with crimson.

"You cut me…"

"Despite not looking like it, I am Mistress Luna's most skilled assassin. You will not defeat me."

"Is that so…? Huhu… huhuhuhuhu… hahahahahaha!" Kirihime laughed. Her voice rang throughout the convention hallway as she giggled mirthlessly.

Taer took a step back.

"Yes! This pain! This feeling!" Kirihime felt her blood boiling. Her desire to kill hadn't been this strong since she'd fought that strange machine seven months ago. "Let me experience more of it before I kill you!"

Kirihime swung the blade in her left hand at Taer's face. Jerking her head back, Taer avoided feeling the same pain that she had inflicted on Kirihime—or so she'd thought.

"A-ah!" Taer gasped when Kirihime stabbed the other blade into her left thigh before yanking it out.

Despite the pain that she must have been feeling, Taer still managed to turn her tumble into a roll. Landing back on her feet, she gestured as if to swipe at Kirihime despite being two feet away.

"Water Art: Silk Threads."

Kirihime yelped when several threads of water wrapped around her wrist and tightened, biting into her flesh. These things were harder than steel!

Taer yanked on the threads, which were attached to her fingers like silk from a spider's thorax. Kirihime moved with the strings. She winced when they dug into flesh, but avoided having her wrist cut off. Blood ran down her hands, making her grip on the knife slippery, yet she tenaciously kept a strong hold on her weapon.

Raising her other hand, she slashed at the strings with a reinforced swing. The threads may have been harder than steel, but they were still water. They broke. Swinging her blade, blood flying everywhere, she swiped at Taer, who backpedaled to avoid having her throat slit. Blood splashed on Taer's clothing as she moved back.

"Water Art: Silk Threads."

Kirihime's maniacal laughter echoed as several threads of water slashed through her chest. The wounds were not deep, for she'd reinforced her body with youki, but they still bled, and that blood dripped onto the floor. She tried once more to spill Taer's blood. The woman deftly avoided her attacks and responded with more threads, which cut into Kirihime's skin and shed more blood.

Giggling like a schoolgirl, Kirihime smiled widely. Her eyes were pools of lunacy.

"Do you know what I specialize in?" Kirihime asked.

"I do not," Taer answered.

"Let me ask you another question: What liquid travels through the veins of every sentient creature?"

"Blood," Taer stated surely before her eyes widened.

Kirihime giggled. The wounds littering her body hissed as they quickly healed over, leaving behind unblemished skin.

"Water Art: Blood Stakes."

Kirihime's blood, which littered the ground in small puddles, became stakes that jutted up and impaled the surprised Taer. The mocha-skinned woman stared at her in shock before falling limp. Kirihime stood still for a moment, to see if the Taer before her would disappear and reveal herself to be an illusion. When that didn't happen, she nodded and dropped the technique, letting Taer's body fall to the floor.

"Now, to find My Lady Camellia and the others."

Reverting to her usual demure mien, Kirihime's posture shifted from maniacal joy to worry. Calling out her lady's name, she left Taer's body where it lay. The hallway became still once more.

***

Kiara laughed as she smashed apart several lances that came at her. Water sprayed all around her before evaporating from her intense aura.

She didn't know how long she'd been fighting. It could have been seconds, or it could have been hours. She didn't care. All that mattered was that she was having fun.

"Water Art: Fire Hydrant."

Large quantities of water gathered in front of the kitsune, rotating like a whirlpool. The water then barreled toward Kiara, who inhaled a lungful of air and then expelled it in a ferocious roar. Hurricane-like winds crashed into the water with the fury of a storm. The water was unable to withstand the wind's destructive power and exploded.

The wind continued on.

Christian leapt out of the way as the storm-like winds tore apart the ground. When he landed, Kiara was there to greet him with a powerful hook. The four-tailed kitsune barely avoided having his head crushed by reinforcing his left arm and bringing it up in a guard.

"Kk!"

Christian grunted as the strike made his feet slide along the floor. Kiara followed, keeping up a relentless pace, her fist blurring as she lashed out at him. Jabs and straights were mixed in with hooks and power punches. Despite Kiara only having one arm, the kitsune was barely able to keep up with her.

Kiara grinned when Christian avoided her latest blow by redirecting her fist over his head. This didn't deter her, and she followed up with a powerful low kick aimed at taking out one of his knees. Christian hopped backwards, thereby dodging the blow—or so he'd thought.

"U-ugh!"

Christian grunted as red youki extended from Kiara's foot and connected with his leg, which gave out and made him drop to a knee. Kiara rushed up and kicked him in the head.

The sound of clapping thunder was preceded by Christian being thrown backwards. He plowed into several booths, breaking through multiple tables, and sending posters and various paraphernalia flying in all directions. Kiara watched with immense satisfaction as the kitsune's body dug a trench in the carpet. He did not get back up, though she could see him trying.

She walked up to the kitsune struggling to rise, stopping in front of the man who, upon noticing her presence, glared up at her.

"You're nearly out of youki, aren't you? That's why you were forced to take my last few attacks instead of using an illusion." Kiara paused, then chuckled. "Well, that, and your illusions don't work on me anymore, as you've no doubt realized."

"H-how…?"

"How did I defeat your illusions?" Kiara quirked her lips. "I just had to constantly circulate youki throughout my body. Your youki is nowhere near as potent as my own, so when it enters my body, my own youki destroys it, thereby breaking your illusions before they have time to take hold."

It was almost amusing, the jaw-dropping gape on Christian's face. Kiara chuckled at the expression.

"Are you going to kill me now?"

"Naw." Kiara shook her head. "I don't kill people who can't defend themselves."

"I could recover and try to kill you again."

"You could try, though you wouldn't succeed. Don't get me wrong, you're pretty crafty, but you're not strong enough to dance with me." Kiara's fangs glinted in the light as she grinned. "However, if you want to wait another hundred years to gain your fifth tail and try again, I certainly won't stop you."

"You…" Christian's face contorted, as if he was trying to decide whether he was angry or resigned. "You never took our battle seriously, did you?"

"Not until you proved to be better than I expected," Kiara admitted. "Even then, I'll admit to holding back a lot. I've only met a few yōkai who can fight me on even footing, much less beat me."

Christian sighed. "I see…"

"Anyway, you just stay put for now. If you have the strength, you might want to think about putting up an illusion for some extra protection."

The kitsune didn't answer. Kiara was not bothered by this.

"Well, maybe I'll see ya around some time."

Tossing a wave over her shoulder, Kiara left Christian to his silent contemplation.

"Now, then," she muttered to herself, "I should probably look for the others. I wonder where they all went?"

***

"Water Art: Water Combustion."

Kotohime narrowed her eyes as a surge of water exploded in front of her. She slid her feet apart, lowering her center of gravity. While her left hand held her sheath, the right went to the hilt of her katana.

The water closed in.

449

Moving quicker than the act of thought, Kotohime unsheathed her blade, slicing it across the surging wave of water. The liquid split down the middle. Salty droplets hit her face as the two waves splashed against the wall behind her, which crumbled as it was struck.

"Water Art: Water Spikes."

Several dozen spikes of water shot up from the ground where Kotohime stood.

"Transient Counterforce."

The spikes dissolved before they could touch her, the water splashing harmlessly to the ground, as Kotohime counteracted his technique by breaking it apart with youki.

"Water Art: Whirlpool."

The water on the floor coalesced into one large puddle and began to spin. Faster and faster it moved, until it had reached maximum velocity. A cyclone of water then shot off the ground before enclosing around Kotohime, threatening to rip her flesh from her bones.

"Ikken Hissatsu."

Spinning around in a counterclockwise circle, Kotohime tore through the whirlpool with her blade. A ripple spread along the water seconds before it exploded in all directions, creating numerous puddles. Kotohime looked at all of the saltwater that now surrounded her.

"With a disadvantage like this, it would appear that I'm going to need to take you a little more seriously, especially since I do not want to be here when your matriarch shows up."

"It doesn't matter how seriously you take me," Kaine said. "You're not leaving until Mistress Luna gets here."

"We'll see about that."

With her katana held in her right hand, Kotohime reached behind her with her left hand. She felt the cloth of her wakizashi's handle. Wrapping her fingers around it, she unsheathed the short sword and set herself into a new stance, feet shoulder-width apart, knees bent, her katana held near her face, and her wakizashi held in a reverse grip in front of her.

Kaine tensed at the sight of this new stance, and he recoiled when his eyes landed on the wakizashi. Kotohime understood. Something repulsive wafted off of the blade. It was fear made tangible, terror manifested on the physical plane. Chikiri no Ken. The Blood Mist Sword, which had killed so many that the steel itself exuded the stench of blood.

"I'll finish you off in one blow."

Kotohime's stance lowered further. Then she disappeared.

"What?!"

"Ikken Hissatsu."

Kaine's eyes widened. That voice had come from behind him!

"Eien Ni."

Kaine screamed as he was wounded by an indeterminate number of sword slashes and stabs. His body jerked back and forth like a marionette controlled by a spastic puppet master. Holes and slash marks appeared all over his flesh and blood arced from his body, staining the carpet crimson.

The assault ended, and Kaine turned his head, one half-lidded eye peering behind him, where Kotohime stood. "I… never stood a chance, did I?"

"No, you did not," Kotohime agreed. "But you did better than most people have, if that's any consolation."

"Heh… I guess… it'll have to do…"

Kaine's eyes glazed over as he fell onto his knees and then pitched forward. His head hit the carpet, and he lay unmoving in an expanding pool of blood.

Kotohime did not spare the corpse a second glance as she turned around. She needed to find the others and leave before Luna showed up.

***

After Heather finished explaining everything to a stunned Alex and Andrew, they made their way across the street.

Christine noticed the wide eyes of her friends, the way their arms shook, how their knees jittered. She didn't blame them for being afraid. They were humans—civilians. They had no experience with the yōkai world. Even Eric and Lindsay knew nothing about this world, despite having been aware of the existence of yōkai for months now.

Fortunately, Heather was experienced in these matters. She led the group to the bus, dual-wielding a pair of Glocks that she'd taken from a dead soldier. No one contested them, however, leading Christine to believe that everyone who might have been a threat was inside the convention center.

The barrier was gone, so they were able to reach the parking lot and enter the bus. Christine sat with Lindsay. The tomboyish girl was shaking. Knowing that this situation wasn't something her friend had experience with, she wrapped an arm around Lindsay's shoulder. The other girl did not hesitate to lean into her.

...

...

"A-are you rubbing against me?" Christine asked.

"No," Lindsay said innocently, her cheeks turning a faint red. "I'm just trying to get comfortable."

"Oh, yeah? Well, you're making me uncomfortable. Stop it."

Lindsay flinched at her tone. She also stopped rubbing herself against Christine, who sighed in relief.

I guess she's just afraid. Lindsay was probably trying to use her as a makeshift teddy bear, something that she could hold onto for comfort. The thought annoyed her, but since they were friends, she guessed it was okay.

"Hold on tight, everyone!" Heather called back as she started up the engine. "We're going back to pick up the others. Then we're getting out of here!"

The squealing of tires preluded the bus tearing out of the parking lot. Christine grimaced as everyone shouted in terror. Her grimace turned into a wince when Lindsay's arms tightened around her until she thought she heard her ribs snap.

If we get out of this alive, I am never getting in a vehicle that Heather's driving again, she promised herself.

***

Like a man who'd been dying of oxygen deprivation, Kevin gasped as he jerked awake.

His eyes snapped wide open, and he looked around, startled and frightened. The world appeared blurry, but it quickly snapped into focus. He noticed that he was propped against a wall. The gaping hole in his stomach no longer hurt, and Kirihime was kneeling in front of him.

She was covered in blood.

"K-Kirihime." He gaped at the woman. "A-are you…?"

"Hmm?" Kirihime tilted her head quizzically before noticing what had caught his attention. "Ah, don't worry, Lord Kevin," she tried to reassure him. "Since the air here is very salty, I had to use blood for my techniques. Please do not be startled by my appearance."

Her words were not reassuring.

"S-so I see." Kevin's mind took a while to reboot. He was having trouble comprehending his situation, which he sought to rectify by questioning Kirihime. "W-what happened?"

"I am not quite sure, to be honest," Kirihime said. "But from what I can infer, it seems that you got into a fight with an Ocean Kitsune—the two-tailed one over there, if I'm not mistaken."

Kevin blinked. He turned his gaze toward the kitsune in question, and he was startled to see Ken dragging himself up the stairs, a smearing trail of blood on the floor behind him.

"Would you like me to kill him for you, Lord Kevin?"

"Ah, um, n-no, that's fine. Let him go."

Kevin was not comfortable with the idea of killing people, and he didn't want Kirihime killing anyone either, though judging from the blood staining her outfit, he guessed it was a little late for that.

"Very well." Kevin couldn't be sure, but Kirihime seemed depressed by his request. He shuddered. "Still, I must commend you on your martial prowess. For a human to match a kitsune in combat, it is most impressive."

"I didn't match him," Kevin muttered bitterly. "I was destroyed. Ken beat me with simple illusions and a few kitsune techniques."

It was almost startling, how easily he'd lost. Their first battle had ended in his complete and utter victory. Kevin had been so sure that it meant he was getting stronger, that he could match a yōkai in combat. This battle had proven him wrong.

It was a humbling experience, this defeat. With Ken's mind unclouded by rage, the two-tails had been able to fight exactly as a kitsune should, using illusions and misdirection to mask his true attacks. Kevin had been thrashed—beaten before the battle began. All of that training, all of the effort that he'd put into becoming stronger, was it all worthless? Maybe it really was impossible for a human like him to match the powers of a yōkai.

Really, what had I been thinking?

"I believe you are giving yourself too little credit, Lord Kevin," Kirihime said, giving the boy a comforting smile—or at least, a smile that would have been comforting were she not covered in copious amounts of blood. "It is true that you received a life-threatening injury that would've killed you—"

"Thanks for making my point for me."

"However, it is just as true that you injured him far more than a single human should have been able to," Kirihime continued as if he'd not interrupted her. "One of the things that you must understand is that we yōkai are beyond humans. We possess powers and abilities that you cannot begin to fathom. Only your vast technological advancements have kept us from revealing ourselves to the world at large."

She nodded towards where Ken had been. The two-tails had already disappeared.

"Even that two-tails has more power than you do," she continued, "powers beyond anything that any human will ever have. Despite that, you, a teenage boy who's only gone through several months of martial arts training, managed to gravely injure him—a feat that normally takes four or five humans. That in and of itself can be taken as your victory."

"Is it?" Kevin asked in a whisper. "Then how come I don't feel very victorious?"

Kirihime shook her head. "I cannot answer that. However, I believe that you are being too hard on yourself. You cannot expect a human to be capable of defeating yōkai after only several months of training. That you have managed to defeat one and tie with another is nothing short of astounding."

There was truth to Kirihime's words, but in that moment, all Kevin felt was disappointment—in himself, in his powerlessness, in his lack of ability. He'd promised Lilian that he wouldn't lose, but he hadn't been able to keep it.

I really am worthless.

"Now, let us be off, Lord Kevin." Kirihime slung his left arm over her shoulder and helped him stand. "We must find the others. I defeated the person who created the barrier, so we should be able to make our escape now."

Understanding that their situation was still dire, Kevin shoved his depression to the back of his mind. "All right. Let's go."

As they slowly waddled down the hall, Kevin felt befuddled as something that Kirihime had said hit him.

"Wait. What's this about a barrier?"

***

Lilian watched as the dark flames of the Void consumed everything in front of her. She shivered but didn't look away. Standing beside her, Iris gritted her teeth, sweat beading down her forehead, as she forced the flames to disperse.

"Do you think that got her?" Lilian asked.

"I… I imagine so…" Her breathing labored, Iris straightened. "I hit her… head-on. The only person who could survive an attack like that is someone with better control over the Void than me."

"Or someone who dodged before it hit her," a voice said above them.

"Right." Iris nodded. "Or someone who—what the hell?!"

Lilian and Iris's heads snapped up to look at the ceiling. Their enemy hung there, her body crouched down like a cat. Her claws were embedded into the ceiling's surface and kept her anchored in place.

"That was an awfully dirty trick you two played, nya," she said. "If that had hit me, I might've actually died."

"That was kind of the point," Iris groused.

"How did you survive that?" Lilian asked. "I saw you get consumed by the flames! There's no way you could have dodged that in time."

"And I didn't, nya." she admitted.

"Then how—?"

"Hellfire clone."

"Eh?" Lilian blinked. So did Iris.

"You were never fighting the real me, just a clone I made from Hellfire, nya," the nekomata explained. "My original plan was to trick you two into attacking it at the same time and making it explode in your faces, but you always kept it at a distance, nya."

"Ugh." Iris grimaced. "So, you're telling me we've been fighting a clone this whole time?"

"That doesn't do much for my self-confidence," Lilian mumbled.

Their opponent's claws retracted and fell back to the ground, flipping around so that she would land on her feet. She stood up from her couch and gave them a grin. "That's what happens when you try to fight the amazing Cassy Belladonna, nya."

"Belladonna? Seriously?" Iris looked disgusted. "What an awful name."

"Nya!" Cassy hissed like a cat being threatened with water. "Take that back, nya! My name isn't awful!"

"It's hideous," Iris countered. "Though I suppose we should just be grateful your name's not something really stupid like McFluffin. Still, Belladonna is a pretty dumb name."

Cassy hissed some more, but Lilian spoke before the nekomata could retort to her sister's insult. "Why are you after me?"

"Nya?" Her anger dissipating, Cassy tilted her head. "I thought I made that obvious already. It's nothing personal, just business."

"It is not just business," Lilian said, glaring. "You've been attacking me like I've committed some great sin against you, and you mentioned Kevin last time. What does he have to do with this?"

"You wanna know why I'm attacking you, nya? Fine, then." Cassy crossed her arms under her chest. "You're right, this is personal. I was so excited when I received this mission because it was in Arizona."

Lilian didn't get it. "What's in Arizona that would make you excited?"

"Master lives in Arizona, nya."

"Master?"

Lilian and Iris shared a look.

"Master Kevin, nya."

"Master…" a deadpan Iris started.

"Kevin?" Lilian finished, looking just as confused.

"Is it just me, or does the stud know way too many yōkai?"

"It's not just you," Lilian muttered. "I'd like to know how he knows so many yōkai myself. For someone who didn't even realize we existed until I came along, he seems to know an awful lot of us."

Cassy ignored the two as they spoke. She was off in her own little world.

"I didn't really care about killing you, to be honest," the nekomata continued. "I just wanted to see Master. Nya, Master Kevin." Releasing a dreamy sigh, Cassy placed her hands on her cheeks. "I remember our first meeting like it was yesterday, nya. He was so kind, and he gave me a place to stay and lots of milk. It was heaven, nya."

Her expression darkened.

"But then that stupid landlord found out about me, nya!" She hissed. "That stupid, fat, insensitive jerk! He forced Master to abandon me! Nya! Oh, how I just wanted to wring his fat nyeck!"

Lilian and Iris stared at the older yōkai with matching wary expressions.

"Ne, ne, Iris, I think this woman's crazy."

"You think? She's obviously insane."

Cassy didn't seem to hear them. She was in her own little world. "So, when I had been told that I'd be going to Arizona to kill off some kitsune, I thought to myself, *This is my chance to see Master again, nya.* I had it all planned out. I would appear before him as a cat, for the sake of nostalgia, nya. He would treat me just like he used to back then, and I'd get a bowl of milk and then, and then when we went to sleep, I'd change back so when he woke up, I'd be in my human form. It was the perfect plan, nya."

Her eyes narrowed.

"And then I discovered that Master Kevin had a mate, nya. He had a kitsune mate, and her entire family was living with him. Not only that, but his mate was the very target I was hired to kill, nya." Cassy pointed at the redhead, her expression a rictus of rage. "You ruined everything!"

"I fail to see how any of this is my fault," Lilian said. "You only have yourself to blame for what happened."

"What?" Cassy growled.

Iris nodded, agreeing with her sister. "You should have been more assertive. Really, you can't blame my Lily-pad for being quicker to nab the stud than you."

Cassy hissed. Her muscles bunched as she bent her knees. Lilian and Iris tensed, preparing for the battle to start up again. A trickle of sweat ran down their faces as the air became thick with Cassy's killing intent. They tried to ignore the shaking in their legs that came from knowing they'd be fighting the real Cassy and not a hellfire clone.

"Lilian! Iris!"

"It's Kevin!" Lilian said jubilantly.

"Does that mean he beat that kitsune?" Iris wore a half-smile. "Not bad. Not bad at all."

"Nya, Master?!" Cassy hesitated for a second before glaring at Lilian. "This isn't over, nya! Just you wait! I'll come back to finish the job, nya. Then Master will be mine!" With one final "nya!" the woman ran off, leaping out of a nearby window and disappearing.

Lilian and Iris noticed her disappearance, but most of their attention was on Kevin—more specifically, on the bloodstains covering his shirt.

"Beloved!" Lilian rushed over to him and began checking for injuries. "Inari-blessed! Look at all that blood! A-are you alright? Does it hurt anywhere?"

"Ah-hahaha!" Kevin chuckled nervously. "I-I'm fine. Kirihime healed my injuries."

"I see…" Lilian sighed in relief. "That's good."

She wouldn't disrespect her mate by showing anything but the utmost confidence in him, but she had been really worried when she'd left him alone with the two-tailed fop. Speaking of…

"What happened to the fop?"

"Ah, um, h-he escaped," Kevin said. Lilian blinked, then looked at her mate more closely. He seemed… depressed? No, disappointed was a better way of putting it.

"Did something happen during the battle?"

"No… nothing serious, anyway."

Lilian's frown grew. "You're sure?"

"Yes."

Kevin gave her a completely unconvincing smile. Lilian worried her lower lip. Something was definitely wrong with her mate, but she supposed now wasn't an appropriate time to call him out. She'd do that in private—preferably while she was cuddling into his side after losing themselves to lust and passion.

"I think you two should continue this conversation later, Lord Kevin, Lady Lilian," Kirihime said. "We should make haste in leaving this place."

Kirihime handed Kevin off to Lilian, who was more than happy to take his weight. Iris also decided to help by getting on Kevin's other side. Lilian was positive that her sister's reasons weren't as altruistic as her own.

"You sound like we need to hurry or something," Iris said as she reached down and placed a hand on Kevin's backside.

"Eep!" Kevin squeaked before tossing an annoyed look at the raven-haired beauty. "Did you just pinch my butt?"

"You're imagining things," Iris replied blithely, ignoring the looks that she received from Kevin and her sister.

"We are in a hurry," Kirihime said gravely. "Someone is coming, and we do not want to be here when she arrives."

***

Kevin's group met up with Kotohime and Kiara before they all made their way outside of the convention building.

"You know, the damage doesn't look as bad from the outside," Kevin commented. Indeed, the convention building's exterior was unblemished. No one would have realized that a battle was taking place inside simply from looking at it.

"All of the fighting is happening inside," Kotohime said. "It makes sense that much of the exterior has remained pristine thus far. Now, then, let us move. I would like to reach the vehicle before the Mul Clan's matriarch arrives."

"Oh, no," a voice said behind them. "That simply won't do. You cannot leave just yet—not until I've had a chance to greet you after all these decades."

Kotohime froze. Everyone else turned to see a woman behind them. She was pale, not porcelain like Christine, just pale, as if the sun had never touched her. The dark clothing that she wore, a black sleeveless shirt, skin-tight pants, and equally black boots, made a startling contrast with her skin. Her long hair seemed to change colors in the sunlight. It shifted from dark blue, to black, then back again. Six black tails swayed behind her.

She strode toward them with an indefinable elegance. The way she moved made the hairs on the back of their necks stand on end. There was something dangerous about this woman; they could all feel it, even if they could not identify why they felt this way.

She stopped several meters from them, her lips curving delicately, her eyes lighting up. Despite her resplendent beauty and gorgeous smile, everyone remained tense.

Kotohime remained frozen solid. Her body seemed unnaturally stiff. Standing beside her, Kirihime's breathing picked up as if she was having an asthma attack.

"Hello, Tsuki-chan," the woman purred. "It's a pleasure to see you again."

CHAPTER 15

Remnants of a Painful Past

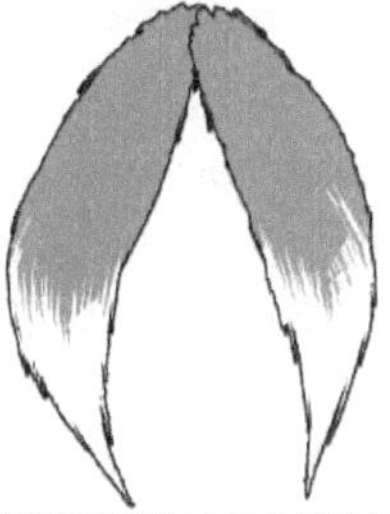

"Luna…" Kotohime whispered in a weak voice.

"It's been a long time, hasn't it, Tsuki-chan? Ah, you don't go by that name anymore, do you?" Luna's smile was so pleasant that it made the hairs on Kotohime's neck prickle. "The last time you and I saw each other was about one hundred and fifty years ago, was it not? You were just a cute little three-tails back then. Look at how well you've grown. You've become quite the beautiful woman."

Kotohime shuddered in disgust and—Kevin thought—maybe even a hint of fear.

"Are you not happy to see me?" Luna asked.

"It had been my hope that you and I would never cross paths again," Kotohime admitted.

Luna's smile took on a twisted quality. "Now that is not a very nice thing to say."

A strange pressure suddenly filled the air. If Kevin had to describe it with words, he would have said that it felt like a several-fold increase in the Earth's gravitational pull. His knees buckled. Were it not for Lilian and Iris holding him up, he would have fallen over. A glance at the two revealed that they were also feeling the effects of this strange force. Their bodies were shaking.

"W-what is this…?" he asked, his voice a hushed whisper, as if he was afraid that Luna would hear him.

"It's killing intent," Kiara answered. "You know what that is, don't you? It is the manifestation of a person's intent to kill or cause physical harm. Humans can use it to some extent, but it's far more powerful when a yōkai does it, because ours is infused with youki."

So this was killing intent—true killing intent and not the kiddy stuff that his peers used to toss at him when Lilian had first shown up. It made Kevin sick. His stomach threatened to empty its contents onto the pavement, and only his iron-clad will and desire not to look weaker than he already did kept him from giving in.

"Kirihime," Kotohime's voice broke through the fog of fear that had penetrated Kevin's mind. "Please take Lilian-sama, Iris-sama, and Kevin-sama back into the convention center."

Kevin observed Kirihime. For a moment, it looked like the three-tails was about to argue. However, after a second of indecision, she accented with a nod. "Very well. Be careful, sister."

Kotohime's smile was tremulous. Kevin had never seen such a look on the woman's face. Something unsettling squirmed around in his gut.

"I will," she assured her sister.

Somehow, Kevin knew that she was lying.

***

Kotohime watched as Kirihime led the trio of youngsters back inside of the convention center. She felt a brief bout of relief. Though there was likely still fighting going on inside, they would be safer in there than they would be out here.

Kiara stepped up beside her, wearing a grin that combined excitement and anxiety. "It seems I'll be getting that ultimate challenge I always wanted."

"I wish your ultimate challenge would come at a time when I'm not around," Kotohime stated.

"Aw, you're no fun, spoilsport."

Luna's eyes flickered from Kotohime to Kiara and, in a derisive tone, she said, "I am disappointed in you, Tsuki-chan. To think you'd have fallen so low as to befriend a dog." Kiara bared her fangs in a snarl, but the gesture went ignored by the six-tails. "And not just any dog, but the very one who was responsible for the death of your dearly departed Corban."

Kotohime felt a surge of hatred that made her blood boil. "Don't you dare speak his name. You are the reason my mate died— you and no one else."

Luna's smile dripped with condescension. "Don't be ridiculous, girl. We both know your mate would never have died were it not for this dog. After all, the reason he died was because it decided to follow you. It was only thanks to your mate sacrificing himself that this mutt is still alive."

Kiara flinched, but Kotohime stood firm. "If you had not kidnapped my sister, I would have never gone to her rescue, Kiara-san would have never followed me, and my mate would have never been killed. Do not try to pin the blame for Corban's death on someone else. We all know who is truly responsible."

"To think that you would still blame me for his death." Luna seemed genuinely regretful, but Kotohime knew better. "It seems trying to talk sense into you will not work."

The air grew thick—not just in a metaphysical sense, but literally thick. Moisture gathered in the air. Streamers of water coalesced all around them, traveling toward Luna, until they were swirling around her tails.

"Though I do so despise combat, it seems fighting is the only way I'll be able to get through to you." Luna's merciless smile made Kotohime's insides quake. "Do be sure not to die on me… Tsuki-chan."

***

Kevin, still being half-carried by Lilian and Iris, followed Kirihime as she led them further into the convention center.

All around them, the dead bodies of kitsune and humans lay. It looked like the battle had come mostly to a close, though they could still hear the sounds of combat further in.

"Kirihime, are you sure we should leave those two alone? Isn't there anything we can do to help them?" Lilian asked as they continued to run.

Without breaking her stride, Kirihime turned her head and gave the redhead a sad smile. "I am afraid that in a battle of this caliber, all we would do is get in the way."

As if to emphasize her point, the entire convention center was shaken to its very foundations. The windows that remained intact shattered in an explosion of water, which poured into the building. Kevin, Lilian, and Iris almost fell as the rapidly rushing water crashed into them. It was only thanks to Lilian and Iris reinforcing their bodies that they didn't fall on their faces.

"Quickly, you three," Kirihime said. "We need to reach higher ground."

They continued to move as the convention center was rocked again. More water flooded into the building. They took a staircase and ascended to the next floor, where they ended up in a hallway. Turning a corner, they were forced to stop in their tracks when another group of people almost crashed into them. Three of them were clad in spandex. One of them was quite familiar.

"Hawa! It's my family!" Camellia's smile was brighter than a star as she waved at them. "Kirikiri, Iris, Lilian, Kevin-kyun! Hullo!"

"Um, hello, Camellia," Kevin muttered, warily eying the soldiers, who were looking at them stupidly.

"My Lady, are… are you well? You're not hurt, are you?" Kirihime asked, her fingers twitching, clearly longing to reach for the daggers under her dress.

"Um!" Camellia nodded joyfully. "These nice people kept me company."

The "nice people" that Camellia mentioned snapped out of their fugue. They looked from the group of kitsune to Camellia, then back to the kitsune. Camellia again. Then the kitsune one more time. For good measure.

"So, wait, these are the people you're looking for?" one of the soldiers asked.

"Yes!" Camellia's sunny smile hadn't changed in the slightest. She was completely unaware of the heavy tension pervading the atmosphere. "Those two are my daughters, and that's Kevin-kyun, and that one is Kirikiri."

"Daughters," one of the men muttered, eyes straying to the tails writhing behind the backs of the three kitsune. "Your daughters are kitsune."

"Of course," Camellia said as if the answer should have been obvious. "I'm a kitsune, too."

As she spoke, five tails emerged from underneath her magical girl skirt, and her ears sprouted fur and became long and pointed.

The group of spandex-clad men eyed each other. Anxiety was written all over their faces. They looked at Camellia's still smiling face, then at the other four people. Kirihime had now taken out her knives, Lilian had several orbs of light orbiting her, and Iris had summoned some void fire, which hovered over her tails. Kevin didn't have a weapon, or superpowers, but that didn't stop him from preparing for combat.

"We're screwed, aren't we?" asked one of the men. Everyone sans Camellia nodded. "Thought so."

***

Several tons of water crashed into the bus before it could reach the convention center. Glass shattered and objects flew as they were thrown from their shelves. Heather swore as she cranked on the steering wheel, and the teenagers screamed as they were tossed out of their seats, smacking into the walls and floor.

Christine held onto Lindsay as her friend screamed. Creating a protective shell of ice, which was hard on the outside and soft on the inside, she softened the blow to her back as she was slammed into a wall. She barely had time to register the pain before her entire world flipped upside down. The world outside tumbled past her. It was a dizzying display that made her stomach do backflips. She would've hurled, but her throat had closed.

And then everything stopped. Inexplicably. Unexpectedly. It stopped.

With her head spinning and her back aching, Christine blinked the fuzziness out of her vision. She belatedly realized that she was lying not on the floor, but on a wall. That meant the bus must have tipped over. Lindsay still lay curled up against her, only now the blonde was lying on top of her.

"You okay, Lindsay?" she groaned.

"I… I think so," Lindsay said, her voice shaky. She placed her hands on either side of Christine and pushed herself up. Their faces were barely an inch apart. "You protected me."

In the face of such a sincere expression, Christine could only blush. "O-of course I did. We're friends. It's only natural that I would protect you."

Lindsay smiled. "Thank you."

"You're welcome," Christine muttered, trying to play Lindsay's words off as if they were nothing. She was embarrassed, but at least the person thanking her was just a friend and not Kevin.

Several feet away, Eric sat up and rubbed his head. "Ugh, what the hell hit us?"

"Don't know," Alex said as he also righted himself. A cut ran along his forehead, and the blood that leaked out made a trail down his face. He wiped at it, then blinked several times as he looked at his now red hand. "Huh, I appear to be injured… and I feel kind of dizzy. Is that natural?"

"For someone as dumb as you—"

"Oi!"

"—probably," Andrew finished despite the interruption. He had several scratches on his hands and a bruise on his arm, but he was otherwise unharmed.

"Lindsay," Christine said.

"Yes?" Lindsay whispered. Dark brown eyes looked onto Christine's as Lindsay lowered her head ever so slightly.

"Can you get off me please?"

"… Eh?"

Lindsay blinked several times. Then her eyes widened as she seemed to realize how close their faces were. With a loud squeak, she shot off Christine, her cheeks beet red.

As her friend stuttered out apologies, Christine sat up and checked herself over. Her clothing was a bit scuffed, and her back was wet—not to mention cold—but she didn't appear to have any injuries. She'd probably be sore tomorrow, though.

Considering what just happened, I can live with being a little sore.

"Master, what should we do now?" Eric asked his teacher. When Heather didn't answer, he made his way over to the front. "Master, are you—Master!!"

At Eric's startled shout, everyone moved to the front to find an unconscious Heather. A large cut ran lengthwise along her forehead, leaking massive quantities of blood. The area around the cut was a dark blackish-purple. Because she was still strapped in, she hadn't fallen out of her seat when the bus had tipped over, but while the seatbelt kept her from falling, it also left her hanging in an awkward position.

Christine acted quickly, creating a small knife out of ice and cutting the seatbelt straps. She dismissed the knife and caught

Heather before the woman could hit the ground. Grunting as her muscles strained under the added weight, she slowly lowered Heather to what should have been the wall.

"Does anyone know first aid?" Christine asked.

Her words snapped Lindsay into action. "I do. Eric, see if you can find a first aid kit somewhere in this bus. Alex, Andrew, I want you to take Heather and put her on the couch…" She trailed off upon remembering that they were standing on the wall. "Um, grab some pillows and put her on those. Make sure to keep her head elevated."

"Right away!"

"Aye, ma'am!"

Lindsay looked at Christine. "I'm gonna need you to create an ice pack after we bandage her head."

"I can do that." Christine hated using her powers, but considering the circumstances, using them a little more wouldn't hurt.

Everyone got to work. Alex and Andrew pulled the mattress out of the small bedroom, which they laid Heather on; Eric found a first aid kit in the bathroom; Lindsay used the supplies inside to disinfect the head wound before wrapping it in bandages. It would need stitches, but they hoped that this would keep Heather from bleeding out until they could reach a hospital. Afterward, Christine made a small ice pack, which Lindsay had Eric keep pressed to Heather's forehead.

"What should we do now?" Christine asked.

"The only thing we can do," Lindsay gave her a grim smile, "wait and hope that Kevin and the others find us."

***

The battleground had become submerged in a layer of water. To keep from sinking, Kiara and Kotohime had to channel a constant, steady flow of youki to their feet, which allowed them to stand on the water's surface.

"How do you like my **Watery Paradise**?" Luna asked, her lips curling as her half-lidded eyes glimmered. "I thought it would be a more suitable battleground, seeing how at least two of us are kitsune whose techniques rely on water—oops." The smile widened. "You can't use saltwater, can you, Tsuki-chan?" A giggle. "My apologies."

Kotohime grimaced. All of this saltwater would make it difficult to use specialized techniques—not that they would do much good. A mere four-tails such as herself would not be able to defeat a six-tails in battle by trying to match fire with fire—or water with water.

"This bitch is just as arrogant as I remember." Kiara sneered in disgust. The sneer was a mask to hide her nervousness, Kotohime knew. The last time they'd met, Kiara had nearly died by this woman's hand.

"She has a right to be." Kotohime caressed the hilt of her katana, using the comforting feel of cloth against her hand to calm her mind. "She's more powerful, has more experience, and knows more techniques than either of us. We are severely handicapped."

"Huh, never thought I'd hear you speak with such a defeatist attitude."

"I am merely being realistic."

"And here I was hoping you'd be—"

"Water Art: Feeding Time."

Their conversation ceased when several sharks composed of water broke the surface and leapt at them. Kotohime's katana and wakizashi flashed, cutting each watery shark that came at her into dozens of pieces. Kiara met the sharks leaping at her head-on. She pounded them with a youki-infused fist, demolishing them.

"You know I don't like being ignored," Luna said with a smile.

"We're not gonna be able to beat her without a solid plan," Kiara said, warily eyeing their opponent.

"Agreed."

"What should we do?"

"Let's play defensively," Kotohime suggested after a moment. "It's been one hundred and fifty years, and we do not know what she is capable of now that she's gained her sixth tail. I don't envy the idea of attacking her head-on without knowing what I'm up against."

"I'm not usually one for defense," Kiara admitted. "But I think I'll make an exception this time." She looked down at her missing arm and grimaced. "I'm beginning to regret losing that arm. That's going to make this battle ten times more difficult."

"Would you like me to say I told you so?"

"Naw, I'm good."

"Water Art: Severance, A Bed of Stakes."

Kiara and Kotohime danced across the water's surface as several dozen stakes burst from the water. The stakes followed them, branching off as they separated and continued haranguing the two.

Growling, Kiara leapt into the air. She channeled youki into her fist and let loose with a ferocious punch. A great red ball of energy erupted from her extended fist, blowing straight through the stakes and smashing into the water's surface, causing it to burst like a geyser.

"Ikken Hissatsu. Hein."

Spinning about, Kotohime slashed at the stakes with her wakizashi, which she quickly resheathed. A small distortion seemed to pass through the incoming water stakes. Nothing happened at first. The ripple flew through the stakes unimpeded and came out the other side. A second passed, then two, before, like shattering glass, the stakes exploded.

Upon landing back on the water, Kiara launched herself at Luna, who saw her coming and turned to face her. She didn't attack, and the feral-haired woman leapt over the older yōkai. She'd drawn back her fist.

"Take this!"

Kiara unleashed a massive amount of youki with her punch, creating what appeared to be a large cone-shaped beam, which descended upon Luna.

"Water Art: Quicksilver Barrier."

Water rose up and over Luna, creating a barrier between her and the beam of violent energy. The beam crashed into the dome-shaped shield, hissing and spitting as the superheated youki caused the water to evaporate.

"Ikken Hissatsu. Ichi no Ougi."

While the dome protected Luna from the attack above her, it could not protect her from Kotohime, who charged in at speeds even faster than when she'd been fighting Kaine. Her katana and wakizashi came out of their sheaths too quickly to track. She swung them at Luna, seeking to overwhelm her foe with an uncountable number of sword strikes.

They were blocked. Kotohime stared in mute shock at the pillar of water deflecting her swords. Luna looked at her, a mocking smile tugging at her lips.

"Did you actually think I wouldn't be able to block an attack of this caliber? How amusing. You may be an excellent swordswoman, and I certainly wouldn't want to fight you in close combat, but do not think that means I am helpless—even in a two-on-one battle such as this."

Kotohime's eyes bulged as the water crawled up her swords. She flared her youki, channeling them through her swords and causing the water to explode off them. Leaping backwards, she skidded along the water's surface, eventually coming to a halt several yards away. Luna didn't attack.

Kiara landed next to her. "That didn't work out as well as I thought it would."

"Indeed." Kotohime grimaced. "It seems the extra tail has increased her power exponentially. I had expected that, but I did not expect to see such a vast increase in skill. Luna never was the type who enjoyed combat."

"Just because I do not enjoy fighting does not mean I can't learn," Luna said in a mocking tone. "Being the matriarch of a great clan means that I need to be strong enough to fend off attacks both from within and without."

Kotohime kept a calm outer facade, but she felt her spirits waver. It was true. Luna was now the matriarch of a great clan, which meant that she had proven herself to be the strongest and most capable among her clan. One did not reach heights like that by neglecting their ability to fight.

"Now then." Luna smiled. "Let us continue, shall we?"

***

After running into Camellia, Kevin and the others made their way to the rooftop.

Standing next to a series of large generators that thrummed with life, Kevin and his companions watched the battle taking place down below.

"Things aren't looking good," he muttered, a pair of binoculars stuck to his eyes. He'd grabbed them off of one of the spandex-wearing soldiers that had previously been escorting Camellia, all of whom were currently tied up and unable to move. "It doesn't look like their attacks are having any effect on that woman."

"That is only natural," Kirihime said. Unlike Kevin, she didn't seem to need binoculars. He assumed she was reinforcing her eyes with youki. "That woman has six tails. Each tail a kitsune gains multiplies their power by the square root of the number of tails that they have."

"I get it." Kevin winced when Kiara was smacked harshly by a large geyser of water that shot up from underneath her. "When a kitsune gains their third tail, the power they possess is multiplied by three times the amount they had when they were a two-tails, and when they gain their fourth tail—"

"It's multiplied by four times the amount they had when they were a three-tails, yes." Kirihime nodded.

"That's a lot of power," he muttered.

"Kitsune power levels are pretty ridiculous," Iris cut in.

The raven-haired vixen sat down on the roof's lip, one leg crossed over the other. Even with the situation being what it was, Kevin still found his eyes drawn toward the expansive amount of leg. He quickly shook his head and looked away guiltily. He had a mate. He shouldn't be ogling Iris just because she was hot.

Something is seriously wrong with me.

"Kotohime has four tails, and this woman has six," Iris continued. "That means the Ocean Kitsune has more than three times the amount of power that Kotohime does."

"B-but she's also got Kiara with her," Kevin blurted. "Surely that means they're on even grounds with her, right? Kiara is pretty strong, too."

"Doubtful." Iris shrugged. "Having never really paid attention to the dog, I don't know how strong she is. But, regardless, even if she's as strong as Kotohime, it won't make a difference. It just means that the six-tails has three times the power of them both."

Lilian stood next to Kevin and gazed down at her maid in concern. "Do… do you think they'll be okay?"

Kevin looked at Lilian to see the girl worrying her lower lip between her teeth. Her expressive green eyes were drawn toward the battle like moths to a flame. Those normally bright and vibrant irises trembled, just like her voice had. She was afraid—afraid for the woman who'd helped raise her, afraid that she'd lose someone who meant so much to her and would be helpless to do anything about it.

Kevin moved behind her. He wrapped his arms around her waist, letting his hands rest on her stomach, and pulled her to his chest. Lilian leaned into him, accepting the comfort that he had to offer.

"I'm sure she'll be okay," he said, hiding his own worry behind a mask of confidence. He was weak: a powerless human surrounded by beings beyond his mortal mind's ability to decipher, but at the very least, he could do this. "We have to believe in her—believe in them. They're not so weak that they'd lose to that woman."

Lilian smiled at his optimism, even if they both knew it was forced. "You're right. I need to believe they can win."

"I wish I had your guys' confidence," Iris said.

Several feet behind the trio, the group of spandex-clad militants sat, bound together by a thick strand of rope composed of water. They didn't look too pleased about their situation, but they also seemed resigned.

Camellia pouted at her maid. "Do we really have to keep these nice people tied up like this?" she asked, and the anti-yōkai faction members looked up in hope.

Said hope was trampled on by Kirihime. "Of course we do. These people belong to a group that hates our kind because of their own misguided beliefs about how we're a danger to humanity."

One of the soldiers, the captain, sneered. "Say that when there aren't yōkai tearing apart a convention center in the middle of—ow!"

"Quiet you," Kirihime muttered, retracting the tail that she'd used to smack the soldier on the head with. Addressing Camellia, she added, "The only reason I didn't kill them is because they helped you. However, that's not enough to make me trust them, especially when the only reason they helped you is because they didn't know you're a yōkai."

"Ugh." The spandex-clad men winced in unison.

"Had they known what you were beforehand, they would not have been so kind."

"Kuh!"

"I do not doubt that they would have riddled your body with bullets, remorselessly killing you simply because you are not human."

"Geh!"

With each harsh word spoken, the group of militants sank further into themselves, until it looked like they were trying to hide in their spandex.

"Hawa." Camellia had nothing to say in the face of such flawless logic.

With Lilian still in his arms, Kevin turned his attention back to the battle.

***

"Water Art: Swarm of Piranhas."

The pounding of her own heart rang loudly in Kiara's ears as she dodged a swarm of water piranhas that flew through the air. She spun around as they moved past her and unleashed another blast of energy from her fist, which consumed most of the swarm. Those that had not been destroyed went back into the water, only to separate and leap at her from all sides.

To avoid having them feast on her flesh, she leapt into the air and let loose with a ferocious roar that caused a hurricane-like gust to emit from her mouth. The piranhas were promptly destroyed. The gust of wind hit the water next, causing a hole to appear as the liquid was pushed away, right before it was sucked back up and launched into the air like a bomb going off.

Several feet from where Kiara faced off with the water constructs, Luna was giving Kotohime some personal attention.

"Water Art: Water Explosion."

"Ikken Hissatsu. Bunkatsu."

As a giant explosion of water made to sweep her off her feet, Kotohime narrowed her profile and slashed at it with her youki-infused blades. Much like the name suggested, the attack,

Bunkatsu, which meant "divide," caused the water in front of her to separate into two halves. Each half flowed around her, providing Kotohime with the opportunity to rush at her foe.

Kiara landed back on the water. Luna's back was to her as Kotohime put pressure on the six-tails, striking at her with attacks so fast that even Kiara couldn't see them. Water rose up and blocked the attacks, but Kotohime didn't seem concerned, and the reason became clear when their eyes met.

So, that's it, huh? Okay, then.

Her muscles contracting as she bent her knees, Kiara burst into an all-out sprint at the same time that Kotohime launched herself at Luna. The two of them closed the distance with their foe in an instant. Kiara launched her fist at Luna's back. Kotohime was already swinging her katana and wakizashi.

"Water Art: Spike Explosion."

Kotohime felt her heart racing as she channeled youki into her legs and leapt into the air. Kiara followed her. They both avoided impalement as the Luna that had been standing before them erupted into hundreds of spikes. Landing back on the water, which rippled under their feet, she and Kiara warily observed their surroundings.

"When did she have time to replace herself with a water clone?" Kiara asked.

"I think the more accurate question should be why didn't you two notice it," Luna's voice echoed around them. "There were plenty of chances for me to work my magic. You were both so distracted defending against my attacks that neither of you even noticed me replacing myself with a clone and casting an illusion to conceal my presence. How shameful of you."

"Tch!" Kiara clicked her tongue. "Listen to this bitch talking about what she did as if we aren't even a threat."

"You aren't a threat. A mutt and a four-tails cannot hope to match my power," Luna's voice echoed again.

Kiara growled. Kotohime closed her eyes, blocking out her partner's frustrated noises, and focused instead on feeling the ripples on the water's surface. While Luna had done an admirable job of masking herself from sight, she still had a presence. And because she couldn't be anywhere but on the water, it meant that Kotohime should be able to feel her out via the ripples she released by standing on it.

Where is she? She must be here... somewhere...!

Her eyes snapped open when she felt a massive surge of youki.

"Jump!" she shouted.

She and Kiara leapt away from each other just as something blasted out of the water. Long and sinewy, Kotohime wondered if Luna had created a giant sea serpent to battle for her.

Is that a... oh, no...

What at first glance appeared to be a giant stake was actually a tentacle—a very large, very thick tentacle that undulated as it moved. Another tentacle shot up from the water, forcing her and Kiara to leap backwards. This was followed by another, and then another, until Kotohime saw six massive tentacles towering over them.

"Water Art: Kraken's Fury."

Kotohime and Kiara were soon forced into a flurry of movement as the monstrously-sized tentacles descended upon them with the fury of a sea god. The tentacles crashed into the water's surface. Great bulges generated by their splashdown created massive tidal waves that sent water everywhere. She and Kiara moved, trying to avoid getting swept up by the waves, which loomed over them like goliaths.

The waves fell. Kotohime gnashed her teeth together in concentration as she skated across the water. She sheathed her blades, slid into an *iaijutsu* stance, then just as quickly unsheathed them.

"Ikken Hissatsu. Hikisakimasu."

Split—a technique that cut everything before it in half. The wave was no exception. Kotohime swung her two blades upwards, cutting the wave before her in two.

Several feet away, Kiara was launched into the air when one of the tentacles splashed down near her. The tidal wave that it created slammed into the convention center. At the apex of her jump, she brought her hand near her face and coated it in fiery-red youki. She fell back down. With a roar that sounded more animal than human, she launched her fist into the giant water tentacle.

A ripple spread across the tentacle, which undulated and bulged. Kiara leapt off just as the entire thing exploded. Grinning, she landed back on the water.

"That wasn't so hard," she said—only for the grin to fall away when the stump sprouted two more tentacles. "What the hell is this thing? A Hydra?!"

The two tentacles shot toward her, faster than before, and Kiara was forced into a deadly dance. She swerved around them, trying to avoid the sharp-looking tips that kept attempting to impale her. Because she was so busy dodging the two tentacles in front of her, she didn't see the one coming in from behind until it smacked her in the back, hard.

Kiara's world exploded with pain as she was sent skidding across the water's surface. She hit the water face-first and tumbled across it like a broken doll, eventually crashing into the convention center with enough force to plow straight through the wall.

Kotohime wove between three tentacles that tried to kill her, using her incredible speed to her advantage. These things were ponderously slow. Dodging them was easy. The only problem she had was the waves they made, which disrupted her ability to skate along the water.

She had already discovered that the tentacles sprouted two more when severed, having already cut one with her sword. Now

she was dealing with three tentacles, all of which seemed eager to either squash her like an insect, or impale her with their sharp tips.

One of the thinner tentacles came at her from the left. Kotohime ducked and glided along the water, dodging the massive limb, which crashed into the kitsune-made lake. She then used the wave it produced to launch herself into the air, thereby avoiding another tentacle that tried to stab her.

Her feet hit the water. A splash went up. Kotohime rotated her body so that she was moving backwards. The three tentacles were in front of her now—two trailing after her while one rose high into the air.

Instincts warned her of impending danger. She bent her knees and, sending youki into her legs, she jumped into the air—just in time, too. Less than a second later, a fourth tentacle shot up from below and came at her. Gritting her teeth, Kotohime sheathed her swords and prepared to counterattack.

"HYA!"

It wasn't needed. Like a rocket, Kiara barreled into the tentacle. Her fist hammered it with a blow that caused ripples to appear along its surface. It didn't burst apart, however, showing that she'd learned her lesson, and instead it was forced back into the water where it landed with a massive splash.

"Da… dammit," Kiara swore, even as she sucked in a heaping gulp of air. "I don't… don't know how much longer I… can keep this up."

Kotohime, also breathing deeply, had to agree. Her friend looked like she'd taken quite the beating. Her face and body were beginning to bruise, and her business suit looked like it had been put through a paper shredder. It hung off her frame in tatters, barely covering her unmentionables.

"**Kraken's Fury** is a technique that creates tentacles by infusing a large body of water with youki and controlling it like an extension of oneself," Kotohime explained. "If we can defeat this technique, Luna will have no choice but to reveal herself."

"So, what you're saying is that we need to get rid of all this water somehow."

"Correct. The water has been infused with her youki, which is why it hasn't dispersed into the rest of the city. We need to break the technique and drain the water."

"How do we do that?"

"I have no idea. **Kraken's Fury** requires at least six-tails to use, so I'm not well-versed in its application beyond what I just told you."

"Gee, how helpful."

"Your sarcasm is unnecessary," Kotohime muttered—seconds before all eight tentacles descended upon them.

****

Kevin continued to watch as Kiara and Kotohime fought against the giant tentacles. He remembered mentioning tentacle monsters during their time at the beach. There was a twisted sort of irony at seeing them now. Unfortunately, any humor that he might have felt was nullified by the fact that these tentacles were trying to kill two people that he admired.

He stood on the roof with Lilian and Iris, feeling the weight of his own powerlessness press down on him. For months now, he'd been training his butt off, working out every morning with Kiara and getting trained in hand-to-hand combat. He thought he'd been doing well, that he'd been getting stronger.

His defeat at Ken's hands had left a bad taste in his mouth, but he'd thought that if he just worked a bit harder, became a bit stronger, he could overcome his weaknesses.

Now he knew better. Watching Kiara and Kotohime fight against a kitsune who could drown an entire area in water and create abominable tentacles to crush her foes, Kevin realized that he truly was powerless.

So he stood there, trying to offer Lilian all the comfort he could, but on the inside, he was drowning in his own despair.

For how could he hope to stand against a creature whose power was so far beyond the reach of a mere mortal like himself?

***

Five tentacles tried to reach for Kotohime, coming in at different angles from different trajectories and at different times. She leapt over the first one. Landing on top of it, Kotohime slid along its slippery surface, using her own youki to propel herself forward. The second came in from the left. She noticed it out of the corner of her eyes and crouched low. Her hand touched the tentacle that she was on, acting as a dorsal fin and altering her path until she was upside down. The other tentacle missed. Still gliding along the first tentacle, she made a full rotation around its circumference.

Three more tried attacking her at the same time. One grabbed at her ankle from behind, but it was avoided when Kotohime slid away. The other tried to impale her. She tilted her body at an almost humanly impossible angle and allowed it to soar past her, the tip ripping open the front of her kimono. The last came at her face. She used her own unique kitsune ability to stop it.

"Kitsune Art: Transient Counterforce."

Transient Counterforce was a specialized technique that she had created decades ago to defeat techniques that were stronger than her own. It projected two thin layers of youki, and then rotated them in opposing clockwise and counterclockwise motions. The two rotating layers of youki acted like a shredder, forcefully cutting any technique apart.

The tentacle reared back after unsuccessfully trying to stab her, its tip now gone. Because the limb had not been severed entirely, it could not sprout two new tentacles and had to be reformed by pumping more youki into it.

Leaping into the air, Kotohime was given a moment of reprieve as the tentacles became tangled together. Because they were composed of water, they simply merged together and reformed, but it still took several seconds.

Kiara was dealing with her own single tentacle. The woman avoided its monstrous crashes as she channeled tremendous amounts of youki through her body, producing the bright red aura that she was known for.

This was the plan that they had come up with. Kotohime would draw most of the tentacles' attention. Meanwhile, Kiara, who possessed more raw power, would charge as much youki as she could into an attack that would hopefully destroy Luna's technique. She didn't know if it would work, but it was their only option.

The moment of rest came to an end when the tentacles reforged and rose into the air. Five began their swift descent, while one rose up and attempted to catch her by surprise. Kotohime sliced off the tip of the one that attacked from beneath her. She then moved back to dodge one of the smaller tentacles as it tried to spear her. Spinning to the left, she avoided the descent of another, but she was unable to avoid the wave that it created.

Rather than let herself get swept up, she rode the wave. It proved difficult; the salt kept interfering with her control. At the wave's apex, she leapt off, just in time to dodge the fourth tentacle as it smashed into where she'd been standing. Skating along the water, she outpaced the second wave that the fourth tentacle created, while the fifth and sixth tentacles came at her in horizontal sweeps— one high and the other low.

Flitting sideways, Kotohime leapt into the air and twisted her body, allowing the two tentacles to pass above and below her. At the same time, she sliced into them both with her katana and wakizashi. It was not enough to sever them. That was not her goal. The extra damage meant that it would take time for the tentacles to reform. Landing on the ground as the two tentacles reared back, she stood up—

—and her eyes widened as a seventh tentacle filled her vision.

Acting out of desperation, Kotohime crossed her katana and wakizashi defensively in front of her. The tentacle smacked her. Hard. Pain erupted in her arms as her bones were shaken. She felt herself being launched into the air. Her mind overridden by pain; she was unable to reorient herself before plowing into the water.

Several meters away, Kiara finished charging as much yōkai into her fist as she could. She leapt onto the tentacle as it came at her and used it as a springboard to launch herself into the air. When she had ascended high above even the convention building, Kiara oriented her body, twisting around, until she was pointed face-down at the water.

Then she extended her fist.

Then she began to fall.

Unleashing a ferocious battle cry, Kiara plummeted to the watery paradise. As if they had minds of their own, all of the tentacles turned on her, attempting to swiftly strike her down. The moment they touched Kiara, their amorphous bodies disintegrated. The overwhelming heat of her youki caused the water composing their bodies to evaporate on contact.

Kiara struck the large body of water seconds later to devastating effect. Water sprayed into the air like an erupting geyser. A large hole appeared where she had fallen, all the way to the ground, which her extended fist struck without mercy.

An explosion of youki blasted the ground apart, tearing through the cement like it was made of paper. Debris flew everywhere. The ground was upheaved, cracks spreading across it before the ground caved in. All that remained was a massive hole.

Kiara leapt away as all of the water was sucked into the hole. Her youki-infused attack hadn't just created a large hole, but created a large hole that led into the sewer system underneath the city. The once watery battleground soon vanished.

Kiara landed several yards from the hole. Kotohime appeared next to her, looking a little worse for wear. Her kimono was soaked while the obi had come undone, leaving much of it open and also showing off ample portions of her voluptuous chest, which Kiara noticed was bruised.

"Your boobs are black."

Kotohime twitched. "Now is not the time for jokes. We may have defeated Luna-san's technique, but we still haven't beaten her."

"Indeed, you have not," Luna's voice bounced across the now waterless clearing. "Nor will you. You may have defeated my **Watery Paradise**, however, that was merely a distraction designed to drain you of your youki—and to amuse myself. You've both already lost and just don't realize it yet."

"What was that?!" Kiara growled as she took a step forward. "Listen here—don't think we've been beaten just because you've managed to weaken us a little. I've still got plenty left in the tank, and I'm sure Kotohime does too. I'm more than ready to take you on if you'd just show your face!"

"You think that because you've beaten a single technique, you've got me on the ropes. How cute." Something ominous drifted in on the wind: a feeling of oppression and danger. "Allow me to rectify your misguided beliefs."

It happened before either of them could even move. Several dozen spears of water shot up and pierced their bodies. The ground became stained with blood.

***

"Kotohime!"

Lilian tore herself out of Kevin's grasp and ran back into the convention center.

"Lady Lilian, where are you going?! Come back!"

"L-Lilian, wait!"

"Hawa!"

Kevin made to take off after her, but he paused when his feet kicked something. He looked down and saw the gun that he'd used to shoot Ken with. He must have dropped it. Scooping it up, he ran after Lilian, the others following close behind him.

Please, Kevin begged whoever was listening. *Please don't let anything bad happen to Lilian.*

***

Kotohime's mind was overcome with pain. Her entire body hurt. She could feel the holes in her flesh, feel the blood leaking from her wounds. She'd stopped most of the bleeding by controlling her blood flow with youki, but that didn't stop it from hurting.

Lying next to her, Kiara wasn't as well off. Blood poured from the many puncture wounds in her body, gushing forth and creating a large puddle underneath her. She was still alive. Kotohime could see her chest rise and fall, but she wouldn't last long without medical attention.

Kotohime was confident that she could heal Kiara's wounds, if given the chance. Unfortunately, judging by the sound of approaching footsteps, she would not be getting that chance.

Luna's amused visage appeared in Kotohime's vision: eyes half-lidded, lips curved in delight, as if the agony that she felt was the six-tail's greatest pleasure.

"Look at you, Tsuki-chan, lying on the ground, utterly defeated by me." The woman sighed in rapture. "This… this is how it should be, how it should have always been: you lying at my feet. It really is too bad it had to happen in such a manner. This moment would have been much more pleasurable for us both had you prostrated yourself willingly."

Kotohime bared her bloodstained teeth. "I would never… submit myself… to you…" Her body shook as she went into a fit of coughing. Blood welled up in her lungs and trickled down her mouth.

Luna's smile widened. "And that, my dear, is why your life is going to end here."

Kotohime tried to move, tried to get up, tried to do something, anything. But her body refused to obey her commands. All she could do was lie there.

"Ha…" Kiara wheezed. "I always knew I would die in battle… but I used to think it would be against my old man… not some chick who'd been holding a century-long grudge…"

"I'm sorry you got involved in this," Kotohime apologized.

"Heh." Kiara smirked at her. "Why are you apologizing? None of this is… your fault… everything that has happened up to this point… has been my choice."

Despite the situation, Kotohime smiled. "That sounds like something you would say."

"Are you two done having your disgustingly touching moment?" Luna asked, her lips contorting into a sneer. "Because I think it's about time you both met your end."

Several spears of water appeared in the air, each one poised over Kotohime and Kiara. Kotohime sighed, resignation entering her soul. She couldn't move, her life was bleeding out, her youki was nearly depleted, and she was at the tender mercy of a woman whose love she'd spurned a century and a half ago. There was nothing left that she could do.

She was going to die here.

Images flashed before her eyes: memories of her most recent past. She recalled the day that she'd met Delphine Pnéyma-denka; the day when the Great Ghost Clan matriarch had offered her and her sister sanctuary in exchange for their loyalty.

She remembered being introduced to Camellia, whose mind had barely started degrading back then. She also remembered becoming the bodyguard to a recently-turned two-tailed Lilian.

Watching the redhead struggle to find her place in the Pnéyma Clan; watching her suffer as dozens of male kitsune were presented to her a decade after she'd gained her second tail; watching her after her first meeting with an, at the time, six-year-old Kevin, and the subsequent strength that she'd gained from that encounter.

Of the more recent past, she remembered her first time meeting Kevin. She recalled the boy's struggle to accept his feelings toward a creature that was beyond his understanding, knowing that doing so would be an irreversible choice. The relief that she had felt at seeing him make a decision was something that she'd planned on cherishing forever.

Would those two be alright without her? She still had so much left to teach them. Kevin especially needed to know more about kitsune culture—and yōkai as a whole. Would Kirihime be up to the task of fulfilling that role?

Probably not. She loved her sister dearly, but Kirihime was too insane to properly teach anyone.

"Well," Luna said, and Kotohime's mind returned to the here and now. Only a few seconds had passed. "I think I've given you enough time to lament your misfortune. Be sure to greet Lord Shinigami for me."

Kotohime did not close her eyes. She met the originator of her end head-on with a glare. She would not allow this woman to defeat her, even in death.

To think I would die like this. There's still so much I wanted to do.

"KOTOHIME!"

Her eyes widened.

No. No, no, no, no-no-no! What is she doing here?!

Luna leapt back as a sphere of light passed the airspace where she'd been standing.

"Get away from her!" Lilian screamed. She tossed several more spheres, but a wall of water rose up and blocked them.

"L-Lilian… no… get away…"

Luna looked down at her and smiled coldly. "You care for this girl, don't you? I see. Yes, yes. Would it not be a shame if she were to die?"

The water shifted, transforming from a wall into a spear.

"N-no… please…" Kotohime begged.

Luna's smile widened. "But it would be even more of a shame if you two didn't get to join each other in death."

The spear flew forward. Lilian saw it coming. She moved, avoiding the attack, and continued running. She never saw the spear as it curved around and came at her from behind.

Blood splattered along the ground.

"Ah…" Lilian gasped, looking down at the watery spear, which had pierced her back and was poking out of her stomach. "Ah…" She fell onto her knees. Then she pitched over, falling face-first to the ground.

Lilian did not get back up. She did not move. She didn't even so much as twitch.

Kotohime opened her mouth to scream.

"NOOO!"

The sound did not come from Kotohime. The voice was male, and it served as a prelude to several loud thunderclaps that Kotohime vaguely recognized but couldn't quite identify.

Blood rained down on her body and face. It was not her blood, she realized, but someone else's. Luna's. She blinked, focusing on the woman above her, whose body jerked and twitched as blood spurted from holes that opened in her flesh. Thunderclap after thunderclap echoed across the courtyard. More holes appeared on Luna's body, until the sound ceased, and the six-tailed kitsune stood there, her eyes glazing over as her body swayed.

The last thing that Kotohime saw was Luna falling backwards and hitting the ground with a dull thud.

CHAPTER 16

A Loss of Innocence

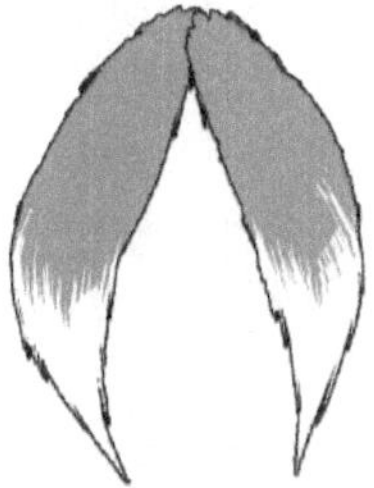

KOTOHIME WOKE UP TO discover that she was lying on a bed in a room filled with white; white walls, white ceiling; the floor was probably white, too, but she couldn't see it. The smell of alcohol and antiseptics hit her olfactory senses—a hospital, then.

What am I doing here? Did this mean that she was alive? But how? And what about the others? Lilian… was she okay?

Kotohime tried to move but couldn't. Though her body didn't hurt anymore, she felt sluggish, weighed down, as if someone had strapped hundred-pound lead weights to her limbs. She recognized the symptoms of youki exhaustion: when the body had so little youki left that it could barely function.

Blinking when something squeezed her right hand, she looked down to see her sister's head resting on the mattress. Kirihime's eyes were closed, and her mouth was partially open. She was holding Kotohime's hand tightly.

"I see you're finally awake," a vaguely familiar voice said. Kotohime recognized it, but she couldn't recall who it belonged to.

She turned her head to see long black hair, dark green eyes, and a voluptuous figure dressed in a kimono similar to her own.

"Kuroneko-dono," she greeted the older yōkai, who stood several feet from the bed.

"That was quite the battle you and Kiara got into," Kuroneko said, half-amused, half-exasperated. "You don't know how much trouble it was covering this incident up. The media is going crazy. We're incredibly fortunate that very few people were there to actually witness the battle. We were able to wipe the minds of the people who saw it, and edit the videos to make it look like a localized earthquake caused a rupture in the sewer system, but it took a lot of work."

"I see," Kotohime murmured as she sank back into the bed. "My apologies for making your task harder."

"Ma, it's okay," Kuroneko said, shrugging. "I was kinda bored anyway. This is the most exciting thing that's happened to me since a shit-faced Nurarihyon came to my café and started hitting on an oni."

Kotohime blinked. She was sure that she didn't want to know.

"Where am I?" she changed the subject.

"You're at one of the hospitals owned by yours truly." Kuroneko gestured to herself and smirked. "You didn't think I was just in the café business, did you? I had you, Kiara, and the others transported here after your battle."

"The others?" Kotohime needed a second to ponder what Kuroneko meant. "Lilian—"

"Is fine." Kuroneko pushed her back down when she tried to get up. "Her wound honestly wasn't that serious. I had a River Kitsune under my employ heal her right up. She's sleeping in the next room with her sister, her mom, and that human boy."

Kotohime felt relief wash through her. *I'm so glad she's alright.*

"Thank you," she whispered.

"There's no need for that." Kuroneko gestured, waving her thanks away. "I couldn't just let the heiress to the Pnéyma Clan die in a city under my watch, could I? That wouldn't do at all. Besides, that girl intrigues me, as does her mate."

Kotohime would've felt worry over the tone that Kuroneko used when talking about Lilian and Kevin, but she was too relieved to care. There were other matters to attend to anyway.

"What happened to Luna?"

"Dead," Kuroneko said. "That human boy—Kevin, I think his name is—killed her."

Kotohime felt shock course through her like she'd stuck her finger in a light socket. "W-what? Kevin-sama did?"

"Yes." Kuroneko chuckled. "When Lilian was struck down, the boy completely lost it. He brought out a pistol and pumped Luna full of holes. She was so shocked that she didn't even have time to even put up a defense." She grinned. "I'm gonna have to find some way to thank that boy. Luna was an absolute pain in my side. I was never able to pin her down for anything, and I couldn't find her hideout because, I suspect, it was under a multi-layered illusion. Her death is a huge weight off my shoulders."

Kotohime wondered how Kevin was doing. That had been his first kill. Knowing humans as she did, he must have been feeling sick.

GRRGEGRGHLLGG!!!

An earth-shaking snore rumbled throughout the room, rattling the windows and shaking the bed. Kotohime looked to her left to see Kiara sprawled out on a bed, snoring away, with a snot bubble blowing out of her nose.

She felt a trickle of sweat run down her face.

Kiara snorted. "Think you can beat me... punk... come on... I'll beat you into next week..."

"Kiara-san, must you make such unsightly noises while you sleep?"

Kiara didn't answer. Naturally.

Kuroneko smiled. "It is good to see that two hundred years hasn't changed the woman much."

Kotohime wouldn't admit it, but she had to agree that it was kind of reassuring to see Kiara acting just like she always had, despite what they'd gone through—even if it was only in her sleep.

"Ha!... Stupid jabroni... I'mma shove my foot... so far up your ass... you're gonna be shittin' in a bedpan for months..."

It didn't change how annoying she could be, though.

***

Lilian woke up in a bed, with a body snuggled into her side. She looked around, noting the white walls and white ceiling, and the smell of antiseptic. There wasn't much in the way of color, just a small potted plant near a brown door. She noticed the cabinet full of medical supplies and deduced that she was in a hospital.

How did I get here?

Sitting up caused the body against her to shift and mumble. Lilian looked down and twitched. It was Iris. She had been expecting—and hoping—that her mate would have been the one sleeping with her.

A glance at the foot of her bed revealed her mother dozing away in her fox form, her five tails lying sprawled on the bed behind her, hanging off the edge. Glancing around the room some more, Lilian finally caught sight of the person whom she'd been hoping to see the most.

He stood near the open window, the light from the dying sun playing off his blond hair. His back was turned to her, so she couldn't see his face, but she could tell from his slouched shoulders that he was deep in thought.

Being careful not to disturb her sister or mother, Lilian climbed out of bed. She padded along the tiled floor. It was a testament to Kevin's state of mind that he didn't hear her approach. The young man only responded when she hugged him from behind.

"Lilian," he said softly. It pleased her to no end how he seemed to know it was her without needing to look. "I'm glad you're awake."

He reached behind him, giving her a reverse hug. Lilian nuzzled her face into his back. She was always happy when he said things like that. However…

"What's wrong, Beloved?"

Kevin sighed. "It's nothing…"

Lilian frowned. She unwrapped her arms from around him and moved to stand in front of her mate. Her green eyes sought out his, locking them in place. When Kevin tried to look away, she reached under his chin and forced him to maintain eye contact.

"It's not nothing. I know you, Kevin. Something is bothering you." It was easy to see. His shoulders were stiff, his eyes had bags under them, and they contained a haunted demeanor. "Please tell me what's wrong. I can't help you if you don't tell me anything."

For a long moment, Kevin was silent. Lilian didn't break this period of stillness and introspection. He would tell her in time. This was just his way. He was thinking, determining which words would best convey his thoughts and feelings.

After another moment of silence, Kevin pulled her into a hug. Lilian felt confused, but she accepted the hug nevertheless, burying her face into her mate's chest and breathing in his scent. It was comforting in ways that still astounded her.

"I'm just… really glad that you're okay," Kevin said finally. "When that spear pierced you, I was so worried. I was so, so incredibly worried. It felt like a part of me had died, and when I saw you fall and not get back up… it felt like my entire world had come to an end. I was so relieved when Kuroneko arrived and said that you'd be okay."

Lilian absentmindedly wondered who Kuroneko was, but there was something else that was bothering her. Kevin was not being entirely honest. His words rang true, and yet, it felt as if he was purposefully leaving something out.

She lifted her head. "Kevin—mmph!"

Before she could say anything, Kevin leaned down and hampered her lips with his own. For one second, she thought about pushing him back so that she could ask him about what he was hiding. It only lasted for a moment, then Kevin, his mouth still grazing hers, spoke the words that stroked her passion more than anything else.

"I love you so much, Lilian."

Lilian kissed him back. Her arms went around his neck, and she pulled herself as close to him as physically possible. She didn't want even an inch of space left between them. She locked her lips with his in a voracious kiss, opening her mouth and allowing his tongue entrance.

Soft moans and delicate whimpers slipped out of her mouth as Kevin grasped her butt and began kneading her cheeks, sending delicious arcs of pleasure through her body. One particularly loud yet pleased gasp escaped when he caressed her tail, stroking the underside where her weak spot was. Wanting—no, needing more of this feeling, she leapt on him and locked her legs around his waist.

As Kevin continued to kiss her, Lilian forgot about what she wanted to ask him. It probably wasn't important anyway, and if it was, then she'd most definitely remember it and ask him later. All that mattered to her right then was enjoying her mate's actions.

She did feel a moment of confusion when Kevin suddenly stopped kissing her, however.

"Beloved?" she asked breathlessly when Kevin pulled back, his face scrunching up. "Is something wrong?"

"I don't know," he admitted, his frown deepening. "It's weird, but I feel like we're forgetting something."

Lilian also frowned, but she couldn't think of anything they might have forgotten. "It's probably just your imagination."

"You're right," Kevin agreed. Then he began kissing her again.

*****

They'd been stuck in there for hours: her, Lindsay, the twins, Heather, and Eric. The twins were sitting together. They'd been quiet for a while now. She would have wondered what they were thinking, but she honestly couldn't bring herself to care. Heather sat on the mattress and leaned against the wall. She hadn't recovered from her head injury, but she was at least conscious.

Lindsay had yet to leave her side. Christine wondered about the girl. She seemed to have become abnormally clingy, though Christine chalked it up to their experiences of the past few hours.

Justin was missing. None of them knew where he was, nor did they know when he'd gone missing. It was like he'd just mysteriously vanished sometime during the chaos. Christine wanted to say that she was worried about him, but they had never really interacted outside of group activities. That said, she still hoped he was okay.

"Where are they?! How come they haven't come to rescue us?! My Lord, where is your divine protection?!"

Sitting on the wall of their overturned bus, Christine's right eyebrow twitched violently as she watched Eric freak out. The perverted male ran along the wall like a chicken with its head cut off.

"Oh, God! This is it, isn't?! We're all going to die here!"

The twitching increased in intensity, and it brought friends.

Her left eyebrow began twitching as well.

"I don't want to die! I still have too much to live for! I haven't accomplished my goal of peeping on every girl in Desert Cactus High School, or groping that kimono-babe's titalicious tatas, or rubbing my face against Goth Hottie's marvelously flat chest— guwagh!"

"SHUT UP!"

Eric fell to the ground and curled up in the fetal position. Christine dismissed the ice hammer that she'd slammed into his gut, which created a small puddle on the floor when it dissolved back into water.

"God, that idiot pisses me off," Christine declared. "Seriously, is the only thing on his mind boobs and butts?"

Alex, Andrew, Lindsay, and Heather all stared at her.

"Are you seriously asking that?" Andrew asked.

"Yeah, you should know by now that nothing is more important to Eric than a nice pair of tits," Alex added, nodding his head.

"My apprentice is indeed a most lecherous young man." Heather wiped a small tear of pride from her left eye. "He takes after his Master."

Lindsay eyed the sniffling woman, then turned to Christine. "I've got nothing to add. You should know how Eric is by now. That's just... how he is."

"That doesn't make it any better!" Christine scowled.

"Hawa—gyah!!"

"Don't use other people's catchwords!!"

***

Still decked out in his costume reminiscent of a certain Solid Snake, Justin walked through a brightly lit hall made of metal. His boots *clunked* along the grated floor. There were no doors in this hall, and only a few people walked past him. Several noticed him and nodded in acknowledgment, but most ignored him. He reached the end of the hall, where a plain-looking door sat, with only a small plaque etched into it to signify its importance.

He knocked precisely three times.

"Enter," a voice called from the other side.

Justin entered the room. It was a spartan office with next to nothing in the way of decoration. The walls were bare, and there was hardly any furniture. There was only a desk situated near the back and a pair of metal chairs in front of it.

Sitting behind the desk was a man. His bulky frame strained against his military-esque uniform. His buzzcut did nothing to hide the large scar that started from his widow's peak and traversed along his right eye, over his mouth, and past his jaw. Justin could only wonder at what had given him that wound.

Justin stood in front of the desk, hands clasped behind his back, feet spread shoulder-width apart, and his back straight. The man looked up, revealing hard blue eyes.

"Commander Paine, I've come back from the field."

"At ease, Lieutenant," Commander Paine said in a gruff voice that reminded Justin of an onikuma—a bear yōkai.

Justin did as told, his posture slumping into a half-resemblance of his lazy mien that he used at school. Commander Paine scowled, but he didn't say anything. Justin mused that the commander more than likely realized that nothing he said would make him act differently

"I will have your report now, Lieutenant."

Justin nodded and began his report.

AFTERTAIL

Hello, everyone! It's been a while since I've done an afterword. This time, I thought it would be prudent to talk about kitsune: Their history, their place in mythology, and how kitsune fit into my story.

Since ancient times, oriental nations such as China, Japan, and Korea have told stories about spiritual beings that took the form of foxes. In Japan, these creatures are called fox spirits, or fox yōkai. I call them kitsune to make it easier in my story, but the truth of the matter is that kitsune just means fox in Japanese.

There are many different beliefs on the types of powers kitsune possess, though all are known to have certain powers regardless: Superior intellect, the ability to shape-shift into a human form, and magical powers.

In American Kitsune, kitsune are given three basic abilities. Known as enhancements, illusions, and enchantments, these are abilities that all kitsune learn to one degree or another. Beyond these three powers, each kitsune has a specific affinity for one element based on the principle of thirteen elements: Fire, earth, river, wind, thunder, forest, ocean, mountain, spirit, time, sound, celestial, and void. Outside of their element and the three aforementioned abilities, a kitsune is no more powerful than a human.

I tell you this now to explain how a kitsune with six tails can be killed by a mere gun. Kitsune are not all-powerful beings. If a kitsune is cut, they will bleed. If hit, they will bruise. If shot through the heart or head, they will die. A kitsune's physical defense is no more powerful than a human's. Even when using enhancement to increase their strength, they do not receive a major boost in defensive capabilities. The only way a kitsune could survive being shot was if they were using their affinity to create armor. For example: If an ocean kitsune had encased their body in armor hardened with their own youki, they could theoretically block bullets, depending on how much youki they had fed the armor. That said, without the armor, no kitsune can withstand getting shot.

This also explains how Luna Mul was killed by Kevin Swift. Without any sort of armor protecting her, Luna was left open to attack. Perhaps if she had been aware of him from the beginning, she wouldn't have died. However, kitsune live for hundreds of years, and Luna, with six tails to her name, had been around for over six hundred years.

Something interesting about a race of tricksters that live for generations is that they tend to grow arrogant. The longer they live, the more arrogant they become. This is due partly to age giving them a sense of superiority over the Homosapien race, but it is also because of the boost in power they receive. A kitsune gains another tail every hundred years. This tail multiplies their power by the number of their tails. A three-tails has three times the power of a two-tails, and a four-tails has four times the power of a three-tails. By six tails, kitsune are powerful enough that very few yōkai can match them in terms of raw youki. That sort of unbridled power is bound to make anyone arrogant.

Well, now. I hope you all had as much fun reading this book as I had writing it. This story took a dark turn, but I believe it made for an interesting twist. If you did enjoy this story, I would be grateful if you could leave a review on Amazon, Goodreads, Barnes and Noble, or wherever you bought this from. Thank you all again for supporting me!

~Brandon Varnell

HAVE A SNEAK PEAK AT THE AMERICAN KITSUNE MANGA ADAPTATION THAT BRANDON IS MAKING ON PATREON!

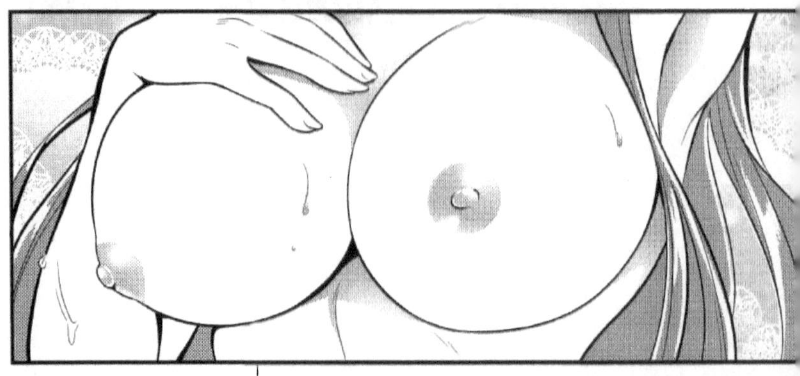

HAVE YOU EVER EXPERIENCED ONE OF THOSE LIFE-CHANGING INSTANCES? AN EVENT SO MOMENTOUS THAT, YEARS LATER, YOU'RE STILL MARVELING AT HOW IT CHANGED YOUR LIFE?

I HAD ONE OF THOSE. IT HAPPENED A WHILE AGO

EVEN TO THIS DAY, THROUGH ALL THE CHANGES THAT HAVE HAPPENED, THROUGH ALL THE EXPERIENCES THAT I'VE BEEN THROUGH, I STILL CAN'T BELIEVE HOW THIS ONE MOMENT CHANGED MY LIFE FOREVER.

NO MATTER WHAT CAME AFTER, OUR FIRST MEETING IS SOMETHING THAT I'LL ALWAYS REMEMBER.

ESPECIALLY SINCE, AT THE BEGINNING OF THIS TALE, I THOUGHT SHE WAS NOTHING BUT AN ORDINARY FOX WITH, UNORDINARILY ENOUGH, TWO BUSHY RED TAILS.

LIFE

. . . .

IT HITS YOU WHEN YOU LEAST EXPECT IT TO.

American Kitsune

American Kitsune
A YOUNG MAN UNWIT-
TINGLY DISCOVERS THAT
YOKAI ACTUALLY EXIST.

WIEDERGEBURT
LEGEND OF THE REINCARNATED WARRIOR

HE RETURNED TO THE PAST IN ORDER TO CHANGE THE FUTURE.

catgirl doctor

THE STORY OF A YOUNG
DOCTOR-IN-TRAINING
AND CATGIRLS.

INCUBUS
BUFF
VERTICAL
THE WORLD'S ONLY INCUBUS MUST BOND WITH SEVEN WOMEN!

A MAN DESPERATE TO SAVE HIS LOVER JOINS FORCES WITH A WOMAN LOOKING FOR A WAY OUT OF AN UNWANTED MARRIAGE.
MAN MADE GOD

He just wanted to be a hero.
She didn't want to be stuck in a loveless marriage.
A Most Unlikely Hero

Want to learn when a new book comes out?
Follow me on Social Media!

 @AmericanKitsune

 +BrandonVarnell

 @BrandonBVarnell

 http://bvarnell1101.tumblr.com/

 Brandon Varnell

 BrandonbVarnell

 https://www.patreon.com/
BrandonVarnell

www.ingramcontent.com/pod-product-compliance
Lightning Source LLC
Chambersburg PA
CBHW030656190726
48286CB00001B/42